FORCE OF BLOOD

ALSO BY JOSEPH HEYWOOD

Fiction:
Taxi Dancer (1985)
The Berkut (1987)
The Domino Conspiracy (1992)
The Snowfly (2000)

Woods Cop Mysteries:
Ice Hunter (2001)
Blue Wolf in Green Fire (2002)
Chasing a Blond Moon (2003)
Running Dark (2005)
Strike Dog (2007)
Death Roe (2009)
Shadow of the Wolf Tree (2010)

Non-Fiction:
Covered Waters: Tempests of a Nomadic Trouter (2003)

Praise for Joseph Heywood and the Woods Cop Mystery series:

"Heywood has crafted an entertaining bunch of characters. An absorbing narrative twists and turns in a setting ripe for corruption."

—*Dallas Morning News*

"Crisp writing, great scenery, quirky characters and an absorbing plot add to the appeal. . . ."

—*Wall Street Journal*

"Heywood is a master of his form."

—*Detroit Free Press*

"Top-notch action scenes, engaging characters both major and minor, masterful dialogue, and a passionate sense of place make this a fine series."

—*Publishers Weekly*

"Joseph Heywood writes with a voice as unique and rugged as Michigan's Upper Peninsula itself."

—Steve Hamilton, Edgar® Award-winning author of *The Lock Artist*

"Well written, suspenseful, and bleakly humorous while moving as quickly as a wolf cutting through the winter woods. In addition to strong characters and . . . compelling romance, Heywood provides vivid, detailed descriptions of the wilderness and the various procedures and techniques of conservation officers and poachers. . . . Highly recommended."

—*Booklist*

"Taut and assured writing that hooked me from the start. Every word builds toward the ending, and along the way some of the writing took my breath away."

—Kirk Russell, author of *Dead Game* and *Redback*

"[A] tightly written mystery/crime novel . . . that offers a nice balance between belly laughs, head-scratching plot lines, and the real grit of modern police work."

—*Petersen's Hunting*

A WOODS COP MYSTERY

To Jeff & Leah —
Enjoy your sojourn
J.

FORCE OF BLOOD

JOSEPH HEYWOOD

LYONS PRESS
Guilford, Connecticut
An imprint of Globe Pequot Press

Copyright © 2011 by Joseph Heywood

Lyons Press is an imprint of Globe Pequot Press.

Text design by Sheryl Kober
Layout by Melissa Evarts

Map by Jay Emerson, Licensed Michigan Fisherman

Library of Congress Cataloging-in-Publication Data is available on file.

ISBN 978-0-7627-7284-1

Printed in the United States of America

10 9 8 7 6 5 4 3 2 1

To Jambe Longue

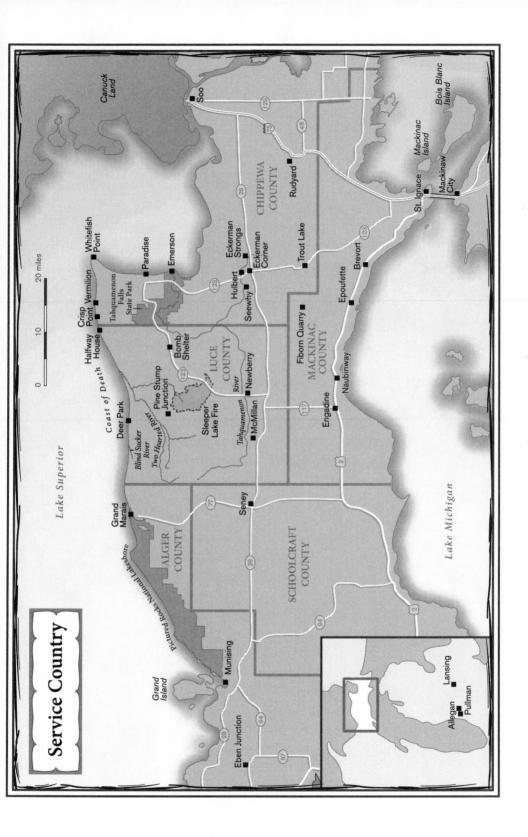

Service Country

. . . there never was so much as a single Indian that could be brought to relish our way of living. Children have been taken even in their swaddling clothes, and have been brought up with a great deal of care . . . all of these precautions having been fruitless, the force of blood having ever got the better of education: The moment they found themselves at liberty, they have torn their clothes to pieces, and have gone across the woods in the quest of their countrymen, whose way of living seemed preferable to ours.

—*Pierre de Charlevoix*
Journal of a Voyage to North America. Undertaken by Order of the French King. Containing the Geographical Description and Natural History of that Country, Particularly Canada, Together with an Account of the Customs, Characters, Religion, Manners, and Traditions of the Original Inhabitants (Printed for R. & J. Dodsley, London, 1761)

Once an Indi'n, always an Indi'n.

—*Waino Kempennen Ahola*
The U.P.'s first known Finnish trapper, quoted in the *Mackinac Island Straits Times*, 1794

PROLOGUE

Mackinaw City, Cheboygan County

FRIDAY, APRIL 27, 2007

Grady Service glared at Milo Miars, forcing his lieutenant to look away.

"Are they out of their gourds in Lansing?" Service challenged. "How do we do the job on fifteen hundred miles a pay period? That's a hundred and fifty miles a day. Hell, it's a hundred miles just to cross Mackinac County. You can't cross most UP counties on that mileage."

Miars stared out the window of the Kuppa Joe Kafe. "We're trying to cut every corner to avoid officer layoffs," Miars said. "And you're overstating the mileage restriction?"

"Yeah, well, convince me."

Miars continued to stare out at the parking lot and Service grimaced. "Seriously, El-Tee, what's the point? Are we supposed to just go through the motions, throw together a Potemkin village?"

"What the heck are you talking about now?" Miars shot back, turning to look at his subordinate.

Service knew he perplexed his boss most of the time. "When Catherine the Great would go out into Russia to see her people, her officials would make sure new facades got put on the crumbling villages she would pass by, just to make them look new and good. But they were pure shit, damn fakes, just like these mileage restrictions."

The lieutenant grinned crookedly. "That's an unsupportable allegation."

Service snapped, "What about Lori?" He was referring to Lorelei Timms, the state's embattled governor.

Miars sneered. "You'd know that better than me. She's *your* friend."

Service had met the governor under trying circumstances just prior to her being elected, and they had become friends. She was his biggest fan, which did not help his deep desire for anonymity. "Does she even *know?*"

"For Pete's sake, Grady, she's trying to save General Motors, Chrysler, *and* the darn state. We're just a pimple in the big picture."

1

"Who the hell is Pete? And why do we give a damn about his sake? Tell me what the hell I'm supposed to do, Milo. I'm a detective, not a patrol officer. I go to where my cases are, no matter where that takes me. If we're gonna redefine the whole shooting match, now's the time to tell me."

Miars scratched his clean-shaven chin. "Work the cases in range, and let the others hang until the fiscal picture is clearer."

Service shook his head. He didn't blame Milo. "The state's drowning and taking us down with it."

Miars said, "You could get out now and think about the young kids. They aren't even considered essential state workers and don't have a pension—the same 401(k) as a DNR cafeteria worker in the Mason Building."

A few years before, the Michigan State Police had lost some top officers by transfers into the DNR; they had carped to their patron saint in the legislature, who then pushed through a law that quietly removed DNR law enforcement from the same retirement package as the Troops. The intent was to give the MSP a recruiting and retention advantage. Officers from the two organizations still worked together and backed up each other, but it was a sore point, growing sorer.

"At least the Troops have a fifty-mile limit," Miars said.

"That's no consolation, Milo."

"Have you considered retiring?"

"Not with the outfit teetering on the edge of the shit can."

"Does this job mean *that* much to you?"

"Doesn't it mean that much to *you*, Milo? If it doesn't, turn in your goddamn badge. The last thing we need are a bunch of damn fence-dancers."

"Remember who you're talking to!" Miars said with a growl.

"Man-to-man, 'boss' is just a paper title, Milo. That's *all* it is. Officers follow those who lead, not those who *play* leader."

"What're you going to do?" Miars asked, obviously looking to end the conversation.

"Drive my Tahoe to the edge of my mileage limit and travel from that point in my four-wheeler. I can get a helluva lot of miles on the ATV for not much gas money. Maybe I'll double up with other officers and we can double our daily miles."

Miars shook his head and rolled his eyes.

Service planned to pay for his own gas, no matter what limits the department levied. He had way too much money thanks to a bequest from his late love, Maridly Nantz, and he'd already taken care of those who depended upon him. He had barely touched the cache since Nantz's murder.

Maybe it's time you did, he told himself, scribbling something on a napkin with a ballpoint pen that was beginning to run dry.

After Miars left him to head for his office in Gaylord, Service telephoned Charles "Chas" Marschke, Esquire, the Detroit-based whiz who managed the money Service had inherited.

Per usual, the uber-composed Marschke listened politely as Service outlined what he wanted.

"Have you thought this through, Grady?"

"Just do it, Chas."

"Let me make sure I have this right," Marschke said. "Houghton, Marquette, Menominee, Ironwood, the Soo, St. Ignace and Mackinaw City, Traverse City, Mount Pleasant, Port Huron, Lansing and East Lansing, Ann Arbor, Ypsilanti, Allendale, Grand Rapids, Kalamazoo, New Buffalo, Flint, Bay City, Saginaw, Midland, and Monroe?"

"That should get us started."

"First thing is that people will laugh, and after they think about it, they're likely to get real annoyed."

"Good," Grady Service said. "Annoyed is good. Pissed-off is even better."

"Do you have a time frame in mind?"

Service thought for a moment. "July third, the day before Independence Day. People will be off work. It will catch some attention."

Service looked at what he had written on the napkin, and smiled. *"Fellow violators—poach away. Michigan's game wardens don't have the $$ to come after you."*

• • •

On the way west on US 2 in the Upper Peninsula, Service stopped at Duquette Lake. A large dog was in the water off a sandy spit, pawing and hopping like it was overrun by mosquitoes, flies, fleas, or an evil spirit. Deer went to water when overwhelmed by bugs, but this was a pit bull, maybe seventy-five pounds of muscle, gristle, and blocky snout, and it was hyperactive in its splash-fest. His heart began to race.

"She's a beaut, eh?" a voice said from behind him.

Never heard him. An old man, bent, white hair, leather skin. "She have a name?" Service asked.

"Kevin," the old man said.

A joke? "Not your normal female name," Service said.

"I want her to think she's a male, so she can have the power gender confers without earning it."

Sheesh. Is the old coot batty? Hard to say. There was a certain eloquence, something in his voice. "What's she got in the water?"

"A large rock," the man said. "It's a metaphor for the lives we all live— fruitless, without meaning, filled with activities that consume time and accomplish nothing. She rolls the rock onto the beach. Then she rolls it back into the water. She will do this without pause until I call her back to me. I am like her five o'clock factory whistle, but of course I would never work her like people work each other. It's in the pit bull's blood to do this without revolting. As with most humans."

"Big rock," Service noted. *One that looks like a human head, the dog a cannibal diligently tenderizing it for the stewpot.* He looked away.

"Something we can do for you?" the old man asked.

"Nothing I can think of," Service said. Over his years with his own dog, Newf, his irrational phobia about dogs of all sizes had finally begun to relent, but seeing this pit bull had brought it flooding back, full force.

"Would you like to meet her?" the stranger asked. "She's a gentle, affectionate creature."

Eva Braun probably said the same thing about Hitler. "Maybe another time."

"Ah," the man said. "The ubiquitous social lie. There will never be another time. We hear this all the time. Mankind clings to appearances over substance, even when a different species is in the mix."

The Yoop draws hink kings like rotting flesh draws blowflies to lay their eggs. He found himself shaking over the brush with the pit bull when he got into his unmarked black Tahoe, and lit a cigarette to settle his nerves.

PART I: HUNKUSLAND

1

Lansing, Ingham County

MONDAY, APRIL 30, 2007

Pulling down Washington Avenue in downtown Lansing, horns honking, traffic hurtling and jerking everywhere—the state's worst drivers, hands down—Grady Service was still steaming from last night's phone message from DNR law chief, Lorne O'Driscoll. No reasons, no hints; just be at HQ by 1000 hours.

It was ten till, and Service found the chief in uniform, sitting on a stone bench in the lobby of the Mason Building. *Weird,* he thought.

The chief stood and extended his hand. "Grady."

"Chief, what's going on?"

Longtime chief O'Driscoll chuckled softly. "No foreplay for you. Right to the heart of things. I'm retiring, Grady. Effective midnight tonight. The new chief wants to see you."

What? There had been no more rumors than usual. Nothing. Milo Miars had said nothing last Friday. Not even hinted at it. What the hell is going on? This is too sudden. "You're okay, right?"

"My health's fine. But it's time for others to fight the battles and wars."

They took the elevator to the fifth floor. Several other passengers warmly greeted both men.

An older woman with close-cropped silver hair was seated behind the desk formerly occupied by O'Driscoll's administrative assistant.

"Meet Luna Pinchot," the chief said.

The woman reached up to him with her hand and nodded. She had a firm grip. "Detective," was all she said. No smile, no emotion, just one word spoken in a neutral voice.

O'Driscoll pushed him toward the door.

"You coming with me?" Service asked.

"You're on your own, Grady, just the way you like it. Try not to nuke him on your first meeting," O'Driscoll said with a raised eyebrow.

For one of the few times in his life, Grady Service began to feel dread. He had no idea what was happening, a rare and unusual circumstance. He inhaled deeply, exhaled slowly, knocked once, and went through the door.

"Michigan Man," the unshaven man with pale gray eyes said from behind O'Driscoll's desk. "Yew done yew any dandy floods lately?"

"Eddie Waco?"

"Some dogs cain't 'splain how they get from there to here."

"*You're* the new chief?"

"Vex you some, does hit?" Waco asked, smirking.

"Not sure," Service said. He had worked with the Missouri conservation agent in the wake of the murders of his girlfriend Maridly Nantz and son Walter.

"How's Cake?"

Cake Culkin was Waco's shadow agent, his ersatz partner, the unofficial Missouri version of Michigan's now-defunct Volunteer Conservation Officers, a program missed by just about every uniformed officer.

"Jes' fine las' time I seen 'im. You wonderin' why I'm sittin' here, do ya?"

"My head's not clear enough yet to question anything," Service said.

"Ain't gonna blow smoke up your backside, Grady. I didn't come lookin' for this job. Hit come lookin' for me, and I said yes, on the condition I call all the law shots—and I do mean *all*."

"*Who* came after you?"

"Natural Resources Commission."

This was the body of political appointees who directed conservation policy in Michigan. "Not their call," Service said.

"They're about to name a new director."

"Eino Teeny's leaving?"

"Already done cleared out his kit, I hear."

This was all major, long-expected news. Teeny had been a toady of past governor Sam "Clearcut" Bozian. Teeny and Bozian had been equally loathed at all levels of the DNR. Once Bozian was term-limited out of the gubernatorial job and headed for the nation's capital, everyone expected Teeny to follow, posthaste. But he had hung on, which suggested how bad his reputation was. Nobody wanted him, not even Sam Bozian.

"Who replaces Teeny?"

"Betwixt us boys, Mizz Doctor Belphoebe Cheke."

"Never heard of her."

"They're bringin' her in from Wyoming—wildlife management type."

"Cheney country."

"Word's out the Veep's *mucho* pissed, but the woman can't stand him."

"Well, that's a big point in her favor," Service said.

Waco smiled. "You and me once made a good pack."

"True," Service said.

"I'll be blunt. I'm askin' you to take a step up the organizational ladder."

Service shook his head. "Up isn't the direction I'm interested in, Eddie. I'm thinking more about sliding gracefully out—into retirement."

Waco shook his head. "Retirement would bore the britches off'n the likes of you."

"Sorry."

"I'd like you beside me as captain and assistant chief. You might want to think on this some, before you say no. You could do a lot of good for the department and for me. I'm the new guy and I get a honeymoon. You know where all the bodies are buried. Together we can do good things."

"Eddie, if I spent any more time in Lansing than I already have, you'd probably end up arresting me for homicide. You need someone smart you can really count on."

Waco pursed his lips and paused. "Got a name?"

"Lieutenant Lisette McKower."

"No reservations?"

"None. She's the best we have."

"Okay, then. I ain't one for twistin' arms. Okay if I call you and check in with you from time to time?"

"Hell, come ride with me—but if you call me, it's on your own dime."

"Wouldn't think of spendin' guv'mint money," Chief Eddie Waco said. "You can count on seeing me again real soon."

"Congratulations," Service said, and added, "I think. Why did you take this job?"

"I got jumped to second captain back home and finished my PhD. First captain's a good man. Didn't want to compete against him. This looked like an innerestin' job, and I figured with you here, we might just make us a difference. This state's got the longest history of all when it comes to salaried professional game wardens—a long, proud history."

"I hope your future analyses are better than that one," Service said. "This state's in financial freefall and the whole place is going under."

"Never figgered you for such an optimist," Eddie Waco said.

The two men laughed together and shook hands.

O'Driscoll was waiting outside. "You approve?"

"Probably."

"You turn him down?"

"Yep."

"And then you recommended McKower?"

"Yessir."

"Think she'll take it?"

"If the chief has any say in it, she will. He was a helluva officer down in Missouri."

"He says you're the best he ever worked with."

"He's chief, not God."

2

Rock River Headwaters, Alger County

TUESDAY, MAY 1, 2007

Grady Service was passing Vanderbilt when his cell phone rang. "This here's Kinkaid," the man's gravelly voice croaked into the cell phone. "Santinaw says he needs to see you right away, like most ricky-tick, eh?"

Grady Service's first response was an uncommunicative sigh. Santinaw was Huronicus St. Andrew, a Munising Ojibwa, who had served in the Pacific in World War II and returned home in late 1946 after spending some time in Japan. As a boy, St. Andrew had pronounced his name *Santinaw,* which had stuck ever since. He lived mostly alone, never married, and occasionally worked as a hunting and fishing guide.

Grady Service's old man, a once-famous Michigan conservation officer, had known the Indian well, but Service hadn't talked to Santinaw since a bizarre bear-poaching case some years back. The old man had to be pushing ninety, and the message to come see him "right away" left the Department of Natural Resources detective scratching his head. No phone, of course. St. Andrew lived in another century; pinpointing the exact one was impossible. Kinkaid, the messenger, ran a small general store in Eben.

Service finally spoke. "*Right away* as in today, or as soon as I can reasonably get there?"

Kinkaid sighed. "You know the old sonuvagun's never that specific. He wants his groceries fetched out to him."

Service closed the cell phone. Vintage Santinaw—always killing multiple birds with the same shot, and never a *please* uttered on the front side: Just do it. Santinaw, a revered, powerful tribal elder and holy man, was not one for vacuous social graces or empty gestures.

Grady Service called Tuesday Friday from St. Ignace and told her about the meeting with the new chief. Friday—more than a girlfriend, less than a wife—was a homicide detective with the Michigan State Police in Negaunee, divorced, with a young son. Probably their relationship could be more precisely defined, but for now they were both comfortable with the arrangement as it stood. Both had hyperkinetic cop schedules and they got together when they could. Shigun, her son, often stayed with him when she was working.

"You know the new chief?"

"Worked together once."

"Life sure can be odd," she said. She had been expecting him for dinner that night, but he told her he had to stop in Alger County and would be later, and not to hold dinner for him. He thought about trying to explain Kinkaid's call about Santinaw, but it was impossible to accurately define the old Ojibwa, so he told her he'd talk more when he saw her again.

"Give Shigun five for me," he said just before hanging up, and she laughed.

"When I see you again, I'll be giving you a lot more than five," Friday purred seductively.

• • •

As he drove toward Eben, Grady Service reflected on the fact that work in recent years had taken some distinctly dark and unexpected turns. It seemed that his ability to control outcomes, or even to ensure justice, was diminishing. The nagging question in his mind: Was this despite him or because of him?

Not having the answer didn't keep him from wondering how after nearly three decades, law enforcement seemed to be getting both richer and more complex, with more and more people counting on him, which meant having answers for them. Right? He *hated* this aspect.

Kinkaid was a short, slightly stooped, gnomelike man with a thin, florid face, and crooked teeth stained by tobacco. He had a carton of Basic cigarettes on his counter ready to add to a canvas pack. "Santinaw's groceries— and his smokes."

A young woman stepped up and hooked the pack with her arm. "I'm Lacey Lucey," the woman said. "Santinaw's woman. I'll carry the load if I can catch a ride."

Service looked at Kinkaid, who shrugged.

"Who pays for the old man?" Service asked the grocer.

"Running tab."

"Cleared recently?"

"Not in a couple of years."

"What's it up to?"

Kinkaid told him. Service shook his head and wrote a check to the man. Even with the recent stock market debacle he still had more money than he would ever be able to spend. The amount the Indian owed on account didn't seem like that much for more than two years, and Service suspected that the old bastard did a lot of "natural harvesting" near his cabin, meaning illegal hunting and fishing. How somebody that old could still get around in winter woods was beyond him, but he admired the old man for sticking to his own lifestyle and not bending to the demands of others.

Lacey Lucey said nothing during the drive from Eben, and when they got out of the truck, she grabbed the pack again and looked at him. "You want me to lead?"

He nodded. Last time here CO Jake Mecosta had led the way, and both of them had gotten turned around. Mecosta was retired now. All the old-timers were hanging up their boots. *Why not you?* he asked himself.

"Known Santinaw long?" he asked the woman.

"Long enough," she said, ducking into the trees at a brisk clip.

Two miles of tortuous verticality and poor footing took a lot of effort, and when they finally reached the old man's cabin on a rocky promontory, Service was sweating and felt slightly winded. The woman showed no effects. She stopped at the door and knocked loudly.

"Santinaw, it's Lacey," she called out.

The Indian said. "Go away. I ain't got no time for the funny business."

"You're my man," she said. "There's more than the funny business in a relationship. We've got your groceries."

"What about my smokes?"

"Them too," she said.

St. Andrew opened the door and squinted. He nodded and grunted when he saw Service. "*Bojo* . . . come in," he said, and when the woman hung back, the old man shook his head, held up his right index finger, and said, "You can come in, but this here's gonna be some serious man-talk you ain't part of."

"I won't interfere," the woman said, proffering the carton of cigarettes.

The cabin had not changed since Service had last seen it. There was a woodstove, ricks of logs piled in an orderly fashion outside the cabin walls, the overall effect that of a whole, well-maintained operation. There were cured furs on the walls, an oiled crosscut saw, a shelf filled with old crocks and bottles, and a rack of bamboo fly rods turned orange by age and use. The floor was shiny from decades of boots, and there wasn't a visible speck of dust.

There was a bed in one corner, and a small table with four simple wooden chairs painted basic red.

Santinaw cracked opened the carton with his thumb, ripped open a pack of Basics, removed one, and lit up before offering the pack to Service, but not to the woman.

"You come along pretty quick."

"Your message said right away. What's up?"

Huronicus St.Andrew said solemnly, "Our ancestors are being defiled."

"*Our* ancestors, as in yours, and/or mine?"

Santinaw grinned. "I always liked *wabish* sense of humor. My people think of you as almost one of us, so I guess that makes this about *our* ancestors. Back when our people fought the Lakota, war parties would appoint one of their bravest to be a runner, who would return to the tribe afterward and tell them what happened. Even if everyone survived, the runner always spoke first because he stayed at a distance, didn't get involved like the others, and could see the big picture. You're like a runner. And you're known to be fair—for a paleface."

Service stifled a laugh. It had been years since he'd heard that word.

Santinaw had always been an odd and mysterious figure, and Service understood him no better now than when he had been a boy and come to visit with his father. "What is it I'm supposed to be watching?"

"Bleedin' sand," Huronicus St. Andrew said. "The sand is bleedin', and only you can stanch it."

"Are there going to be more details?"

"My son, Four Hawks, and my people need you, Service."

"*You* have a son?"

"Even Santinaw can't defy odds all the time. Whiteman's weinerboots ain't a hundred percent, eh? His name is Four Hawks, but in your world he is called Duncan Katsu, his mother's name."

Service smirked and took a drag on his cigarette: Santinaw's exploits with much younger women was legendary in the central U.P., and probably throughout the entire Ojibwa populace of the United States and central Canada.

"Where is this son of yours?"

"I seen him up there on that Coast of Death."

"You were up there?"

Santinaw tapped his head. "I got the gift."

Death's Coast. It had been years since he'd heard the term. White men called the south shore of Lake Superior the Shipwreck Coast, and the Chippewa called it Coast of Death because of a bloody battle fought with marauding Iroquois centuries back, which may have happened or could very well be bullshit. With the tribes you never knew for sure what was real and what was a figment of group imagination and the inaccuracy of oral history.

Technically, the area stretched from Munising to White Fish Point, but the main Shipwreck Coast ran east from Grand Marais to Whitefish, a largely uninhabited coastline rarely visited except by a few tourists and agate hunters.

"He lives way out there?"

"Between Crisp and Vermilion," Santinaw mumbled, "near the halfway house."

"You visited him?"

"I seen the whole thing."

Service inhaled deeply. *Stay calm; he's an old man, and he's seen—and believes—things you don't know about.*

Service tried to recall what he thought he knew. In the old days there had been a string of U.S. Life-Saving Service stations stretched around the coastlines of the Great Lakes and down the Eastern Seaboard, and every day surfmen had walked the beaches, looking for flotsam and jetsam from wrecks. The surfmen were very tough hombres. One man would walk halfway to the next station and the next station would send a man the other way, and the two would make contact in the middle, compare notes, spend the night, and walk their return routes the next morning. Crisp Point was about as isolated a place as one could find in the U.P.

"He have a camp up that way?"

"Ain't none of us own land 'cept in *wabish* thinking. He treats the land with respect and it takes care of him. The boy lives the old way and practices the traditional ways. He's headstrong, but a good boy. He went off to try the *wabish* way, but he came back. We always come back."

The traditional way? Bleeding sand? What the hell is he talking about?

"Am I supposed to go see him?"

"A man is free to choose," St. Andrew said.

Bullshit. Santinaw was putting the bite on him, leaving him no choice. "Think you could cough up a bit more detail for me to go on?"

"Look into your heart," the old man said, turning and gently patting the younger woman's firm left buttock. She responded with a lascivious laugh.

"I take it you won't be hiking out with me?" he said to Lacey Lucey.

She raised an eyebrow and said, "My old man and me, we got important things ta take care of."

Service nodded and smiled. It had been a week since he'd last seen Friday and he could empathize.

By the time he got to his truck he was winded. *Need to step up your workouts*, he told himself. His sinuses had been plugged for more than a month, which sometimes left him feeling like he was living inside a gelatinous atmosphere. If this kept on, he'd call Vince Vilardo and try to get the sinuses cleared.

The internist and retired medical examiner for Delta County was an old friend and collaborator, and despite retirement, still seeing a few patients. He'd probably bug him to get a full physical, but he'd been avoiding this for years and saw no reason to give in now. *You take your truck to the dealer and it comes out with more problems than it went in with. Same thing happens when you go see a damn doctor. It can't be coincidence.*

3

Newberry, Luce County

WEDNESDAY, MAY 2, 2007

Grady Service called District Two's Lieutenant Lisette McKower during his drive east. His former partner and sergeant, one-time lover, and now district lieutenant, remained a close friend.

"Lis, Grady. You hearing any rumbles about tribal problems up on the south shore?"

"Should I have?"

"Not sure. I got summoned to Santinaw's, and he wants me to go visit his son. He says the boy lives the old way up on the Coast of Death."

"Huh," she said. "That's Jingo Sedge's area."

"Sedge?"

"Two academy classes back. Good kid, and really serious, so go easy. The young officers in this department believe you walk on water. Shows you how poorly we recruit for judgment."

"Liquid shit can easily be mistaken for water," he said.

"Grady, you can't duck leadership responsibilities your whole career. You're the best at this job. Think how much you could help our young people."

"There are lots of ways to do this job and make cases," he said defensively. He wasn't in the mood for one of her lectures, no matter how well-intentioned.

She sighed dramatically. "There're a lot of young officers who could use your guidance in teaching them to do things your way . . . the old way . . . the right way."

He immediately changed the subject. "Where's Sedge live?"

"Right on M-123, about four miles west of Tahq State Park, just east of CR 500. The place is an old service station, a cinder-block hovel with a Mobil Oil sign. The other officers call it the Bomb Shelter. Nobody can believe the

Department of Environmental Quality or the EPA haven't condemned it. Sedge likes to run solo. None of us has ever been inside."

"What's Sedge's call?"

"Two One Thirty."

"What's Sedge like?"

"Same as you when you began—storm trooper, takes no prisoners."

I was like that? Always hard to tell if McKower is jabbing for fun or for real. "You in the Newberry office today?"

"I promised Sergeant Bryan I'd work with him and one of his new officers between Trout Lake and Fibre."

Six-foot-six Sergeant Jeffey Bryan, Service recalled, had been a cub CO when the two of them had gotten into the middle of a strange shooting incident between Amish and Mennonite hunting parties some years back.

"Later."

"Bear in mind that what you say to young officers gets passed around like gospel."

"Just fucking great," he said, and hung up. Would Eddie Waco promote her to Lansing? He was an idiot if he didn't. As for him and Lis, she'd find ways to keep track of him. She always had.

4

Halfway House, Chippewa County

THURSDAY, MAY 3, 2007

Grady Service spent the night in the Newberry office, studying the area top-ographical maps he'd spread all around the conference room.

He had been to Vermilion Point where the feds once had a top-secret wolf-training operation, but never anywhere near Crisp Point or between the two sites. He considered giving Jingo Sedge a bump, but ruled it out. Santinaw had come to him for a reason. Until he had a better feel for what he was going into, if anything, it would be better to not complicate matters.

He tried to find a plat book for Chippewa County, but the back of his truck was trashed beyond description. *Probably left the damn thing at home. You've got to clean out your truck*, he lectured himself. He looked at a topo instead. Five-Pack Creek seemed to parallel Lake Superior, north of what was listed on one of his maps as the Vermilion Rod and Gun Club property. It had been there when he worked in the district, but he had no idea if the club was still in operation.

Halfway House—he learned from a clerk who worked at Pickelman's General Store south of Newberry on M-28—was the site of a shack, of which there might or might not be anything left. There was no way to know because the place was rarely visited by anyone the man knew of, and every winter seemed to eat more of the shore and embankments out that way.

Service made his way north on Old Maple Block Trail, where it angled north off the East Town Truck Trail. It was just after 4 p.m. when he stashed his truck a mile or so south of the old Rod and Gun Club property, hoisted his ruck, secured the truck, and headed north on foot through the sandy soil, jack pines, and scrub oaks. He figured the hike to be about three miles, maybe a smidge more. No way to tell where Duncan Katsu's camp was, but there couldn't be many places up this way, and somewhere ahead he expected there would be a county fire number or a camp sign.

Within an estimated quarter-mile of Lake Superior, and easing through a heavily wooded area of scrub oak on a steep barrier dune, he caught the faint sound of voices and stopped to try and pinpoint the source. *Damn sinus condition made hearing unreliable. Gotta go see Vince, get this ear shit taken care of.*

Voices ahead, somewhere to the left, not close. Wind's out of the north. Hearing was a key sense in the woods, and a lot more difficult to use accurately than your eyes, but often more reliable. *Move cautiously*, he reminded himself.

His Automatic Vehicle Locator rolling map and his topo charts had shown Five-Pack Creek flowing out of Brown's Lake to the west and meandering eastward and north, sort of roughly paralleling the coast. He'd never seen Five-Pack Creek, but guessed it would be cold and narrow with a steady current and a mostly loon-shit bottom, tag alder banks, and probably a lot of woody debris. *Probably will have some native brook trout in it, but too far off the beaten path for most anglers to bother with. Can feed me if I'm hungry enough.*

He had a hand line stowed in his ruck, and if he got the opportunity and was in the mood, he told himself, he might get up a brook trout meal tonight. After hiking, he was feeling slightly winded again, and already hungry. The last real meal he'd had was yesterday's breakfast, when he'd made one of his giant shroomelets. He patted his stomach. *You can afford to miss some meals, pal.*

This morning he'd telephoned his granddaughter in Houghton and had enjoyed a nonsensical conversation with the two-and-a-half-year-old, which left him feeling kingly: *Little Maridly.* Just the thought of her made him smile and feel warm all over. She talked nonstop and smiled at him nonstop and would stand beside him and pat his back like he was an old dog. *Which you are*, he reminded himself.

More voices, this time further right. *Could be wind*, he reminded himself. Wind tended to whip off the lake into the barrier dunes and send fractured sound scrambling.

Five-Pack Creek turned out to be exactly what he'd expected, and as he walked westward he found a shallow place with hard-packed gravel. There was an orange plastic cap stuck in the grass. *Assholes who litter!* He picked it up, stuffed it in his pocket, waded across, and made his way northeast through an immense expanse of chest-high horsetail ferns. His mind was on fish. The gravel area suggested fall salmon and spring steelhead runs. Law-abiding anglers might not make the effort to get out this far, but violators surely would.

Halfway through the ferns, the plants suddenly erupted into life and his heart began pounding as something began running tight, fast circles around him. Instinctively he pulled out his .40 cal and held his breath as a gangly, long-legged young wolf popped onto a grassy hummock ten yards away and stared at him before loping away.

Calm down, he told himself. Then, *What the hell is a single wolf doing here? This time of year the packs are usually in their rendezvous areas, teaching their pups how to hunt and kill beaver.*

The terrain rose steadily as he moved north until he crested a ridge and could see a dense marsh below and the big lake beyond that, its swells slopping lazily against the beaches. He couldn't actually see the beaches or shore, but he could hear Lake Superior.

What made the most sense was to get down to the beach, look around, backtrack into the cover of the tree line, and make temporary camp. If he decided to go for brook trout, he could hike back to the creek. There should be natural bait in abundance along the stream's edge.

From the trees, Service looked eastward and saw smoke wafting from below—from where he guesstimated the beach to be. Actually, he thought he'd caught a faint smell of smoke before, but the wind was shifting to the northwest now and curling the smoke away from him. No law against fires out here, but it seemed uncomfortably close to the water's edge, and if the wind came up or a tanker passed, even a half-mile offshore, whoever was tending the fire would get swamped by incoming waves, or worse. Unless his mental picture of the beach was different than reality. At least the fire seemed close to the water, which meant not much fuel for it to get into.

Preferring not to show himself, he walked eastward and moved downhill through the trees. A couple of hundred yards east, he froze when he saw two apparently naked men jog quickly through the trees, headed south. Both were shirtless and had feathers in their hair. They wore ankle-high moccasins, he thought, but he wasn't sure. It was pushing twilight now. *Something weird for sure. But it is the U.P.,* he reminded himself, shaking his head, as if this explained all aberrations.

Allowing the pair to move on, he saw what appeared to be a clearing on the edge of the tree line where a small fire was flickering. One man was sitting alone on a log, smoking a cigar, his face painted red and black. *Jesus, what the hell is this?*

Service watched from concealment as three more men came up from the woods to the north, mumbled a few words to the man by the campfire, and continued southward, same as the first two men. These three wore loin-cloths and just *looked* naked. Probably the other two had been the same. Still, it was peculiar.

A tiny fire was an Indian's fire, not a white man's. Service found himself nodding off. *Sign of age; unable to maintain focus like when you were young.*

He fell asleep and kept nodding awake and checking on the man. He finally woke with a start not to sound exactly, but to motion, moving air or something, someone or something cutting through dune grasses, *something afoot*, vibration. *Not that damn wolf again.* Blurry-eyed, he saw the fire still flickering on low, but its tender nowhere in sight. *Damn. Jesus, did I sleep all night? Doofus!*

Looking around frantically and trying to shake off sleep, he saw stooped black forms moving through the eelgrass around him, not running, but not walking either. Lots of them, spread pretty well, good discipline. Nobody could get a whole bunch of them with one shot. *Why such discipline? Ass-hole militia types?* The U.P. had plenty of them. *I hate gun-nut militias,* he thought.

A light touch on his shoulder startled him so badly he nearly yelled, but he managed to contain himself. A voice said, "You gonna sit there in the sand, old man, or deal yourself in?"

Female voice, confident, in charge. Before he could ask, the voice added, "Jingo Sedge. And you'd be Service, the legend himself."

Before he could answer, she had moved on. He struggled to his knees and got up, semi-stumbling through the loose sand until he got his bearings and began to get his mind focused. By then, Sedge was moving like a grey-hound and he had to hump to keep up. He only reached her as all hell broke loose in the form of a collective human scream that was more penetrating than any lynx he'd ever heard—and one lynx was way more than enough to stop the unsuspecting heart momentarily. This was like that, only a lot louder and more penetrating. Somehow, over the top of the crescendo, he could hear a female stentorian voice commanding, "Touch this man and you *are* going to fucking jail!"

Service caught up to the crowd and pushed his way between the painted men without shirts to find Sedge holding the arm of a small man and glaring at the rest of the group.

A tall man with wild hair was in front of her. Service tapped his arm and said, "DNR," and eased over to Sedge's side. *Why the hell didn't Lis tell me Sedge is female?*

Light was beginning to draw pink in the eastern sky, most of the landscape blackening like buried coal. *Morning on the way. How much did I miss last night?*

The man had long black hair tied back in a long braid, and the bright red print of a human hand across the bottom half of his face.

"*Bojo.* This like some sort of Shinob Halloween?" Service asked. "Seems a little early for costumes." *Shinob* was an obscure slang word for the Anishinaabeg, the tribe white men called Ojibwa or Chippewa.

The man grunted. "Just like *em-shii-goo-shee* to have the cultural sensitivities of a reptile." The man looked up at Service and held out a cigar. "*Wa-bish-kis mis-sabe.*"

"My Shinob's a hair rusty," Service said, ignoring the cigar and sitting down cross-legged on a hummock of grass. "Talk fucking English."

Sedge said, "White Giant, the White Shadow Wolf."

Service ignored her, said to the pony-tailed man, "You Katsu?"

The man nodded. "One seed of many planted by Huronicus St. Andrew, master manipulator."

"Santinaw told me the sand is bleeding."

"Obviously not for him, or he'd be here as a matter of honor."

Service held up his hands. "Listen, I haven't got a clue what any of this is about, or even what the hell 'bleeding sand' is. Your old man asked me to come see you, and here I am."

Sedge said, "White Giant super dick rides in to rescue incompetent rookie CO and savage Shinobs."

The chip on her shoulder wouldn't fit into the bed of an oversized pickup truck. Service added, "Santinaw doesn't send anyone without a good reason. 'Course, sometimes he's not too damn good about saying what those reasons are."

Katsu chuckled and once again held out the cigar. "That's Santinaw, the backwoods puppetmaster—certain he's pulling all the strings, even when they don't exist."

Service accepted the cigar and lit it. "*Megwetch*," he said with a head nod. "Thanks."

Katsu offered nothing to Sedge, who harrumphed indignance.

As it grew lighter, Service saw that all the men with Katsu were painted, some of them frighteningly so.

"This public land?" Service asked after a while.

"Define 'public,'" Duncan Katsu said. "There's been Anishinaabeg here since time began."

"Bullshit," Sedge interjected. "If you're referring to your people, they have *not* been in this area since time began. They migrated from northeast Canada around 1500 and pushed the Sioux westward over a hundred years or so. Your ancestors were interlopers, same as the Europeans. You, me, us— same-same, dude; run people off, take over their property."

"You gonna bust us for trespass?" Katsu asked in a challenging voice.

Service said, "Hell, I don't know exactly where I am, which means if you're trespassing, I guess I am too." He added, "You want to ask your people to all step up where I can see them? I don't much like people hanging back in the dark when I'm in the light. Nothing personal. Think of it as an occupational courtesy."

Katsu's people spread out until Service counted twenty-four of them, all decked out in breechcloths or deerskin leggings, their loosened hair long, with lots of feathers, and more than a few traditional weapons, the curved clubs called "breakheads" looking especially lethal. All of the people wore paint in a wide variety of designs, but the colors tended mostly to be black and red, like Katsu's, and Service wondered if this was meant to signify something.

"If I didn't know better, I'd say this looks like a war party," Service said.

"Could come to that," Katsu said. "If the others choose, we'll happily oblige."

Katsu glared at Sedge.

What others? "As in *your* others, or *other* others?" Service asked.

Katsu said, "You wear a badge. It should be obvious."

Little about tribals was ever obvious, and about the time you thought it was, they knocked you off balance with subtleties so deep they were often inexplicable, and certainly unfathomable to one not raised in Native traditions. "I can't even solve my granddaughter's jigsaw puzzles," Service said. "And she's just going on three."

"A white member of the Shadow Wolves can't figure things out?" Katsu said, leering at him. "That's bullshit, *wabish*."

"Yeah, total bullshit," Jingo Sedge added.

"No, it's apples and oranges," Service countered. *God, Sedge is a total pain in the ass. Like a damn Jack Russell always on the attack.*

At that moment Service heard a poorly muffled ATV coming down the beach toward them. Katsu's painted and feathered people immediately charged eastward, screaming.

Sedge surged after the group and Service followed. She somehow got past the lead Ojibwa and charged into a man who was getting off the four-wheeler, hitting him with a violent head-on tackle that put him on his back on the ground with a loud thump.

She grabbed the individual's arms, twisted them behind him, cuffed him, and yelled at Service, "Secure the driver!"

Service grabbed the driver as he tried to restart the machine and knocked him off the seat, jerked him to his feet, and only then discovered he had just rough-dusted a woman, skinny as a rail, loose hair, wild eyes, shaking like a leaf.

That's when the infernal shrieking began anew, screams so penetrating they shot a chill down Service's spine, the sort of screams he had once heard from fanatical North Vietnamese troops charging to their deaths through the jungle at night.

But this morning there was no crackle of gunfire or grenades popping, and all he could hear was a voice shouting angrily. Soon Sedge appeared, escorting a small red-haired man with a goatee and long hair. The man was struggling vigorously and hopelessly against Sedge until he saw Service.

The woman Service held was about the man's age, skinny and mean-eyed.

"You white?" the cuffed man asked. "Or one of *them?* So damn much mixed blood in the tribes nowadays, can't hardly tell who's real anymore."

"I'm Detective Service, Department of Natural Resources, and I'm real."

"Sedge, conservation officer," his partner of the moment announced.

"*Detective?* Game wardens? Where the hell are the real cops? Listen, tell these bloody Shinob cretins to leave us alone."

"Who are *you?*" Service asked.

"We call him Cool Ghoul," one of Katsu's people called out.

"*Professor* Delmure Arcton Toliver," the man said. "*Dr.* Toliver to these troublemakers."

"You a doctor who treats patients, Del?" Service asked.

"My doctorate is in history, my thesis on the Anishinaabeg migration."

"Up here you've gotta treat patients to be called 'Doctor.' "

"You don't mean up here . . . you mean *out* here. This place is on the edge of the Earth."

"He's desecrating our ancestors," Katsu said with a hiss.

Toliver took a deep breath and said measuredly, "We've been through this before, Katsu. This land is *not* a burial ground. There are no bodies here. This was a fishing village and a safety refuge from bad weather. There were never more than twenty or thirty people living here at any given moment, and there were *no* burials."

"There are hundreds of remains here," Katsu replied. "*Na-do-we-se* bodies."

Toliver snorted. "Jesus, man. The oral traditions of your own people say the battles between Ojibwa and *Na-do-we-se* took place at least forty miles southeast of here. *Remember*—Iroquois Point?"

Katsu examined the small man. "And the Menominee claim they killed a thousand enemies on Green Bay, but the Menominee are liars. The real battle was *here,* and my people were in it."

"Whatever," Toliver said dismissively. He shook his head and looked to Service like he had more he wanted to say, but couldn't summon the words.

"The professor wants to dig for artifacts," Katsu said. "If I wanted to go and dig for pots in Arlington National Cemetery, you think your *wabish* government would allow that?"

"Arlington *is* a cemetery," Toliver said.

"This place is no less," Katsu said with a steely voice.

Toliver sighed. "I have been issued the requisite state permits to sink-test cores."

"Permits issued by whom?" Service asked.

"The Office of the State Archaeologist," Toliver said righteously.

"Toliver and the State both deny the truth," Katsu said.

Toliver keened, "Your own state authorities agree that there are no bodies here. I have *permits*. Everything is legal and in order. Katsu is obstructing a legally sanctioned archaeological dig and academic field program."

"There will not be digging here," Katsu said. "None."

"I'll be back with *real* cops," Toliver said.

"*We're* both real cops, dipstick," Sedge said angrily, nodding toward Service, "and, more to the point, the DNR grants the right to dig, *not* the state archaeologist."

"I'm not going to stand here and argue pointlessly or be insulted anymore," Toliver said. "These people assaulted us. I want to file charges."

"Do what you feel you have to do," Katsu said flatly.

Toliver said, "We want our machine back."

Service's eyes narrowed. "You illegally used that thing, so we'll just hang on to it for now. The walk out will probably do you good."

"Illegally?"

"Riding double, no helmets, nearly plowed into a group of people, riding on the beach, which is against the law—we could keep going with the list, but we'll leave it at careless operation and just warn you on the other things."

He looked at the driver. "Who're you?"

"Jane," she said in a quavering voice.

Toliver said, "Good God, man—do you realize how far we are from our vehicle?"

Service said, "More to the point, do *you?*"

When Toliver and the woman turned and began to trudge east, several Ojibwa blocked their way. Service intervened, separating Toliver and the woman from Katsu's people. "Okay, fun's over. Let these people pass." He nodded at Sedge, who gave the woman named Jane a nudge toward Toliver.

The four of them walked down the beach.

"You saw everything," Toliver said. "The assaults."

"I'm not sure what I saw," Service said. "How long has this pissing match been going on?"

"We had the first encounter with Katsu last summer. Flin Yardley, the state archaeologist, had already given permission, but we went back and asked again if he was certain there were no remains here, and he told us we were clear to sink-test holes. Now, every time we show up, Katsu and his thugs are here blocking us. I don't understand how they always know we're coming."

"A professor where?"

"Hibernian College near Cleveland."

Service had never heard of it. "You teach there?"

"Twenty years, and I'm curator of the campus museum."

"So, if there are bodies here, you can't legally dig?"

"If there are bodies, we can dig, but the dig would then have to satisfy federal regs in addition to state regs, and because of NAGPRA, the feds would formally bring Native Americans into the process."

"NAGPRA?"

Sedge blurted out, "That's the Native American Graves Protection and Repatriation Act, which says nothing can be done to bones without direction by and from the Indians." Her voice betrayed extreme frustration.

"Tribals do tend to complicate some things," Service said, speaking from experience.

"You've dealt with them?" the professor said.

"The thing is, mostly they just want people to think about what they're doing."

"Bloody hell, man, I *study* them and think about them and their past all the time."

"And you're certain this was no more than a fishing village?"

"Right—a distinctly minor one, more a safe refuge from inclement weather than a serious, established fishing settlement."

"How can you *know* that?"

"Various European accounts, including the *Jesuit Relations*, all of which formalize the Native oral traditions."

Sedge said, "Katsu says you're wrong."

"What does *he* know? These people didn't even have a written language until Europeans came along, and even that took a couple of centuries. This group of Katsu's isn't a federally recognized tribe. They call themselves the Five-Pack Creek Band of aboriginals under the Grand Island Ojibwa but it's all made up, with absolutely no historical basis. I know; I've made a career of studying these people."

"Did you two have helmets?" Service asked.

"No need. We're on sand, and I drive carefully."

Service stopped walking, took out his ticket book, opened it, and started writing.

"What do you think you're *doing?*" Toliver asked.

"Giving you a ticket for riding your machine on the beach. That's against the law. But I'll just issue warnings on the helmets."

Toliver said. "You think this is a joke?"

"A joke? Professor, there's about two dozen tribals back there, decked out in war paint and carrying some very nasty-looking weapons. The last thing I think is that this is funny. You stir a hornet's nest, you've got to expect to get your sad butt stung."

Dr. Toliver set his jaw. "That knife cuts two ways, buddy boy."

Katsu was alone by the time Service and Sedge got back to him.

"Toliver seems pretty insistent about his permits."

Katsu said, "I'm telling you, the Office of the State Archaeologist *can't* permit him legally because there *are* remains here. It would be a violation, a desecration—not that such things ever stopped *wabishi* in the past."

"Have you talked to this archaeology office?"

"They only talk to other archaeologists. Seems to us the State *wants* Toliver to dig here, only we can't figure out exactly why."

"Historical reasons?"

"Or black-market artifacts," Sedge interjected.

Service stared at her. "*Artifacts . . .* here?"

Sedge walked over to the four-wheeler and opened a storage case mounted on the handlebars. "If Toliver's honorable, why's he carrying a shovel? Archaeologists don't dig in the dark."

"Emergency kit for the four-wheeler?" Service countered.

Sedge extracted a trowel, a whisk broom, and a small bucket with wire mesh across the bottom. "This stuff look to you like four-wheeler emergency equipment?"

She had a point, and Service felt a rumble in his stomach, a sure sign that he had rolled into the middle of something he sensed he was totally unprepared to deal with. They chained the four-wheeler to a tree, told Katsu to keep his people away from the machine, and headed out.

Sedge said nothing during the long hike back to their trucks. Hers was parked next to his. Suddenly she pivoted sharply and raised a fist. "Who in the *hell* do you think you are, horning in on *my* case!"

Holy shit. She's a damn wildcat. "Whoa," he said, raising his hands. "I'm not horning in on anything."

"I've been working this goddamn case for months. I just got an assistant attorney general up to speed, and *that* asshole jumped ship to another job without a goddamn word. Now I have to start all over."

Once some of her fire had been tamped down, Service said, "Look, you don't want me in this, I'm outta here; color me gone. It's that simple."

She looked up at him and gnawed the inside of her cheek. "No, you'd better come to my place after we patrol and let me bring you up to speed."

"That mean you want me in?"

"Take my word," she said strangely. "You'd like that."

He had a feeling she wasn't talking about the case. Talking to her was like running through an unmarked minefield. *Keep your mouth shut,* he advised himself. It was Friday, and he was tired.

5

Bomb Shelter, M-123, Luce County

SATURDAY, MAY 5, 2007

They did not get to her place until well after midnight. Service felt vaguely sore from hiking, and he was famished.

As McKower had told him, the old gas station was right on M-123, just before the Middle Branch of Linton Creek. A large and rusty metal Mobil Oil sign squeaked as the morning wind pushed against it. "That thing looks like it's gonna come down someday and cause some damage," Service said, trying to look at the woman without being obnoxious. She stood no more than five-foot-five, had her hair stuffed under her law enforcement baseball cap, and looked like she was borderline anorexic. "You follow my tracks in last night?" he asked her.

"By the Five-Pack," she said, adding, "I'm Donna Sedge, but call me Jingo." She did not stick out her hand. "Saw your truck on the AVL."

"Jingo's a different kind of name," he said.

"I'm a different kind of person," she muttered.

Service sensed that the anger that had surfaced earlier was still there, but now she was holding it back. *Measuring me?* he wondered. *Regretting inviting me back here?*

"You want me to rustle up some coffee?" she asked.

They were still outside, between their two trucks. "That'd be good," he said.

She made no move to open the door to her place. "Toliver was in Paradise yesterday. Someone I know heard him say he was headed to the beach again."

"Were you following Toliver?" Service asked.

"I don't have to follow him. Katsu has a plant at the motel where Toliver stays. The informant calls Katsu, then me. Until I saw your truck pop up on the computer and cut your trail," she said, "I had everything under control. Been up to me I'd never have let Toliver get that close to Katsu's people, but I saw your call on the AVL and figured I'd already had this out with Katsu; he knows he can't be messing with Toliver or anyone else who comes out there. It's public land, and moral right isn't synonymous with legal right."

She seemed on the verge of boiling. "I didn't intend to interfere. I've looked into Toliver's background. He's not some scribble-school chump, Detective. He's highly respected and damn powerful in academic circles."

It dawned on Service that Sedge was deeply involved in all this, whatever it was, and that maybe she had neglected to inform her lieutenant. "Have you talked to the state archaeologist?" he asked her, intentionally switching directions to see how she would react.

She made a growling sound. "Those clowns don't talk to mere cops. We're the equivalent of dog turds under their flip-flops."

"You know, we have good senior people in Lansing to run interference for such things."

"Yeah, and we all know what a big fan of Lansing *you* are," she said sarcastically.

"Does McKower know what's going on?"

"Know *what?*"

"About Katsu, Toliver, any of this."

"Don't you *get* it? Eight weeks ago *I* didn't know anything. All I heard was that a bunch of tribals were harassing four-wheeler types out here, and I came out to investigate. Katsu and his people had erected a fence with signs asking all non-Indians to stay away out of respect for his ancestors' remains."

She added, "The old village was in a bit of a sandy bowl, eh. Ass-bags on four-wheelers like to rip up and down the dunes, and they were obliterating everything. If you look around in daylight you can see for yourself." She continued, "I asked Katsu to take down the barriers and to explain to me what the heck was going on, and since then I've been meeting with him and learning. I don't know enough yet to officially talk to anyone downstate, but my instinct was to first go to the attorney general's office and find out what they knew about this sort of situation. This couldn't be the first time this sort of thing has happened."

"The state archaeologist won't talk?"

"*Hell-ooo!* They talk, but what they say is that cops do *not* have a right or a need to know where historic sites are, or to know what's in them, *unless* a crime is committed on such ground, and if we detect a suspected crime, we're to report it to them. Only then will the SAO verify a site's existence. *Maybe.*"

What the hell was she telling him? "That makes no sense," Service said. "How the hell do we patrol something if we don't even know it's there?"

"They're afraid we'll reveal secrets the public isn't entitled to know. Or steal the artifacts ourselves."

"We patrol and take care of underwater preserves," he said.

"The ones we know about," she countered. "There's a whole lot out there we don't know anything about."

Santinaw had propelled him into something that smelled like it could carry him down to Lansing and create a nasty bureaucratic food fight. The thought made Service weary. His every interaction with Lansing was less than satisfying. Last year he had worked a case involving possible graft among personnel in the DNR itself, and he was still disappointed and bitter about the outcome. He had put civilians in jail, but insiders had retired and escaped unscathed.

"You said you talked to the AG's office?"

"I did, and they didn't know shit, but they handed me off to a deputy and I did a whole bunch of research and got the assistant AG up to speed. Last week, absolutely out of the blue, the sonuvabitch retired and joined an association of archaeologists as its executive director." She sighed. "My problem is that according to the records Toliver cites, this place was pre-Ojibwa, and abandoned *before* the Ojibwa even migrated to this area."

Service asked, "What about the Iroquois remains he talked about?"

"As far as I know, nobody's ever looked for them at that location," Sedge said. "Only Katsu claims there was a battle here, and even he doesn't know exactly where. The stories say the Iroquois camped in this region, dragged their canoes onto the sand, and got drunk. They were headed west on the war road. Katsu claims his people first spotted them to the east, closer to Bay Mills, and followed them west, maintaining a safe distance. The enemy force was nearly three hundred strong, plus some captives they'd collected along the way. The Ojibwa had help from their Odawa brothers and some others, and fell on the *Na-do-we-se* before sunrise. It was over almost before it began. According to the legend, the attackers killed all but three of the enemy, cut the heads off the dead, lined up the severed heads on the beach, and told the survivors to go back to their homeland and tell their people that if they ever again came onto Ojibwa land, the Ojibwa would build a road of skulls all the way back to their land."

"Very dramatic. Did they come again?"

"Apparently not," Sedge said.

"Santinaw says humans can't own land."

"There's so much damn Native American crap to sort from fact," she said.

Service said, "Katsu claims occupying is temporary ownership even by old tribal standards, occupation and stewardship being synonymous in some cases for some people."

She nodded. "I listened to the same story and told him it's *public* land, and he can't legally block the public from using it. Katsu said to me, 'Even if they are tearing up our heritage? Every time they shoot through here on their machines, they destroy remains.' "

"I corrected him. 'Artifacts, *not* human remains.' "

" 'Don't quibble,' he told me. He insists there are bodies out there."

"Corroboration?" Service asked.

This earned him another sour face. "Not exactly, but I learned that about ten years ago a professor from Whitewater State in Wisconsin conducted a dig there. No bodies were found, but months later—the next spring—she reported finding remains that the winter storms and sand-shifts had uncovered. More likely she was back digging again, the second time without authorization, but, having found a body, was afraid someone would find out, so she reported it as being found on the surface. She said she reburied it, but refused to say where."

"Who'd she tell this to?" Service asked.

"State archaeologist's office, in writing, and the SAO wrote its own report, in effect declaring, 'No harm, no foul.' I had to get the damn thing through FOIA—on my own dime. The department's lawyers in Lansing were too busy to help me."

"But you figure she was digging without proper clearance."

"I wasn't there, but it smells that way to me. There were some known artifact caches that disappeared at that time. The DNR even knew where they were—we'd cataloged them ourselves—then word got out about the remains and the artifacts went missing."

"Wouldn't it make sense to locate the *Na-do-we-se* burials and push the State to reclassify the ground?"

"Katsu insists the remains are there and that it's wrong to disturb them."

"You could've called me on the 800 last night, let me know you were in the area," he chastised her.

"Back at you! *Listen to you!* Yeah, sure," she said, "I *could* have done, but I saw your number and I thought, Holy shit—why's the Big Dog lifting his leg in *my* backyard?"

Big Dog? "Katsu's father is an old friend. He asked me to look into this."

"Katsu's *father?*"

"His name's St. Andrew, but he's known as Santinaw."

"You should have checked in with me," she said. "You know, professional courtesy, trust, teamwork, all that other good shit?"

"Don't be so territorial," he said. "I called McKower. She doesn't know anything's going on out here, and she asked me to give you a bump, but I wanted to see what I was dealing with first."

Sedge, clearly exasperated, stared at him. "I think you'd better come inside."

"The Bomb Shelter?" he said to her.

"Intelligent people usually have good reasons for what they do," she countered, "even if others are too thick to understand them."

"No doubt," he said, as Sedge opened the door to the cinder-block building and flipped on tracklights.

Service stepped inside and tried to keep his mouth from hanging open. The walls were covered with brightly colored paintings of exceedingly hirsute pudenda. *What the hell is this!*

"Cat gotcher tongue?" Sedge asked with a shit-eating grin.

"Unique," he managed to mutter. *What the . . . ?*

"All self-portraits, studies in light."

"Uh, I guess I'm not much of an art aficionado."

"Do tell," she said sarcastically. "The el-tee tell you anything about my background?"

Service tried to not stare at the paintings, but he couldn't help himself.

"My old man's a tribal cop at Isabella. I grew up in Mount Pleasant, went to college at MSU on an academic scholarship, did a stint in the army, got discharged, and went back to East Lansing where I majored in fine art and went all the way through to my MFA, when it dawned on me that I needed a paying job to support my art, so I took a master's in law enforcement, applied for the academy, and here I am."

"That doesn't explain *everything*," he said, nodding at the paintings.

"Ah," she said with a grin. "A big-time gallery in Indianapolis wants them, and so does another in Minneapolis, so I'm going to take some days off and personally deliver the stuff. Meanwhile, I don't want my colleagues all coming in here to gawk at my pussy."

Service was dumbfounded.

"You ought to know that Katsu and his bunch hate my ass," she said.

"It didn't show."

"They aren't going to let some white badge know there's a rift, but they resent the hell out of a woman with a white man's badge walking into their deal and maybe controlling their fate. Behind my back they call me *no-je-mik bishi-gwadj-ik-we*."

"Like I said earlier tonight, my Shinob vocabulary isn't all that current."

"Female Beaver Whore," she said with an ironic grin. "Is that totally sophomoric and lame, or what? Someone broke into my place and saw the paintings. I wasn't surprised, and I still resent you going at me over my el-tee. But you might as well call me Pocahunkus."

Service stepped back, his mind reeling. "I didn't go *at* you or over you. Pocahunkus . . . You mean Pocahontas?"

"I mean what I say, Service. My mother use to call a woman's privates her hunkus. That's the title of my collection: 'Hunkusland.' "

"Are you nuts?"

"No, but I can draw a pair if you like. Listen, I may be new by your dinosaur standards, but I *know* what I'm doing, and I especially know how to deal with my *own* turf."

He couldn't believe she had once again ignited like a match. *How the hell had she gotten through the academy and field training with that temper?* "Really," he said, trying to placate her. "I was just asking obvious questions."

"Don't patronize me with small talk!" she shot back at him. "I say what I mean and mean what I say. You do the same."

"That so?"

"Yeah, and I heard you were similar, which is obviously bogus information."

He was too hungry to listen and tired of her anger, and it was nearing daylight. "Knock it off, Sedge. If you want to paint pictures of your twat and call it art, that's okay by me, but I'm done being polite. This thing with Katsu and the artifacts doesn't have anything to do with *your* people or *my* people.

It has to do with a dispute between a state agency and Toliver, and Katsu—who I can't sympathize with—has no official role or rights in any of this."

"Figures," she said.

"*What* figures?" *Calm down*, he told himself.

"You write a guy off because he's done time."

"*Katsu* did time?"

"Vehicular homicide—five years in a state lockup in Minnesota."

"I didn't know that."

"Neither did I until recently, and he didn't tell me. It was a friend who put me on to it, and then I checked. When I confronted Katsu, he went ballistic."

Service thought for a moment. "With a felony he's risking his ass by protesting this thing."

"Which might also just suggest how sincere he is?" she countered. "One plus one doesn't always equal two."

Grady Service couldn't disagree, but he didn't know Katsu well enough to judge. He turned toward one of the walls and pointed. "I think I like the purple one best," he said.

Sedge laughed out loud. "You don't have a clue about art."

"*That's* not against the law, is it?"

"Depends on your intentions."

"I think getting the hell out of here as fast as I can is at the top of my list."

"Do you find all this disturbing, Detective?"

"Uh-huh," he mumbled.

"Geez, you're probably gonna hate my next project. Wanna know what it is?"

"Not a chance," he said, bolting for the door.

She followed him out to the Tahoe. "Sorry," she said. "This isn't easy for me, but I need help. I know I've got something, but I'm not sure what, or where to take it next."

"Get in," Grady Service said. He looked over at the young woman. "We've all been where you are."

"Even you, the Big Dog?"

"*Especially* me. Nobody's born a big dog."

6

Paradise, Chippewa County

SATURDAY, MAY 5, 2007

Early morning twilight in the east. Service allowed Sedge to stew in silence as he drove east on M-123, past the entrance to Tahquamenon Falls to Paradise.

In town he pulled into the lot of a place called the Bay-O-Wolf Coffee Emporium and ordered plain black coffees, which earned a look of disapprobation from their waitperson.

"Okay," he said to Sedge, "tell me succinctly exactly what you think you have."

"Were you not paying attention?"

"I was listening, but humor me."

"Removal of historical artifacts from public land and an archaeological site."

"That's it?"

"That's not enough?"

"Once taken, what happens to the artifacts?"

"I don't know," she said with a shrug.

"You've *seen* these artifacts being taken?"

"No, afterwards. I saw where they had been."

"But you saw them *before* they were removed—for whatever reason."

She was stumbling a bit. "Some of them. It's hard to explain."

"Did Duncan Katsu come to you with this?"

"No. Like I told you, I got word that he and his people were causing a goat-rodeo, illegally blocking public land. I went out there, found signs warning people away, and a rudimentary camp. Then I called Katsu and asked to meet him."

"*Called* him? He lives there, right?"

"No, he lives near Strongs on Indian Trust Land, near where Creek Number Eight flows into the East Branch of the Tahquamenon."

Service knew that the feds owned land set aside by treaties for various tribal uses. Why the tribes did not have ownership of such parcels had always eluded him—some arcane point of law, no doubt. "His old man told me he lives on the Coast of Death."

"No, Strongs, like I just said."

"Have you been to his place?"

She frowned. "Are you insinuating—"

"Stop being so damn prickly. I'm asking about his lifestyle, his house, what you saw there."

She calmed. "Simple camp, one-story, your basic box in the woods. He drives a ten-year-old minivan."

"How did he react when you called?"

"He was polite. I told him what I had found at the site and that I wanted to know what was going down, that I had drawn no conclusions. He asked me to meet him on the beach and I did. He took me around the site and showed me how to recognize artifacts. They're everywhere out there, and he's devised a clever way to mark what's what. There was even a ten-inch-long copper spear point that was stunning."

"Valuable?"

"I assume, but I don't know. It disappeared before I could talk to anyone to get it appraised. But I got photos." She took out her digital camera and showed him.

"Nice," he said. "This is at the place he claims is a battle site *and* burial ground?"

"Yes, but the copper point wouldn't be part of that. It's older."

"Site of the old road of skulls story?"

She nodded. "He claims."

"You buy it?"

"I don't know enough to accept or reject."

"You trust Katsu?"

"I want to. The day I met him out there I told him he couldn't block the public, that he'd have to tear down his stuff."

"Was he alone?"

"No, he had his usual entourage of assholes and hangers-on, but they did as I directed, and took everything away."

"When was this?"

"Last fall. I spent all winter trying to get more information on the site."

"And?"

"A retired Michigan State professor provided some help, but nobody is certain where the actual battle took place. Or even *if* it really happened. My people are prone to hyperbole and intergalactic metaphor."

"Okay," Service said. "Jump to Professor Delmure Arcton Toliver of Hibernian College."

"Legit, substantial professional rep; he's dug all over the Midwest, the Northeast, and Canada, and he has lots of papers to his name, not to mention a CV as long as a tiger muskie."

"You think he's lifting artifacts?"

"I don't know. A little voice tells me he is who he claims he is, and it's all legit—a noted archaeologist wanting to dig and having the permission of the State, and having jumped through all the hoops and red tape resents Katsu's intervention."

"That would be understandable," Service said.

Sedge nodded. "For sure."

"What about the digging gear on the ATV?"

"I don't think it's what Katsu claims. I think that stuff is part of the professor's field kit for sinking core samples, which he has approval to take."

"But Katsu thinks Toliver's your guy."

"Maybe, but Toliver's handy, and I'm not sure Katsu really thinks it's him. It could be that Katsu wants us to make an example of the professor, and that could be enough to back off the real thieves, even if Toliver isn't part of it."

"*If* there are thieves," Service said.

"Oh, there *are* thieves," she said resolutely.

"What about the state archaeologist?"

"My only contact was in regard to the Whitewater State professor."

"The one who uncovered remains and allegedly reburied them God knows where?"

"That would be her: Dr. Ladania Wingel."

"You talked to her?"

"I mostly listened as she ranted and accused me of being a chauvinist and a racist."

"Indian?"

"African-American," she said.

"Over-the-top reaction?"

"*Queen Mary* when a jonboat would have done the job."

He found himself laughing. Sedge could be funny. "So Katsu takes the law into his own hands and blocks Toliver, who denies there are any remains on the site. Who told you about Wingel?"

"Katsu. I'm also guessing he has his own archaeologist guiding things from behind the scenes."

"His band's not federally recognized."

"But they have filed. I checked."

"You've confirmed it?"

She nodded. "I talked to the feds who talked to Katsu. They don't have the paperwork, but the feds say this is standard—that pulling together the evidence for an application is a huge and exacting job."

"Have you asked Katsu if he has his own archaeologist?"

"Not yet."

"Okay, so you went to the state archaeologist to confirm the business with Dr. Wingel and the State said, 'No harm, no foul.' What the hell does *that* mean?"

"Got me. I never actually met or talked to the state archaeologist. I sent my letter in December, which was not answered until April—April first, to be precise. He made it clear that law enforcement is persona non grata and not entitled to know the location of archeological sites *unless* we detect criminal activity, in which case he could confirm a site—if necessary."

"Then what?"

"Spring came, Katsu headed back up to the coast, I got word Toliver was coming, and that's where you and I ran together in déjà-vu-all-over-again-land."

"What do you want to do next?"

"I asked for *your* help."

Rephrase it dummy, she's nervous. "What don't you have?"

"I don't have shit."

"*Sedge.*"

"Evidence of artifact theft," she said. "I guess."

"You checking trout fishermen yet?"

"Water's still too high from runoff, and blackflies will hatch any day."

"As a department we don't have all the mileage we want. What do we have?"

She looked at him and he could see the lightbulb come on. "Time," she said, "Surveillance time?"

"Count me in," he said.

"What exactly do we surveil?"

"Katsu showed you around the site, right?"

"He showed me some of it, but he's also admitted he's not really sure where the main site is."

"You want me to quote his nitwitship Don Rumsfeld's silly shit about knowing what we don't know versus not knowing what we don't know?"

"I don't know," she said, making both of them laugh.

"Let's go take a look, make our plan based on what we find."

"Today?"

"No; I need to get home, pay bills, hug my dog, all that good stuff. Three days from now, sunrise, the Bomb Shelter."

"I'll have coffee waiting."

He held up a finger. "Just not inside, please."

"Art's an acquired taste."

"Don't even," he said, leaving cash for the waitress.

7

Harvey, Marquette County

SATURDAY, MAY 5, 2007

The wall clock read 11 p.m., straight up, and Tuesday Friday's leg was draped over his hip. "Boyohboyohboyohboy," she said breathlessly. They were still slippery with postcoital sweat. "I vote for a frequency greater than weekly," she whispered playfully. "I like you Grady Service. A heap. How long do we get you?"

"Tonight and tomorrow night. You want to bring Shigun out to my place?"

"Sure," she said. "Where are you headed next?"

He laid out the story and she listened, and when he finished, she said, "Odetta Trevillyan, Marquette County Historical Society. Grew up in Calumet, educated at Smith, retired distinguished professor of history from Yale, now living at Shot Point."

"Indian specialist?"

"I don't think so, but she's a polymath and interested in all things Native American."

"Odetta Trevillyan?" he said.

"Honest-to-God Cornish. Chances are she'll ask you a lot of questions that will help you refocus your own ideas more clearly. You want to fool around again?"

"Is that rhetorical?"

"What do *you* think?" she asked, kissing him with the sort of ardor that kick-started his heart rate and all that cascaded from there.

8

Marquette, Marquette County

SUNDAY, MAY 6, 2007

Service called the historical society's office and a volunteer gave him Trevillyan's personal cell number. She would not be working today, but she answered her cell phone. After hearing what he wanted, she suggested he join her for coffee and pastries as soon as he could get there. "Shot Point Road, directly across from Lakenland," she said.

He knew Lakenland, a scattering of more than three dozen whimsical and nonsensical statues created from scrap metal by a retired pipefitter. Some of the more conservative elements of local society called the place an eyesore, but Service admired such whimsy, and knew that artist Tom Lakenen didn't charge admission or try to hawk his creations. He made stuff for people to enjoy purely for his and their pleasure, and Service considered it an almost sacred calling.

"Less than half an hour?" Service suggested. He was at his office in the regional DNR building called The Roof because of its unique architectural design.

"I'll be waiting," Trevillyan said. She had an alert, pleasant voice.

The house, which overlooked Lake Superior from a height, was humongo—three stories, giant orange logs (the real deal, not half-logs in facade), windows everywhere, a huge deck looking out on the big lake, which at the moment was rolling lazy soft blue-gray swells onto the rocks below. The house had a three-car garage with only one vehicle, a four-door PT Cruiser, but there were several bicycles nearby.

The woman who came out through the garage weighed no more than a hundred pounds and moved like air. She had short white hair and wore spandex running shorts and red-and-gold Asics running shoes. She looked muscular and fit enough to run a marathon uphill.

She introduced herself, insisted he call her Etta, and invited him into the house. "Do you like blackberries?"

"Sometimes," he said.

She turned and looked at him momentarily, sizing him up. "Always speak your mind?"

"Not always."

"Good. These are Texas blackies, which can't hold a candle to our Upper Peninsula berries, but in a pinch, eh? Most of the year I have to content myself with less than optimal substitutes—sheer impostors!"

She laughed out loud and placed a cup of coffee and a small turnover in front of him. "I can warm it, if you'd prefer."

"This is fine," he said, nibbling the turnover.

"No sugar in the crust. I make a thin crust of sugar as I take them out of the oven. That way the sweetness doesn't overwhelm. Enjoy."

The flavor was indescribable.

"You like?" she asked.

He nodded.

"Good, now try this." She opened the oven and pulled out a pasty, one that had already been cut. She gave him a chunk on a small plate. The flavor coursed through him like a bolt.

Trevillyan nodded happily and raised an eyebrow. "The trick is to freeze the lard, then grate it fine. The juniper berries I picked last year, and froze. The morels are last year's whites, dried and hung. You can use either Marsala or Madeira, although I prefer the latter. I call it a U.P. shroompasty."

"You could market this."

"Then the fun would be gone," she said. She took two pasties from the oven, put them in a cloth bag, and set it on the table by him. "For later," she said, sitting down and refilling their coffee cups.

"Iroquois and Ojibwa wars," she began. "Like most things historical, it seems a simple request, but one fraught with complications."

"Such as?" he said.

"Dates, to begin with; aboriginals don't think in terms of calendar years. History places your battle in 1662, thirty miles east of the mouth of the Tahquamenon, but that's European white history, not Native American history, and I doubt white men were in the fight, so what we get from Europeans is all secondhand—which is to say, *their* slant or spin. I think that's the word nowadays, *spin*."

"Suggestions?"

"One, definitely look at the *Jesuit Relations*. All Jesuit missionaries were required to file annual reports—so to speak—to their home offices, which they called mother houses. All the original reports from Upper and Lower Canada reside in Quebec City, but most reports from Canada have also been translated into English. There's a chance one of the priests reported the battle, and while it's unlikely he was an actual witness, he might have heard an early version of the oral account. It might be useful for you to compare that with the story as it is spun now in more contemporary retellings."

"*Jesuit Relations.*"

"Don't be intimidated by the title. The reports make fascinating reading."

"Where do I find them?"

"The J. M. Longyear Research Library in the Peter White Library, right here in town," Trevillyan said. "I'll call and let them know when you're ready to do some reading. I have to tell you . . . there are aspects of the legendary battle that have always bothered me."

He let silence work.

"Mainly, it's the scope. Instances of large belligerent aboriginal forces going head-to-head to the death are exceedingly rare in history. War back then was a way to scare up more women and manpower for the tribe, and for personal aggrandizement, rarely for territorial conquest or acquisition. Some accounts report three hundred dead Iroquois, which would make the size of the war party and the fight unprecedented, perhaps for the entire Midwest. Scholars believe at the height of their power the five tribes of the Iroquois Confederation could marshal no more than five thousand warriors—tops. After smallpox began to decimate the Iroquois, their war-fighting capacity was a helluva lot less than that. Seriously, who risks six percent of their army in *one fight?*"

"What about the bit with the road of skulls?"

"*No-te-pe-ti-go*? It's plausible, but not probable. Aboriginals were and are big into symbols. . . ."

"But," he said, anticipating her pause.

"The fight could have been in 1662, or '72 or '52, or none of the above. It could have been no more than baloney and wishful thinking, and *if* it happened, it might have happened at what we now know as Iroquois Point—or not. Nothing is certain. The Ojibwa had no written language at that point in their history. The Iroquois did, but they weren't going to write about getting their butts kicked. For the Ojibwa back then, everything was moved by word of mouth, and as a police officer, you know what historians know: Oral tradition and hearsay might be interesting, but they aren't worth a damn in court or as an accurate verification of fact."

"If you were trying to pinpoint the site, how would you go about it?"

"You can see that I like to run?"

"I guessed that."

"I run because I like to eat even more. By running a lot I can eat a lot and not gain weight. It's a way to offset my weakness with strength. The point is that the Ojibwa had no written language in the ordinary sense, but their Midewiwin Society used a form of pictographs that are quite detailed and rich. You familiar with the Mide?"

"They were medicine men, elders mostly, rarely accepting of whites. You know a Mide priest?" he asked her.

"Sorry, ethnography isn't my forte, but what I can say from my limited knowledge is that virtually none of the Ojibwa oral history checks out factually. Let me repeat: I've got serious doubts, though I admit up front I've never given any of this serious thought or scholarly focus. We are left with something like three hundred dead Iroquois warriors, give or take, which would be about one in twenty of their total amalgamated fighting forces. The accounts don't mention Ojibwa losses. I doubt the victors would have left any of the dead to scavengers, but Ojibwa and Iroquois burial practices were different. The Iroquois buried the dead in the flex position—sitting up —facing east. The Ojibwa put their remains aboveground in spirit houses. After time, the Iroquois dug up the bones, cleansed them, and put them all in a community ossuary with great reverence and ceremony."

"If the Iroquois weren't buried?"

"The remains would have been scattered by scavengers and weather. Porcupines would have eaten some of the bones. There's something else that strikes me as odd. According to what I know, which admittedly is not that much, the Iroquois were a top-down military society, and it was their custom—if their leader fell in battle—to melt away to regroup and fight another day under a new leader. They didn't stick around leaderless in the hope of some Pyrrhic victory."

"What if someone dug up remains that had been buried?"

"I'd assume they were Iroquois, and that the victors buried them to honor them."

"After removing their heads."

"That's not unusual or odd for aboriginal thinking, but hell, we do the same sort of things. We kill our enemies by the millions, then rebuild the vanquished countries. It's thoroughly human, and therefore without logic. Human beings make *Alice in Wonderland* look like a veritable documentary."

Grady Service laughed. *I like this woman.* "*Jesuit Relations*, that's your recommendation?"

The woman spread her hands in resignation. "Got a card?" He handed one to her.

"In case I think of something else."

Nice words, he thought, *but just words. No conviction. She's the kind who doesn't like to disappoint.* "How extensive are these *Jesuit Relations?*"

"Close to two hundred years' worth."

This is helpful?

9

Slippery Creek Camp

SUNDAY, MAY 6, 2007

Newf, his 130-pound Presa Canario, a Canary Island mastiff, stared at him with a look that said, "Where have *you* been, jerkwad?" Even misanthropic Cat hissed spitefully, which she did, happy or angry. She had only one mood: bad. The dog had been a gift from a former girlfriend who thought it might help him get past his fear of dogs, and he'd thought it was working until the pit bull the other day.

On the way home he'd stopped at Econofoods in Marquette and bought boneless chicken breasts. Since Nantz's death he tended to cook in multiple batches, freezing what he didn't eat for road chow. Friday enjoyed cooking, but where he and Nantz had been wild and sexual in the kitchen, Friday was more restrained, measured, orderly, and she was also always on time.

He would have shopped closer to his camp, but the Upper Peninsula's independent grocery stores in small towns and villages were dying fast because of the competition of big chains and the crush of the state's failed economy.

Service whipped up a salad of lettuce, English cukes, grape tomatoes, slivers of Spanish onion, California golden raisins, dried apricots, chopped dates, ground pecans, fresh avocado and clementines, and scallions. He set the salad aside and began assembling the meat. He would microwave sweet potatoes for them. He got a dozen Thai red peppers out of the freezer and chopped them finely. He mixed hot curry powder, salt, and pepper and rubbed the mixture into the chicken breasts. He set a nonstick frying pan on the stove while he grated lemon zest. Finally, he poured two glasses of Barolo and looked out the front window.

With Friday's entry into his life he had once again put away the footlockers he'd slept on for years, replacing them with a king-size bed in the upstairs bedroom (which he had finally gotten around to finishing).

When Friday pulled into his road he went outside to help her and the baby, who clung to him as he bounced him happily. Newf jumped and whimpered, wanting her own share of kid time.

"Gotta feed His Majesty," Friday said, after giving Service a lingering kiss. She carried a bag with bottles and baby food. Service packed more formula into the fridge.

The solidly built Shigun was a placid, happy eighteen-month-old toddler until he was hungry or needed a diaper change.

"You want me to start cooking?"

"Go ahead, the kid eats like you—fast. What's on the menu?"

"Something new."

"I don't need fancy," she said, meaning it.

"It's basic," he told her.

"I bet," she said, rolling her eyes. "Shigun can sit with us while we eat."

He handed her a glass of wine. "Trying to ply me?" she asked.

"I don't know that exact word, but if it means making reckless boom-boom, yeah."

He put four chicken breasts in the pan and cooked them six minutes a side, cooking until three batches were done. He spooned two small breasts on each plate and left the rest of the meat to cool on the counter. He'd put the remaining eight breasts in plastic freezer bags after dinner. *Which reminds me—I need to pull some meals out of the freezer for Sedge and me.*

Service combined lemon juice, water, and sugar-free apricot jam in a saucepan and heated and whisked until the mixture was smooth. Then he spooned the sauce onto the plated breasts and sprinkled them with lemon zest and finely minced Thai red peppers.

"Jesus, Grady. That smells unbelievable. What's it called?"

"Curried apricot-lemon chicken."

"You call this *basic?*"

"Have I ever led you astray?"

"Kehh!" she said with a snigger. "Every chance you get."

"I meant gastronomically," he said, correcting himself.

"No."

"Eat."

He watched her sample the chicken and close her eyes.

"Damn," she whispered.

They ate in earnest for a while, quiet, no talking. When Friday had the hungries, conversation went bye-bye.

After a while she said, "This Sedge kid, what's she like?"

He told her about the paintings and got her laughing so hard she nearly choked. "Jesus! Her *hunkus?*" Friday punched his chest with the heel of her hand and laughed out loud. "You're making that up!"

"It's true, and let me say at the outset—and for the record—that I cannot testify to the veracity of her work."

No laugh this time. "Better keep it that way, buster." Then, "I noticed you left the little detail of pussy paintings for our second night together."

He shrugged.

"Our case last year involved eighty-year-old remains; now this. Has it ever struck you as odd, the range of your responsibilities?"

"This archaeology thing is entirely new to me, and probably it's the same for most officers on the force."

"Sedge up to the challenge?"

"She seems to have a lot of gears. I talked to Etta Trevillyan today."

"Can you believe that woman is seventy-five? She dates a forty-five-year-old emergency-room physician from Munising."

"No *way* she's seventy-five," he countered.

"Way, dude. Was she helpful?"

"Yes and no."

"The old 'academic balance' deal?"

"More or less."

"Heading east tomorrow?"

"Early. Sunrise at Sedge's place."

"Conservation officers keep shitaceous hours," she said.

"No argument from me. Is that a real word?"

"It is now. You gonna call Little Maridly tonight?"

"After dinner and the dishes."

"Sure you're up to it?"

His granddaughter, who would be three in December was precocious and already exercising the vocabulary of a balls-to-the-wall ten-year-old.

"She's gonna be a load when she's a teeneager," Friday said.

"Shigun isn't?"

"Boys are way easier to raise than us girls, dude."

They loaded the dishwasher and Friday took Shigun for his nightly bath while he picked up the phone and dialed Houghton.

A tiny voice answered, "Pengelly residence, this is Maridly."

Don't tear up, he told himself. "This the rugrat who eats dirt?" he challenged her.

He heard her giggle and inhale. "I only *eated* it once and I *did not* like it, and I am *a pretty little girl—not* a rugrat."

"Better a rugrat than a rat on a rope."

The little girl squealed with delight. "*Bampy!*" she screamed into the phone. "When are you coming to see me?"

"Soon baby. Where's your mom?"

"Mum's right here."

"Can I talk to her?"

Pause. "She says she guesses. I love you, Bampy."

"Shigun's here."

"We *like* Shigun," the girl said. "He's cute!"

"I know we do, hon."

Maridly's mother had been his son's girlfriend. Karylanne had been pregnant when Walter was killed, and he had taken the girl and her baby into his life as if they were his own, which, in his mind, they were.

Karylanne Pengelly was trying to finish a master's degree at Michigan Tech, and when that was done she'd begin looking for a job. The thought of her moving away with his granddaughter made his stomach roll.

Friday met him upstairs, wearing nothing but a backwards baseball hat.

"Shigun's asleep already," she said, smiling. "How's the kiddo?"

"Steering the planet through space," he said. "What's with the hat? You calling balls and strikes tonight?"

She lowered an eyebrow and said, "Just balls."

10

Coast of Death, Luce County

MONDAY, MAY 7, 2007

Sedge looked half-asleep, but as promised had a thermos of fresh coffee sitting on the tailgate of her work truck. "Big Dog," she greeted him.

"Pocahunkus," he replied.

"You ready to roll?" she said, eyeing the trailer with his Polaris RZR. "Holy shit!" she said with a yelp. "Eight hundred XP, Bimini roof, winch, spare tire, full windshield, steel deer guard—that bitch is totally tricked out. Lemme guess: This is *not* department-issue."

"Mizz Einstein. Grab your brain bucket."

"Don't need one in the RZR."

"You haven't ridden with me."

"Point taken." She went into the Bomb Shelter and came out carrying her helmet bag. "Take off from here?"

"Let's take the truck and trailer north, unload up there. Toss your gear in my truck. No point taking two."

Sedge said, "Let's cruise up CR 500, head into the area from Crisp Point."

"Rationale?"

"Luce County is a magnet for every ATV outlaw and moron for five hundred miles. Good PR to be seen, and let them see us with the RZR, which will get them to thinking."

"Head-bending is good," he said. "The endless psyops between good and evil."

Despite early snowmelt and no spring rain, back roads were in terrible shape, county graders not yet deployed. Service drove slowly over the endless washboarding, preferring to be off on two-tracks, but Sedge wanted to fly the department flag, and as her partner he was all for it.

"Ever hear of *Jesuit Relations*?" he asked.

"I thought those dudes were celibate," she quipped. Then, "No."

He explained what they were and ended with, "The super-sensitive Dr. Ladania Wingel—you know where she lives?"

"Jefferson, Wisconsin."

He stared at her. "Are you kidding?"

"Hardly. What's the big deal?"

Jefferson was home to the late Wayno Ficorelli's ferocious aunt, Marge Ciucci. Wisconsin Warden Wayno, who had worked with him on a case, and had been murdered by the same person or persons who killed Nantz and his son. Ficorelli had been a hard-charging Wisconsin game warden. Ciucci had wanted vengeance against her nephew's murderer, and had not danced around it with delicate language.

"Might be good to visit Dr. Wingel, give her the up-close eyeball."

Sedge said, "There's no budget, and that sounds like a nasty trip to me."

"I know someone I can stay with for free in Jefferson."

"What about *me?*"

"You'd probably want to paint your hunkus—or something."

She smiled. "I might just."

"I'll call my contact over there, see if she knows Wingel, can fill us in on the professor's local reputation."

"*She?* You keep a 'she' in Wisconsin?"

"No, my *she* is in Marquette," he said, thinking, *And not kept.* "Aunt Marge Ciucci is in Jefferson. Last time I saw her she told me in Italian not to break her balls and nobody fucks her in the ass." *My 'she.' I wonder how Tuesday would like that description.*

"Sweet," Sedge said. "My kinda gal."

"Did you ask Wingel about the body?"

"She never gave me a chance. She said the wind uncovered it and she reburied it, end of story."

"That makes you racist?"

"I might have mentioned something about empathy. That's when she went off."

"Follow-up?"

"No point then, but she's on my list. What is it we want from her?"

"Not sure. How'd the body look, what position it was in, anything with it, was it just bones, wrapped? You know . . . stuff?"

"She'll just default to weather."

"How people deny things is often a statement and a clue."

"Sometimes deniers are telling the truth. Maybe winter did uncover the remains. Katsu says it brings new artifacts to the surface every spring."

"Maybe," he said. "What're those handmade signs I keep seeing?"

"LOL?" she said. "Laughing Out Loud."

"Really?"

She grinned. "Only in the computer world. Out here it means Lands of the Lord—a religious camp," she told him. "Catholic wilderness retreat over toward Bear Lake, a few miles south of where we'll be. What religion are you?"

"Earthling . . . mostly."

"I was raised Baptist-Fundamentalist-Agape-Evangelical—you know, no sex standing up 'cause it just might could lead to dancing."

He laughed.

"My church is out here," she said, with a wave at the woods.

"Mine too," he said.

• • •

They left his truck parked off a faint two-track about two miles west of the old Crisp Point lighthouse, unloaded the RZR, and headed east, keeping south of Lake Superior in the woods beyond the barrier dunes. Service carried his handheld GPS to capture the route and final destinations for future use. He'd dump all the data into his truck computer when he got time. He parked the RZR precisely 3.6 miles east of Crisp Point, dismounted, and looked around, stretching his stiff muscles. The four-wheeler pounded your back, even if you were taking it easy.

"I think I came up from the south last Thursday—east of this hill we're on."

"You did," she confirmed.

"You spend a lot of time out here?" he asked her.

"Some, not a lot. But I figure whenever I'm up this way it makes sense to poke around to see what I can see and learn rather than waste gas going back south just because."

"How far is Katsu's spot from here?" Service asked.

"Half-mile, max," Sedge said, "mostly downhill."

"Let's leave the RZR and hump it on foot," he said, grabbing his ruck.

At the top of the hill he stopped and squatted.

"Problem?" she asked.

"No. You know standard military hand signals?"

"I think so." They reviewed them quickly and he nodded. "Delay like this is an old fly fisherman's habit. You never wade right into the river. It's better to stand back, watch, and see if you can figure out what's happening before you jump into action."

"Sounds applicable to a lot of things," Jingo Sedge said.

"It is. Show me our target from here."

"Eleven o'clock, to the right of that scrub oak stand."

"What's over at one o'clock?" he asked.

"Sand. That's where the ATVs have been tearing up shit."

"Beyond that, see the outline?"

"Sort of."

"What's it look like to you?" he asked.

"Amoeba?" she ventured.

"Yeah," he mumbled. "That's as good as anything I can think of." *But there's something swimming in the back of my mind, just out of reach*, the voice in his head said, *something crucial and not so obvious.*

An hour later they were in the sandy area and she was pointing out artifacts, flint chips, pottery shards—some decorated with impressions. "There's stuff *everywhere*," Sedge said.

"The copper point was *here?*"

She pointed. "Over there, right on the surface, Katsu said. See all those little bunches of vertical twigs?"

"I see them."

"They're Katsu's idea: two means tools, three means pottery, four means weapons—stone points, hammers, stuff like that. There's a lot more pottery than anything else."

"What's a one?"

"Put there by chance and wind."

The things she's showing me are certainly interesting, but are they valuable? "Why would people steal this stuff?" he asked her.

"Because they can?"

"Is there a market?"

"Katsu says there is, but I haven't really looked into that yet. The thing that sticks in my mind is that if all this little stuff is on the surface, what sort of big stuff is there, and how much is still below the sand?"

"I hear you," Service said.

"You're sure we want to sit on this place?" she asked.

"I think we need to mark some things, come back every couple of days, see what happens. If stuff gets scarfed up, then we'll sit on the place."

"That's closing the barn door too late," she said.

"Most people aren't smart enough to limit exposure. If they score early, they'll come back again. Greed usually blinds: A thief is a thief. Trail cameras," he added.

"The district's only got three," she said.

"Lucky for us, I've got six in my vehicle," he said. "Starmites."

Sedge's mouth hung open. "From where?"

"My dime."

"At seven big a pop?"

"Hey, they work, high-res, day-night range to sixty feet."

"Wildlife Resources Unit?"

"My own," he said. "We'll have to go back to the truck and fetch them. With six I think we can ambush any bad boys."

"Let's go," Sedge said.

Returning, they put everything in place. With the cameras set, there would be no need for close on-site surveillance. The cameras had built-in motion-detection triggers. Some cameras they set for still photographs, a couple for motion clips. And then they left.

"You going to stick around?" Sedge asked.

"No, I'm thinking I'll use my pass days to talk to Aunt Marge, find out if she knows Wingel. And spend some time in the libes in Marquette."

"Sounds like a plan."

"The library in Marquette has English translations of the *Jesuit Relations*."

"Is detective work satisfying?" Sedge asked.

"Mostly it's scut work, dotting i's, crossing t's, all that regular police detail work. But once in a while all the sour notes fit together and you get some very cool music."

"I like solving puzzles," she volunteered.

"You've found a good one here—which reminds me, you need to brief your el-tee, and I also need to brief mine. Never know; somebody somewhere may know more about this crap than we do."

"What do I tell McKower?"

"The same things you told me—the truth."

"She intimidates me."

"She'll be your biggest booster if you trust her; she's so smart it's scary."

"I heard you two were close."

"You heard right," he admitted. "Tell her what's going down."

"It's still my case, right?"

"Absolutely. Yours all the way."

"No sneaking back here without me."

"Paranoia is unprofessional."

"What do you expect from someone who paints her you-know-what?"

"I hear what you're saying. What's the fastest way back to this place?"

"There isn't a fast one, but there are clearer routes. I'll show you on the AVL when we get back to the truck. Why?"

"I don't believe in approaching a place from the same direction or route every time."

"That also sounds applicable to a lot of things," she said.

Service tried to ignore her. Her youth, candor, and ways of thinking were unnerving, and he needed to adjust to her. *Keep your mind out of the gutter*, he told himself.

11

Marquette, Marquette County

TUESDAY, MAY 8, 2007

The bound facsimile set of the English translation of the *Jesuit Relations* were shelved, a neat row of black books with gold type and a layer of dust suggesting they were seldom touched, much less read. Service went through the index, found VOL. XLVIII, "Lower Canada, Ottawas: 1662–1664." He went to the shelf, pulled out the book, and took it to a table.

It began with a preface written by Reuben Gold Thwaites, listed as secretary of the State Historical Society of Wisconsin. The preface was dated 1899. Chapter IV was entitled, "Various Iroquois Wars, and Their Results." The report was dated September 4, 1663, submitted by one Hierosme Lalemant, S.J. *The old froggies had interesting names.*

He did the math in his head. He was looking at the facsimile of a report written 344 years before—nearly three and a half centuries, photos of the original French-language letter beside the English translation. The report was to the point, and, after a quick skimming, Service found several terms he didn't understand. He decided to write down the part that he wanted, which was less than half a page long, and chase down the unknown terms later.

He began copying Lalemant's words:

Last year the Agnieronnons and Onneiochronnons, the haughtiest of the five Iroquois nations, formed an expedition of a hundred men to go and lie in ambush for the Outaouax, who constitute our upper Algonquins, and to fall upon them when engaged in passing some difficult rapid. With this purpose they set out early in the spring of the year 1662, depending on their muskets for provisions, and using the Woods, which lay in their path as a courtyard, kitchen, and lodging place. The shortest paths are not the best, because they are much traveled; he who loses his way makes the most successful

58

journey, because one is never lost in the woods without finding wild animals, which seek a retreat in the remotest forests.

Definitely way before GPS, and a reminder that Native Americans had no word for wilderness *until we gave them one.*

After following the Hunter's calling for a considerable time, they turned into Warriors, seeing that they were approaching the enemy's country. So they began to prowl along the shores of the Lake of the Hurons, seeking their prey; and while they were planning to surprise some straggling huntsmen, they were they themselves surprised by a band of *Saulteurs* (for thus we designate the Savages living near the sault of Lake Superior). These latter, having discovered the enemy, made their approach toward daybreak, with such boldness that, after discharging some muskets and then shooting their arrows, they leaped hatchet in hand, upon those whom their fire and missiles had spared. The Iroquois, although they are very proud and have never yet learned to run away, would have been glad to do so had they not been prevented by the shafts leveled at them from every direction. Hence only a very few escaped to bear such sad news to their country, and to fill their villages with mourning instead of joyful shouts that were to ring out on the warriors' return. This shows clearly that these people are not invincible when they are attacked with courage.

Service signed onto a library computer and quickly translated *Agnieronnon* and *Onneiochronnon* to Mohawk and Oneida. He took his notes and went outside to smoke a cigarette and think.

The Saulteurs were obviously Ojibwa in the Soo. This had to be the battle, but this invading force had been made up of one hundred warriors, not three hundred. Also, Father Lalemant's report was secondhand, not eyewitness, regarding alleged events that had happened six months before. Still, the nut of the report seemed right, and would probably pass Etta Trevillyan's notions of a reasonable-size attack force. The Iroquois had started up the coast of Lake Huron looking for Ottawa victims and had ended up in Saulteur territory. As far as he knew, the Ojibwa had controlled turf all the way down the St. Mary's River to Drummond Island. How had the Iroquois gotten *around* the Soo if the attack had gone down near Crisp Point, or even if it had happened at Iroquois Point?

Something about this didn't jibe, and there was nothing in the priest's secondhand report to provide direction, other than making it clear that the invading Iroquois had been effectively surrounded and dispatched. No mention of actual casualties on either side, and the statement that only a very few escaped. What about the old stories of the triumphant Ojibwa purposely releasing prisoners to take the word back to their home nations? The Jesuit said some Iroquois managed to escape. Presumably on their own, through luck.

Do the Iroquois have a version of this story in their oral histories? He made a note.

He wished he knew more about Indian logistics and such. A hundred warriors: Did that mean fifty canoes? Or were they in the larger Montreal canoes? With five per Montreal they would need only twenty craft, though either fifty or twenty would be damn near impossible to conceal along the coasts. No wonder the Saulteurs found them.

He wished he could read French, but guessed any French he'd recall now would not make reading the seventeenth-century version any easier. Every language tended to shift and vary greatly through the centuries. In college he'd once looked at Old English and could hardly make it out, much less understand it without a lot of sweat, thought, and a lexicon.

Returning to the reference room, he read a subsequent account of eight hundred warriors from the other three confederation tribes going against the Susquahannocks, only to be once again ignominiously banished. After an initial armed skirmish, the Susquahannocks in April 1661 withdrew into their impregnable village. The Iroquois sent twenty-five armed ambassadors into the village to negotiate terms, only the Susquahannocks immediately took them prisoner, put them on stakes on platforms, and burned them to death in front of the other seven hundred–plus warriors waiting for the signal to attack. These warriors reportedly withdrew to their own country with the Susquahannocks screaming they were coming there to burn all of them the way they had burned the first twenty-five.

Had this story and Iroquois Point somehow gotten mixed up? If three hundred is unrealistic, isn't eight hundred even further off the damn charts?

Further on, Father Lalemant indicated that smallpox began to ravage Iroquois "towns," which effectively curtailed any significant future forays on the war road.

Service guessed it wasn't the threat of a road of skulls that kept the Iroquois from coming back: It had been smallpox.

Damn interesting reading by a writer who pulls you right back into his century, but not much there for a police case. Except for the tactical note of the Iroquois being surrounded. As a recon marine in Vietnam he had seen his share of ambushes on both sides of the equation, and to make one happen with totality you needed the best possible terrain, steady nerve, and a helluva lot of luck.

He was sitting there tapping a pencil on his chin when Etta Trevillyan sat down across from him and said, "You look perplexed. Something you read?"

"What if the ambush didn't happen at all, or it happened south of the Soo, not to the west?"

"I think that's exactly the kind of doubt I was trying to convey when we talked. There's just no way to know for certain unless someone stumbles upon the actual site. Artifacts and remains would reveal most of the truth." She smiled. "I wouldn't mind helping you with this. Native American history has always fascinated me, and anything an old historian can do to to bring clarity to disputed events is a good thing."

"I could use some help," he admitted. "Do you know Dr. Wingel of Whitewater State?"

"By reputation."

She's holding back. "Which is?"

"Professionally or personally?"

"Both."

"Professionally she's said to be very ambitious and somewhat competent. Personally she's described as paranoid, cowardly, self-serving, and petty."

"But her cats probably like her," he said.

"Based on what I've heard I'd find it difficult to believe anyone or anything could do more than tolerate her."

"I get the sense you don't appreciate directness."

The retired professor smiled. "Sometimes, with some people, there just ain't no way around the honest-to-God, knock-you-twixt-the-eyes truth. What do you want me to do to help you?"

"I want to try to nail down whether this vaunted Iroquois-Ojibwa battle actually took place, and if so, roughly when. Father Lalemant in the *Jesuit Relations* puts a certain battle in the spring or early summer of 1662, which seems to relate to the general story, but anything you can do to clarify would help."

"And if the battle didn't happen?"

"Then it didn't happen." *Which would make Katsu's whole effort null and void, clearing the way for Sedge to hammer him with charges if he kept interfering with archaeologists whose work was approved by the State. Approved by the State? Does this mean the state archaeologist alone, or are others involved?*

"The other day you said both the Iroquois and Ojibwa buried their dead?"

"I did."

"If you found remains, how would you know which was which?"

"The Ojibwa tended to dress up their dead and have viewings much as we have before burying them in their best clothes. The Iroquois wrapped their dead in birch bark because when the rotting process was done, they would dig up the bones, clean them, and rebury them with a big ceremony. You'd also know by any implements with the remains. . . . Well, not exactly *know*, but you'd have evidence for an intelligent guess."

"Thanks, Etta."

"You want to stop for pastry and coffee next week and I'll share what I have?"

"Sounds good to me."

"I'll call or send an e-mail when I have something," she said.

"Have you ever worked with the state archaeologist in Lansing?"

"No."

"Do you happen to know if the SAO is the sole government agency to grant approvals to excavate?"

"I think DEQ gives the approval, based on the SAO's recommendation. After all, someone is asking to alter the environment, aren't they?"

12

Slippery Creek Camp

TUESDAY, MAY 8, 2007

When Grady Service saw Limpy Allerdyce's battered Ford pickup parked next to his cabin, he winced. Allerdyce was one of the U.P.'s most notorious poachers, a felon, the leader of a feral tribe with a remote camp in the swamps of extreme southwest Marquette County, his father's alleged one-time snitch and now his informant as well. All of this was bad enough in its own right, but what hurt most was that Limpy had somehow eliminated the people who had killed Nantz and his son, Walter, which by unbending Yooper ethical standards now left him indebted to the creep.

He found Allerdyce in a stare-down with Newf on the porch. "Yore dog t'ward me ain't so frien'ly, sonny," Limpy said.

"Good for her," Service said. "You want coffee or arsenic?"

"I don't like da flavors youse got in dere." Which meant the old poacher had been inside his cabin. Keeping him out was like trying to cut off air.

"Why're you here, Limpy? I'm busy."

"Yeah, youse ain't here much dese days. Youse still porkin' dat cute little state trooper?"

Service glared at Limpy, who greeted the glare with a bobblehead grin. The old man was here with a purpose. He never showed up without a reason. "Spit it out, Allerdyce."

"Word out youse're lookin' for errorheads."

"The ubiquitous 'word,' huh?"

Allerdyce ignored Service's sarcasm. "I had me dis call from pal over Raco, eh."

"That so?"

"Said red niggers campin' up Vermilion way got somepin' in da ground dey don't want white men ta have."

Jesus, the U.P. swamp drums are unbelievable. "*What* sort of thing in the ground?"

Allerdyce shrugged. "I ain't no monocle like dat ole Nekkidbuttgeezer."

The poacher's often sloppy language, twisted logic, and malapropisms made him seem a fool, but he wasn't. What the man lacked in formal education, he overcame with prodigious natural smarts, raw intelligence, and highly refined woodcraft, the sort of combination that made him a formidable cedar swamp lawbreaker. "What *have* you heard?" Service asked.

"Hectorio, El Spicko Grande, word is he put out word for copper errorheads. You know Hectorio, eh?"

"Can't say I do."

"Lives Spicklansing, owns tamaletacoteria, nort'side."

"You mean Lansing?"

"I just said."

"Never heard of him."

"Youse need get out, circle-eight, check 'round more."

"I'll keep that in mind. You ever find any 'errorheads'?"

"Pfft. All over bloody place up here, I guess. Not wort' shit."

"This you know from experience?"

"Just say I mebbe heard it oot in woods."

"This Hectorio, he wants copper?"

Limpy sighed. "I never learned ta think Spick."

"You heard this from your friend in Raco?" Raco was near Bay Mills, which was just east of Iroquois Point. Once a Bomarc missile base, it was now an EPA Superfund Site.

"Dat's close nuff, but all he tole me was red niggers up da lake, makin' shit pies."

"And your source for Hectorio?"

Allerdyce stared at the roof. "Somewheres, don't member 'sackly."

"Seriously, you know about such places?"

"You don't? Dey're everywhere, 'specially by big lakes, rivers, eh."

"And you never picked up artifacts?"

"What I want armyfax? Stuff's ugly, wort'less junk. You pick rotted bloobs?"

Service shook his head.

"Den youse unnerstand, sonny," Allerdyce said, hopping down from the porch snarling and growling at Newf with such realism it pulled Service up short.

But Service didn't understand anything except that Limpy was trying to give him information, and obviously the old man knew about Katsu and the fracas with the archaeologist from Hibernian.

Limpy stood beside his truck. "Dat big red nigger dey call Katsu? He done hard time."

"For what?"

"Ain't healt'y walk around yard axing why somebody inside, eh. Dat ginch squeeze you got, word is she good gal, fair, not no Dickless Tracy."

"We were hoping for your endorsement," Service said sarcastically.

"Youse just take a shot at me?"

Service held out his hands and Allerdyce got into his truck and disappeared.

Oddly enough, he found himself pleased by Limpy's visit. The fact that the old poacher knew about Katsu suggested the deal on the coast was, first, a big deal, and second, that big money was in play, or Limpy, reformed or not, would be unlikely to have the slightest interest. Allerdyce knew just about everything that went on in the U.P., and although he'd spent seven years in prison for shooting Service in the leg during a scuffle, the detective couldn't think of anyone who would make a better governor of the U.P., if there was such a thing.

• • •

Back at his office in The Roof he checked his private telephone directory on the computer and called Marge Ciucci.

"Aunt Marge," she answered after one ring.

"Grady Service, Aunt Marge."

"Ah!" she exclaimed. "You done it, boy. *Grazie grazie, prego prego, bravo bravo,* Grady."

"Am I interrupting anything important?"

"You interrupt? Not possible. *Never.* Anything you want, you get."

"Dr. Ladania Wingel."

Long pause. "What you want *that* for?"

"You know her?"

Marge Ciucci let loose a long hiss. "*That* one. *Femmina!*"

"What's the deal, Aunt Marge?"

"She sweet-talk her way onto school board, get 'erself appointed to an open term. Then all hell she breaks loose, *si?* Only she knows how schools should be run, and if anyone disagree for any reason, she screams racist!"

Wingel's consistent, at least, always leaning on race. If Tree was here now, he'd kick her in the ass. Luticious Treebone was a black man, his best friend, a fellow Vietnam veteran, and a retired Detroit cop. They had served in the Marine Corps in Vietnam together. "You know the woman personally?"

"She lives in a condo south of town, only mixes with muckmucks."

"Any other Whitewater faculty members in Jefferson?"

"*Professore* Crispin Franti—he teaches soil science at the college, works the state extension service here in town."

"Good guy?"

She made a smacking sound with her lips. "*Numero uno*: the best."

"Got a phone number?"

"*Minuto*," she said, left the phone, and came back with the number.

"Thanks, Marge."

"You gonna be in Jefferson, you stay with me, you hear? Marge take care of you like her own bambino."

"Yes, ma'am," he said hanging up.

He walked outside to have a cigarette.

Persia Hunger was already outside. She was his age, a longtime employee in the Department of Environmental Quality. "You know anything about DEQ permits for archaeological digs?" he asked.

"I'm water. You need to talk to dirt—Verlin Ponozzo—but he's in Lansing all week." After a moment of silence she said, "You think DEQ and DNR will ever be merged again?'

"I ain't no monocle like old Nekkidbuttgeezer," he said, quoting Allerdyce.

"*What?*"

"Sorry, that was a poor play on words. I really don't know the answer, Persia."

He knew she asked because he was a friend of the governor. Everyone assumed he and Governor Timms talked a lot. Everyone assumed wrong.

He called Friday at her office. "I think I'm headed to Wisconsin," he told her. "What's your day been like?"

"Like a week of water torture—phone calls, witness reports, transcripts, files, all the glory of law enforcement in one day."

"The kid okay?"

"More resilient than us. How'd things go for you?"

" 'Puters and phones, 'puters and phones. Oh, and Allerdyce showed up at camp."

"My, aren't you blessed."

"Believe it or not, I think he was trying to tip me on the artifact case."

"That *creature* is scary," she said.

"Yeah, but every cop knows him."

"Don't remind me."

"He asked if I'm still porking you."

"Are you?"

"Not often enough."

"Did you tell him that?"

"He thinks you're cute."

"Well I am, right?"

"And hot."

"Hold that thought until I have energy again. When to Wisconsin?"

"Tonight maybe, back later this week."

"That should work good. I should be brimming with energy by then."

"I would hope so."

• • •

Professor Crispin Franti was at home, seemed friendly, and agreed to meet him for lunch at the Havelock Café in Jefferson the next day at noon.

A call to Marge Ciucci got him a bed for as long as he needed it. "You mind if I bring my dog?"

"He's welcome too."

"She."

"Even better."

The last task of the day was to follow up on Allerdyce's statement that Katsu had done time, and a quick check showed it to be true. He immediately called Jingo Sedge.

"Sedge? Service."

"S'up?"

"Tell me more about Katsu's criminal record."

"Grand theft. He was in a bar, drunk, bought a car from a drunk cowboy for two hundred and fifty bucks, cash. Katsu drove it away. The cowboy staggered home, sobered up, and his old lady wanted to know where the fuck *her* wheels were. Hubby calls the cops, claims the ride was stolen. The cops pick up Katsu that same day. He had a previous conviction for aggravated assault. He was barely twenty then. The prosecutor in the car case got the previous conviction into the record, and Katsu's public defender stood mute with his thumb up his ass. The jury found him guilty in twenty-five minutes flat and the public defender told him, 'Better luck next time around, chief,' and bogeyed into the sunset. This was in Montana, state of Big Sky and tiny minds."

"This doesn't bother you?" he asked.

"Quite the opposite. Given his background, it takes some balls to knowingly protest what he considers to be a moral and social travesty."

Service said. "Okay, if that's your gut, go with it. But consider the flipper: Maybe the bigger magnet for his interest is the amount of money at stake."

Silence on the other end. *Good, she's listening.*

"You got something specific?" she asked, after a long pause.

"Allerdyce dropped by my place to specifically tell me about the goings-on, and that Katsu's an ex-con."

"Based on what that scum told you, you assume Katsu's out for money?"

"That *scum* knows more about what goes on up here than you and me combined. He would not have dropped by unless there was substance for us."

"So you trust one con's word against another's?"

"Yep, that's a tidy description of our work. I'm on my way to Wisconsin."

"To see Wingel?"

"Probably. Later, Sedge." He heard her suck in breath just before he hung up.

13

Jefferson, Wisconsin

WEDNESDAY, MAY 9, 2007

Crispin Franti was sixtyish and white-haired, but had a pencil-thin, coal-black mustache, which looked like it had been painted on.

The Havelock Café was plain and small, and filled with people who dressed like farmers just in from fields or tractors, or whatever it was that they did.

"You know the word 'havelock'?" Franti asked.

"No."

"It's that cloth sunshade doodad hanging down the back of a hat, which means this place is here as the refuge from the sun, which is the farmer's friend and his foe. But you want to talk about Ladania Wingel."

"How did you know that?"

"Aunt Marge called me after I agreed to meet you. Everybody around here knows Wingel: On campus she's a banshee howling in a bugle factory, and nobody pays her any mind because she can't get her voice heard above the academic din. But here in town on the school board it's different, and she's cut herself a real swath in the town's collective feelings. I just read that the IRS says an estimated 75,000 people make their livings as ETAs—Elvis Tribute Artists. Can you believe that? Ladania is a blowhard. She loves to go bitchcakes in public and watch people cringe. Me, I think she's entertaining, but then I know to not take any of her shit personally."

"If people don't agree with her?"

"She inducts your ass into the Universal Club of Racists. You met her yet?"

"No."

"Wingel has dinner every Wednesday night at the Bounty House. She's the ultimate control freak. She'll be with the school board president, who is a dandy piece of work in her own right, but well-intentioned. Walk in on them and she'll have no choice but to play nice. Her public rants are mostly directed at teachers, students, parents, administrators and so forth, but she publicly and verbally kisses the school board president's ass."

"You don't care for her."

Franti grinned. "The only reason we don't shoot some people is because it's against the law. I'm hungry. Let's order."

• • •

Aunt Marge tried to feed him another lunch after the lunch with Franti. She and Newf were already bonding. "Crispin, he's a good guy, eh?"

"You were right."

"What you want for supper tonight?"

"I've got a meeting."

She frowned and shook a finger at him. "Work, work, work, the same as Wayno, and look where that got him, *capisce?*"

• • •

The Bounty House was in downtown Jefferson, across the street from an old firehouse, which now housed a national agricultural PR firm.

Finding Ladania Wingel wasn't difficult. She was the only black person in the restaurant. The woman with her was attractive, spiffed and polished, a high-upkeep type in a tight, bright-red top and red fuck-me heels.

He approached the table. "Excuse me . . . Dr. Wingel?"

"We're in a meeting here," she said tersely, through a forced smile.

He flopped open his shield. "Detective Service, Michigan Department of Natural Resources."

"You have no jurisdiction in Wisconsin."

"Actually I do. I'm also deputized as a federal marshal. You want to see those credentials too?"

"Would you care for a drink?" the other woman asked. "Razzie martoonis here are yummer-yums."

Wingel sighed. "This is about the dig."

"It's about the remains you harvested and mysteriously reburied."

"I reported all this. Winter unearthed the remains, not me."

"So you wrote in your report."

"Oh good, it's nice that you can read. If you've comprehended what you read, then our business is concluded. Good-bye."

Service pulled out one of the two extra chairs at the table and sat down. "I'll say when we're finished, Dr. Wingel." He turned to the professor's companion. "I'm Grady Service—I won't be long."

"Marldeane Youvonne Brannigan. Stay as long as you like. You don't have to hurry on my account. Can we girls buy you a martooni?"

"I'm on duty, but thanks for offering," Service said.

"Shame," Brannigan said. She ordered a raspberry martini and drained the drink in hand. There were already two empty glasses on the table. As soon as the waiter brought her a new drink, Brannigan got up and left the table.

Service looked over at Wingel. "Before you find some bullshit reason to accuse me of racism, I want to do something." He pushed the speed-dial number for Treebone and put the phone on speaker. "You all set?"

"Good to go, man."

"Dr. Wingel, Lieutenant Luticious Treebone of the Detroit Police Department is on the line. He is a black man. If I say anything to you that is in the slightest bit racist, he will jump in. Shall we proceed?"

"I'm good," Tree said.

"This is highly irregular," Wingel said.

"I know," Service said, "but Tree and me are highly irregular guys: We spent a long time together in the marines in Vietnam, we were state cops and game wardens together, and I'm godfather to his kids, so there's no bullshit between us."

"We gonna jaw-jaw or do this thing?" Treebone complained impatiently.

The woman's eyes were wide, a deer in the headlights.

Service took out a piece of paper he'd prepared earlier at Aunt Marge's. The map he'd sketched included the area with the sand bowl and the place Sedge had described as an amoeba. He put the map on the table in front of Wingel and handed her a pen. "Where exactly did Old Man Winter cough up said corpse?"

Wingel said, "You don't intimidate me—*either* of you."

"Wrong answer. Where exactly was the corpse?"

She studied the drawing and finally, tentatively, made a small, shaky x, the ink barely legible on the paper. The mark was on the southwest extremity of the amoeba.

He tapped the area. "Any idea what that is?"

"It's not written anywhere, but the late chairman of the Madeline Island Reservation once told me that according to oral tradition, there once was a small, protected harbor there. Obviously time and weather have closed it in and filled it up."

"Madeline Island?"

"Wisconsin," she said haughtily.

"Did this alleged chairman make a dying declaration?"

"Don't be an ass," she said.

"When you conducted your first dig, were you aware of the harbor?"

"There was only one dig."

"I take it the answer is negative?"

"Don't presume answers on my behalf. Winter brought up the burial bundle, not my digging."

"There was a bundle?"

"I believe I just clearly stated that."

"Describe it, please."

"I don't remember. It was years ago."

"I'm not trying to twist your thong," Service said. Then, at the phone: "Did that qualify as racist?"

"Could be a bit sexist, but definitely not racist. How you know she wearing a thong? If she commando, you'd be inaccurate. Sister, listen to me: Cops, we don't buy into convenient memory lapses."

"You heard him," Service said. "About that bundle?"

"It was wrapped in birch bark—the remains were enclosed in what appeared to be bark."

"Is that significant—professionally speaking?"

"*Na-do-we-se.*"

"Iroquois, right?"

"Yes, correct," Wingel said with a slight nod.

"You didn't think that worthy of follow-up?"

"The season uncovered it and it needed to be put back."

"Where'd you rebury it?"

"I don't remember."

"Tree?"

"Before she gets on the racism or sexism horse, your professor there needs to tell truth, hear?"

She took the pen and made another tentative mark—across from the filled-in harbor where the bundle had been found.

"Why rebury it there instead of closer to where you'd found it?"

She shrugged, stared at the wall.

"You *did* rebury it, yes? I mean, if we get search warrants, we're not going to find bones in your house, or your office at school?"

"I reburied it," she said coolly.

"Immediately?"

"I think I want to call my lawyer."

"So you didn't bury it right away."

"Of course not. I examined it before putting it back."

"But you didn't put it back where you found it? Technically that's not putting it back, is it?"

"How long must I endure this?" she asked.

"Answer him, sister," Tree commanded from the phone.

"Where did you dig the first time?"

"There was only one time," she said again. She tapped her finger on the north side of the sandy bowl, which was close to where Katsu had been.

"You find much?"

"Quite a lot."

"All Ojibwa?"

"No. Of course, there were certain items that came from trading with other tribes."

"Where's that stuff now?"

"It was turned over to the State of Michigan, which is what the laws require."

"I see. Describe the remains."

"I did—in my report."

"Sister," Tree chimed in.

"What is it you want to know?"

"Bones, a skull—what?"

"Most of an entire skeleton."

"Skull too?"

"No!"

"The skull wasn't with the bones?"

"A few feet away."

"In what condition?"

"It had been interred underground for a long, long time."

Service looked her in the eye. "You're trained to observe. So am I."

"The skull appeared to be fractured," she said cautiously.

"In what way?"

"Broken."

"By what?"

"I wasn't there."

"Guess."

"A projectile."

"Pointed or round, large or small?"

"Round, small."

"Like a musketball?"

"That would not be an unreasonable conclusion."

"You think this is where the 1662 fight took place?"

"That could not possibly be determined without further excavation."

"By you?"

"My days in the field are long done," she said.

Dr. Wingel's companion Marldeane Youvonne Brannigan came staggering back to the table with another fresh drink in hand, put a card under his hand-drawn map, and loudly blew back the strands of hair hanging in her face.

"Thank you for your cooperation, Dr. Wingel. Tree, we're done."

"Cool," Treebone said, and hung up.

"I hope our next meeting isn't in a courtroom," Service said. "If it is, I won't be nearly so polite."

"You poor-white racist trash," she said with a snarl.

"Later, ladies." He got up and walked outside. He looked at Brannigan's card, on which she had scribbled "I'm discreet—are you? Have a nice day!" She had written a cell-phone number under the name and added a smiley face.

I hate smiley faces. He dropped the card in a curbside trash bin.

14

Newberry, Luce County

FRIDAY, MAY 11, 2007

Sedge wanted to meet at nine. Service decided to drop by the district office. Sergeant Jeffey Bryan met him at the unstaffed reception desk. There was no room in state budgets for such positions anymore.

"S'up?" the six-foot-six officer asked.

"Dunno. Just drove in from Wisconsin."

"You hear we have a new chief? Just announced yesterday. And Teeny's gone."

"Huh," Service said noncommittally. "Your el-tee in?"

"She's with the new chief. For a while they were yelling at each other."

"You think they need a ref?"

Bryan grinned. "El-Tee can take care of herself."

Service headed for McKower's cubicle and got there as Eddie Waco stood up, shook McKower's hand, and departed, looking tired. He nodded to Service as he passed.

"*You*," McKower greeted him. Her tone was menacing, and the blood drained out of her face as he stepped into the office.

"Me what?"

"You know damn well what."

"I heard there was some kind of ruckus back here."

"Ruckus my ass. This is *your* doing."

"Lis what are you talking about?"

"I saw you two exchange the secret boys' club nods just now. This was your idea. You two are in cahoots!"

"You need to calm down."

"He just asked me to be assistant chief."

"Who asked?"

"Chief Waco."

Service looked behind him. "Was *that* him?"

McKower pounded her table with a fist. "You know damn well who he is. You two are pals."

Service held up his hands. "Did the man tell you that?"

"He didn't have to."

"Well, there ya go."

"You numbskull. I read all the case reports from Missouri, his and yours, remember?"

Damn her memory. "One case, way back, does not constitute friendship."

"For Christ's sake, Grady. I talked to Lorne. He told me you met the chief in Lansing on the thirtieth."

Time to clam up. "Old business. You accept?"

"What do you think, Geppetto?"

He nodded. "Yeah, you'll do it."

"Which you knew."

"All I know is that everyone in the department thinks you're destined to be chief one day, and here it begins."

"My kids will *hate* Lansing!"

"Live outside the city. Assistant chiefs can choose."

"What I should do is kick your ass," she said.

"But?"

"The chief and I have a better idea."

Don't like this. Don't like this one bit. "Which is?"

"You'll see. By the way, Sedge briefed me on the artifact case."

"Good officer," he said.

"And eccentric," McKower added.

"True that. Got any advice?"

She smiled. "I briefed the chief. Know what he said?"

"You're gonna tell me?"

"He said let Grady run with it."

"He did not say that. It's Sedge's case."

"You'll never know, will you?"

"Geez, rank going to your head already?"

She seemed amused.

"So what did you and the chief argue about?"

"We had a discussion, not an argument."

"About?"

"You."

"What about me?"

"Time will tell."

Service stood. "I've taken enough abuse, thank you." He turned to leave but spun back and held out his hand. "Semper fi."

"That's not our outfit," she said.

"It's you and me, Lis. Always will be."

"Stay where you are, Detective."

She moved some papers on her desktop, revealing two sets of chevrons, each with six stripes, one of them with a diamond in the middle. She held that set out to him.

"I believe these are yours, State Chief Master Sergeant Service."

"Not a chance," he said, taking a step back. "No way."

She smiled. "You knew I'd take my job, and I know you'll take this one. Besides, it's an order, you big jerk. Your first job is to select the state master sergeant."

"What the hell is going on?"

"Coasting time's done, big boy. Time's come for you to step up and lead."

"Master sergeant. Who?"

"That's your choice." She glared at him triumphantly. "You can't help doing the right thing. Usually."

"Grinda gets the detective opening," he said.

"Talk to Milo—persuade him."

He held up his hands. "I will *not* waste time in meetings in Lansing."

She smiled, clearly enjoying herself. "Your job is to move around the state, work with everyone. Figure out which officers should be groomed for sergeant, which sergeants for el-tee. Weed out the bullshitters, lightweights, and politicians. Chief Waco and I both want only the best officers moving up."

He hesitated for a long time. *You have to say something, asshole.*

"But no meetings. I mean it."

She wiggled the chevrons. "Fine, no more plainclothes stuff. Wear your uniform."

"Hey, you want me to do this damn job, I'm going to do it my way. What about Sedge's case?"

"You always finish what you start, Grady. I can't see you changing now."

"Bite me," he said, snapped a salute, turned, and fumed out of the office.

15

Coast of Death, Chippewa County

FRIDAY, MAY 11, 2007

They parked on Lake Superior State University property and hiked west down the beach from Vermilion, three sandy miles to the dig site.

"Could make better time on four-wheelers," Service groused. He had called her from Wisconsin and briefed her on the Wingel meeting.

"If you don't care about destroying orchids or piping plover nesting colonies," Jingo Sedge pointed out.

Service looked at the peregrinations of four-wheeler tracks crisscrossing the terrain. "Doesn't look like much of a priority for some people," he said.

"*Post hoc, ergo propter hoc:* Four-wheelers aren't people," Sedge mumbled.

"What?"

"Never mind."

They sat side by side on a fallen cedar at the northeast extreme of the amoeba.

"Wengel said this was once a harbor," Service said.

"Toliver said the same thing. Musketball in the brainpan?"

"Claims Wingel."

"But found *across* from where we're sitting."

Service nodded.

"Why not bury it where you find it?" Sedge asked.

"Panic, cunning, stupidity—take your pick."

"Cunning?"

"Assume it happened the way she says it did, and winter regurgitated the remains. But having found the corpse, she clearly and quickly recognized its importance historically. That being so, you just might put it somewhere else to mislead people in case it showed up again."

"Based on wind patterns, there's a good chance that if it did surface here, it would end up where she found it, over there," Sedge pointed out.

"By that logic, the bulk of the Iroquois burials are beneath our butts," he said.

"That's sort of creepy."

"She *knew* the bundle was Iroquois," Service said. "She understands the significance, and you have to wonder if she happened to mention that to the state archaeologist. Did you see her written report?"

"No. Only the brief summary."

"What do the regs require?"

"What regs?"

"Surely there *are* regs. We have regs for everything in this damn state."

She shook her head. "The state archaeologist is like God."

"I wouldn't waste my time praying to the bastard," Service said, adding, "Wingel knows the truth about this site."

"You're jumping the gun, dude. She may have lied to you about the bundle."

"Doesn't matter. My gut says she did more than rebury remains. By her own admission, I'm guessing there are photos, diagrams. She may even have some of the bones."

"Too big a risk."

"I've looked in her eyes."

"Do you think she might have continued digging here for all these years?"

"We don't know if anyone has been digging here," he said.

"Katsu says—"

"His motivation is not yet clear."

"But you know his old man."

"His old man's totally batshit, but a man of honor. Nobody *knows* Santinaw."

"Katsu doesn't seem to think much of him."

"The old man thinks enough of the kid to send me here," Service said. "It's not easy to parse father-son relationships." His own son Walter and he had not had time to establish a pattern in their relationship before his murder.

"Well, here we are. What do we do? Check the cameras?"

"No, leave them for now. Let's play in the sandbox, see what we can find—record our findings, make our own chart, mark everything. They teach you about this kind of work at the academy?"

She guffawed.

Over the next six hours they found seventy artifacts (mostly small bits and pieces), but there also was a most impressive small copper ring that had oxidized a powdery blue-green. Each item was marked, sketched, and put back with a marker using Katsu's scheme.

"Is it possible we'll catch a thief this easily?" Sedge asked.

"Possible, but not probable. Complex cases sometimes break on small things that initially seem entirely unrelated."

"But all this is worth the effort?" she asked.

"You bet. We already have a better understanding of the site and the surrounding terrain."

"Sit on it tonight?"

"No, let's leave it, come back in a few days. I want to do some more walking around."

"I'd love to stay," she said, "but I need to get over to the Blind Sucker river mouth west of Deer Park. Four-wheelers are cutting new trails over there between the mouth and the campground. Addicted four-wheeling types are such major assholes. I write one, and he says, 'Got ticketed for the same thing down home, so I come up here.' I said, 'Hey buttwipe, it's also illegal up here—duh!' "

Service laughed and she asked, "You good here?"

"I'm addicted to what the French call *dériver*," he said. "It means to wander aimlessly."

"Really?" she countered.

"I like to wander."

"I doubt that."

It was late afternoon before he had cleaned the site of all signs of their presence, and he was meandering south quite a distance before he turned east toward Vermilion and his truck. At first he thought he was imagining the sound, a thin voice crying *Help!* When he heard it again he knew it was real, though the source was not apparent.

Ahead and right, maybe? Lower than me, slightly muffled. "I hear you!" Grady Service said. "Say something louder if you can."

"Help me!"

Not louder, but two words instead of one. Sometimes progress comes in small steps. "One more time, please."

"Help me, dammit!"

"Okay," Service said. "Gotcha."

The voice was floating up from chest-high ferns, unusually lush and high this early in the year. It was like a leprechaun or some silly thing deep in the green, and when he found himself looking down at a frail, naked elfin man, he had to fight back a laugh. The man had matchstick, unsteady, bandy legs.

"You hurt?"

"Weak, undernourished—nothing I haven't anticipated."

"Want water?"

"Is it pure and unadulterated?"

"Is anything?"

"Point conceded," the man said, holding out his hand, which seemed to glow in the low light in contrast to the darkening air.

Service handed a water bottle to the man and listened to him slurp and cough.

No point telling thirsty people to drink slowly. They never listen.

When the man tried to return the bottle, Service said, "Keep it. I carry several. I'm Service, DNR."

"Godfroi Delongshamp. People call me God, which is meant to be a joke, but turns out to be not so funny. You or I could have created an equally failed world. So much for perfection and other exalted claims for Him. Why not either one of us as God, eh?"

"I don't want the job."

"You pass judgments like God. It's the nature of a cop's work."

"You don't know me."

"Which only increases the mystery. The religious thugs love the mysterious. The more bizarre and utterly unbelievable, the better."

"Are you with the religious community?"

"That's difficult to answer. Are rejects technically part of a group? Or castaways?"

"Does either condition pertain to you?"

"More like I'm just a lousy joiner."

"Like that community believes in wearing clothes and you don't?"

The man cackled. "I like you. You can assume part one is true, but part two isn't. I had clothes, but the fools who pranked me left me like this."

Pranked? Strange man.

"How'd you get out here?"

"I have a camp."

"Close by?"

"To be frank, I'm not entirely sure. I've got end-stage macular degeneration and don't see as well as I once did. Think you could help God find his way home?"

"Shouldn't be a problem." Service lit the man with his SureFire, saw he was covered with insect bites and welts.

"Those hurt?"

"No. I'm trying to ignore them."

"How's that working?"

"Not well."

Service took some Adolph's Meat Tenderizer out of his ruck and used a water bottle to mix a paste that he applied to the man's bites.

"Holy cow," the man said. "Instant relief!"

"It's temporary, but it'll help for a while." Service gave him a long-sleeved tee and sweatpants from his pack.

"I'm going to leave you here and find your track. When did you leave your camp?"

"Late yesterday. My camp overlooks the Shelldrake River."

Service gave the man a chocolate oatmeal PowerBar.

An hour later Service found a ten-by-fourteen log cabin, ancient by the look of it, in bad need of re-chinking. The door was open, the interior trashed. He had followed the man's trail, saw no sign of anyone else. He'd look again in daylight to be sure, but the old man's story wasn't holding water.

Deslongshamp looked relaxed and had not moved from where Service had left him. "You got neighbor problems?"

"Not with all those lame God Squadders on the other side of the river. My reality is out-of-control kids on four-wheelers buzzing all over my place, night and day."

"Your camp's been trashed. Were you here when they came?"

"No. Every day I take a walk—same route, just to sit and listen. They jumped me, took my clothes, slapped me around, but I'm not hurt. I'm tougher than I look."

Who the hell is this guy?

"You have family?"

"Used to. Been living in my camp for nearly twenty years."

"Year-round?"

"Not every year, but most of them."

End-stage macular degeneration? What the hell is that?

"How do you get in and out?" Service didn't know of any nearby roads.

"Peewee Bolf over to the Falls brings groceries, keeps me in firewood, always looks in on me. I have a well and a generator. It's not as bad as you think, and most of the time it's quiet."

"Excepting four-wheelers."

"Alas and alack. Peewee is a good man," Deslongshamps said.

Service told the man, "Okay, let's get you back to camp and I'll clean it up. For convenience, I'm going to carry you. That dent your pride?"

"Not in the least."

• • •

After the camp was put back together, Service sat down to talk to the man. "Any idea who the night-riders are?"

The man shook his head. "One machine runs rough. The other one has a problem with its sound baffling."

"Two machines?"

"Just two. If there were more, I'd hear them. When one sense goes, others compensate."

"But you didn't hear them this time."

"I happened to be meditating. I thought I heard footsteps but pushed the thought aside, and then they pounced on me."

"They jumped you out there?"

"Yes, during meditation."

"They say anything in particular when they jumped you—use any names, anything?"

"They were laughing with glee, but no words."

"They've trashed your camp before?"

"Twice, each time while I was on my walk. They never bothered me before."

"Have you reported the previous incidents?"

"To what end? I'm too far out for the law to protect me."

"Mr. Bolf's your only regular visitor?"

"He is. But I hear four-wheelers in summer and snowmobiles in winter."

"All kids?"

"No, the others are well-maintained machines, quiet ones. I can see the vague flash of their headlamps sometimes."

Okay, he has partial vision.

"This is a nighttime thing?"

"Always."

More here than meets the eye. But what? He's off-bubble, but that's also irrelevant. Aren't we all off-center in our own ways?

"Would you mind if one of our officers stops by from time to time?"

"It's not really necessary. Are you leaving?"

"I am."

"Watch your step," the man said. "This country can be downright treacherous."

Some sort of message? "You bet it can."

16

SeeWhy, Chippewa County

SATURDAY, MAY 12, 2007

Sedge had sounded out of sorts when he'd called her the night before to tell her about his encounter with the eccentric Godfroi Deslongshamps.

"What am I supposed to do about it?" she'd asked with a growl.

"Just check in on him once in a while."

"I'm not a goddamn nursemaid."

"He claims there's night activity out there."

"You told me that, and you also told me he's going blind. What good is he to us?"

"You never know. Be patient. He's alone."

"Which got his ass kicked. I'm not too good with touchy-feely crap, Service."

"Listen to me," he said. "Katsu thinks something's going on, and he thinks it's Toliver. But you're not so sure Toliver's a bad guy. Delongshamp claims stuff is going on at night. He's all we've got, Sedge."

"All right," she said. "What next?"

"I'm going to see SuRo." Summer Rose Genova was the premier animal-rehab specialist in the Eastern Upper Peninsula. A veterinarian, she had a facility fifteen miles east of the Mackinac Bridge in western Mackinac County.

"Major bitch," Sedge said.

"No argument. She can be touchy, but she's good at her job, and she's connected to the whiffer-ding tree-hugging crowd."

"Big whoop," Sedge responded.

"What's your problem?" Service shot back at her. He was quickly losing patience with her, along with his civility—never his strong suit.

"Figure it out," she said, and hung up.

This morning she had called while he was having coffee with SuRo. "Sorry about last night," Sedge said. "You with Genova?"

"Yeah."

"Someone wants to see us noonish."

"Who?"

"Toliver's lady friend."

"Her idea?"

"Wasn't mine. She's a total skank."

Service thought for a moment. "I never caught her full name."

"Jane Rain," Sedge said.

"You *know* her?"

"Not so much. She showed up in Paradise late last summer, works at Punk's."

A bar south of Paradise, near Eckerman Lookout on M-123. "Waitress?"

"You sexist dinosaur. She's the summer catering *manager!*"

Boy. "Okay, when and where?"

"SeeWhy. You know it?"

"Fountain of Youth," Service said. "Why SeeWhy?"

"She wants anonymity. Noon work for you?"

"I'll be there."

"There's an old cabin site," she told him.

"Listen to me, Sedge: Luce and Chippewa were my first areas."

SuRo Genova had nothing for him.

SeeWhy was named for the postmaster of the village, which once had featured a sawmill, general store, and train stop for the Duluth, South Shore and Atlantic Railroad. As Service remembered, it stood for the postmaster's initials, "C.Y." Years ago, an artesian well just east of the location had been dubbed "The Fountain of Youth," and the name had stuck. Years back a secondary road came into the area along the Tahquamenon River from the south, but the entrance to the road was now private, the route blocked off and heavily posted. The only way in now was over the abandoned rail bed, which had been stripped of ties and rails and was used mostly in winter by snowmobilers.

Why is Sedge so edgy? First she called the woman a skank, and then she jumped me for assuming she's a waitress.

• • •

Jingo Sedge was leaning against her truck when Service parked beside her. He got out, checking his watch. It was noon, straight up. "She late?"

The young officer answered by looking past Service toward the woods. He looked back and saw a ghost stepping out of the brush, zipping his fly.

"Ye gods!" Cornwallis "Smoke" Ghizi yelped. "Bro, when I heard you got out of 'Nam alive, I called it a miracle, first-fucking-class. What happened to that big black sonuvabitch you used to run with?"

"Treebone made it too. He's a retired Detroit cop, el-tee."

"Gadzooks and ye gods—you two assholes surviving the shit *and* the suck! That's gotta beat all odds."

In Vietnam, Ghizi had always whispered and acted like the enemy could come in at any moment. He was an odd combination of relaxed and wired, but suspicious of everything and everyone, and always asking penetrating questions in his soft voice. As an intelligence officer he liked to work alone, and he moved like shade in the shadows. Service and the other marines called him "Smoke." Son of an Egyptian diplomat father and an Anadarko Indian mother from Oklahoma, he was slight in stature and maestro of his own emotions.

The man now before Service looked a little gray, but otherwise pretty much the same as he had been all those years ago. But this Smoke was much more verbal and outgoing.

"What the hell are you doing *here*, Smoke?"

"Long story. I retired some years ago from Fish and Wildlife, but they called me back as a consulting agent, which means damn good pay but no bennies."

"Where's Jane Rain?" Service pressed.

"No need for her to be here."

Service considered events. "She works for you?"

"Not exactly. I'm just a consultant, but she's a helluva agent."

"You know Carmody?" Service asked. "Barry Davey?"

"No games, Service. I am who I say I am. Yes, I knew Minnis and ten other aliases he used, and Davey too. Minnis is dead."

"When?"

"Just last year. His stump never healed right."

Minnis/Carmody was an Irish-born Fish and Wildlife undercover agent who had worked a wolf case with Service some years back, and lost a leg in the process.

"What's the deal with Jane Rain?" Sedge interjected.

Ghizi wagged a finger at her. "*I'm* talking, girlie." He turned back to Service. "You people got *tombaroli* operating here."

"*Tombaroli?*" Service said.

"Italian for tomb raiders."

"This isn't Italy," Sedge said.

"Brits call them nighthawks," Ghizi said, ignoring Sedge. "National Park Service estimates the country loses half a billion bucks a year to these asswipes. Given government accuracy, it's probably twice that."

"Lost to people like Dr. Delmure Arcton Toliver?"

"We're not sure yet about Toliver, but we're pretty sure some bent archaeologists, amateur pot hunters, and relic dealers are working deals. This shit is going on in virtually every state, and we're just beginning to figure out how to get our noses into the dragon's shit."

"Not much here of value."

"Pricing is an art unto itself. So is finding real relics. There's a boatload of skilled assholes out there making and selling relics in their shops and over eBay as legit crap."

Service saw that Sedge was listening.

"Duncan Katsu?" Service asked.

"Possible bad boy," Ghizi said. "A good possibility."

"He claims he's protecting a historic site," Sedge said.

"Words are cheap, girlie."

"Don't call me girlie," she snapped, stepping toward him with her fists clenched.

Ghizi raised his hands, took a step back, and smiled. "The relic snatchers in national parks call nine-one-one to distract law enforcement with bogus calls, then they swoop into sites and take stuff they've already scouted. The parks don't have enough people to patrol or to enforce everything."

"Evidence on Katsu?" Service asked.

Ghizi tapped his chest. "Hunch."

"Our judges don't issue warrants on hunches," Sedge said.

"Not on *your* hunches, maybe," the man shot back. "But mine? Diff deal."

"What the hell do you want, Ghizi?" Service asked to stop a brewing fight. *God, every time I get into a case up in this country, the fucking feds show up. What's that about?*

"Rain said you two were in the middle of their shit the other night. She did some checking and found out you both have reputations as hard chargers who won't let go."

"Are you asking us to let go?" Sedge said.

"No, we just don't want to be gettin' in each other's way."

"How do we prevent that?" Service asked. "Give you the lead on the case?"

"By talking and no swoop-and-scoop unless we clear it with each other."

"Same for your side?" Sedge challenged.

"We're all on the same side," Ghizi said.

"How long you people been after this?" Service asked.

"On Toliver, two years, but Katsu was new as of last fall."

"You got somebody in Katsu's camp?" Service asked.

"No comment," Ghizi said.

"Same team?" Sedge challenged with a scowl. "Bullshit."

"What kind of relics are we talking about?" Service asked.

"So far, none. But they'll show up. Count on it. They always do, if you know where to look for them."

"And you do?" Sedge asked.

"We're learning as we go. There ain't no DIY book on this deal, and the academics are scared shitless of spoiling their colleagues' reputations, so they pretty much clam up when badges get pulled out."

Sedge said, "I got into this because Katsu was blocking access to public land. When I confronted him, he backed off."

"You *think* he backed off."

"Dude," she said.

Service cut her off. "Let the man talk."

Ghizi seemed to weigh every word. "August of 2005 Toliver acquired five breakheads." Ghizi looked up. "Know what I'm talking about?"

The two Michigan officers shook their heads. Service did not want to let on what he knew to any fed and decided playing dumb was best.

"Spike club. Club with a knob on it, used to beat the bejeezus out of your enemies. One of them was made of a bear-leg bone and fit with a big agate as the striking surface. He also got a carved elk horn stone-blade knife, a primo thing, worth beaucoup bucks to the right collector. It was all Iroquoisian, and Toliver allegedly got them from a dealer in Milwaukee, who verbally swore to a certain provenance for the items he couldn't prove on paper. Toliver got suspicious and called the FBI. The dealer claimed he had bought it all at a relic collectors' swap meet, but he copped to amnesia about time, place, seller, and so forth."

"What law did Toliver break?"

"None we know of, and neither the Feebs nor us could build a case against the dealer, so he was released. Six months later he died suddenly."

"Cause?" Service asked.

"Campylobacter," Ghizi said. "Animal shit in the water supply."

"Not uncommon up north," Sedge said.

Ghizi raised an eyebrow. "True enough, but at the time the dealer was having dinner with Toliver at the dealer's cabin in Ashland, Wisconsin."

Service's turn to raise an eyebrow. "But Toliver reported the dealer to the FBI."

"Right, and nighthawks like to call nine-one-one to divert attention."

"Toliver wouldn't kill the guy so obviously."

"That's our conclusion too. It looks like somebody wanted to pin it on him, but it didn't work. However, the breakheads disappeared from the dealer's collection. After suspecting they were bogus and calling the FBI, the agency took them as evidence, but when they couldn't make a case, Toliver told the Feebs to give the stuff back to the dealer because his college was only interested in legit relics."

Service rubbed his face. "The dealer say where the stuff came from?"

"No. Claims he made it all up, which isn't unusual in this game. Every artifact has to have a story to help it sell. Where there isn't real history, stuff gets fabricated."

"Anybody else look at the items?" Sedge asked.

Ghizi nodded. "We had experts from Yale and the Smithsonian. They said the items were legit, and they managed to date them to mid-seventeenth century, give or take."

"Iroquois?" Service said.

"Yep," Ghizi said. "Baddest motherfuckers in the Northeast, and then they moseyed out this direction into the Midwest and got their asses handed to them, and that pretty much ended all that."

"Smallpox got the Iroquois," Service said.

Ghizi nodded. "You've been doing your homework."

"Where are the clubs now?" Sedge asked.

"No clue. They disappeared," Ghizi said.

"Your people got any notions about the source of the relics?"

"Kinda hoping you might have some," Ghizi said.

Service looked over at Sedge, who said, "If we come up with something, we'll let you know."

Ghizi said, "Figured you'd say that. Repeat—we're on the same team."

Service asked, "You want us to stay clear of Jane Rain?"

"Please."

"We supposed to meet regularly like this?" Sedge asked the Fish and Wildlife consultant.

"Works for me." He handed the two Michigan officers business cards and waited to receive theirs.

"That dating's certain?" Service asked.

"As certain as carbon dating can be."

"What's Toliver have to say about the dating?"

"We never told him. In fact, you two are the first to hear it."

"Other suspects?" Service asked.

"Not yet."

"Something in the works?"

"Possibly. We'll let you know. Thanks for this meeting, and Service—tell that ole boy Treebone I'm glad he made it."

After Ghizi left them by cutting south into the forest, Service looked Sedge in the eyes. "Thoughts?"

"You know *Alice in Wonderland?*"

"Neither personally, nor biblically."

"Not funny," Sedge said.

"Not sure I ever actually read it."

Sedge took a deep breath and continued. "Alice is talking to the Cheshire Cat and she says, 'Would you tell me, please, which way I ought to go from here?' The Cat says, 'That depends a good deal on where you want to get to.' And Alice said, 'I don't much care where.'

" 'Then it doesn't matter which way you go,' said the Cat. '—So long as I get *somewhere,*' Alice explained.

" 'Oh,' said the Cat, 'you're sure to do that, if only you walk long enough.' "

Service grunted. "You want to know where *somewhere* is, or how long it will take us to get there?"

"Hell, I think we know where *somewhere* is. Don't we?"

"Nighthawks," Service said. "Maybe we need to revisit Mr. Delongshamp and find out more about what's been buzzing around out by his place at night."

"Sunday work for you?" Sedge asked. "Tahq Park, tall-falls area, at two?"

"Works for me."

17

Harvey, Marquette County

SATURDAY, MAY 12, 2007

"This gives hit-and-run a whole new meaning," Tuesday Friday said, her leg draped over Grady Service's hip as it invariably was after sex. "Do you *have* to go back tonight?"

He rubbed his eyes and yawned. "We're in mole mode with the case," he said, fighting sleep.

"Progress?" she asked.

"Maybe," he said, not wanting to talk.

The next thing he knew it was morning, they had made love again, and her leg was back over his hip.

"Good thing this is the weekend," Friday mumbled. "My brain is like in atomic Jell-O-mode."

Service looked at her clock radio. "It's the next day!"

"God, you must be a *detective!* You were in a deep sleep and I couldn't bring myself to wake you up."

"You woke me just fine this morning," he said.

"That was for my mental health. How long will this darn case go on?" she asked.

He shrugged, lay his hand on her flat belly. "You know," he said.

"Yeah, it is what it is. She good-looking?"

"Who?"

Friday punched his upper arm. "Sedge, you jerk."

"I think so. Are you jealous?"

"Should I be?"

"Not yet."

She laughed out loud. "I asked for that one."

"Probably."

"Is she competent?"

"I think so, but she's young."

"Do you remember what it was like to be young and new in your job?"

"I was born old."

"I remember," she said. "We normals are filled with insecurities, so go easy on her."

"You *are* young," he said, giving her a playful shove.

"An me so *haw-knee*," she keened. "So *haw-knee* . . ." taking the lines from a Vietnamese Vietcong hooker in *Full Metal Jacket*.

"No time," he countered.

"Make time to make time," she whispered, kissing his shoulder. "Make me."

18

Tahquamenon Falls State Park, Chippewa County

SUNDAY, MAY 13, 2007

Sedge would meet him at the state park at two o'clock, but first he wanted to find a more-direct route to Delongshamp's cabin on the Shelldrake River. He trailered his RZR up to West Betsy Road, unloaded it, locked his truck, and headed north, halting at a gate marked LAMBS OF THE LORD A bearded man in faded blue jeans was kneeling in a flowerbed, but popped up to greet him.

Service, in civilian clothes, showed his badge. "DNR."

"Charlie Nickle," the man said. He was thin, tall, straight-backed, well past sixty.

"You in charge here?"

Nickle smiled. "The Lord's in charge."

Service wished he had not stopped. "Do you know a man by the name of Godfroi Delongshamp?"

"Yes, of course—The Lost Sheep."

"Part of your group?"

Nickle smiled again. "Not part of any group, at least not one I can identify."

"What can you tell me about him?"

"Why?"

"Just wondering."

"In a litigious society with privacy laws, nada. Sorry, Officer."

"Hard feelings between Delongshamp and your group?"

"Not on our part."

"How many people are here?"

"That particular number varies. Right now it's seven, maybe eight."

"Young folks?"

"Not at the moment."

"Have you ever had problems with vandalism or break-ins out here?"

"The Lord protects us from youthful indiscretions."

Youthful? "What's your role here, Charlie?"

"Priest-handyman—Father Fix-it, if you will." Nickle shrugged. "Actually, I don't have all that much to do. God sends us retreaters with a magnificent array of skills. What can we do for you, Detective?"

"Just wanted to introduce myself. You mind if I work my way north across your property?"

The priest frowned. "No motorized vehicles are allowed. Silence is the cornerstone of solace and introspection. I'm sorry."

"That's okay, Father. We all have our rules."

"Call me Charlie."

"Okay, Charlie. Is there a ford near here?"

"Section Fifteen. Cowlspel owns the property, and there's a bridge for snowmobiles and four-wheelers. He doesn't mind people using it. It's a half-mile north of our property line."

"Thanks."

"You ever need a truly quiet place, son, we're always here."

"I appreciate that, Charlie."

"If you happen to see a disrobed woman walking around north of here, please don't be alarmed. She's trying to work through some personal issues. This behavior is part of her recovery, but it can be rather upsetting to some people."

Say what? "In other words, don't bust her for public nudity."

"If you would be so kind," the priest said.

• • •

The Delongshamp cabin was empty and trashed again. Service found two four-wheeler tracks nearby and covered them so he and Sedge could pour plaster casts later. There were no footprints, only griddle-like markings in some soft dirt patches. He had no idea what had caused the cross-hatching, but something inside told him he ought to know.

Service followed the four-wheeler trails northeast toward Vermilion, and when he cut across a soft sand two-track, he saw where the machines had been loaded on a trailer and hauled away.

• • •

Sedge met him in the parking lot of the "tall falls," her term for the Upper Tahquamenon Falls. A man in a dark green DNR shirt was with her.

"Jeremy Cugnet, Grady Service. Jerry's the park manager," she explained.

"Bolf works for you?"

"He works here, but not directly for me. He's seasonal—cuts grass, does miscellaneous maintenance chores."

"Been here long?"

"His third season."

"Before here?"

"Sleepy Hollow State Park, Clinton County."

"Clinton?" This was downstate, near Lansing.

"Yep, that's the one."

"What did he do there?"

"Pretty much the same job."

"Why'd he move?"

"Divorce, wanted a change of scenery."

"Somebody recommend him?"

"Sammy Pinto, my counterpart down there. Said he's a good worker, doesn't cause trouble, shows up every day, never a problem. Why?"

"He's the friend of someone we have an interest in."

"Huh," Cugnet said. "Bolf isn't the pally type. Stays to himself. He's a trapper."

"Is he a good employee?"

"A little slow by my standards, but reliable enough."

"Working today?"

"Nope. Works twelve-hour shifts, Tuesday through Thursday."

"Do you know Godfroi Delongshamp?"

Cugnet pursed his lips. "Can't say I do."

"What about Father Charlie?"

"You mean Father Brightsides out at LOL? Yeah, I know him."

"Brightsides?"

"Power of positive thought, God is always at your side, the glass is half full, bad shit is good, all that sunshine-lights-up-your-ass stuff."

"You disapprove?" Sedge asked, intervening.

"I'm opposed to zealotry in service to ambiguous celestial beings."

"Where's Bolf live?" Service asked.

"Fire number 32 on West Lost Lake Road, about six miles east of here," Cugnet said. Sedge wrote the address on a piece of paper. "He's got a pack of dogs," Cugnet added. "Pit-bull mixes."

Fuck, Service thought, feeling his stomach lurch.

• • •

There was a red fire number on West Lost Lake, but no name. A grassy two-track led back through some trees. The trailer sat at the far end of what looked to be a ten-acre parcel. No vehicle at the trailer, no Bolf, no dogs.

"This is productive," Sedge said.

"Let's take a good walk around before we decide what to do next," Service suggested. Moments later he added, "No fresh dog shit. Looks like no dogs have been here for a while."

"Maybe I wrote down the wrong fire number," Sedge offered.

"Or Cugnet had it wrong," Service said. "Bump him on your cell. Find out."

Sedge walked down the grassy road, looking to get enough bars to call out.

"This is the right number," she said when they met again.

Service circled the trailer, looking into dirty windows. "The inside looks dusty, lots of spiderwebs. It looks abandoned."

"So he moved," Sedge said.

"Possibly. Call the County, see if they have the same fire number."

"That's paranoid," she said.

"Just filling squares," he told her.

Service found steel stakes, no chains. He could see where dogs had been restrained, but the worn areas looked old, and what dog feces he could see were dessicated and faded white with age. *Dust to dust*, he told himself. Animal scat was a preview of the process that lay ahead for every living thing.

Walking a spiral route he found two rectangular holes, eighteen inches by three feet. Sedge caught up with him. "There's no such fire number. What're the holes—graves for elves?"

Service knelt and felt around in the holes, coming up with a wood sliver, which he showed to her. "Military footlocker," he said. "Whatever was here was temporary. Government footlockers rot fast in the elements. Cheap Chinese knockoffs rot even faster. Let's walk a rough grid from this point," he suggested.

"Are you thinking warrant to get into Bolf's trailer?" she asked.

"No evidence of a crime and no missing person report. I think we'll have to wait until he's supposed to report to work Tuesday."

She said, "Forty-eight hours is a long time."

"The law and the Constitution can sometimes be downright inconvenient," he said. "I think one of us needs to talk to other employees about Bolf, and the other one needs to talk to Chippewa County, tell them we might be looking for warrants. Find out if they've had contacts with Bolf or Delongshamp."

"I checked the Retail Sales System," she said. "Bolf doesn't have a fur harvester's license. Didn't have one last year either." RSS was the database for all state outdoor licenses and a quick way for officers to determine if people were off the legal reservation.

"Cugnet says he traps."

"Interesting," Sedge said. "I'm tight with some deps, the undersheriff, and the magistrates."

"Okay, the park's mine."

"My place tonight?" she asked as he drove her to her truck at Tahquamenon. "The paintings are down and packed for transport to the galleries. You afraid you can't control yourself?"

She likes to throw people off balance. "You walk around your joint in your whoopee suit?"

"Of course."

"Good," he said.

"You don't want to see hunkus painting, but real hunkus is okay?"

"I like reality shows," he said, fighting a smile.

"You are one strange dude," she declared.

"Takes one," he said, making her laugh.

"Check in around five," she said. "I've got elk steaks we can grill."

"Sounds like a plan," he said, watching her drive away.

• • •

Service found Cugnet in his office. "You sure Bolf still works here? There's no recent sign of dogs or habitation at his trailer."

"He's still on the payroll."

"The fire number you gave us doesn't exist with the County, but the sign is there and it looks legit."

"And?"

"The sign is identical to others like it. Someone went to a lot of trouble to make it look legit."

"Can you translate that to park-talk?"

"Money."

"What about it?"

"That's the part I have to figure out. Who's his boss?"

"Ingo Sailinen, up at the maintenance shop on M-123. I'll let him know you're coming."

● ● ●

Sailinen looked mean, with splotches of gray hair and a thick white mustache. "You interested in Bolf?" he asked.

Service nodded.

"Nobody knows the man. Does his job okay. Always looks like he's deep in thought, though I always had the impression he don't have a lot between the ears, eh?"

"Cause any problems?"

"Nah, he tows the line. Like I said, slow, but he's not lippy or nothing."

"You know he was a trapper?"

"I seen traps in his vehicle from time to time, but he don't talk about it."

"What's he drive?"

"Ten-year-old white Datsun that's more rust than metal. I think the thing's held together with Bondo, duct tape, and baling wire."

"You ever see his dogs?"

"Once, and they scared the hell out of me. Aggressive sonsabitches. We all stayed clear of his place."

"You were there?"

"Just the once."

"You ever hear of Godfroi Delongshamp?"

"Should I have?"

"Nope, just asking. Bolf working Tuesday?"

"Always does."

"Okay, thanks."

Sailinen nodded once and marched away.

• • •

He got to Sedge's five minutes before her.

"The deps know him. Bolf drinks like a fish over in Bay Mills, but he's never been busted for operating while intoxicated or under the influence. One of his dogs got loose last fall and killed a hunter's English setter. The hunter threatened to kill Bolf's dog and Bolf threatened to kill the hunter."

"No cops?" asked Service.

"Later the hunter got to thinking and called the sheriff, and they talked to Bolf, who denied the whole thing. No evidence, just 'he-said' claims. The cops couldn't do anything. The hunter threatened to sue in civil court, but so far he hasn't."

"You talk to the deps who handled it?"

"Yes, Tailor Tate handled the dog deal. She says Bolf's a ticking time bomb, but he's got no record."

"And no trapping licenses."

"What're you thinking we do next?"

"Grill the elk steaks. I brought beer."

"Works for me. You make it down to SuRo's?"

"Nothing there. One request?"

She looked at him.

"Keep your clothes on," he said as she opened her front door.

She grinned from ear to ear. "He breaks first!"

"You've got major pain-in-the-ass written all over you," he mumbled, stepping past her.

"Why Chief Master Sergeant, I do declare . . . and here I was thinking you hadn't even noticed little old me," she vamped.

PART II: NIGHTHAWKS

19

Sault Ste. Marie, Chippewa County

MONDAY, MAY 28, 2007

He had not seen Jingo Sedge in two weeks, but they had talked by phone several times. She had gotten an unexpected late steelhead run up Lake Superior feeder creeks, which acted as a magnet for several crews of fish cheats.

Meanwhile, he had finished interviewing a Diorite man whom a Montana game warden alleged to have illegally taken two elk and a grizzly bear. It had taken several heated conversations with the man and the creation of a case that looked more menacing than it was real to convince the man to cop to charges, which he finally did in a flood of tears. And then he wanted a hug and totally disgusted Service. *Damn fools in the woods.*

Michigan was part of the Interstate Wildlife Violator Compact, which meant if a hunter had his hunting privileges revoked in one state, twenty-seven others in the IWVC would follow suit and also revoke. Service told the man Montana would consider not asking for revocation if the man confessed. This was partly true. The game warden he'd talked to repeated the words as Service dictated them to him, but drolly added, "I reckon that SOB won't ever hunt the Big Sky again, even with a dang slingshot."

Service didn't feel sorry for the hunter. He'd known better, and two elk and a griz were, in his opinion, equivalent to grand larceny. In fact, the man had cried when Service had confiscated the elk meat and bearskin, which had been salted and packed in plastic. But what set the man off most was the confiscation of his hunting rifle, which he'd gotten from his grandpa when he turned twenty-one. Taking "grandpa's gun" was often the straw that broke the camel's back.

For two weeks, Friday, Shigun, and Service had lived in some semblance of normalcy, spending one week at Tuesday's place and one week at Slippery Creek. Karylanne and Little Maridly had driven over from Houghton one Sunday and he had grilled hot dogs and they'd had s'mores over a campfire by the cabin. Shigun would be two in November, Maridly three the following month, but already she assumed the bossy role of older sister and fussed over the little boy, lecturing, and scolding him.

This morning Friday had snuggled in close. "Can you believe some families live like this *all* the time?" she had whispered. "How long will you be gone this time?"

"Sedge wants me to meet a retired assistant AG who's gone over to the dark side, and I need to get down to Lansing to meet the illustrious Hectorio."

"The one Allerdyce told you about?"

"One and the same."

"Your case seems to lack focus."

"Most of them are this way, and so far there's no evidence of a crime." He'd not told her about the USF&WS involvement in the background of the case. *Maybe later.*

"How do you justify working it?"

"I don't bother. I just stay with it. You remember the old story about the worker who keeps leaving his clock factory at quitting time with an empty wheelbarrow, and security always let him pass?"

"He was stealing wheelbarrows," she said.

"Right, and somewhere, somehow, someone in this case is stealing wheelbarrows."

"Says your gut, not the evidence."

"My gut's good enough for me at this point."

"Well, don't go getting your big butt shot or anything stupid," she whispered.

"Not to worry."

"We women are wired to worry about our men, you insensitive lummox."

"Worry about things that need worrying about," he countered.

"I do."

• • •

He met Sedge in the parking lot of the Soo Troop post near I-75. Sedge looked different, but he couldn't figure what exactly had changed. If anything.

"I will never understand how and why people will risk life and limb for damn fish," she said disgustedly. "Four crews yesterday, all jerks—fifteen tickets and I took all their damn gear. Boy, you should have heard them bitch!"

"There's no logic to greed," he said. "Your AG pal expecting us?"

"Former AG, and no. He's at the Kewadin, and I thought we'd just pop in on him. He moved to Ottawa, Headquarters for the First Nations Archaeological Society."

"He's Canadian?"

"Dual card. Born here, raised there, came over here for college, law school at Wayne State, prosecutor in Wayne and Oakland counties, then assistant AG with the State. Now he's back in Canada."

"He got a name?"

"Elvis Y. Shields."

"What do you hope to get from him?"

"An explanation? I educated the man, and he used what I taught him to get a new job."

"You know that, or speculate that's how it went?"

"It feels that way. I just want to hear what he has to say."

The Kewadin hotel conference center casino was on Shunk Street, not far from the St. Mary's River and the ferry to Sugar Island. The French, who showed up at what the Indians called Bawating in the early seventeenth century, saw that it was the strategic entrance to Lake Superior, settled in, and named the area Sault Ste. Marie. The area had retained strategic importance and the name ever since.

"Why's Shields here now?"

"Personal trip to gamble. He owns a camp on Raber Bay."

Raber was south of the Soo, about halfway toward Drummond Island and Detour. "Who told you he was here?"

"The handyman who looks after his camp."

He was impressed at her network. "What's my role here?"

"Ears and eyes."

"I can do that."

"He'll be playing blackjack," she said, leading them inside.

"Per your handyman?"

"A dealer I know."

She's young but understands the importance of multiple irons in the fire.
As predicted, they found Elvis Y. Shields hunched over a blackjack table.

Sedge left him alone until a hand was played out and he raked in a substantial pile of chips. Service thought the man looked unhappy to be disturbed, which was understandable, but he picked up his chips and walked with her into a plush corridor.

"Elvis Shields, meet Grady Service."

The man's eyebrows shot up. "The governor's big dog," he said, and looked at Sedge. "What do *you* want?"

"To ask some questions."

"Make an appointment."

"I tried."

"I'm a busy man."

"Not too busy for this two-bit casino. You wasted all my time," she added sharply.

Shields looked at Service. "Hey, Big Dog, explain to the little girl how life works," the man said.

Service said, "How about I smack a blunt instrument up the side of your greasy fucking head?"

Shields recoiled. "Are you threatening me?"

"Not at all. Apologize to Officer Sedge, or I'm going to knock your fucking head off. That's a promise, asshole."

Shields said unconvincingly to Sedge, "Sorry."

"Why?" Sedge asked. "I want an explanation."

The lawyer shrugged. "An unexpected career opportunity arose. I had enough time in, I pulled the plug and moved on, end of story. Someday you'll do the same thing."

Sedge said, "I was counting on you to help me move my case along. I *invested* in you."

"You have no case," Shields said. "And Katsu's a bloody felon. You ought to take a closer look at that."

"No case?"

"The state archaeologist says your site was not one for burials, and thus NAGPRA doesn't apply. Professor Toliver can dig. If you were to come up with human remains—something solid, anything—you might be able to develop a lukewarm case."

"What's the First Nations Archaeological Society?" Service asked, intervening.

"Just what the name implies."

"It implies nothing."

"Maybe to the uninformed."

Asshole. "You own property on Raber Bay?" Service asked.

"Is there a point to this inquisition?"

"It's implied," Service said. " 'Course, I know all your taxes are paid, right, and everything is according to Hoyle?"

"Don't even," Shields said. "You might be the big dog out in the cedar swamps, but in a courtroom against me, you'd be dog food."

Service felt Sedge pinch his hip and pull him, and let himself be led away.

"How'd I do?" he asked.

"I don't think he was impressed," she said.

"He heard me," Service said. "Loud and clear."

"Why didn't I?"

"You just haven't sorted it out yet. I just let that bastard know we're going to put him under the microscope."

"You said that?"

"It was implied."

She shook her head. "I suppose I should call his caretaker, check out the property."

"That's good. I'm heading down to Lansing for a tête-à-tête with the infamous Hectorio."

Sedge stared at him. "Who?"

"Allerdyce says Hectorio trades errorheads and he's looking for copper."

"*Limpy* Allerdyce, the old scumbag who *shot* your ass?"

"The one and only. And it was my leg."

"Too much information," she said. "I'm heading for Raber Bay."

"Later," he said to her back.

20

North Lansing, Ingham County

MONDAY, MAY 28, 2007

Just last year he had bumped into Limpy Allerdyce's former daughter-in-law and sworn enemy, Honeypat, once thought dead; instead, she seemed to be prospering as a high-end madam in the Lansing poon-trade, servicing politicians and bureaucrats in addition to regular citizens. Honeypat was one of the sexiest, craziest women he had ever met, and for years before disappearing, she had tried relentlessly to get him into bed with her. Ironically, she had been a big help on a case, and afterwards he had gotten a handwritten business card in an envelope in his mailbox. All it had was a phone number, but he was pretty sure it was from Honeypat—her way of letting let him know he could get in touch with her if he wanted to. Given her concern for personal security, it was a huge concession to allow him such access.

He called the number from St. Johns on his way south.

"Leave your name, number, and a short message," a recording said. *Not her voice.*

"This is Service."

He heard an immediate click. "Talk about unexpected," she said. "Where youse at?"

"Headed into Lansing."

She growled like a starving cat. "Where youse staying?"

"Haven't thought that far ahead yet."

"You want a room, I can help youse."

"I'm more interested in information."

"A room's free, and so am I. But information, she costs, eh?"

"How much?" he asked.

"You know."

"Never gonna happen, Honeypat."

"You say," she said. "What is it you want?"

"Hectorio."

A long pause ensued. "What about *that one?*"

That one? "You know him?"

"Self-declared *jefe* of the North Lansing *barrio*. Me and him, we got this understanding. You don't got, he runs you out. Or worse."

"I heard he collects arrowheads and Indian relics."

"Can't say I heard that, but wun't surprise me none. Some say he's part Indi'n, Chocktaw or Comanch, or something, and real proud of it. What's your interest?"

"Mainly I'd like to talk to him. Where's he hang?"

"Mictlantecuhtli, a café on ML King and Shiawassee. You can't miss it. Got colored skeletons all over the front of the building."

"Sounds appetizing."

"Food's good and cheap, but Mictlantecuhtli is the god of the dead, and that fits Hectorio."

"Bad dude?"

"The baddest of the bad, hands down."

"Worse than Limpy?"

"Don't go there."

"You know Hectorio well?"

"Enough."

"I'd like to meet him."

"That will cost you," she said.

"How much?" he asked, guessing the answer.

"Yo, like youse already know. The cost is *me.*"

"Too high," he said.

"Your loss," she said.

"So how do I find Hectorio?" he asked, persisting.

"Let me get you a room; I can set it up. He don't like movin' around in public, and he don't much like gringos."

"It was Limpy who told me to talk to the man."

"Shit," she said. "And you called *me?*"

"Hey, I'm not too proud to ask for help."

"There's a motel in Holt called Carolo's. Right off I-96, can't miss it. Go there. A room will be waitin' in your name."

"This going to happen tonight?" he asked.

"Somepin' will," she said, "but my crystal ball's kinda hard to see into."

"Thanks, Honeypat."

"I ain't done nuttin' yet."

"Thanks for nothing then."

She laughed out loud. "Youse always make me laugh, Service. And, I get hot when I laugh."

"Well," he said, "let's dial it over to sad."

She laughed even harder. "It don't work that way."

"Carolo's in Holt, off I-96."

"Youse in uniform?"

"No."

"Keep it that way."

• • •

Carolo's in a former life was called the Albert Pick. It was two stories, and clean. The night manager was a Latino woman who avoided eye contact. Service gave his name. The woman glanced up and handed him a key to Room 214 without saying a word. Not a plastic, electronic, programmable key, but a metal one, like the old days. And bent and scratched, showing its age.

The room had faded from once-bright colors. The furniture was cheap, the carpet a fibrous scab over a tile floor. A small TV sat on a high stand on the wall. He sat down in a chair and faced it toward the door to await whatever would happen next. He hoped Honeypat would not show up. He had been fending her off for years and it was tiring, because the truth was that he had sometimes been tempted. Even thinking this, he felt guilty because of Friday. *Honeypat's like Typhoid Mary!*

There was a noise in the hall, but a door to the adjoining room opened suddenly and a tall, handsome Hispanic man stepped in and stared at him. "*Que onda.* You him?"

"I'm Service." He thought he could see the man's Indian blood.

"What you want?"

"You Hectorio?"

"I *look* like Hectorio?"

"I've never met the man, so I've got no idea what he looks like."

"*Bueno.* Think of me as Hectorio if that make it easier for you, hombre. Me, I like ambigoolity. What it is you want? I don't have all night."

"Native American artifacts."

"What about them?"

"You buy and sell."

"You buyin' or sellin'?"

"Inquiring, looking for help."

"Who told you this thing?"

"A mutual acquaintance."

"Why a fish *placa* interested in that stuff?"

"Call it a sideline." Honeypat must have told the man he was DNR law enforcement.

"Maybe I do it as service to my people."

"What kind of service?"

"You know, man. Buy tings, return them where they belong."

"Like Robin Hood of the antiquities business."

"You might not be too far off, hombre."

"I'm trying to determine if there's been a theft."

"Of what, from where?"

"Can't share that. You understand."

Hectorio smiled. "I'm cool. What you do if there's theft?"

"Catch the bad guy, and return the items to their rightful owners after the courts are done with them."

"Word's around you straight-up dude, no bullshit."

"Makes things easier," Service said.

"Where this stuff is, you want?"

"Above the bridge."

"Port Huron?"

"Mackinac."

"Shinob turf."

"Some of it," Service said.

"All of it till you whites stole it."

"Paid for it."

"Paid little dirt for a lot of dirt."

"I'm not interested in renegotiating history," Service said. *Or reinterpreting it.*

"Ain't neither. You talkin' jes Shinob shit?"

"Probably."

"Low-ticket, man."

"I believe there are exceptions."

"Could be," Hectorio allowed. "Like what?"

"Copper points, carved-bone breakheads."

Hectorio looked interested, sort of leaned in. "Shinob war clubs?"

"Maybe Iroquois."

The man's eyes narrowed. "Somebody break into a cache?"

"Could be."

"*Mucho feria, hombre.*"

A lot of money? "How much is a lot?"

"Carved-bone Iroquois war club, up to a hundred K, maybe."

"That sounds way high."

"Supply and demand, dude."

"You buy direct?"

The man cocked his head. "You a fucking fed or what, man?"

"State, and we're not interested in you."

Hectorio grinned. "You lie, you die."

"Understood. You buy direct?"

"I walk the middle, *esse*, hand between buy and sell, *comprende?*"

"You seen anything like I described?"

"Could be somebody *heard* about some shit, but a lot of bullshit gets buried in the ground, sayin'?"

"You know of anybody who's put out a call for such things?"

Hectorio shrugged nonchalantly. "I might."

"Care to share?"

"I look stupid? What in this for Hectorio?"

"Don't know yet. You thinking stipend?"

"Fuck is stripend, man?"

Service rubbed his thumb against his forefinger.

"*Si*, bueno. I think stripend. How much that stripend is?"

"Depends."

"Like on what?"

"Where a name takes me, who it is, like that."

"I lose a good buy, I need big stripend. Businessman, he, like, got espenses to take care of."

"Could be it would make you a hero."

Hectorio snarled and leered. "Dude, Hectorio *already* a hero. You can't spend no fucking hero."

"Big-time public hero."

The man seemed to consider this. "No man, big stripend enough. How I get to you, I get a name? You skank *puta?*"

Service handed him a business card.

The man grinned, showing a flashy gold tooth in front. "Mr. Dicktecative."

"Leave a message and I'll get back to you."

"We'll see, man. You call me, say how much this stripend, okay?"

"No need to call. How's twenty-five K strike you?"

"I get four times that."

"You got nothing to sell.

"What if you dirty, want make deal, cut me out?"

"I lie, I die, right?"

Hectorio nodded, tapped the business card against his gold Rolex. "Maybe I call you, *esse.* Twenty-five large, si? Old bills, no new cash, no check shit."

"Old bills, however you want it."

"Adios, fish cop. You call me, ax for Aitch," the man said, and was gone.

Honeypat stood in the doorway where Hectorio had been.

"You want it rough and dirty, or sweet and soft?"

"Neither," he said. "As in none."

"Thank God," she said.

He stared at her. "What?"

"I'm not Honeypat, you cretin. I'm Honeypet, her twin sister."

Service could only stare. "Are you trying to fuck with my head?"

"Don't use that language around me," she said. "I'm a righteous Christian woman, born again. Honeypat says to tell you that you two aren't over."

"We never started."

"That's not how she tells it, but then we all know how the woman exaggerates everything."

"Like hell."

"I'm not going to tell you again about foul language. She'll talk to you soon."

"Her or you?"

"Hard to say."

"I doubt it."

"Count on it, Service. Hectorio gets what he wants, my sister needs something too. Fair is fair."

"Are you like her psychic pimp?"

The woman spat at him as he escaped through the door. He found his hand shaking as he got behind the steering wheel. Jesus! *Honeypat's twin sister?* He punched in the speed-dial number for Sedge.

"I'm out on foot," she answered in a whisper.

"Anything?"

"Talk later. You coming north?"

"Should I?"

"My place, soon as. I know I'm close to something, but I can't quite find it."

"Be safe," he said, closing the cell phone.

21

Bomb Shelter, M-123, Luce County

TUESDAY, MAY 29, 2007

It was the faintest stage of early-morning twilight, and Service found Sedge sitting in her truck, her face glowing with green light from her computer.

"You just get here?" he asked.

"No, I'm just clearing e-mail."

She looked sleepy.

"You doze off?"

"Maybe for a little while."

"You can't work twenty-four seven," Service said.

"Everyone says you do."

"Everyone's full of shit. I'm telling you I don't."

He lit a cigarette and let her finish on the computer.

"I was gonna call the handyman, but I decided showing up unan-nounced at the property might be better."

Same choice I would have made. "And?"

"Bait piles all over the place, some of them lighted, but the lights weren't connected. I also found a blood trail and followed it to an outbuilding, which is padlocked."

"What next?"

"I called Shields. He said he knew nothing about the property, that in fact it is for sale, and that I should call his watchman."

"Whom you already know."

"This time he gave me a different name—John Root. My guy is Kindal VanFen."

"How does Shields explain that?"

"Claims he fired VanFen because he was hearing some, quote, 'unsavory and disturbing rumors,' end quote. Naturally he refused to elucidate. I called VanFen. The firing was news to him. Said he got a check last Friday. I asked him if he knows John Root, but he's never heard the name before, and he's lived up here all his life."

"Did you talk to Root?"

"I wanted to, but Shields didn't have the man's phone number, because, he said, 'It's in my flat in Ottawa.' He'll call me when he gets home. I called Information. No John Root listed in the Eastern Upper Peninsula or the Upper Lower. I called Shields back and he said Root has a cell phone, that he just moved here from Indiana."

"Let me guess: Shields is headed into Canada today."

She nodded. "The asshole called me from Sudbury."

"Want to bet on getting a phone call from Ottawa?" he asked.

"I think not."

"Are there 'For Sale' signs out on the property?"

"Not that I saw, and if there are, they're not prominently displayed. I already checked online listings. Nothing there. I sent a note to the county board of realtors, but I doubt I'll hear back from them for a few days."

Service tried to weigh options, but he was groggy from driving. "Sure you can trust VanFen?"

"As much as anyone."

"Did you get a blood sample from the property?"

"And some hair."

"Deer?"

"Not sure. Think I should send it to the lab?"

The DNR's state forensics lab was located at Michigan State University, in East Lansing. "No, hold the sample. The lab's too jammed up for such a small thing."

"What happened in Lansing?"

"I met Hectorio, offered him incentives to provide us a name."

"Think he'll come through?"

Service sighed. "No clue."

"Good news. I talked to a Luce County dep. She said she knows a Bolf with a camp on Teaspoon Creek, south of Newberry."

"Our guy?"

"Could be. She said there's lots of dogs there, and the guy's a mega-boozer."

Before Service could speak, Sedge added, "I called Cugnet. He confirms that Bolf has had some bottle problems—beer, not hard stuff. You want to head over to the Teaspoon to take a look?"

He tried to hide a yawn, but failed. "I need a nap."

She led him inside and pointed to an oversized, understuffed couch. He looked at the bare walls around him. "Lacks cachet," he said.

"You want them back on the walls?"

He held up his hands. "I love it just the way it is."

He had a thought he wanted to share with her, but the next thing he knew she was shaking him. "Sarge, it's noon and we're burning daylight."

He groaned as he sat up and put his feet on the floor. "You hurt yourself?" she asked.

"When you get to my age you'll understand. Why'd you call me Sarge?"

"An e-mail came through today. DNR's first chief master sergeant. Congratulations. Does that mean you're moving on?"

"This case comes first," he said, adding, "*your* case."

"Just how old are you?" she asked.

"Too old to joust with you. Point me at a head."

"You want lunch?" she asked.

"Shiny shoes food, or real stuff?"

She laughed. "Shiny shoes?"

"Suits, people with expense accounts that *do* lunch instead of eat it."

"It's real, dude."

"We'll see," he said, limping slowly toward the bathroom.

22

Houghton, Houghton County

WEDNESDAY, MAY 30, 2007

Sedge volunteered to creep the potential Bolf camp on Teaspoon Creek and check in with him afterwards. Grady Service had driven to Houghton to spend the night with his granddaughter, who kept poking his ear with her forefinger and chanting. "My Bampy, my Bampy, my Bampy."

"She likes the rhythm," her mother explained. "Don't worry, she'll have a new mantra tomorrow."

"I won't be here," he said.

"Your loss," Karylanne said. "You going back to Marquette?"

"That's the plan."

But Chas Marschke had called to let him know that the billboards were all set to go. "Do you want to review final wording?"

"Too tied up," Service said, and gave his financial advisor-manager a thumbnail of the case.

"Taxes," Marschke said.

"What about them?"

"Rich people give artwork to museums and take substantial tax deductions. It's often a dodge. What they claim for certain pieces isn't even close to actual market value, and a lot of times the stuff is either fake or stolen with virtually no provenance."

"Stolen?"

"Yes, and usually the collector-donor and recipient—and sometimes even the IRS—knows, or suspects the truth."

"Case of the rich getting richer?"

"That, and museums living off the ill-gotten gains of certain collectors. By the way, you now more than qualify as rich," Marschke added.

"I don't feel rich."

"Some people never do," Marschke said. "If you want, we can pull the trigger on your project earlier."

"How much earlier?"

"June first."

"Do it," Service said. "The sooner people start talking and bitching to their politicians, the better I'll like it."

• • •

Service had known the peculiar Zhenya Leukonovich since late 2004 and had worked a couple of cases with her. She was a star investigator for the IRS, and well connected in the miasma of the federal alphabet soup bowl. As she often did, she answered on the first ring when he called.

"Special Agent Leukonovich is most pleased to hear from the mysterious woods cop in Michigan's wilds."

He had come very close to a less-than-professional involvement with her, but had somehow steered clear. "This is strictly a business call, Zhenya."

"Zhenya is of course unsurprised. The wilderness peace officer invariably leaves her disarticulated."

She loved to wade endlessly in verbal sludge.

"Artifacts," he said.

Silence on her end. Then, "Artifacts or relics?"

"Either, both—what's the difference?"

"Humans make artifacts. Human remains over time *become* relics."

"People give such stuff to museums and get tax breaks," he said.

"Deductions, not tax breaks. Technically there is no such thing as a tax break. That is the inexact language of the ignorati mass media."

"Whatever. Some of the stuff is stolen."

Leukonovich said nothing. Then, "Why are you making this inquiry?"

"I need a name, someone to guide and advise us in a potential case."

"Where?"

"Here," he said. "Close."

"Artifacts or relics?"

"Either and both," he said. "We're not sure yet."

She paused. "Professor Ozzien Shotwiff, University of Chicago, emeritus, an archaeologist of great repute, *the* authority on Native American cultures east of the Mississippi River. Be warned: This is not an individual to be trifled with, and he can be most difficult in his relationships."

"The fat part of the Mississippi, or the headwaters?" Service countered.

"If that is an attempt at humor, be advised it is wide of the mark."

"Duly noted. How do I reach Professor Shotwiff?"

"I believe he lives from May through October at his Lake Superior cabin near a reputedly quaint village called Silver City. Do you know such a place?"

Ontonagon County. He knew it. "Yes, I know. Thanks, Zhenya."

"Zhenya clings to the hope the detective might wish to thank her in a more intimate way at some juncture."

"I'd probably like that in a different life, but I don't think that's going to happen in this one."

"Zhenya never says never," she said, and hung up.

Service called Sergeant Joe Delucca, newly promoted and covering four western U.P. counties. "Joe, Grady. Professor Ozzien Shotwiff of Silver City—you know him?"

"We call him Ding Dong Disney. The dumb bastard thinks he's St. Francis of Assisi incarnate, feeds goddamn bears, wolves, you name it, right out on the beach in front of his bloody cabin. His wife of forty years got slightly clawed by a bear last fall and she immediately divorced his clueless ass. There's no law against the lack of common sense—or feeding bears. We've tried to convince him to stop, but he insists he has a higher duty to care for God's lesser creations."

"Your guys ever talk blunt to him?"

"Tried, but he's one of those glass-half-full assholes who never sees the downside of anything—for people or animals."

"I need to talk to him."

"Yeah, good luck with that, man. His other nickname with the folks in Silver City is Ozone. You want me along?"

"We can do bad cop, terrible cop," Service said.

Delucca laughed. "I'm all over that shit. Everyone knows about the coot. Some local businesses have started feeding bears to attract tourists. This is a potentially dangerous situation, but our hands are tied."

Service guessed he'd need a hook to get the professor interested and feeling helpful. He sat at a table on the front porch of Karylanne's house with Maridly in his lap. "*Doing*, Bampy?"

"Rewriting history, honey. You know what history is?"

"Un-unh, but I do it too, okay, Bampy?"

She was already a pill and not yet three.

The *Jesuit Relations* talked about another battle south on Lake Michigan, toward Green Bay, he thought, but he wasn't sure. What if Iroquois Point involved the same group heading home *after* the battle farther south, looking to redeem egos and bent reputations? His eyes locked on the map where the Whitefish River emptied into Little Bay de Noc in Delta County. He ran his finger north along the river; the more he thought about it, the more possible it seemed. Probability, he knew, remained a major issue, but Katsu was insisting the Coast of Death was the actual battle site, and while the Ojibwa had no written history, their oral tradition was strong, and sometimes accurate.

"Bampy needs a smooch-smooch," he announced to his granddaughter.

She rubbed her little hand on his chin and shook her head. "Whiskers too *scratchy*. Smooth first!"

God.

23

Gull Point, Ontonagon County

WEDNESDAY, MAY 30, 2007

The ancient-looking cabin had been built of hand-hewn square logs creo-
soted black to prevent rot. Thick moss covered the roof and plants grew out
of the moss. It sat less than fifty feet from the water's edge, and about six feet
higher. There was no garage, no carport, and only a small lichen-covered
toolshed. *How the hell does this place escape obliteration during November
storms?* Bird feeders were all over the grounds. The cabin faced north at Lake
Superior. The ground around the buildings was matted with thick brown
pine duff.

Service knocked on the door several times. "Around back," a muffled
voice called out.

"Here goes nothin', " Joe Delucca muttered.

Service paused at the corner of the cabin and looked west. A sow bear
and four cubs were moving up and down the beach. A male voice was calling
softly, "Your babies are okay with me, Mama."

The voice came from a tall man with a shock of wavy black hair and
dark, leathery skin.

"Professor Shotwiff? I'm Grady Service." He motioned for Delucca to
keep watch for other bears. Where food was being handed out, crowds could
be anticipated.

"You come to dissuade me from feeding my animals, or to take me to jail?"

Service walked over to him, careful to keep the sow in sight. "You like to
play with hand grenades with the pins pulled, Professor?"

The man glanced over and shook his head. "That would be pretty damn
foolish."

"The pins are out of these bears, Professor."

"Nonsense, young man. I've known this sow since she was a cub coming
in with her mama. I've been doing this over multiple bear generations now.
They all know me and trust me."

"I'm not a young man, and don't you patronize me. You may think you're doing a good thing, but you're setting up these animals for premature deaths. You're killing them."

"Poppycock. Are you going to arrest me?"

"Nossir, but I wouldn't mind beating some sense into you."

The old man grinned, stood up, and turned to face the conservation officer. "Bring it."

Service saw Joe Delucca's eyes popping and focused to the east, and just as quickly the other officer was pointing. Service looked and saw a rangy young male emerge from the woods, and just as fast the female lunged at the professor and Service ran toward her, waving his arms and screaming. She stopped and clacked her teeth in warning, saliva cascading out of her mouth, a signal for everyone to back off.

"You brought that on," Service told the professor.

"Patent nonsense. You enticed it, *sir*."

"She came after *you*," Service pointed out.

"It's just a false charge. I've seen this before."

The professor's hands were shaking so badly that Service guessed he was about to keel over. He took the man's elbow, steadied him, and helped him sit on the edge of the deck.

"Easy," Service told the man.

"I don't understand."

"Joe," Service said.

Delucca chased the bears west down the beach until they fled into the trees. The boar loped in pursuit of the other animals from the east, following at an unbelievable speed.

"I think you need a drink for your nerves," Service said. "That boar is looking to kill one or all of those cubs."

"There's a bottle of Calvados on the kitchen table."

Delucca brought brandy in water glasses.

Service could faintly smell apples in the drink, didn't like the burnt aroma or the harsh flavor. Too much like antiseptic mouthwash.

The man's hand was still shaking as he tried to sniff the drink.

"You familiar with the boar?"

The old man shook his head.

"Tell him, Joe."

"The male wants to rub out all potential competition."

"What's the story here, Professor? You're a smart man. You have to know this is how it is."

"But they're *my* animals."

"They're *not* yours, but you could end up as *their* meal."

"I will not accept that."

"It doesn't matter what you reject or accept. Because of you, others in town are now feeding bears, which means the bears you think you know will have to compete against animals they don't know. We've seen this scenario play out before. Right, Sergeant Delucca?"

"There it is," Delucca said. "These deals always end up the same way."

"Why're you two here?" the retired academic asked.

"Iroquois Point," Service said.

"What about it?"

"You're familiar with how it was named?"

"Of course; what's this got to do with bears?"

"Absolutely nothing to do with bears, but what if it's misnamed?"

The man pursed his lips. "I'm listening."

"How does a war party that large move by water westward past the Soo in the first place?" Grady Service asked. "If they came up the St. Mary's from the east, the fight would more likely have been east of the Soo, not west."

Professor Shotwiff had a crooked grin, his eyes tight. "Is that your professional theory, and, if so, why should either of us care?"

"I just can't buy it happening to the east, but how the hell did they get past the Soo without being seen? I'm thinking it might have taken place farther west."

"The thing about amateurs is that they can let fantasy captain their imaginations."

"What if someone found a bear-bone-handled breakhead with an agate striking head, or several of them?"

"*Did* someone? Items, plural?"

"Theoretically," Service said.

"First, such artifacts would be quite valuable to collectors and archaeologists. Second, their presence at a site would strongly suggest *Na-do-we-se* presence."

"Ever heard rumors along those lines?" Service asked.

"In my business I used to hear all sorts of peculiar and equally asinine things. I ask again: Why are you here?"

"Zhenya Leukonovich."

"Never heard of him."

"Her."

"Same answer. No joy."

"She knows you, and recommended you as *the* authority on Native American cultures east of the Mississippi River. We need an expert to advise and guide us on a case we're working."

"Involving relics or artifacts?"

"That's not yet all that clear. Maybe both."

"How much does this consultancy pay?"

"It doesn't."

Shotwiff smiled. "Are you always so abrasive with the public?"

"My superiors have tried real hard to reform me. And hell, here I thought I was treating you with kid gloves."

"Stubbornness can be a virtue," the professor said. "I've always harbored doubts about Iroquois Point, but not for your reasons. What're you thinking?"

"I barely qualify as an amateur with this stuff."

"Presumably you're not an amateur at solving puzzles; amateurs have made a lot of important historical discoveries."

"Father Lalemant in the *Jesuit Relations* wrote about a battle that might be the one we're talking about, but he talks of one hundred Iroquois warriors, not three times that many."

"Of course. I've read Lalemant; all Jesuits exaggerated all things— especially when exaggeration would promote a heroic image for the often-infamous Society of Jesus."

"Then you know he talked about another fight on La Baie des Puants." This was French for Bay of Stinkers and referred to modern Green Bay.

"I remember there were no details."

"Meaning it didn't happen?"

"Not necessarily. The Iroquois attacks drove Potawatomi, Huron, and even some Ottawa westward, all the way down the Bay of Stinkers, which refers to the Winnebago tribe at Green Bay, living in mud huts. *Winnebago* translates in Algonquin to 'evil-smelling.' The Winnebago, or Ho-Chunks, seemed to rub everybody the wrong way. Let me hear *your* theory."

Am I amusing the old bastard? The old man was hard to read. "What if they had the scrap over toward Green Bay, and on the way east and home decided to cut north to the Soo, trying for a little payback?"

"An attack on either side of the Straits of Mackinac would be too risky. Too many people, no way to come in unseen, too many tribal fragments in the area. Please continue."

"You can run all the way up the Whitefish River, make a short portage to the AuTrain River, and pop into Lake Superior west of Munising. From there they could work eastward toward Bawating."

"Why would they go to such extremes?" the professor asked.

Service found himself caught short and blinking in the face of the professor's challenge. "Too hard to get past the Soo. Too narrow there, too much chance of being discovered."

Professor Shotwiff smiled. "At the time you're talking about, there wasn't a permanent village there. Years of attacks by the Iroquois had pushed Nipissing, Saulteur, Ottawa, and Huron way west, even when the Saulteur won all the battles. At the time you're talking about, I believe the main Saulteur force and their allies from Sault Ste. Marie were staying with their Keweenaw kin near L'Anse."

Service felt deflated. "Sorry to waste your time, Professor."

"You haven't wasted anything, son. Some accounts report the Saulteur et al. had traveled east to Bawating to fish and hunt, and that's when they bumped into the Mohawk-Oneida force, which presumably had come up the St. Mary's looking for a village to eat, but this isn't necessarily the final word on that. It's only the account endorsed by the Jesuits and other French reporters, none of whom were in attendance at the event. You're a detective. What would you do to find the truth?"

"In our terms this one is a really cold case—like frigid."

Shotwiff chuckled and nodded. "Welcome to the historian's world."

"I'd talk to the Iroquois, see if that side has a different memory of the battle. All we have now are secondhand accounts from the Anishinaabeg side.

Shotwiff grunted. "The Whitefish route," he said tentatively. "You're sure you don't mean up the Manistique-Fox, with an east portage to the upper Tahq?"

"Nossir, the Whitefish."

"You've floated this route?"

"Full length, several times. Over the years I think I've floated all the major river courses in the U.P."

"I'll be damned," the professor said. "You think they could have come north from Green Bay?"

"Afterwards, if they prevailed, they could have shot the rapids eastward past the Soo, or they could have reversed course and come back the way they'd come in," Service offered.

Shotwiff said, "Distance was meaningless to *Na-do-we-se* war parties. They often left their towns for two and three years to travel the war road. What do you think you have?"

"An old harbor, sanded in, but once open and a good place for an ambush."

"Somewhat west of Iroquois Point, I presume."

"Fifty miles on crow fly, more by canoe."

"Huh. Artifacts?"

"Copper points, but mostly pottery shards."

"The breakheads?"

"Maybe, maybe not. They were found, but precisely where isn't yet clear, and nobody seems to know for sure. What would such weapons be worth?"

"Anything from a thousand dollars to fifty times that—or more. But if you have a group of them, the collection could be worth a whole lot more, depending on the quality."

"People have that kind of money?"

"Private collectors and museums. What about bodies? How many?"

"Only one we know of, allegedly turned up by winter weather and wind."

Shotwiff sniggered. "Could happen, but it's also the old dodge of ambiguity used by archaeologists when they get caught off the reservation. Where're the remains now?"

"Reburied."

"Huh. Photos?"

"Not acknowledged."

"Trust me, there *are* photos. Archaeologists and treasure hunters are like Nazis—they can't help keeping detailed records even when they're enthusiastically committing crimes against humanity."

"Do a lot of archaeologists break laws?"

"One is too many," Shotwiff said, "but most of us are wimps *and* greedy, at least for ego reasons and professional reputations. The big-money jackals in the archaeological business are looting crews."

"You know about them?"

"In my line of work, we all know. It used to be a bunch of raggedy-ass local pot hunters looking for easy cash. Now they're well-equipped, experienced, professional looting crews. They can dismantle and empty a site in no time. Is it possible to see this site of yours?"

"To what end?"

"I can probably tell you if professionals have gotten to it."

Grady Service sensed opportunity. "No more bear feeding?"

"Goddammit, that's blackmail!" the professor said.

"Pretty much. Do we have a deal?"

"I suppose. What if they keep coming back?"

"Call us. We'll trap them and move them."

The professor's face contorted. "What are *game wardens* doing policing archaeological sites?"

"One of our many unacknowledged services. You ever deal with the state archaeologist?"

"Flin Yardley? I know him," said Shotwiff.

"Opinion?"

"Bureaucrat, paper pusher, neither a first-rate scholar nor overly experienced field man. Barely more than a glorified high school history teacher with family political connections to Clearcut Bozian."

"Honest?" Bozian was former governor Sam Bozian.

"Can you define that word?"

"Not absolutely," Service said.

"Therein lies the rub with values," the professor said.

"You ever deal with looting crews?"

"I have, and it's often unavoidable. Some are technically quite good, so we ask ourselves: Is it better to buy from them with some sense of provenance, or to let amateurs simply strip away history and make it disappear? There's no simple answer."

"Honesty and law pitted against reality."

"The classic conundrum."

• • •

Service tried several times to call Sedge on his way east but couldn't raise her by cell phone, radio, or computer.

He called Sergeant Jeffey Bryan. "Sedge talk to you and Lis about her case?"

"Briefly."

"She's trying to find a camp on Teaspoon Creek, but I can't raise her. Think one of your guys could see if they can find her truck?"

"You got it. Where are you?"

"West of L'Anse."

"Okay, I'll roll and get other help if needed. Bump me when you get closer."

"Clear," Service said, closing the cell phone.

24

Teaspoon Creek, Luce County

THURSDAY, MAY 31, 2007

"Headed east," Service told Friday as he flew past Marquette. "Sedge went to creep a cabin. She's not on her radio, she's not answering her cell phone, and her truck hasn't moved."

"Be careful, Grady," Friday said.

"How's the kid?"

"Keep your focus," she said. "He's fine, I'm fine, we're fine. Keep your head in the game."

Her ability to prioritize sometimes amazed him. "I'll be back," he concluded.

"She'll be okay," Friday said reassuringly.

My gut's not so sure, Service thought. He called Sergeant Bryan as he passed Seney on M-28. "She show?"

"Not yet."

"Where am I going?"

"Turn north in MacMillan on 415, go till you hit the tracks, and park. The captain will meet you in her RZR."

Captain Grant? He was confused for a moment, then realized McKower was now Grant's equal, and to some extent, his superior officer. Talk about a changing world.

• • •

McKower looked worried. "Bring your rifle," she ordered as he strapped his field ruck and cased .308 on the back of the Polaris. Her hard plastic rifle case was already strapped down. He did as he was told and lowered himself into the right seat. The tracks ran east and west. McKower ran on the left side in the cinders where other four-wheelers had gone before. In Luce County the damn things went anywhere and everywhere, a constant pain in the ass for conservation officers, county deps, and state police, all of them.

"How far?" Service yelled over the motor.

"Three miles to the Teaspoon on the tracks, then cross-country a third of a mile downstream to the Oxbow."

"Bolf's Camp?"

"No, a man named Delongshamp."

"Godfroi Delongshamp?"

McKower had the hammer down and they were being shaken violently, but she managed to stare at him.

"Why there?" he yelled.

"Her cell-phone chip."

"What chip?"

"Do you *ever* read your damn e-mail?"

"Don't need to. You're telling me what I need to know, right?"

She glowered. "Test program. Sedge and five other officers have GPS tracking chips in their cell phones."

"Let me guess," he yelled. "They don't have to be on."

"A gold star for our techie-boy," McKower said.

"No other contact?"

"None."

"The phone isn't on?"

"No, the system's designed passive."

"Big Brother," he said.

"Don't start," she yelled.

"She briefed you on her case?" he shouted.

McKower stopped the machine on a low bridge, took out a topo map, and handed it to him. The coordinates of Sedge's cell phone were written on the plastic cover over the map. "Must be hard ground on that finger," he pointed out, thinking out loud, trying to decipher what he was looking at. "The rest looks like swamp," he said, sliding into his ruck and slinging his rifle across his chest, barrel down. "My radio will be off until I see what's what. Where's Jeffey?"

"Working his way in from the other side of the Teaspoon."

Service entered Sedge's cell-phone coordinates in his handheld GPS and plunged north on foot into the dense swamp, finding himself knee-deep in dark water with a root-and-black-mud bottom. *Careful,* his mind warned. *Move steadily, not fast.*

Thirty minutes later he heard three shots, the reports muffled. He had his earbud in but he had heard it, and touched his chest to activate the transmitter on the mike. "Two One Hundred, Twenty Five Fourteen. Shots fired, forty-cal."

"Copy," McKower said. "You there? Clear."

"Gotta be close. Clear."

When he heard the shots, he had immediately lifted his hand and pointed to where he thought the point of origin was, a technique he and Tree had learned in the marines, and which had persisted over his career, as a lot of his marine training had.

"Twenty Five Fourteen, Two One Oh Three."

"Go, One Oh Three." It was Bryan.

"I'm with Two One Thirty. She's okay. Where are you?"

"Edge of the high ground south of the Oxbow," Service said, looking ahead. "You?"

"Other side of the Teaspoon. It's got a fair bottom if you look upstream about twenty-five yards. You'll see where Two One Thirty crossed back. Clear."

Service found the location and crossed holding his rifle and ruck above his head, mosquitoes crawling all over his sweaty body. "Left," Jeffey Bryan yelled from above.

Sedge was kneeling on one knee, her face beet-red. "You all right?" Service asked.

"She's mostly pissed off," her sergeant said, pointing at a cedar next to her. Service saw a crossbow bolt protruding from the reddish bark. Bryan held up three fingers.

Service squatted beside her, got water from his pack, held it out. "What's the deal?"

"I found the damn camp is what's the deal."

"Bolf?"

"Never saw him, but *someone* was living there. It's on the north edge of that low ridge and down, well camouflaged. It's just a shanty, but it's damn near invisible."

"You spook someone?"

She looked at the bolt in the tree. "Ya *think?*"

"Talk us through it," Service said, trying to calm her.

"Luck. A laser sight crossed my arm and I hit the deck as the bolt pounded the tree. I heard two more go through the foliage. I actually saw the last shot and then I saw him, and put three rounds over there."

"*Him?* Can you describe him?"

She chewed her lip. "He was green."

"Green?"

"Yeah, like Kermit the fucking frog."

Whoa, he thought. "You did good."

"I missed the bastard."

"You backed him off."

"I wanted to take him off the fucking *planet!*"

Change the subject. "Where's your truck?"

"On County 434 where it crosses the tracks. East-northeast of us."

"Where's your four-wheeler?" her sergeant asked.

"At the Bomb Shelter."

"Any description at all?"

"I told you. He's fucking *green!* I felt like I'd landed on the set of *Predator,* for Christ's sake."

"That bolt isn't Hollywood shit," Sergeant Bryan said.

"You saw a laser?" Service asked.

She pointed at her left arm.

"What direction was it moving?"

She paused to think. "I was stationary. It moved right to left," she said. "I can't figure out why he was scanning. All he had to do was put the dot on me and squeeze off the shot."

Service watched her. *Upset, but remarkably under control, reacting much the way I would.* "Where was this Kermit?"

She pointed.

"Keep guiding me."

He followed her hand signals to a thick cluster of tag alders, separated the trees and branches, and looked down at the ground.

"You're there," Sedge said.

"Got him," Service said. "Frog tracks."

"You *asshole!*" Sedge screamed.

"Swear to God," Service said, sorry he'd provoked her with a bad joke.

Bryan joined him, leaned over, looked back at her. "No shit, Sedge, but they ain't man-size. You think your boy might've been decked out in camo paint?"

She buried her face in her hands.

"Let's go see the camp," Service said.

Sedge didn't respond. Service looked at the sergeant and nodded toward the creek.

The two men waded the river and found the shack. They searched methodically, finding nothing.

"Fish camp?" Bryan asked. "Locals say the brook trout in this stretch are something special. It's one of those cricks they don't talk about to outsiders."

"Trapper," Service said. "This swamp and lower marsh are first-class muskrat habitat."

Bryan sniffed the air. "Eau de skunk. You're probably right about a trapper."

Skunk was a base ingredient in just about all liquid attractants. Service could smell skunk, but wasn't yet ready to conclude anything. He searched along the water and found a pipe driven deep into the bank. The end of the pipe was capped, with a small steel ring welded to it. The ring was wrapped in rubber to keep it quiet. "For a boat," he told the sergeant. "Where the hell would you put in a canoe?"

"Carlson Creek or off 405, but way upstream. We're almost down in the main Tahq here."

"What's this place remind you of?" Service asked the other officer.

Bryan shrugged.

"Something you built when you were a kid."

"A fort . . . a hideout?"

"Yeah, a hideout. This isn't the sort of place you stumble onto. Even if you come down in a canoe, you'd have to know it was here."

A hideout was what Bolf needed.

"Let's put out a BOL," he told the sergeant. "We might as well get the rest of law enforcement worked up over this."

"Be On Lookout by name?"

"Hell, by shoe size, IQ—whatever it takes."

Bryan made the radio call to McKower. "She's fine. We need a BOL for Peewee Bolf." He gave her the specifics and heard her immediately get on her radio and call the Luce County and Troops dispatcher, who covered several counties.

They found Sedge almost where they had left her, but she was smiling. A broken crossbow lay at her feet in the weeds. "One of my rounds broke it and he dropped it." She was wearing garish blue latex gloves.

Service saw the laser sight mounted atop the weapon and sucked in a deep breath. Rumors were flying that it wouldn't be long until the Natural Resources Commission liberalized the use of crossbows for hunting in the state. As it was now, it required special permitting.

"Barnett Wildcat C5 crossbow with a Pro-40 Multi-Dot scope, carbon bolts."

"You know about crossbows?" Service asked her.

"Yeah, and I'm betting this ain't your plain brown-envelope Barnett. The feet-per-second power on this sucker has got to be out of sight."

"Be nice to get prints," Service said.

"Like *that's* gonna happen," she quipped, and he agreed.

"Still gotta go through the steps," he reminded her. "You never know."

"I think I'll fix the weapon, and when we catch this asshole, I want to put a pea on his dick and tell him I'm going to shoot it off."

Let her blow off steam, he thought. *But keep an eye on her. She's got quite a temper.*

She tapped his hand and looked into his eyes. "No bull, Service; the perp even looked like Kermit, and I'm neither crazy nor hallucinating.

Sedge was too set on this to argue with her. Let it ride for now.

25

DNR District Office, Newberry

THURSDAY, MAY 31, 2007

Custody of evidence from the camp on the Teaspoon was formally transferred to CO Afton Radaskovich, who was headed to Ishpeming for a National Guard weekend. The Michigan State Police forensics lab in Marquette would try for prints and other micro-evidence.

McKower, Service, Bryan, and Sedge were crowded into the new assistant chief's office cubicle. The air was stale. A BOL had been issued on Peewee Bolf, and it turned out after checking that Peewee wasn't the man's nickname.

McKower was trying to rehash various phases of the case, and asking Sedge a lot of questions. Service found himself tuning out, preferring to contemplate other things. During the hike out with her he'd sensed he was missing something obvious, but the harder he tried to bring it into focus, the dimmer it got. He was hungry and tired and his clothing reeked of creek water and black muck; he just wanted to take a shower and eat a good meal and forget all this nonsense.

"You headed back to Marquette?" McKower asked, breaking his reverie.

"Not sure yet."

"I agree that you and Sedge ought to check the site again, see if there's been any activity."

When had this plan been put forth? Pay attention, you jerk. "Okay," he answered.

Out in the parking lot he asked Sedge, "Why *Kermit* the frog and not some other frog? You saw a face?"

"Sort of; maybe. I'm not sure. Whatever it was, Kermit's what my mind connected to."

Service left her and walked back into the office to find McKower pouring herself another cup of coffee. "That shit will stunt your growth," he said.

"It already has. I thought you two had left."

"You up for something off the wall?"

"From *you?* That won't exactly plow new ground."

"We put Peewee Bolf's description out with the BOL, but we didn't have a photo."

"Standard," she said, sipping the coffee and making a face.

"Can we add a picture of Kermit the frog to the alert?"

She spit coffee and guffawed, but then stopped and stared, wiping her chin. "Jesus, you're *serious!*"

"Call it a hunch."

"I call it ridiculous," Assistant Chief McKower said.

"Have my hunches paid off in the past?"

She rolled her eyes. "We *will* be the joke among law enforcement everywhere."

"And the public," he said. "Don't forget the public. The media will jump all over this."

"Oh God," she moaned. "I *hate* working with the media."

"Are you turning me down?" he asked.

McKower stared at her subordinate for the longest time before sighing deeply and theatrically. "I hesitate to ask this, but do you have a picture?"

"That's what the Internet is for," he said.

"Get out of my office," McKower said, launching a pencil at his back.

Sedge was waiting outside. "Where were you?"

"Frogging around," he said.

.

26

Halfway House, Chippewa County

FRIDAY, JUNE 1, 2007

The sun was beginning to rise from the direction of Vermilion Point. It had been a long night, the air filled with biting, stinging, chewing insects.

After the meeting at the district office, Service and Sedge had driven to the Bomb Shelter where he had taken a long shower. Sedge loaded her four-wheeler into the bed of her truck, he hitched his trailer with his RZR, and they had headed north, leaving their trucks and his trailer hidden in a birch forest at the end of Maple Block Road.

They had come most of the rest of the way to Katsu's site on their four-wheelers, but had dumped them a mile south of the location and hiked the rest of the way, taking up positions above the site. It was dark by the time they had gotten into position, the June night air warm and humid. The insects were bad, but Sedge seemed to ignore them just as he did. He liked seeing this quality in her. Good wardens ignored the weather and all biting insects. They neither saw nor heard any activity down where the artifacts were, and had taken turns sleeping during the night.

With first light coming Service made a small fire and got tea makings out of his ruck. He never went into the woods without tea, a little sugar, and a small tin of Pet milk. *Never milk in tea or coffee at home, but always in the bush. Old habits die hard. Thank you, Vietnam.*

Sedge woke up as he started his small stove. "You did good at the Teaspoon," he told her.

"I don't need your approval," she said with a growl.

"Are you always this social in the morning?"

"Depends on how good last night's sex was," she said with a grin.

After tea they moved into the sandy area. Sedge stood with her hands on her hips, clearly irritated. "The damn markers haven't been touched."

"Maybe," he said. "Let's put new disks in the cameras."

"You got some?"

"In my truck. You have a video disk player at your place?"

"Doesn't everyone?"

"Not me."

She grinned and shook her head. "Why am I not surprised?"

"I have a nice Victrola, though."

"What the hell is that?"

"Record player?"

"What's a record?"

"Never mind," he said, glumly. He wondered suddenly if she could tell time on a nondigital watch. Most youngsters no longer could.

After collecting the old disks and putting in new ones, Service said, "Let's take our time, search the whole area." He walked toward the sandy expanse that looked from some angles like a bowl or sanded-in harbor. He made a point of moving sluggishly, but as at the other site, saw nothing protruding from the sand. At the site they'd investigated earlier, he and Sedge had found all sorts of things. Was it possible that the wind and weather were responsible for uncovering artifacts? Could it be that Wingel was telling the truth about the burial bundle she'd found?

Sedge eventually drifted over to him.

"You trust Katsu?" he asked her.

"Like I said before, I want to."

"How about we ask him to come out here and we put him with Professor Shotwiff?"

"For what?"

"Let them do the male dog butt-sniff on each other, watch the chemistry, see what happens."

"I guess," she said.

"Every case has its doldrums," he told her.

"*Doldrums?* Yesterday some asshole was trying to kill me, and this morning I'm crawling around in a big fucking sandbox."

"You sure he was trying to kill you?"

She knocked sand off her pant leg. "Are you kidding?"

"Think about it." He had.

She looked at him for a long time. "The laser dot," she said. "I was standing still."

"That's what you said."

"At twenty yards that should be an easy kill." She pushed a strand of hair out of her face. "Warning shots?"

"Can you rule it out?" he asked.

"No."

"There you go," he said.

"But why?"

"If we knew that . . ."

"Let's put Katsu with your professor," she said decisively.

"Let me check Shotwiff's availability. We'll try for Wednesday or Thursday. Shark can bring him to us."

"Who's Shark?"

"A very peculiar individual."

"Like you?" she said.

"I'm not the one painting hunki close-ups," he countered.

"*Hunkuses*. If you're gonna take shots, get it right."

"Hunkuses," he said, enunciating and grinning.

"Feels good in your mouth, don't it."

"How did you *get* this job?"

"Ya know," she said, "I ask myself that same question all the time."

27

Slippery Creek Camp

FRIDAY, JUNE 1, 2007

The billboard east of Marquette near the Chocolay River was prominent, with bright red lettering on a pale green background: FELLOW VIOLATORS—POACH AWAY. MICHIGAN'S GAME WARDENS DON'T HAVE THE $$ TO CHASE YOU.

Grady Service smiled as he turned his civilian radio to WFXD, a commercial station in Marquette that carried country music and news.

"Get this," an excited radio jock yelled into his mic. "I'm not kidding! The cops in Luce County are, as we speak, hunting for Kermit da Frock! Details after this!"

A thirty-second ad for a Wildcat Pizza special followed.

The jock came back. "You heard right, boils and goils. The po-lice from Luce County over in the eastern U.P. put out a BOL today, asking all us Yoopers to be on da lookout for Kermit da Frock. The authorities are not providing any details, other than saying the frog is a person of interest. Person? Kermit is a *person?* I guess we all sorta assumed that a long time ago.

"I've got Captain Ware Grant from DNR law enforcement in Marquette on the line. According to him, 'Facial characteristics—even unusual ones, no matter how far-fetched—can help citizens identify the people we want to talk to.' So, Captain Grant, you're not actually looking for Kermit—just some human being who might *look* like the Muppet character?"

"Yes," the captain responded. "Resembles the character."

"Thank you, Captain, and good luck with your search."

Service heard a click, and then the radio jock added, "Ribbit, folks—ribbit. Sometimes weird fact trumps way-out fiction. Hey, we're in da Yoop!"

Service's cell phone buzzed. "Grady, where are you now?" It was Friday. "Marquette."

"Have you heard about the billboards?"

"I just saw one about the DNR," he said. "That what you're referring to?"

"Can you believe *that?* Your department will be a laughing stock."

"We already are. DNR stands for Do Not Respect. Where are you?"

"My office."

"Check BOLs."

She hung up and called right back, laughing. "What the hell is *that* about?"

"Sedge saw a guy who looked to her like Kermit."

"So?"

"Just as he fired three crossbow bolts at her."

"Good God! Is she all right?"

"Fine; mostly pissed off."

"The world is flipping out," she said. "I'll be at camp about seven."

"Wine will await thee," he said.

"To start," she said with a leontine growl.

• • •

Allerdyce's truck was parked at his camp again. Newf sat beside the old violator, wagging her tail. No sign of Cat.

"Word is da spick was impressed, youse Georged right in dere like dat."

"What do you want, Allerdyce?"

The old man opened his hand and a small leopard frog sprang to the ground and hopped away. "Dat da guy youse guys want, or you want bigger?"

"Kiss my ass, old man."

Limpy laughed so hard it sounded like he was choking.

"Go away before I douse you with Oust."

"Lighten up, sonnyboy. It true youse guys got no money?"

"We have money—just not enough, and not in the right places."

"Lotta dat shit dese days, eh."

"Why did you send me to Hectorio?"

"See if youse is serious, mebbe."

"About what?"

"Assholes rob da dead, dat shit."

"You disapprove?"

"Ain't right bodder dead mens."

"What dead mens do you mean?"

"Out dere, Coast of Deads, you bet dere's heapsa dead mens in da sand, eh."

"And you, of course, know the locations."

"Mebbe Limpy know somebody knows more den a few, eh."

"Your chum from Raco?"

"What's it wort' he shows you da place?"

"What's he think it's worth?"

"I check wit' 'im."

The old man seemed to be enjoying himself.

"I saw Honeypet in Lansing."

Allerdyce's head rolled like a Bobblehead. "Holy wah! She pull dat twin sister shit on youse? Ain't no Honeypet, *just* ole Honeypat." Allerdyce wiggled his finger at his temple. "She's batshit, dat one, give you good girl, bad girl, twoferone, you pork her, got dat double twat personality shit goin' on."

"Did she call you?" Service asked.

"What dat bitch an' me got talk about?"

"Ask your pal how much he wants for information and what kind of guarantee we'd get."

Limpy got up and shuffled toward his truck. "How much cash you take for dat big mutt yers?"

"She's not for sale. You can have her if she'll go with you."

Limpy chuckled and clucked at her as he opened the truck door and she charged down from the porch, set her front legs, snarled, and began barking wildly, spraying drool strings all over him. This time the old man didn't respond in kind.

"Guess not," Service said.

• • •

In the hours after midnight, Friday lay beside him, rubbing his shoulder. "Really, Grady. Kermit the *frog?*"

"You've never seen suspects who look like animals or famous people?"

"I suppose," she granted. "But this borders on an awful joke."

"If it gets results, who cares?"

"You always think for yourself," she said.

"I don't like trails that are already there," he said. "Know why?" He didn't let her answer. "Because people who stay on the trails shit on the trails, and I don't like wading through other people's shit."

"A mental picture and metaphor I'd rather not dwell on," Friday said. "How long do we have this time?"

"If I was to say just tonight?"

"I'd say, let's get to it again. Like right now."

"And if I'm here till Monday morning?"

"I'd say the same thing," she said. "I got a ton of unexpressed energy, and I really don't care if I spend the whole damn weekend in Jello-O mode."

Unexpressed energy?

He kissed her tenderly and she responded in kind. He felt whole when he was with her and Shigun.

28

Bomb Shelter, M-123, Luce County

SATURDAY, JUNE 2, 2007

Sedge gave him a contorted look when she opened her door.

"Trouble?" he asked, stepping inside.

She led him to a widescreen TV hooked to a disk player. "Lemme kill the lights," she said.

Service stared at the screen and a grid seemed to materialize, coming in from one side, fading to the other, sort of sagging, blurry, hard to see, but the pattern of squares, whatever it was, seemed pretty evident.

"Any theories?" Sedge asked from beside him.

The camera had been set to snap stills when triggered by motion. *What the hell kinda motion produced this?* "Not really. You?"

"Volleyball net?" she offered, adding, "It is a beach . . . sort of."

No idea what I'm looking at. Hell, it might be a volleyball net for all I know. "What's the other stuff show?"

"I haven't looked at it. I was sort of waiting for you."

"How much coffee we got?"

"Enough to start our engines." She put another disk in the player.

"Nothing more on that first one?"

"Just what you saw."

By noon they were rewatching a disk showing a small bright flash, moving left to right across the screen. "Jingo?" he said.

Her answer was an ambivalent grunt. "Something pink? Red? Can we get this stuff magnified at a lab somewhere?"

On the same disk they had a pretty good picture of a twelve-point buck moving through the field of vision, tail and nose and ears all twitching, looking nervous, moving stiff-legged, all signals he was preparing to bolt. "He's winding something," Service observed.

"God, he's big," Sedge said.

Service agreed. "I'll drop the disks at the Marquette lab on the way home. There's a guy there named Saugus."

"That grid thing seems familiar," Sedge said. "Or should." She rubbed her eyes with the back of her hand.

"Enough," Service said.

"What next?"

"Go back out to Teaspoon Creek and take a real microscopic look, but take reinforcements with you."

"You want to go?"

"No. I'll see if I can get Professor Shotwiff over here Wednesday or Thursday."

"What should I tell Katsu?"

"Leave it at we have someone we think he'll be interested in meeting."

"He may not buy it."

"Persuade him," he said.

• • •

Service was on his cell phone most of the way to Marquette, his last call to Chief Waco. "Where are you?"

"Mason Building," Waco said. "You?"

"Yoop. There's a department called the State Archaeologist, man named Yardley. Could you give him a visit and ask him to explain state policy vis-à-vis law enforcement?"

"Important?"

"Could be. Read his guts if you can."

"How quickly?"

"Not urgent, but soon will do."

"Grady, I think you're right about McKower."

"You two will make a great team."

"You sew on your new stripes yet?"

"That would be a negative."

Eddie Waco laughed loudly in his ear. "Let us know when you've identified your choice for state master sergeant."

"Roger that, Chief. And, thanks."

29

Marquette, Marquette County

SATURDAY, JUNE 2, 2007

Forensic technician Waldmar Saugus was waiting at the Michigan State Police Forensics Laboratory's front door.

"Am I screwing up your weekend?" Service asked, stepping inside.

"Like you people, we don't have weekends. Whachu got?"

Service handed him the two disks, saying, "One is stills only, the other moving. Only three images: a huge buck, a square thing, and a moving pink light. They all could be important."

"Care to say where this is?"

"You mean the twelve-point?"

Saugus grinned.

Service said, "No way."

"Didn't think so, but I had ta ask. Is this urgent?" the technician asked, handing him the necessary paperwork and securing the disks in an evidence bag.

"Soon as you can, but don't break your back."

"You guys busy?" Saugus asked.

"Always. Assholism never takes naps."

• • •

Service relieved Friday's sitter and was holding Shigun when his mom came through the door at her place in Harvey. "You *do* know how to keep a girl guessing," she said, obviously pleased he was there.

Service laughed. "If we're still guessing at this stage, something's seriously wrong with the both of us."

She exhaled. "That's a fact. How long do we get to have you this time?"

"Until Wednesday morning."

"What if we can't stand each other that long?"

"We'll deal with it. I'm going to go replenish food for Cat at camp, and bring Newf back with me."

"That guy Kermit?" she said.

He looked at her. "Did the BOL produce?"

"Not quite, but I checked National Crime Information Center for Deslongshamp, and came up empty. Then I called a Troop friend of mine, Sergeant Ellen Wegerlee out of the Gaylord Post. She keeps an unofficial database—weird nicknames, odd crimes, cop facts. Calls it E-Coplection."

Stupid name, techie humor. "And?"

"There's a male subject cops in Wisconsin nailed on a cattle-rustling charge from Texas. They refer to the guy as Kermit."

He rotated his forefinger like a crank. "Stop dragging this out. And?"

"He was in jail in a place called Paladullah, and Wisconsin was waiting for Texas to send someone to fetch him, but he escaped and hasn't been found. This was three years ago. I have a mug shot."

Friday opened her briefcase, removed an envelope, and held it out to him. He passed a grinning Shigun to her and slid the photo out of the envelope.

Holy shit. He turned over the photo. The name: Joseph Paul Brannigan. *Name's sort of familiar? From where?*

"Sure as hell looks like Delongshamp," Service said. "Does this birdbrain have a jacket?"

"Probably, but I didn't have a chance to pull it. I can run to the post and look at NCIC."

"Hell no, this is our time, and work can damn well go hang. But why does the sergeant in Gaylord have him in her pocket file?"

"CR—cattle rustling—someplace near Dallas. You don't hear that charge very often nowadays. That, and the fact that the man looks like a human clone of Kermie."

Service studied the face again. In some ways it looked more amphibian than human. "How'd you like to go through life looking like *that?*" he asked Friday.

"You know, it's just that sort of perception that tips some borderline personalities into lives of crime." She added, "I'm not joking."

Naturally he started laughing and went out to his truck. He'd met the man. Not seen the resemblance. You're not part of Sesame Street Nation, he told himself.

• • •

He was halfway to Slippery Creek when Waldmar Saugus from the lab called on the cell phone.

"Service, Saugus here. I've looked at the stills, and I'm going to do a lot more manipulations to be positive, but I'm pretty damn sure you've brought me a photo of a net."

Volleyball net, Sedge said. "Net?"

"Yeah. Can't say for sure yet, but it looks like a live-trap net, what they call a cloverleaf snapper."

"How can you tell that?"

"I can't yet—I'm just giving you my first impressions. But I do volunteer every year to help your deer biologist out of Escanaba capture animals to radio-collar them, so they can monitor deer-yard migration routes. My grandpa has a camp in north Delta County. Where'd this photo come from?"

"Does it matter?" Service answered.

"Hey, I'm not talking about the twelve-point. What I'm saying is, it might make sense to ask the biologist from that district if he's running tagging ops out where you got the photo."

"It's the wrong time of year for that, but it's also a helluva good suggestion. Thanks, Waldmar."

"Just a thought, but I figured you'd want to know."

"I do. Thanks again."

He got on his radio and turned to the District Two channel. "Two One Thirty, Twenty Five Fourteen."

"Two One Thirty," Sedge answered.

"Got coverage?"

"Affirmative, for the moment."

"Twenty Five Fourteen clear."

He punched in her speed-dial number on his cell phone and she answered immediately. "What?"

"Is there a deer biologist in the Newberry office?"

"Position's vacant right now. Tina Calabreeze retired in April. No replacement named yet."

"She retire locally?"

"Yes, got a kid who's a junior in high school at Engadine. Why?"

"She run deer radio collars to track migration routes?"

"When she had money in her budget. She retired partly because she felt the job was badly underfunded for essential field work."

"You ever work the collaring detail with her?"

"Once. I couldn't walk right for nearly a week afterwards. Too dangerous to trank the animals, so we ran them into nets and bulldogged them to the ground." There was a pregnant pause. "Oh my God! The net on the camera."

"The technician just called me. He had a similar epiphany. Can you call Calabreeze, find out if she ever worked our target area?"

"You bet. Anything else?"

"Kermit may be Joseph Paul Brannigan out of Wisconsin.

"I thought Delongshamps was Kermit."

"Delongshamp is probably an alias. Brannigan is wanted in Texas for cattle rustling. He was picked up in Wisconsin, but got away."

Sedge was laughing. "Cattle rustling? Are you shitting me, Chief Master Sergeant?"

"CR—that's what the record says.

"Good God. You want me to get out to his little cabin and dust for prints?"

Damn good idea. "Yes, that's good. Can't hurt. You talk to Katsu?"

"He can meet your guy either day."

"Tell him noon at the same place on the Coast of Death. I'll RZR the professor down the beach from Vermilion. I doubt he can walk all that distance."

"Cool. I'll bring coffee and sammies."

"You're a very civilized lady," he said.

"I'm neither," she said, "but when I need food and can't get it, I elevate *bitch* to new levels. I'll let Katsu know and give you a bump after I talk to Tina."

• • •

He put food out for Cat at the cabin, opened some windows a crack to air the place, loaded Newf and her food in the truck, and began the return trip to Harvey.

The cell phone rang. "Waco here. I called that Yardley fellow at his home, which like to give him apoplexy. He refused to talk on the phone on a weekend, so I drove on over there in uniform. Then thet old boy went totally ballistic."

"Disproportionate reaction," Service said.

"By Ozark miles," the chief said. "Once he calmed down he refused to invite me inside, claims law enforcement in the past has revealed historic, archaeologically rich sites, which has led to looting."

"You buy that?"

"I told the man I want names, times, places, dates, evidence, reports— the whole shebang."

"Is he talking about DNR law enforcement?"

"Nope, other agencies."

"When do we get the information?"

"Says he'll work on it next week, but he's short on people and it won't be priority."

"You believe him?"

"Nossiree. Come Monday I speck to have his lawyers wantin' ta palaver with our lawyers."

"Make you wonder what's going on?"

"Sure does, but I don't like connecting dots too soon. You still on the case with Officer Sedge?"

"I want to see it all the way through," Service said.

"That's your call, Grady."

"We put trail cameras on the artifact site."

"Get anything?"

"Got us a real fine photo of some kind of net," Service said sarcastically. "The Troop forensic tech thinks it's the kind of net used to capture deer for radio collaring."

The chief said nothing for a long while. "First, Sergeant Service, do you know what the most lucrative domestic wildlife crime is nowadays?"

"Animal parts? I'm not much on tracking megatrends."

"You need to change your ways, Grady. It's gonna be your job to keep the big picture in mind when our people are focused on the little picture, day to day. The biggest crime is that whitetail deer are being live-trapped from states that have animals of superior size and genetics, and these animals are then shipped to destinations where such fine specimens can fetch up to a hundred grand, cash money."

A hundred grand for a damn deer? What the hell's wrong with people? "Deer from Illinois and Minnesota?" Service asked.

"Kansas, too. U.S. Fish and Wildlife calls it CR, for cervid rustling. We made a half-dozen fine cases in Missouri just last year."

CR? "Michigan doesn't have those kinds of gene pools."

"Don't much matter. You live-trap a monster buck in the 175 class and you're looking at immediate big money, and whatever you have, they all go to the same place: Texas."

The chief hung up. Service sat and thought; closing his eyes, he kept seeing the face of Kermit the frog. *CR . . . cervid rustling . . . CR . . . cattle rustling. CR, CR, CR. What the hell have we stumbled onto?*

30

Coast of Death, Luce County

WEDNESDAY, JUNE 6, 2007

WNMU-FM, Northern Michigan University's NPR affiliate, was filled with stories of D-Day as he drove Professor Ozzien "Ozone" Shotwiff east from Harvey. Shark Wetelainen had dropped off the man last night and headed on to Service's camp at Slippery Creek, which tended to get brown drakes somewhat earlier than other area streams. Shark was married to a Houghton detective and ran a motel, working solely to pay for his endless fishing and hunting.

Shotwiff seemed engrossed in the radio broadcast. "I was there," he announced quietly, "Omaha Beach. I was barely seventeen and literally crapped my drawers going ashore. I remember every damn detail, sight, sound, smell, you name it. You ever been to war, son?" Shotwiff had tears in his eyes.

"Vietnam," Service said. "Marines."

"Combat?"

"Yessir."

"Then you know."

He did, but so far had managed to keep most of the worst memories at bay.

"Who's this fella we're gonna meet?"

"Duncan Katsu. He's trying to get federal recognition for an offshoot of the Grand Island Ojibwa."

"Five-Pack Creek Band?"

"You know them?"

"No, but I've wondered for years why they don't yet have federal status. I just figured there weren't enough descendants."

"They're real?"

"That's not the term I'd employ. But they existed. Crane clan, if memory serves me, which it doesn't always."

"Oral traditions?"

"From a Wisconsin Shinob I know. This where you think the Saulteur Iroquois Point fight took place?"

"Katsu thinks so. I don't know what I think yet."

"You'd have made a fine professor," the retired academic said with a grunt. "I put a bayonet through a man's Adam's apple on D-Day," Shotwiff announced out of the blue. "It sounded like one of those bursts of flatulence people call an SBD. The Kraut killed my buddy at close range and I lost my head. I was never scared again, and all I wanted to do for the next two years was kill every goddamn German I met, in uniform or out. Righteous hate is a fearful force in this world," Shotwiff said. "This country treated you boys like dog dirt on the sole of a new dress shoe when you came back from Southeast Asia. Makes me sick. We old guys knew that, but kept our mouths shut. Some 'Greatest Generation' we are. Bunch of old geezers just wanting attaboys and pats on our backs to never stop. I'm still ashamed. You and your fellas deserved a whole lot better."

Service couldn't think of a reply and remained quiet.

• • •

The professor and Katsu walked over to the edge of a birch copse and sat down, talking quietly while Service and Sedge waited. "You talk to what's-her-name?" he asked.

"Tina Calabreeze. Yeah, I left you a message."

He and Friday had been distracted by diversions other than work.

"She ever do roundups out here?"

"No, but she says these small hills and ridges hold some small winter yards that attract some gigantic bucks from the southern county farm country. Most deer migrate west and south to Schoolcraft County, but a few make the trek up here. She thinks there's a state record in Luce County, maybe more than one, something even most local headhunters don't know."

"Was she good at her job?"

"Far as I know. We've got two distinct things here, don't we?"

"It's looking that way to me, but we need more evidence to know for sure."

Katsu and the professor eventually rejoined them. "We've had a fruitful chat," Shotwiff said. "We're going to play in the dirt for a while now."

"There's sandwiches," Sedge said, pointing at a bag.

"Any preliminary thoughts?" Service asked the professor.

Katsu was staring toward Lake Superior, his mind apparently elsewhere.

"Well, I'm not ready to say your theory holds water, but neither am I willing to just write it off. You know who Ladania Wingel is?"

"I met her in Wisconsin."

"You're a brave man. She attack you in full harpy mode?"

"She tried."

"Wingel started her PhD at Oregon," Shotwiff said. "Her name then was Ence."

Why's he telling me this? "And?"

"Just thought you should know," the old man said mysteriously.

"You know her?"

"*Nobody* knows her. Or wants to."

"She has a doctorate. She must have something going for her."

"Well, that's one way to look at the data. Now you'll excuse Mr. Katsu and me?"

"Sure." *What the hell is going on?*

Shotwiff took one step and looked back. "You know Santinaw?"

Service nodded.

"The man's a giant," the professor said, and walked away.

"What was all that about?" Sedge asked.

"I don't have a clue," Service admitted.

Service and Sedge carefully canvassed the area for deer sign and found nothing significant, or unusual.

Later in the afternoon when Katsu and Shotwiff rejoined them, the professor held up a baggie. "This is undeniably Iroquois."

"What is it?" Service leaned close to look at a brown lump, maybe an eighth of an inch long, looking more like a rock than anything else.

"That, my boy, is a genuine wampum bead. You can't see it, but you can feel it. Only the Iroquois scored their beads with indentations."

Service saw that Katsu was looking absolutely triumphant.

"And we conclude what from this, Professor?"

"Absolutely nothing," Shotwiff said. "But on the basis of this bead and five others we uncovered, I would petition the State to core-sample this area and sink some test pits, see what providence gives up."

"The battle could have been here?" Service said.

The professor nodded. "You know, of course, that Iroquois Point has never been excavated or fully explored for aboriginal artifacts?"

"But it carries the name," Sedge said.

"Gives one pause when it comes to cementing any confidence in history or historians, yes?"

Shotwiff looked up at Service. "Did I mention Miss Ence at the University of Oregon?"

Why doesn't he just spit it out? "I believe you did."

31

Slippery Creek Camp

THURSDAY, JUNE 7, 2007

Shark had taken the professor back to Silver City last night and Grady Service ended up at his camp alone, with his dog and cat. He'd roasted some chicken breasts and thawed mole sauce he'd made and frozen last winter, pouring the dark, unsweetened, peppered chocolate over the meat.

Newf sat beside him with drool streams hanging almost to the floor like stalactites at high risk of breaking away.

Friday had wanted to join him, but he'd needed time to sort out all the case items.

As he cut into the chicken, Limpy Allerdyce walked into the cabin unannounced and sat down. "Geez, it dinnertime already, sonny?"

"Get a plate," Service said with resignation. "You got your teeth in?"

"You seem to do okay with yours out," the old poacher said. Service had fallen into a river some years back, gone through a culvert in spring run-off, and broken all his teeth, all of which had been removed and replaced. He hated the false teeth and wore them as infrequently as he could get away with. Or he wore only the upper halves, when he could.

Service dished up a serving and shoved it in front of Allerdyce. "Don't be sneaking any to the dog."

"Youse decide 'bout dat errorhead stuff?"

"Not yet."

Allerdyce pursed his lips. "Jus' tryin' help."

"You know anything about live-trapping deer?"

"Why I know *dat*? Youse know my job ta kill 'em, eh. Deer ain't no pets."

"Okay, theoretically."

"You mean like make-believe?"

"Yeah, like that."

"Aromatically, mebbe I might heard some pipples use dogs run 'em into nets, and some use four-wheelers."

"Then what?"

"Trank in ass, wrap 'em up tight, and get 'em where dey need go fast, keep somebody in back keep 'em alive."

"Good money in this?"

"Heretically," Allerdyce said.

"How much?"

"Dunno. I don't keep track of no make-believes."

"High mortality from tranks?"

"Speck 'pends on who makin' drug dose, eh?"

He had a point, and a certain degree of practical information that suggested his knowledge was far from just theoretical.

"Theoretically this was done up here in the Yoop?"

"We don't got big deer like da old days, youse know dat."

"You didn't answer my question."

"I 'pose it could happen here or dere."

Service grinned at the man. "I'd love to lock up your ass again, old man, and throw away the key."

Limpy winked. "Youse caught me once, but even youse ain't good enough ta catch Limpy twice, and 'n innyvint, I retarded and reformed, 'member?"

"Whatever."

"Hurts my feelins', dat attitude."

"You've got no feelings, old man."

"Mebbe more den you tink."

"What about your pal and the errorheads?"

"You pay?"

"RAP will pay something. I don't know how much." RAP was the toll-free state Report All Poaching line.

"Errorheads ain't poachin'. What dey gotta do wit' dee-enn-are officers?"

"If it's something illegal and we get a conviction, there will be a reward."

"You guarantee dat?"

"Cross my heart."

"Once upon time," Allerdyce began.

"I didn't ask to hear a fairy tale."

"Ain't fairy scale, is by-God fact. Once upon time might could be somebody fum diffident state pay good cash money fellas dig up Indi'n graveyards."

"That so?"

"Fact, sonny."

"How long ago?"

"Five years at least."

"Makes for old, cold trails."

"Might could if'n weren't stuff ta be found where it don't belong."

"And you're gonna give me a name."

"Homesteader Pioneer Museum west of Trout Lake."

"Never heard of it."

"Private, ain't public. Gotta call somebody ta see it."

"You got a number for me?"

"Got pal who does," the old man said, holding up one finger. "Cost a hundred."

Service dug out his wallet and peeled off two fifties.

Allerdyce studied the money. "Dis crap marked?"

"Jesus, don't be paranoid; it was in my wallet. I didn't know you were coming over."

Limpy folded and pocketed the bills. "You seen billboards 'round town?"

"I see lots of billboards."

"Ones about dee-enn-are."

"Don't think so."

"Well, dey makin' hot talk wit' some—if youse get my point."

"No, I don't." But he did. "Tell me."

"Some pipples, dey tink now's time ta help seffs ev'ting in woods."

"They do?"

"Holy wah, you betcha."

"What about you?"

"I smell rat—some kinda trap."

Service suppressed a smile. This was the legendary sixth sense that made Limpy Allerdyce so difficult to catch.

"Have you shared your paranoia with your colleagues?"

"My *what?* I'm retarded fum all dat. Let udders learn hard way."

"How long to set me up with your pal with the private museum?"

"Ain't pal. Call you in da mornin'?"

"This just a look-and-see place, or do they deal?"

"Wun't surprise me dey deal, but not cheap."

"Who owns the place?"

"Nobody know dat. Guy runs it name Morrie Clatchety."

"He live on the premises?"

"Nobody live dere. Just stuff."

"You ever seen this place?"

"Jes heard."

"They got breakheads?"

"All kinds good stuff."

"Ever hear the name Delongshamp?"

"Frog name," Allerdyce said.

"Frog?"

"Yeah, Frenchie—right? Why you look me so funny?"

Allerdyce. "What about Brannigan?"

"Joe Paul?"

"Joseph Paul Brannigan."

"I know 'im."

"Some call him Kermit."

No reaction. "I call 'im creepy. He 'round again?"

"He was here and left?"

"Heard he was 'ere mebbe ten years back, den nuttin'. "

"He got a specialty?"

"Whatever make money," Limpy Allerdyce said. "Weren't picky."

The poacher shoveled down his food, got up, belched loudly, patted the dog on the head, and walked to the door. Looking back, he said, "I ain't no Larry Bird."

"Adjust your hearing aid," Service said.

"I ain't got the AIDS neither," Allerdyce declared, and was gone.

• • •

Grady Service called Sedge after midnight. "*God!* What the hell do you want now!" she yelled into his ear. "Don't you ever fuck or sleep?"

"What's either got to do with a phone call?"

"Jesus mercy," she said disgustedly. What do you *want?*"

"Homesteader Pioneer Museum, west of Trout Lake."

"What the hell is that?"

"You never heard of it?"

"Duh."

"A good source suggests the place deals artifacts."

"We going to break down the door?"

"I'm gonna send in plainclothes, see what we can wedge loose with smiles and the promise of cash."

"Who?"

"Gotta check with Milo Miars first. You get any prints yet?"

"Going first thing tomorrow. Partnering with you is a full-time job."

"That's a good thing, right?"

"Don't kid yourself."

"If you get prints, get them over to the Troops ASAP. They can fax them to Marquette or Lansing."

"And the museum? I don't even know where the hell it is."

"Don't worry about that now. I'll get more details, get back to you."

"Okay, done. *Now* can I go back to what I was doing?"

"What was that?"

"That is none of your damn business, Chief Master Sergeant."

• • •

Service next called his former boss, Milo Miars. "El-Tee."

"Jesus, Grady, we're trying to sleep. Congratulations on your promotion. I'm glad I don't have to pry reports out of you anymore."

"I want Elza Grinda to replace me."

Miars was silent. "Does she want the job?"

"She did at one time."

"If she wants it, I'd love to have her. If not, we'll find somebody else."

"I'll have her call you in a few days."

• • •

The next call went to Conservation Officer Elza Grinda in Iron County. Her longtime boyfriend, CO Simon del Olmo, answered the phone sleepily.

"Grinda there?"

"Who the hell is this?"

"Grady."

"Shit, it's Super Sarge himself. Sheena's on patrol," del Olmo said, using Elza's nickname.

"Got her private cell number handy?"

"Burned into my steel-trap mind," del Olmo said, and gave it to him.

Grinda answered after a couple of rings.

"It's Grady; are you busy?"

"I'm sitting on a boat trailer at a launch right now. What's up?"

"I'd like for you to do an undercover job."

"Where and when?"

"Trout Lake. I hope to have the timing set by tomorrow."

"What's it entail?"

"I want you to go into a private museum and see if you can buy Native American artifacts."

"When did *that* become part of our jobs?"

"Always has been."

"Nobody told me."

"Welcome to the ship of the often-misled and massively clueless, but that will change soon—especially if you can get some action out of this dealer."

"I assume there'll be a more-detailed briefing at some point."

"I do too, but that doesn't mean it will happen. You may have to go in with very incomplete information. Would that be a problem?"

"I'd prefer complete, but I can rock-and-roll either way. Should I congratulate you on your new position?"

"Only if you still want my old one."

"Detective? Absolutely."

"Good; think of this as a warm-up."

"Don't tell me this is some half-assed audition or some such crap."

"Nope. You've already got the job; this is just a taste of some of the work you'll be doing."

"Don't tell me I already have the job if I don't!"

"Okay, I won't."

"You drive us crazy," she said.

"Who?"

"Almost all of us."

"I'll bump you when I get the timing squared away—cool?"

"Cool," she said, and he closed the connection.

She'll make a great detective; much better than me.

• • •

He called Tuesday Friday. "Hey, baby, wanna have phone sex?"

"Are you jagging on coffee?" she asked. "We're trying to sleep here."

"Don't know what you're missing."

"In fact I do, and telefornicating is not even close to the real deal. You sound like adrenaline's pumping through you like a high-pressure fire hose."

"Pretty damn close," he said.

• • •

He was way too wired to sleep or even think about it. Zero three thirty: He made a list of names and one jumped out at him. He picked up his hand-held 800-MHZ-radio and dialed in the channel for Station Twenty. "Station Twenty, Twenty Five Fourteen; is Nine One Oh Three on duty?"

"Yessir, Twenty clear."

Service set the freq for District 9. "Nine One Oh Three, Twenty Five Fourteen."

"Nine One Oh Three."

"You got bars?"

"Affirmative."

"Got my personal cell number?"

"Roger."

"Give me a bump; I'm at my residence."

"Nine One Oh Three, clear."

The phone rang minutes later. "First Fucking Shirt, are you shitting me?" Sergeant Bearnard Quinn shouted into the phone.

Bearnard was a Gaelic name that translated to "strong as a bear," and Quinn in Gaelic meant "wisdom."

"Bernie, how long you been a sergeant now?"

"Since me ma spit me from betwixt her legs, ya ugly bastard."

"Well, try this on for size: Master Sergeant Bearnard Quinn, Himself."

"Getouttahere!"

"No, the stripes are yours if you want them. You're the best sergeant in the state. Should be you with my job, so when I go, you'll take it, which is the way it should have been in the first go-round."

Silence on the other end. "What's the mission?"

"Float, evaluate officers for development to sergeants, sergeants to el-tees."

"Just us?"

"We recommend to the chief and his assistant chief."

"Pretty much us, eh?"

"Pretty much."

"We fuck up, it's just our asses and our heads, yes?"

"There it is."

"Then sign me up, ya big galoot, and point me at the guns!"

"You got pass days soon?"

"Old lady and I planned to go to Toronto for a few days, starting next weekend."

"Can you meet me over the bridge?"

"Say when and where."

"Back at you tomorrow. You the man, Master Sergeant Quinn. Congratulations, you old warhorse."

"An' sure if he don't tink ee loiks da sound a' dat," Quinn said in a poor stage brogue.

Quinn had been awarded the state medal of valor at least twice, the only police officer in the state to be so decorated more than once, and he had five or six life-saving awards. He never balked, never took shortcuts, and the people who reported to him would have followed him into the maws of hell. *I'd follow him too*, Service thought.

The dog bumped his leg and he let her out. A wolf sang and Newf answered.

"Get back in the house," Service said. "If I'm not getting laid tonight, neither are you."

Newf had once had puppies by a wolf, and he had been forced to give them to a wolf rehabber in Wisconsin. *No way are we going through that again.*

32

Slippery Creek Camp

SATURDAY, JUNE 9, 2007

Limpy Allerdyce called before sunrise. "Morris Clatchety will meet youse Monday, ten in morning, one person only. Meet front B.J.'s Rock Shop, Trout Lake."

"Price of entry?"

"Hunnert go t'ru door."

"I remember giving you two fifties last night."

"Door-open fee, dat."

"I thought this was a pal of yours?"

Allerdyce asked incredulously, "You Jew me for peanuts?"

Eye on ball. "What's Clatchety look like?"

"Never put eyes on man afore."

"He's the manager, yes?"

"Way I heard. Who youse send?"

"Friend of mine, artifact expert. Think it'll be okay with Clatchety?"

"Only cares sell crap, make money I hear, dat one. Your trooper squeeze be okay."

"I didn't say I was sending a woman."

Allerdyce chuckled. "Know how youse t'ink, sonny."

Service tried to recall the diminutive Trout Lake's village geography. "Rock shop just west of the IGA, right? Old wooden building, needs paint?"

"Dat's da one; been dere long time, eh."

Allerdyce hung up and Service called Grinda at home. "Monday, ten a.m. in Trout Lake, meet first at zero eight hundred at Fiborn Quarry, north end on perimeter road where the karst society has its information boards. Where the old town used to be."

"Uniform of the day?"

"Show skin."

"How much?"

"Hell, it's summer, and don't ask me! Do what will work, right?"

"Sometimes I wonder about you, Grady. I'll drive my personal ride, no radio, computer, nothing."

"Don't forget your snubbie."

"Always close by."

"Better bring your handheld, too, and lock it in your vehicle."

"I'll get a room at the Beartrack in MacMillan Sunday night."

"It's a plan. Be careful."

• • •

Jingo Sedge called. "I just dropped prints at the Post. They were all over the place. Post el-tee wants to know who will pay?"

"Tell him to send invoices to my office in Marquette."

"Your new job carry its own budget?"

He had no idea. "That's a good question."

"Do you have a new call sign?" she asked.

Another question he couldn't answer. "I'll let you know. Use the old one for now. Sheena's going in for us. She'll get a room at the Beartrack Sunday night. Monday oh eight hundred we'll meet her at Fiborn, north side."

"Tell her she can bunk with with me, save motel money."

"She's a bituva loner, but thanks."

"She going in alone?"

"That's the plan."

"Wired or not?"

"Unwired. Too early for wires. We don't have enough for a warrant. This visit's strictly exploratory, and we don't want to trip her up."

"No takedowns, just recce—affirmative?"

"Right," he said. "How long on those prints?"

"Monday afternoon earliest, probably Tuesday."

"You talk to Katsu after we left?"

"He was strutting, but he had an interesting suggestion. He said we ought to ask Toliver to do the digging job the professor suggested, see how he handles it professionally."

"You agree?"

"Makes some sense, I think."

"You want to call Toliver?"

"This all has to be cleared through the state archaeologist."

"I know, but you can walk Toliver through what's under consideration, ask him to come up with a plan."

"And if he uses this as a quid for his own digging?"

"Hell, let him do his own dig. He already has permission, yes?"

"You think about inviting Wingel to the shindig?"

He had not considered this. "Maybe. I'll think on that."

"You do anything about Wingel and Oregon yet?"

"Plan to put an iron in that fire today. If not today, Monday. After Monday's gig we may want Sheena to see the artifact field, brief her into it on-site."

"Good idea," Sedge said. "Think she'll replace you in Wildlife Resources Protection?"

"This is just a plainclothes job, like we all do from time to time."

"You pick the master sergeant yet?"

How can she have so damn much information? "That's in the works."

"Smart money's on Bearnard Quinn."

"You don't say."

"Hey, I want in the pool; give a girl a hint."

"That would be insider trading, which is against the damn law," Service said.

"Tight ass," Sedge muttered. "See you in the morning."

• • •

Oregon. He knew only one person in the state, and that man had been a fish and wildlife trooper named Whybus. Ence/Wingel, Shotwiff claimed, had started her education at the University of Oregon. *Eugene? Corvallis? Can't remember.* He could try going through the university, but he felt more comfortable with law enforcement types, especially those he'd worked with successfully.

He called information and got a number for Oregon Fish and Wildlife in Salem. He dialed it, expecting to encounter a computer menu, and was surprised by a friendly human voice. Like the old days when people were assets to organizations and not mere expenses.

"My name is Service," he explained. "Chief Master Sergeant, Michigan

Department of Natural Resources. I'm trying to locate one of your troopers. Name's Whybus."

"He's not a trooper anymore."

Shit. You keep forgetting how long it's been.

"He's Captain Whybus these days."

"Chook is a *captain?*"

"David Whybus is the captain's name!"

"I always called him Chook."

The operator laughed. "That's him, but not many have the nerve to call him that."

"What do you call him?"

"Captain . . . sir."

Service laughed. "Is there any way I can get in touch with him, a number, leave mine, anything?"

"You say you know him?"

"We worked a case many years ago."

"Ordinarily I'd take down your name and pass it to him, but our captain is a different cat than past captains. Got a pen handy?"

"Yes, ma'am." He wrote down the number she gave him, thanked her for her help, and dialed the new number.

"Whybus residence," his old colleague answered. Whybus was a Northern Paiute, raised in a tribal community on the Malheur River. He had gone to college at Gonzaga in Spokane on a combination academic and basketball scholarship.

"Sorry to bother you so late on a Saturday night, Captain. This is Grady Service."

Long pause. "Are you pulling my leg?"

"Nossir."

"My God, man! How many years has it been?"

"Ten, twelve—I'm not sure anymore."

"Boy, did I get ribbed when they imported a white man to outtrack an Indian!"

"I got lucky."

"Yeah, that's what I told everybody too, but we both know you were a Shadow Wolf. Hell, I'm Indian and I've never gotten that honor. Never will."

Shadow Wolf was a designation bestowed on only a handful of Americans who had demonstrated unparalleled skills in tracking and manhunting. The case he had worked with Whybus had been in the high desert, two lost hikers, one of them a prominent national politician. Service had found them alive after an exhausting four-day search in an unseasonal deluge of freezing rain.

"What can I do for you, Grady?"

"There's a woman, Ladania Wingel, now a PhD, who started school at the University of Oregon, but something happened and apparently she left. I have no idea what happened, but we suspect it has some bearing on a case we're working involving illegal trafficking of Native American artifacts."

"Huh," Whybus said. "Time frame?"

"Sorry—no idea, and to be honest, this could well be a wild goose chase. The tip came from a retired professor who is helping us, and he seems eager for us to follow up with the university."

"Didn't care to spell it out for you?"

"Not even with a broad brush."

"Typical academic—cowed by lawyers and fearing for his reputation."

"The woman, now Wingel, was Ence at the university."

"That's her maiden name, Ence?"

"Sorry, Captain. I just don't know."

"Hey, it's Chook, not Captain. The woman's name is Wingel now?"

"Right, Dr. Ladania Wingel." Service spelled it for him. "She's one of those who screams racism every time something doesn't go her way."

Whybus said, "Next week okay for you, Grady?"

"Yessir. We really appreciate this."

"You must be close to retirement," Whybus said.

"That's what some people tell me."

"Tough to abandon a way of life, old friend."

"Amen to that. What about you?"

"Was on my way out the door when our last captain fell over dead. I was asked to step in on an interim basis, and then they made it permanent. I'll give it a couple more years. You ever think about starting a tracking school when you put away your badge?"

"No."

"You ought to. Hell, every state would send people to you—feds, too.

Great hearing your voice, Grady. Back at you next week. Ence/Wingel, something that happened at Oregon."

"Yessir."

Last year the Keweenaw Ojibwa had extended an unofficial offer for him to head up their tribal game warden force. But a tracking school? *Worth thinking about? Maybe, but not yet. Retirement for any reason's not an option yet.*

33

Teaspoon Creek, Luce County

SUNDAY, JUNE 10, 2007

Grady Service barely fit into a canoe, and found it impossible to squeeze into the cockpit of a standard kayak. In lieu of this, he used a kayak that let him sit on top and keep his legs free. He'd slept for shit last night, and by the looks of her, so had Sedge.

Early morning, heavy air, even though it was dry, birds singing, no wind, the thick scent of fish water and cedar engulfing them. "Pete's Creek," Sedge said. "We float this down to where it merges into Carlson, then follow that to the Teaspoon."

"How far?"

"Three miles, crow, maybe ten river miles; pretty good current, we should zip right along if we don't have to crawl over too many logs. The creeks are real twisty and overgrown.

"Let's get after it," he said, using his paddle to slide his plastic craft into the current.

They drifted and paddled, the only sound the creek's natural flowing hydraulic music or the occasional water dripping off their paddle blades.

Service found himself hardly working, but perspiring heavily. Sedge's face was flushed. "You coming down with something?" he asked her.

"The fabled curse," she said.

"Oh."

"Sorry you asked?"

"Pretty much."

"Have you looked at the vegetation? It's as dry as I've ever seen it," she said.

He had half-noticed, but not made a mental note. Now that she mentioned it, he could really see it. Naturally the entire state was understaffed with fire-control personnel for the woods. "July rain will help," he said.

"I wouldn't bet on that," Sedge said. "Up here Mother Nature always seems to have PMS."

. . .

Five hours of combing the area around the camouflaged cabin produced nothing other than a piece of faded orange plastic cap Sedge found near where the metal ring was fastened to a pipe in the creek. She held it up for Service to see.

"Litter," she said. "You seen enough here?"

"Let's boogie," he said. "What's the plan?"

Sedge said, "Down the Teaspoon to the Tahq, then downstream. Sergeant Bryan and the fire-control officer moved my truck to our get-out. I'll drive you back to yours."

. . .

She dropped him at his vehicle and was leaning against the back gate while he smoked a cigarette. "You know, you've got the same litter I've got," she said, opening the Tahoe's back door and picking up an orange plastic cap.

Service looked at it. "I found that out by the Five-Pack. I threw it back there and told myself I'd dump it with the other trash when I got around to it."

She said, "The same orange cap—one on the Teaspoon, one on the Five-Pack. What're the chances of that? Let's tag 'em and bag 'em."

"Knock yourself out."

"You get the Oregon thing started?"

"I did. Should know something next week, if there's anything to know."

"What are you going to do the rest of the day?" she asked.

"Thought I might drive up to the church camp, talk to the priest there about Delongshamps."

"Kermit the frog," she corrected him.

Whatever, he thought. Tomorrow they would meet Grinda on her way to the Rock Shop. Meanwhile he wanted Sedge to stay calm.

34

Lands of the Lord Camp, Chippewa County

SUNDAY, JUNE 10, 2007

Grady Service found Father Fix-it, Charlie Nickle, where he'd found him the last time—on his knees, pulling weeds already browning without rain.

"Father?"

The priest looked up and wiped his forehead with the back of his forearm. "This ground is hard and dry," the priest said. "Can't ever remember it being this dry this early. What can I do for you, Officer? It's Service, right?"

"Godfroi Delongshamp."

"Yes?"

"Last time here I picked up some vibes. You mentioned something about a litigious society."

"I did."

"I would like for you to spit out what it is you have to tell me, Father."

"It's not that simple."

"Delongshamp escaped from jail in Wisconsin. He's wanted in Texas and we're looking for him. I found him that night out in the woods. Someone beat hell out of him and trashed his camp. When I mentioned this the other time I was here, I asked if you had any vandalism problems. Do you remember what you said to me, Father?"

The priest looked at the ground, a common attempt to collect thoughts.

"How much acreage are you folks gardening?" Service asked, switching directions without segue or warning.

"Uh, several plots . . . maybe seven or eight acres at the most. But in this drought . . ."

"Corn?"

"And beans, and various root veggies."

"Growing season here is really short."

The priest nodded.

"What you told me, Father Nickle, was that God has protected your group from *youthful* indiscretions."

"Is that what I said?"

"I never mentioned kids or youth."

"You're sure?"

"It's my job," Service said.

"This place is beautiful," the priest said, "but it's not paradise."

"Meaning Delongshamp?"

"There were . . . run-ins. . . ."

"Explain."

"Perhaps some of our members were overzealous in trying to bring Jesus Christ into the man's life. In my heart I know it was well intentioned."

Service decided to let the priest talk and work his way to whatever it was he was trying to find the right words for.

"One of our members, a fine woman I would hasten to add, ended up going there a lot, and over time she remained. Not to proselytize, you understand?"

"I think so. Is she married?"

"Yes, with two teenage sons. They went there and tried repeatedly to force their mother back to the family. I told them to trust in prayer, but you know how headstrong teens can be—all those hormones *and* the devil vying."

"Tell me what happened, Father."

"The woman ended up leaving that man, and the area."

"With Delongshamp?"

"No, alone."

"And her sons went after Delongshamp?"

"I really don't know the details, Officer. The boys are gone, and so too is their father."

"Did they confess?"

"If they did, you know I can't talk about that."

"All I need are names."

"Sorry, Officer Service. I can't do that. As far as I'm concerned it's over and done with. I just hope the family can reconcile and find peace."

"A court will give me a warrant to get the names, Father. The church may be tax-free, but you still have to abide by the law."

"Then you will have to get your warrant, and we will still not turn over the names. My bishop will call in our lawyers. All this will have to take place in court."

"You should think about that, Father Charlie. Do you *really* want to fight this in the public, what with all the problems the church has had with some of its priests?"

"This is different."

"It won't be in the public's mind," Service said.

The priest rubbed his mouth. "I must consult with the bishop."

"All we want are names, Father. We'll give you till the end of the week." Service offered a card, but the priest refused it, saying, "I have the one you gave me last time."

"Take this one too, Father. It's free."

35

Fiborn Quarry, Mackinac County

MONDAY, JUNE 11, 2007

The forest condition indicator outside the Newberry DNR Service Center said that fire danger was EXTREME, and that all fires were banned in the eastern U.P. until further notice. Usually it was late summer before such restrictions were levied.

Service made his way south through Rexton and turned north down one of the U.P.'s worst washboard roads until he circled the quarry, which had once mined pure limestone and been owned by a former Michigan governor. It had operated from just after the turn of the century into the mid-1930s. Once there had been a town in the area, and some limestone caves, which attracted adventurous locals.

Grinda's gray truck was parked next to Sedge's patrol vehicle. The two women were carrying on an animated conversation. As far as Service knew, the two had never met. He still didn't understand the social gene in women that seemed to enable them to take up conversation with just about anyone, at any time.

"Morning," he said, getting out and lighting a cigarette.

"The state's super sergeant shouldn't be smoking," Sedge said. "You need to set a good example for the rest of us."

"She's right," Sheena said.

"Knock off the tag team," he grumbled.

"We're serious," Sedge said.

I don't need this. His granddaughter was already riding his ass about smoking—and shaving.

"All right, we have two damn hours, so let's get to work," he said, trying to assert control.

"Jingo's already told me a lot about the possible case."

"I stopped at the Troop house this morning," Sedge added. "They ran the prints. They come back to an operator's license for an Annie Kerse out of

Pullman. No wants or warrants; she's an upstanding citizen. There are also prints for one Andrew and one Allen Kerse, also in Delongshamp's camp," she added.

"Kermit was banging Mrs. Kerse," Service said.

"How can you *know* that?" Grinda asked, scrinching her face.

"I went to LOL and talked to Father Nickle. Last time there I got vibrations something had happened. This time he talked. Mrs. Kerse was trying to harvest Delongshamp's soul, and he ended up harvesting another part of her."

Sedge's mouth hung open.

"The lady has two teenage sons, Andrew and Allen, and they took exception and tried to bring mum home, but she had already bugged out for parts unknown, so they apparently took their frustration out on Deslongshamps—which is when I entered the picture. The prints seem to confirm the priest's account."

"And Kermie hit the road," Sedge said.

"Yeah, well, so did the boys and their father, and the priest refused to give up their names, so I told him we'd get a warrant for his records, and he told me the church wouldn't cooperate. I reminded him that the church doesn't have the most stellar public record in recent years, and that they might find cooperation a better road than a public fight in court. He said he would talk to his bishop, and I gave him until the end of the week. Where's Pullman?" he asked.

"Allegan County," Sedge said.

"We'll let Father Nickle and his bishop sweat. Call the Allegan sheriff and ask if his deps can make contact for us, question the boys about what happened up here."

"Can we get back to the museum?" Grinda asked.

"You meet your contact in front of the old building next to B.J.'s Rock Shop, just west of the IGA. Your contact will lead you to where the collection is housed."

"Museum?" Grinda said.

"Play it straight. You heard from a friend in Epoufette about the place, and you are married to a collector and wanted to see for yourself in case there might be something your hubby would like."

"Jesus," Sedge said. "When did you think that up?"

"Right now. Want to change the story?" he asked Grinda.

"No, that seems pretty straightforward to me. In a twisted way," she added.

"Don't pretend to know anything about artifacts, but probe for values, prices, and so forth."

"I won't have to fake that part," Grinda said.

"Make sure you have your remote panic button in your pocket and if anything difficult goes down, push it and we'll come running."

"This should be pretty routine."

"*Should be* isn't a guarantee of anything."

"How will I know the guy?" Grinda asked.

Service looked down at her shapely legs sticking out of extremely short shorts and said, "With wheels like that, he'll find you."

She rolled her eyes in protest.

"He's male. Don't worry, he'll find you."

"You men can be such pigs," Sedge said.

Service grimaced. "Be glad for that. It makes us playable."

"Afterwards, meet back here?" Grinda asked.

"No," Sedge said. "We want to take you north to see the site. Head north out of town on M-123 and take Wilwin Truck Trail west about a half-mile into a big clearing. We'll wait for you there."

"Any notion how long this thing will take?" Grinda asked.

"Nope, but as long as the guy's not hinky and he's liking your legs and smells potential sales, I'm guessing he'll be downright garrulous."

"Nice word," Sedge said.

"I'm not just a pretty face," Grady Service said.

36

USFS Highway 6633, Chippewa County

MONDAY, JUNE 11, 2007

Noon and no sign of Grinda. He'd called Sergeant Quinn and arranged to meet him in Rudyard later that afternoon. Then thirteen hundred rolled up and Grady Service was starting to get nervous when Grinda came on the radio. "Three One Twenty is turning down Wilwin."

Service sighed and tried to hide it, but he realized Sedge was watching his every reaction and keying off him. *Shit, is this what the future will be like—everyone watching me?*

Elza Grinda got out of her truck and shook her head of giant hair. "God," she said. "Is there something wet to drink?"

"Water," Sedge said, handing her a bottle from her truck cooler.

"I'll write a report," Grinda said after taking a drink. "You cannot believe this place. Three stories and a basement, an old farmhouse three miles from town, packed with artifacts and antiques of every description. I still can't believe what I saw."

"What about Clatchety?" Service asked.

"I doubt he even saw my legs. My gaydar says he's of another pesuasion. This guy is all about money. He drives a ten-year-old Ford pickup, but I saw a photo in the house with him beside a silver Mercedes SL550, and I was able to get the plate number." She handed the note to Service.

"He in business?"

"He was cagey. The museum is obviously someone's write-off. Prearranged, escorted visits only, and only people Clatchety knows or are vouched for get invites."

"But he'll deal?"

"He's nimble on his feet. He made me almost beg him before he'd even speculate on letting things go."

"Let me guess: He has to check with the owner?" Service said.

"Bingo—the owner, who is or is not local."

"Where?"

"Refused to say. He's just buying time, trying to figure out what to do and how to play me. Let's see what that plate gives us."

"Anything else?"

"I made a mental list of all the Native American stuff. There are five or six rooms filled with it: arrowheads, spear points, tools, copper stuff, you name it."

"Breakheads or hatchets?" Service asked.

"Five or six. One of them seems carved out of bone with a large agate laced into the end. Scary-looking thing. Not hatchets or tomahawks."

Agate? "Where'd you leave the buy?"

"He has to confer with the owner, and I am to call him back on Friday. He gave me a number. I'm guessing it feeds into a call forwarder which probably goes to a pay-as-you-go phone he can use once and dump."

"You sense he's that careful?"

"He seems cautious and professional," Grinda said. "Measured, not eager."

"He carry?"

"Nothing obvious if he is."

"Weapons in the collection?"

"Three or four flintlocks in primo condition. I'll write everything down and put it in my report. I wish I'd had a camera."

"Too dangerous."

"Anything else?"

Service looked at Sedge. "Nope, you did great."

"Good. Now I'm getting out of these shorts and sandals and into my uniform and boots. Service looked and saw Sedge bringing Grinda's uniform from her truck.

"I guess that means I should take off," Service said. "I have a quick meeting in Rudyard."

"Meet us where we dropped trucks the first time we went to the site," Sedge said. "You remember where that is?"

"I dropped an AVL marker."

Grinda laughed. "Jesus, Grady; you barely know how to use the computer and we've had it how many years?"

"Only ten," he said, walking toward his truck, trying to block out their laughter.

37

Rudyard, Chippewa County

MONDAY, JUNE 11, 2007

Sergeant Bearnard Quinn's truck was in the parking lot of the town's library, which was attached to the school. Service got out and lit a cigarette.

"Gonna have to knock off the coffin nails," Quinn said through his open window.

"Mind your own business."

"Yo! My boss's business *is* my business."

Service handed his colleague several sets of embroidered chevrons. "You earned 'em, Bernie."

"Word's going 'round you worked with the new chief."

"On one case. He's top-notch, leads from the front."

"Lorne was a good chief," Quinn said.

"He was, and a friend, and now it's time for him to take a rest and let others carry the ball," Service said. "You headed to Toronto?"

"We moved it to Friday. The wife's gonna take personal business days Friday and Monday. We'll make a four-dayer out of it."

"Good town."

Quinn stared past him. "Grady, you been looking at the grass? It's dry below the bridge but it looks downright scary up here."

"Part of the cycle," Service said philosophically.

"We get fires, it fucks up everything," Quinn said.

"Beat it, ya big Mick."

38

North Rudyard, Chippewa County

MONDAY, JUNE 11, 2007

The cell phone was sounding as Service sped north toward M-28. "Grady, this is Eddie."

"Chief."

"The state archaeologist resigned this morning, apparently came into the building over the weekend and cleaned out his office. He sent his resignation by e-mail, and nobody knows where he is."

"Sounds like you hit a raw nerve," Service said.

"My thought too. So much so in fact that I've talked to our lawyers, and I'm asking them to go to the AG and get a search warrant. Something stinks in this deal."

"You want me down there?"

"No point right now. I'll keep you up-to-date. What's going on up there?"

"I got a tip about a private museum, and I asked Officer Grinda to go plainclothes. She said the guy has an old farmhouse west of Trout Lake, loaded with artifacts and antiques. The guy is eager to sell. She's to call him back Friday."

"That's good. Any breaks with the CR case?"

CR case? "We can't even say that's what it is yet, Chief."

"I can smell it," Eddie Waco said. "Shake some trees, see what falls out."

"I have an informant who tells me it's pretty rare, but it has happened in the state."

"Don't doubt your source. One thing you ought to know is that this deal is almost always in isolated places. Rounding up deer in populated areas isn't practical. Too much chance of discovery. If you're way out in the boons and find evidence, you can make book on what's happening."

"We'll keep that in mind." *Made sense, even though the southern part of the state had most of the deer—and almost all of the big ones.*

"Bearnard Quinn is the new state master sergeant."

"District nine?"

"That's him."

"I was pretty sure you'd pick him."

Service didn't understand.

Waco told him, "A lot of leaders don't want strong people near them. They're insecure. Good leaders pick top people and let them push them around to try and make changes. I was right about you, Grady."

"Thanks, I guess."

"You tell Miars about your plainclothes deal?"

"Not yet."

"Brief him so he can be ready to take it over."

"Sir, I don't mind briefing him, but this is Sedge's case, and she deserves to take it all the way. She's young, and big wins early count for a lot."

Eddie Waco laughed. "They sure do. Thank you, Chief Master Sergeant. By the way, your new call is Twenty Four Fourteen."

• • •

As he turned west on M-28 the 800 crackled to life. "Twenty Four Fourteen, this is Three One Twenty."

"Twenty Four Fourteen."

"We're at that place. Where are you?"

"Eighty miles south, roughly."

"You'd better get over here."

"Make my way, or expedite?"

"You got warp speed in that jalopy?"

39

Coast of Death, Luce County

MONDAY, JUNE 11, 2007

He drove his truck far beyond where Sedge had parked hers and jogged cross-country the rest of the way, becoming winded—a reminder that he was letting his fitness slide, a dangerous oversight for a dirt-boot officer in the field.

Service found the two women had stripped down to their T-shirts, their gun belts and vests draped over on a nearby log. There was a huge hole in front of them, and sticking out of it was a hoof.

"I needed warp speed to see *that?*"

Sedge exhaled. "Horses, Sergeant, not deer. What the hell are horses doing buried here? I mean, really?"

"How many horses?" Service asked.

"Nine," Sedge said. "So far."

He looked down. "Whole carcasses?"

"Not that we've seen yet. They look like they were quartered and brought out here."

Service sniffed the air. "Still ripe."

"That's what got us to looking," Grinda explained. "But it's not for them we were in a yank for you to get here."

Service looked around the area. "They look like they're away from the artifact field."

Sedge looked up at him and sighed. "Check that hole over there," she said, pointing.

Service looked down and saw a human skull.

Sedge said, "The horses may not be in the artifact field, but I think they're right in the middle of the Iroquois remains."

Katsu's right. It happened here. "How do we know they're Iroquois?"

"Buried in flex position, wrapped in birch and other barks," Sedge said. "It's got to be them."

"The chief called me today. The state archaeologist cleaned out his office over the weekend and resigned by e-mail this morning."

Sedge raised an eyebrow. "Something *we* did?"

"Something someone did," Service said. Sedge and Grinda didn't need to know that Eddie Waco had gone to the man's house, which no doubt had helped precipitate the hasty departure.

"We should tell Katsu," Sedge suggested.

"Let's think this through first," Service reasoned. "The SA is gone. It will take time for a replacement to be named, perhaps a real long time. DEQ can green-light Toliver's dig. We can ask him to put together a hasty plan for this and let DEQ look at it. If necessary, we can pull in the AG's office and let them ride herd on the whole thing legally. We're looking at crimes here, as well as a new historical discovery. We want both lines of inquiry to lead us somewhere."

"God," Grinda said. "That's pure Machiavellian thinking." Her voice suggested admiration.

"The Native American Graves Protection and Repatriation Act will apply," Sedge said. "Human bodies, yes?"

Service thought about it. "Even on state land? I'm not so sure. Let's let the AG coordinate NAGPRA in the absence of a state archaeology official."

"Who calls the attorney general?" Grinda asked.

"We'll ask the chief to do that for us. Meanwhile, Jingo, you may want to touch base with Toliver."

"What about my idea with Wingel?"

"Let's hold on that. I might have more information coming."

"And Kermit the frog?" Sedge asked.

"He's on the run for the moment. I guess we just let him keep running for now."

"I'll run the plate number I picked up off the photo at the museum," Grinda said. "You want me to head home or stick around?"

"She'll bunk with me," Sedge said. "We already talked about it."

"*Sort of a loner?*" Grinda said to Service, who cringed. "I don't think Simon thinks that," she said.

Service rolled his eyes. *Had Sedge told Grinda? Damn.* Dealing with this pair was a lot more work than he had anticipated. Two sharp minds and tongues to match. "We'll let the church camp stew until Friday, but we need to talk to the family down in Pullman, see what they have to say and, if necessary, we need to talk to their boys.

"Ya know," Grinda said, "the meat's been taken off these carcasses. What do you suppose that means?"

"I don't know. Dog food? More important, how the hell did they get them out here? And why?" Service asked. "Too damn big to haul on four-wheelers, and with all this weight, there must be tracks somewhere."

"You're the tracking dude," Sedge said. "So track."

• • •

Service looked around the area, but found nothing of immediate interest. He began circling, looking to cut sign on something that might suggest what had happened. To the west there was a sandy enfilade leading north, and it looked to him like someone had brushed it with evergreen branches, or something similar. A little handwork in the sand showed faint evidence of a groove, possibly an old drag mark.

He moved down the sandy draw until it opened into a low dune area. From where he stood he looked for the easiest route north and took that, which led him to a spot not more than four feet above the beach. The wind was blasting from the north and the water was up, but he could see in the gravel areas that it had been disturbed by some weight, and that someone had tried to smoother it over, to make it look undisturbed.

Not from hikers. He let his legs hang over the edge of the sandy spit and lit a cigarette. When he dropped an ash, the dry brown grass immediately began to smolder. He jammed the cigarette deep into the sand and slapped some more sand on top of the smoldering area until the smoke stopped.

Holy shit. It's a tinderbox out here. He took his radio off his belt and clicked in the frequency for District Two. "Two One Hundred, Twenty Four Fourteen."

If McKower was there, she would be in her cubicle with her radio on.

"Two One Hundred."

"Has anyone talked about how dry it is north of town? I've never seen it this bad before."

"Fire has warnings at max red," she said. "The rest is up to nature."

"That's not reassuring," Service said. "Twenty Four Fourteen clear."

He played with his cell phone. No bars. *Shit.*

When he got back he discovered that his partners had uncovered another Native American burial. "Maybe you two should leave that stuff alone until the experts get out here," he suggested.

Grinda looked up at the sky. "If we get lightning, the woods out here are gonna blow up."

"Shall we cover up what we've found and mark them?" Grinda asked Sedge, who nodded.

"Good idea," Service said, suspecting he was being tuned out.

"We weren't talking to you," Sedge said with an edge to her voice.

"You want me to wait for you two?"

Neither answered. Both were too busy moving sand.

Time to get out of here, he told himself.

"You going to be around town or back at your place?" Grinda called after him.

"Here somewhere. I'll see if I can bunk in with Sergeant Bryan."

"His new girlfriend may not like that," Sedge said.

"I'll let you know how it works out," Service said, eager to get back to the solace of his truck. *Maybe this sergeant thing was wrong; too much face time with too damn many people.*

40

Deer Park, Luce County

TUESDAY, JUNE 12, 2007

It had been a pleasant night with Jeffey Bryan and his girlfriend, Stella. The two men had kept her laughing for a long time with stories about a deer-season dispute between local Amish and Mennonites some years back, and how they had stumbled into the middle of it and been forced into peacemaking roles, something neither of them was fit for.

Stella taught school in Grand Marais, eighteen miles west by dirt road, and she left for work before he and Bryan were even awake. The couple had an English bulldog they had rescued from a shelter. Its name was Struts, and for some reason it stuck to Service's side, drooling on his bare feet and gasping for breath like it had just run ten miles uphill.

"Struts likes you," Bryan said.

"That makes my life complete," he muttered under his breath. "Are your fire people aware of how bad conditions are around here? Hell, it's only June."

"They know, but what can they do?"

Service had no answer.

"You working on this side for a while?" Bryan asked.

Service briefed the sergeant on Sedge's artifact case, but said nothing about horse rustling.

"You know Father Charlie over at LOL?" Service asked.

"Yeah. He's a pretty good guy."

"You know anyone around here who collects Native American artifacts?"

"Pot hunters? Most locals probably have a piece or two. If you're in the woods you always stumble across things; you just can't count on it happening unless you find a honey hole."

Service stepped outside. Bryan's house was built on a bluff forty feet above Lake Superior. The view and the sound of the waves were astounding.

From the wraparound porch Service checked his cell phone. No bars. Bryan came outside. "End of the porch, last four feet to the east. The phones

189

always work there. Nobody knows why; they just do." The young sergeant spread his hands in exasperation. "Is what it is, sayin'?"

Chief Waco answered his own phone. "Go," the chief said peremptorily.

Service talked him through the discovery of the horse carcasses and the human remains, and outlined the plan to have the attorney general's office oversee an exploratory excavation by Professor Toliver, with actual digging approved by DEQ. It would be the AG's call on bringing in NAGPRA.

"The logic is that Toliver already has a plan for the site and it's been approved by the state archaeologist. Seems to us that he can modify his plan to cover our interests, and DEQ can give him the go-ahead," Service said.

"Without expert archaeological oversight?" Chief Waco asked.

"We could ask Dr. Shotwiff to evaluate the plan. He's the expert for things Native American east of the Mississippi."

"Shotwiff's already been to the site?"

"Affirmative."

"All right. I'll get our lawyers talking to the AG and we'll set up a meeting, our lawyers and them. You may have to drive down here for that. Call Shotwiff and ask if he'll pitch in. We'll put him on a consultant's per diem."

Service had no idea what that per diem entailed, or even that such a thing existed.

"You'd better call Toliver, too," Waco said. "You sure he'll play along?"

"I think he'd agree to almost anything to break ground. When he hears there are bodies in the flex position, he'll jump on it."

The chief hung up and Sedge called. "You still at Bryan's place?"

"Right."

"Sheena and I are at the district office with Tina Calabreeze."

Service looked at his watch. Zero seven hundred. "You guys started early. Calabreeze?"

"The retired biologist."

Start writing stuff down, dummy. "Yeah, okay."

"You gonna work your way in this direction?"

"I am now. More horses?"

"Something more tangible," Sedge said, and broke the connection.

More tangible?

Newberry, Luce County

TUESDAY, JUNE 12, 2007

There was a woman with Grinda and Sedge. She had long auburn hair that hung nearly to her waist. She looked like an over-the hill hippie, at least Service's age, but she inexplicably had the face of a fourteen-year-old.

"More tangible?" he greeted the women.

Sedge held up a plastic bag with a faded orange plastic cap in it. "Remember this?"

Service nodded.

"I'm Tina," the third woman said. "Calabreeze?"

"Sorry," Sedge said. "Should have introduced you two."

"Not a problem," the biologist said.

"Tina saw the cap on my desk," Sedge said.

Calabreeeze stepped in and spoke. "I asked her why she had a trank-dart cap."

"Trank-dart *cap?*"

"You know the cap-gizzy on the plunger?" The woman made a gesture with her thumb. "This one I'd guess is off a Type P practice dart. The other one, I'm certain, is from a DNA dart."

Service sat down. "Can I have all that in English?"

"Sure," the retired biologist said. "Darting animals with tranquilizers comes down to accuracy with the projector, selecting the proper agents, getting the drug combination and dosage right—all skills you acquire over time."

"Projector?"

"Sorry—the dart gun. Could be a pistol or a rifle, but probably the latter if the target's at any distance. Pistols are used pretty much for animals in confined trap devices—boxes and clover nets and so forth."

Scientists. "Uh-huh," Service said, trying to absorb what she was telling him. "You said something about DNA?"

"Right. You can use special darts to collect DNA samples, or for a biopsy. Or you can use a transmitter dart so you can track your animal when it runs. They almost always run," she added, "and increased exertion drives up the heart rate, which increases mortality from the procedure."

"DNA," he repeated.

"Yes. Let's say you want to know if the animal has a certain line of DNA; the dart will take a sample for you, which you can then process in the lab."

"And if the animal runs away, you follow the transmitter's signal?"

"Exactly," Calabreeze said. She looked at the other women and added, "He's not as dumb as you guys said." All three women laughed, and Service wondered what the hell was so funny.

"If you don't want the animal to run, what do you do?" Service asked.

"The question is *not* whether the animal will run, but usually *how far;* the farther it goes and the greater its heart rate increases from fear, the greater your potential problems. So," she continued, "selecting the correct agents *and* dose are of paramount importance."

"And?"

"You estimate weight in pounds and convert it to kilos, which is about point four five. The desired dose for Xylazine, for example, is kilos times five milligrams per milliliter. You have to calibrate every time. The best dart rifles are effective up to ninety yards, but nobody would be so stupid as to attempt that long a shot, right? The drugs you'd use would probably be Xylazine and Telazol, and maybe Ketamine."

Good God. Can she not focus? "I've seen Telazol and Ketamine used on bears," he offered.

"Right, but with deer you need to add an agonist, either yohimbine or Tolazine." Calabreeze looked at the other women. "Yohimbine bark is supposed to help the guys . . ." She made a fist and stiffened her arm. "Yohimbine HCL, you know, indole alkaloid, but the libido deal is strictly anecdotal."

"Viagra sort of put yohimbine in the backseat," Sedge said.

"Deer," Service said. "What about deer and tranks. *Agonist?*"

"Yes, agonist—to undo the anesthetic effect," Calabreeze said. "Like, reverse the pharmacokinetics and pharmacological action?"

"Would you call it a system, the rifle and such?"

"Sure, it's a system, and I only saw it used in grad school. We never used it here. We do it differently: We trank our animals up close and personal. Our way is cheaper and safer."

"If you don't mind bruises and multiple contusions," Sedge chimed in.

"True," the biologist said with a smirk. "It can get pretty physical."

"Back to the orange caps," Service said. "You conclude what from those?"

"Well, it's just an educated guess, but it seems obvious, doesn't it? I'd say someone was practicing to increase accuracy with a practice dart, and wanted DNA to be sure they were targeting the right specimens."

"For?'

"You guys are law enforcement," Calabreeze said. "My job was biology and science."

"How about cervid rustling?" Service offered.

Calabreeze's eyebrow rose at an angle. "Possibly," she said.

"Does Luce County have the right DNA?"

The biologist lowered her voice. "There are state-record racks here," she said in a near whisper. "Plural, as in many."

"Where?"

"She drew a map for us," Grinda said, holding up a piece of paper.

Sedge caught his attention and nodded without speaking.

"Okay, tell us the limits of this approach," Service said. "This *system*."

"You have to find the target and get at least as close as a bow hunter. The target needs to be calm, not harassed. The projectors are loud, and as you no doubt know, even a noisy bowstring will make an animal jump and often cause you to miss. Getting the right drug combination is difficult, and calculating dose is a special challenge, bordering on an art form. Then you have to get good at using the projector."

"Anything else?"

She raised her eyes for a moment. "Projectors are considered rifles and are subject to federal law. Shipment is limited to the military, law enforcement, and holders of federal firearm licenses. If you don't have an FFL, you have to get a local dealer to receive for you. This can be done, but it's a lot of work, and a lot of dealers want no part of all the government's red tape."

"Vets have trank guns, and animal control officers?"

"Some, not all. The systems are fairly expensive, like up to two grand for a good setup."

"Is there a trank rifle here?"

She shook her head. "You'd assume, but the reality is that only a few districts have them. You have to plan ahead and make arrangements to get them on loan. That's why some of your people and regular cops end up needlessly euthanizing animals. They can't get trank guns quickly enough."

"You're familiar with cervid rustling?" he said, changing the subject again.

"Heard of it, sure. Familiar? Not hardly."

"Rumors of it happening in this state?"

"Not that I recall."

The biologist excused herself to check something in her old office area, and when she was gone Service said, "Convenient loss of recall."

Sedge was silent. Grinda said, "That's not fair."

"Hey, it's just us badges now," Service said. "Some biologists don't like working with us. They're convinced we drive away the public, which means they aren't getting the maximum amount of data they want."

"Tina wasn't like that," Sedge said in the biologist's defense.

Service picked up the plastic bag with the orange cap. "Talk about luck."

"The power and mystery of serendipity," Sedge said.

Service stared at her. "Yeah, that too. We need to ask her more questions," he added, and Sedge left the cubicle immediately.

Grinda sat back in her chair. "She's a good one. Know what Jingo's hobby is?"

Here it comes. "No, what?"

"She's a painter."

"Houses?"

"Don't be a moron. Canvases. She's an artist."

"Picures of what?'

Grinda shrugged. "Does it matter?"

Sedge and Calabreeze came back and the biologist apologized for leaving.

Service said, "We're sort of floundering, trying to get a grip on a case. We've all worked with biologists to incapacitate animals for various reasons, but not to relocate deer any extreme distances. Be patient with us, okay?"

Calabreeze smiled.

"We have a deer we want to move and it's down. What next?"

The biologist nodded. "You come up on the animal from behind, always from behind it. Be real quiet, avoid any sudden noises—like your radio squelching. Kneel down, make sure the animal's air passages are clear and that there's no stuff around the mouth or nose that might get inside and cause problems. Then you check respiration and heart rate."

"You have instruments?'

"Right. Then you check circulation. Do you want me to go into the details of each procedure?"

"No, significance is enough," Service said, looking at Sedge and Grinda, who nodded their agreement. "Why check circulation?"

"To help us understand the animal's level of excitement. Elevated heart rate increases mortality."

"Okay. Next?"

"Put a covering over the deer's eyes and hobble its legs A blindfold not only protects, but it also helps calm the animal. Then comes the hard part. You need to help the animal achieve sternal recumbency, specifically ventral recumbency."

"English?"

"Sorry," Calabreeze said with a giggle. "The animal needs to be on its brisket—its chest—with the legs tucked underneath, like it's sleeping."

The three officers nodded.

"If you have to roll the animal over, first put it on its stomach, then move it over to its side. The deer's digestive system is hypersensitive and delicately balanced, and it will twist out of shape and shut down with the slightest provocation. Rule of thumb is that a deer that goes on its back will be dead within three days. The damage from that mistake can't be undone. Questions?"

"What about antlers?" Service asked. "How do you protect the rack?"

"We don't, because we do our work in winter here, and most sheds are off by then."

There were no more questions.

Calabreeze continued. "When you get the animal stabilized on its brisket, you check for any injuries or signs of disease. You also check the dart site. You can hit an artery and bleed them internally into shock. The internal bleeds are hard to spot at first. Deer checked, use the Aniham to move the animal into the transport, secure it in its cradle, and make sure someone is with it to monitor its signs."

"And it will survive?" The process she had just laid out was pretty much what Allerdyce had told him, albeit with less eloquence and technical precision; yet more evidence that Limpy seemed to know what he was talking about.

"A minimum of five percent die, even when you do everything right. Most mortality rates are much higher. Good teams can keep it at five percent or even a little lower."

"You need a vet to do this?" Grinda asked.

"Ideally, because of the drug complexities, but a competent vet tech could also do it."

"Aniham?" Service asked.

"Animal hammock—a fabric carrier under the deer, like a firewood carrier, human carriers on the sides. You lower the Aniham into the cradle under the deer and leave it there until you reach your destination."

"Could you safely move a deer a thousand miles or more?"

"Nonstop, I doubt it. I certainly wouldn't attempt it. More likely you'd have to do it in stages. Go from A to B, release the animal, stabilize it, then after a period of time, move from B to C, and like that until you reach your destination."

Service looked at the women. "Rustlers can get up to a hundred thousand dollars for a trophy buck. Stages of movement, special equipment and transport, the need for highly skilled, specially trained personnel—all this says we're talking high overhead, which means this isn't your basic redneck poaching crew." He turned to Calabreeze. "Are there special vehicles for this?"

"Out west they relocate a lot of mule deer," she said. "They have trucks with built-in cradles."

"What did you use?"

"A temporary, collapsible wooden cradle we could assemble in a pickup bed in ten minutes. Once tightened, it was safe and sturdy."

"The trucks out west, like, livestock eighteen-wheelers?"

"No; they have small ventilated boxes, six to nine cradles max."

"Can you use the vehicles for other species?" Grinda asked.

"Sure," the biologist said. "I once saw them move some buffalo in Yellowstone."

"In cradles?"

"No, they just herded them into the truck like livestock—ya know, up a chute—and let them mill around the cradles inside until they drove them where they wanted to unload them."

Service thanked the retiree for her help and watched her march out of the office.

After the biologist was gone Sedge said, "*Nine* cows. Makes you wonder, eh?"

Service understood. *Trucks with six to nine cradles.*

Grinda punched in her speed-dial number for del Olmo. "Can you call Sommers, ask them how beef is transported to Midwest stores, and from where? No, I'm not crazy," she said. "I don't know," she added. "Yes, that will be good."

She looked at Sedge. "Sommers is a meat shop in Crystal Falls. Simon wants to know when I'll be done with the assignment here, and he says he'll patrol my area while I'm gone."

"He's horny," Sedge said with a smirk.

"Aren't they *always?*" Grinda said.

"Hey, hey," Service muttered.

42

Harvey, Marquette County

WEDNESDAY, JUNE 13, 2007

"Bootie call?" Friday asked with a knowing grin.

It was nearly 5 p.m. "Been bouncing all around Luce County," Service said. Slept in my truck last night. I just wanted to see you and the kid and sleep in our bed," he said. "So you wouldn't mind skipping sex tonight?"

"Up to you," she said with a shrug. Then she pushed him hard in the chest. "Now hear this," she declared. "There *will* be sex in our bed tonight."

He had arrived minutes before and sent the babysitter on her way.

"Your case making progress?" she asked.

"Sort of," he said. "Cases. It looks like two of them. What're you doing?"

"Dude in Skandia caught his wife with his business partner's son and gave them a few exuberant head shots with a pickax."

"Geez," Service said, wrinkling his face. "Intent?"

"Sure, but it will plead down to second-degree, moment of passion, yada yada yada, bargain-deal—you know the drill."

He did.

"You think anyone has any notion how screwed-up our justice system is?" she asked.

"Nope, and as long as it doesn't touch them, they really don't give a shit," he said.

"You here for just one night?"

"Two, I hope." He had called Professor Shotwiff, who agreed to help out. Shark was bringing him again, and Service would take him to Newberry and put him in a cabin owned by a friend of Jeffey Bryan.

• • •

Sedge called to report that she had talked to Toliver about the dig. "He damn near came while I was talking to him," she said.

"No objections to revising his dig plan?" Service asked.

"As predicted, not after I told him about the flex remains."

Chief Waco called next. He and the DNR lawyers were meeting with the AG's people. No need for Service in Lansing. Yet.

"The AG folks keep talking about one of their people who retired and who's the most knowledgeable about archaeological issues. They want to bring him back as a consultant."

"He may not accept," Service told his boss.

"Why?"

"There could be tickets and warrants awaiting his arrival."

"I'll tell them to extend the offer and see what happens. If he shows, you guys can pinch him."

Service called his granddaughter. "*Mad* at you!" she said. "You no call."

"I've been busy, hon."

"Bampy *mean!*" she shouted, and dropped the phone.

"Bituva temper," Karylanne said.

"I should have called."

"No, she's just got a bug. She'll be fine. Don't pay any attention."

Simon del Olmo called. "This is wild! Iron, Dickinson, Gogebic—we're making pinches all over the place. It's like the dirtbags all had brain farts at the same time. Major over-limits of fish, shooting at deer, ATVs all over prohibited federal land—it's crazy! Like the god of nature is for once smiling down on the good guys, and it's not even the full moon."

"Right," Service said. "The god of nature. That would be the relative of the Tooth Fairy or the Easter Bunny? I can never remember."

"Who cares, Sarge. We are busy as hell everywhere right now. Hey, Quinn is a great pick for master sergeant."

Service agreed.

"You look tired," Friday said.

He felt in his gut he was going to get a lot more tired in the days ahead, but he wasn't sure why he felt this way, and didn't care to examine the feeling. *Is what it is,* he told himself.

43

St. Ignace, Mackinac County

FRIDAY, JUNE 15, 2007

Professor Shotwiff arrived with Shark at 4 a.m., and within minutes his bags were in Service's truck and the two men were racing toward Lansing. Chief Waco had called Thursday night. "Need you here, thirteen hundred tomorrow, my office." No explanation offered.

"Professor Shotwiff will be with me. You want us there earlier?"

"Nope, this meeting is being forced, so I'm going to use my ways to control it. My turf, my time. About the time the beer-a-craps and politricks get antsy for Friday drinkies, we'll just be settling in for all-night palavers." He added, "Be careful," chuckled mightily, and hung up.

Beer-a-craps?

Service stopped to refuel on the state card in St. Ignace. Professor Shotwiff stared at a billboard questioning the DNR's ability to chase wrongdoers. "Is that true?" he asked Service.

"Nope."

Shotwiff nodded. "Interesting," was all he said. Then he switched subjects. "I've been thinking a lot about your theory," he said, "and I still think it's plausible that the Iroquois would come in from the west, but maybe they were after something different than white men's history books tell us. You know anything about Iroquois fighting tactics and strategies?"

"No."

"Most of the time they operated in small groups. Big group battles were rare at any time, and reports of huge forces are no doubt overstated many fold. Most of our reports come from the Jesuits, and you can bet the Indian informants would play things way up or way down as events most benefited them. Simply put, you can't rely on aboriginals for anything like dependable or accurate quantitative information. It's nothing sinister; it just wasn't part of their culture."

"Meaning what?"

"Meaning that perhaps one hundred Iroquois makes more sense than three hundred. The real innovators of the birch-bark canoes were the Ojibwa, not the Iroquois. The Ojibwa and Odawa had trade routes in giant canoes hundreds of miles west and north into Canada. The Iroquois had few large canoes, and depended mostly on the under-twenty-footers to scoot about. These craft carried two or three warriors and supplies, so a force of one hundred would amount to thirty to fifty canoes—like you said, pretty damn difficult to hide on river travel, and you couldn't take the damn things too far offshore in the big lakes. If the war party was four hundred warriors, then we're talking a hundred and twenty to a hundred and fifty small canoes, an impossibly large group to hide."

"Unless they were coming from the south and west."

"I'm beginning to put some credence in that thinking, especially when other factors are taken into account."

Service threw a token in the fare basket and sped south up the span of the bridge toward Mackinaw City, pegging his speed at 45 mph.

The old man stared off in the distance as they crossed the Straits of Mackinac. The water was almost azure, and the clouds floating overhead were moving like gigantic, lugubrious airships. "Understand, the Iroquois *were* bloodthirsty bastards. Totally. Agrarian economic base; they had surpluses of food for their families and the women doing all the scut work, which left the men with nothing to do but hunt and fight, so that's pretty much what they did," Shotwiff said.

"But beaver began to run out, and the Iroquois were forced to expand westward for new fur sources. This is when they swept into northern Ohio, west of Toronto, southern Michigan, and parts of northern Indiana, driving some tribes away and killing survivors by hundreds. The destruction was so complete that southern Michigan was virtually without Native Americans for almost fifty years. Some tried to resist and were crushed. Most ran to Illinois, or Wisconsin, or up to and across the Upper Peninsula. The Iroquois rightfully infused everyone with abject fear, all of it deserved."

Service was spellbound.

"The Iroquois, flush with success, got to feeling invincible and decided to go after the Ojibwa, or Saulteur—they're the same tribe," Shotwiff continued. "That's when the proverbial shit hit the fan, irresistible force colliding with unmovable object. The Ojibwa didn't want to talk. They didn't run, and they didn't surrender. They dug in and fought as ferociously and dirtily as their enemies, fighting to the death in every engagement. Such a show of resistance brought grudging admiration—then reinforcements from displaced tribes and the Ojibiwa force soon grew larger as the Iroquois began to shrink from losses. Understand, I'm interpolating history, but this is the gist of how it progressed."

"Losses like they suffered on Lake Michigan against the Menominees and Ojibwa?" Service asked.

"Exactly; attrition at its worst. You are far from home and reinforcements can't be had. My thinking is that they had to begin getting a little desperate for a win to change momentum. The Ojibwa resistance brought almost continuous reinforcements, and between 1640, when the fur expansions began, and 1670 or so, the Ojibwa drove the Iroquois completely out of northern Michigan and back through Ontario to upper New York. The Iroquois didn't stop making war, but they concentrated their efforts on foes in Pennsylvania and Maryland. Late in the century European countries switched alliances and allegiances, and the Iroquois found themselves with insufficient backing or a provider of modern weapons."

"Then smallpox hit?" Service offered.

"Exactly, though European historians prefer to give credit to superior European soldiering. Neither the Ojibwa, nor the disease, get deserved credit for the final one-two punch. Understand, I'm not talking about ritualized, ceremonial wars of previous eras. I'm talking about near-total warfare with ruthless carnage on all sides. There was nothing like it in aboriginal history until then, and very little afterwards—until Custer's days out west—and with such fighting, the Ojibwa took command of upper Michigan permanently. As one of my more-jocular colleagues used to put it, the Ojibwa put the *bad* into badass."

"I don't remember any of this from my school days," Service said, laughing.

"It wasn't taught. All you learned about were *les sauvages* and European contact. To give proper credit, the Iroquois were a brave and clever people, and politically sophisticated with their five- and then six-nation alliances. They liked war, realized its importance, and studied it in the context of their own efforts and those of their enemies. Damn clever. They'd come upriver by canoe, and when they got within striking distance of an objective, they would fill the canoes with rocks and sink them. Then they'd go ashore, form up, and head through the woods on foot to attack the enemy at a vulnerable time or place. Assault over, they'd race back to their canoes, refloat them, and paddle like hell to get out of the area. Sort of an early Nazi blitzkrieg style."

"Does this relate to our site?"

"It could. I'm getting to that," Professor Shotwiff said. "Let's say for purposes of our discussion that they came north as you have speculated. They might very well have landed at your site. The question is why."

Service kept his eyes on I-75 and set the speed at eighty. "Crisp Point is a long way from the Soo."

"Right, my boy. Too far away for accidental discovery, at least theoretically. And that would be one good reason. But perhaps they sank their canoes there, gathered in a camp, and got themselves together for a push against another target to the southeast."

"Southeast?"

"Bawating might not have been the objective at all. The Iroquois liked to campaign, move in a sort of series of strategic thrusts and attacks. I'm thinking it's entirely possible that they intended not to strike Bawating or Bay Mills, but the heavily populated villages of Ojibwa and other tribes from the mouth of the Tahquamenon up to the Upper Falls. Lots of people in those villages. If the Iroquois successfully struck these camps, they could capture food and weapons and begin to advance eastward in greater strength toward Bawating. It would then amount to a concerted, planned military campaign, which was their hallmark. My boy, I think it's quite possible the battle happened at your site."

"Pure bad luck for the Iroquois that the Ojibwa stumbled onto them."

"If the theory is right."

"How can we know?"

"We can never know absolutely, but if the test dig begins to uncover canoe remains and more bodies, we'll start to get a reasonable estimate of the battle's dimensions, casualties, and so forth. The dig is critical."

"Canoe remains and flexed bodies?"

"Possible in this northern landscape. Do you know why the bodies were flexed?"

"No. Respect?"

"Some believe that, but I don't. It was out of fear, not respect. They double the bodies, folded them if you will, in the belief that this would keep evil spirits inside the remains and keep them from being loosed on living humans."

"Which means the dig may release evil sprits?"

Shotwiff chuckled. "You superstitious?"

"Not especially. You?"

"Hell, yes," the professor said, breaking into uncontrollable laughter.

At Wolverine Shotwiff asked, "Any idea what awaits us in Lansing?"

"Nossir," Service said.

"Want my take on it?" Shotwiff asked. "If Native Americans are there, and involved, this will be what we called, in my military service days, a SNAFU. You have a term for it in your line of work?"

"Goat rodeo," Grady Service said. "That's not a compliment."

"You like a good fight, Sergeant?"

Service nodded. "When the stakes warrant it."

"Me," the professor said happily, "I like *any* fight—especially one where the opposition thinks it has the upper hand."

• • •

The cell phone buzzed as they passed Mount Pleasant. "Service? Chook Whybus. Sorry to take so long to get back to you, but Ms. Ence/Wingel is not a subject the university folks want to talk about. Grady turned the phone to speaker so the professor could listen along with him.

"She started her academic career at Oregon, got a BA in biochemistry and an MA in aboriginal studies, and began her doctorate under Professor Cayuga Greysolon, *the* expert on northwest Native American art. Ence is Wingel's birth surname. Seems she got involved in . . . activities, uh, outside the professional? They became a scandal. The professor was married to another heavyweight scholar, who apparently took umbrage. Obviously race was part of the public issue, white professor, young, pretty black female. This woulda been around 1970, '71.

"Then a Salish necklace came up missing from the professor's personal collection. The wife blamed Ence, and filed a complaint with the cops. They came to question the girlfriend. The Salish were a major coastal tribe known for unique arts and crafts. The necklace in question was not just rare, but priceless, one of a kind, the only known Kwakwaka'wakw erotic piece. A pendant of a woman in a compromised position. The police were left with an accusation but no evidence, and the professor died a couple of years later.

"Ence left campus and the state and finished a doctorate at McGill in Montreal under the name of Wingel," Whybus continued. "No idea where that name comes from. She also sued the dead prof's wife for slander and got some sort of huge out-of-court settlement. Ence/Wingel was considered a brilliant student, but also a shady archaeologist, and a rank opportunist. She has a lot of digs to her credit, and far more papers than it seems possible one person could author unless she were a true polymath.

"So that's the story. I've got a couple of young women working for me who can play computers like concert pianists. They found an interesting photo that I've sent on to your chief, along with a second photo. Take a look. I think you'll find them to be thought-provoking."

"Thanks, Chook," Service said. "I owe you."

"Yep, you do," Whybus said.

"How long to Lansing?" Dr. Shotwiff asked. "I gotta drain the old down-spout again."

44

Lansing, Ingham County

FRIDAY, JUNE 15, 2007

The woman had stringy gray hair as coarse as straw and the countenance of an aging wharf rat. Her skin was leathery and brown, obviously from too much time in the sun and the elements. "So this is the Big Dog," she said, looking at Grady Service.

"Dr. Becca Ledger-Foley," Chief Waco said. "Assistant state archaeologist."

Assistant? Sedge never said anything about an assistant. No AG people, no lawyers, just the chief, Professor Shotwiff, and Ledger-Foley. Not at all what I expected. Can't read her stone face. Better pay attention.

"Dr. Ledger-Foley?" Chief Waco said.

"This meeting is off the record," she began, "which is why I requested no lawyers be present. I want to make it clear that my supervisor, Dr. Flinders Yardley, resigned not because of any wrongdoing, but because he cannot emotionally deal with conflict. *Any* conflict. Flin is an honest, caring man who was appointed by Governor Bozian because Flin's father was a major Bozian contributor. Would another governor have appointed him? I don't know the answer to that question. His sudden departure was not meant to draw attention, but to avoid it."

She creeps me out, Service thought, and he saw surprise in Chief Waco's eyes. Ledger-Foley looked dowdy, but her mind was obviously keen, and she seemed primed to fight. *The issue is why.*

"Are you familiar with Professor Toliver's application?" Service asked.

"Yes, I am. I reviewed it for Flin and recommended approval. I reviewed *everything* for him," she added.

Martyr complex? Trouble reading her. "Do you know the history of the site?"

"Of course. Dr. Wingel's discovery of a body after winter disruption and thaw, and reburying it without telling the State where—yes, I know. This happened long before Flin and I were here."

Ducking? "Had Wingel presented her report to you, would you have accepted it?"

"I didn't, and I find theoretical discussion a bore at best. It happened, she filed the requisite report later, end of story."

Eddie Waco slid a manila folder over to Service, who looked inside, opening it to a group photograph. *What am I looking at, and for?*

"These from Chook Whybus?" he asked the chief.

"Yep."

The second photograph in the folder showed a gaudy pendant that seemed to be a female body being penetrated by an erect male member while something seemed to be forming in the female figure's uterine area. Waco motioned for him to flip back to the first photograph, which he did. There were a half-dozen people in evening dress, the men in white jackets, the women in dark gowns. Ladania Wingel was on one end, a pendant hanging from a chain. Service looked at Waco, who nodded. Service looked at the date and location on the photo.

He looked at Ledger-Foley. "Has anyone suggested that Wingel did not rebury the remains?"

"That's presumptuous, preposterous, and outrageous," she said, her voice sliding up.

"Why? It happened before your time. Is everyone you work with honest?" he pressed.

"*Honest* is the wrong word," the assistant state archaeologist said. "If you asked whether all applicants push limits in seeking excavation permission, I would tell you that many of them tend to overextend themselves, which is to be expected. It's not a question of honesty. With money so tight, professionals are sometimes 'forced' by their institutions to overreach. You can't get the brass ring with your hands folded in your lap," she added.

"I disagree," Professor Shotwiff interjected.

"And you are?" Ledger-Foley asked.

"Ozzien Shotwiff."

"Ah yes, I thought you looked vaguely familiar. Your reputation precedes you."

"You have no reputation that I know of," Shotwiff countered sharply.

The woman bristled.

"I'm too damn old for verbal fencing, Dr. Ledger-Foley. We both know there are all kinds of crooks, knuckleheads, and scoundrels in academia, even in top-shelf institutions, so let's drop the holier-than-thou crap."

Service grabbed the opening. "Dr. Wingel started her doctorate under Professor Cayuga Greysolon at Oregon."

"Yes, I know of the late professor. He was a giant, a Kwakwaka'wakw art expert with a worldwide reputation for pristine scholarship."

"When I say 'under the professor,' I mean just that, and not just academically." Service let his words sink in. "A rare necklace came up missing. The professor's wife, herself an academic heavyweight, took umbrage over the scandalous affair and accused Wingel of theft. At the time, Wingel went by the name of Ence. Wingel was naturally offended and left the program and the state. This was at the end of 1971. She subsequently earned a doctorate at McGill in Montreal under the name of Wingel."

Ledger-Foley sighed.

Service held up the photo of the pendant. "This is the missing object," he said. Then he held up the second photo. "This was taken at a conference in Tulsa in 1997. That's Dr. Wingel on the end, to the left, and the pendant around her neck appears to be the one in the first photo. Let's dispense with talk of theoreticals, Dr. Ledger-Foley. Wingel stole the necklace. She's a dirtbag."

"That may well be so, but you have no proof that the necklace she's wearing is the original rather than a copy, and in any event, the statute of limitations surely has expired."

"No argument. But if Wingel stole once, what are the chances it happened again? We know, for example, that she sued her lover's widow and won a large out-of-court settlement. First you steal, and then you sue for being accused of stealing. That takes some big cojones. There's nothing theoretical here, Doctor. Chief?"

"We see this all the time," Eddie Waco said. "Past criminal behavior is a good predictor of future criminal behavior."

"That is not an absolute," Ledger-Foley said.

"Never said it was," Waco said. "But I'm sure a grand jury would give me sealed warrants based on this."

"For what—skeletal remains? The statute of limitations is gone on that as well. Are you kidding?"

"No, ma'am, that's not my way. I talked to the FBI, and the Bureau wants to take a closer look at Dr. Wingel—you know, over time—sort of correlate X with Y and so forth, and see what pops up."

"That's nothing more than a fishing expedition," Ledger-Foley said, "at the public's expense!"

"We're woods cops," Chief Waco said. "The people of this state pay us to go on fishing expeditions."

"I am leaving," Ledger-Foley said.

"No, you're not," Waco said. "Sit back and listen. We are *not* your enemies and we are not trying to ruffle feathers. DEQ is going to give Dr. Toliver the green light to dig. But Toliver is first going to modify his dig plan to look at some other factors that recently have come to light. As acting state archaeologist, which I assume you are until your boss's replacement is named, you are going to review the modified plan, and we certainly *hope* you will approve it."

"Why do you care about this?" Ledger-Foley asked.

The chief handed her a photograph. "Know what that is?"

"Flexed remains."

"Yes—Iroquois—and at the very site where Wingel found the body. The theory of that battle and its history are going to be challenged at this place, and perhaps settled."

"Not necessarily."

"Listen to me," Shotwiff asserted. Then he laid out the Tahquamenon River village raid theory.

Service sensed that the state official was listening attentively to the professor's every word.

When Shotwiff finished, Ledger-Foley said, "My. When will I get the modified plan to review?"

"In July," Shotwiff said. "I would think Professor Toliver could be turning dirt by August first; most of the bugs will be gone by then. It will be clear sailing for the dig."

"That seems reasonable to me," Ledger-Foley said. "We may be on the cusp of a major historical discovery."

"Indeed we might," Shotwiff said. "Thanks in great part to this fella sitting next to me."

45

East Lansing, Ingham County

FRIDAY, JUNE 15, 2007

David Ohgwahoh was a tiny, straight-backed man in his seventies with a shock of short white hair. His Mohawk name meant "wolf." He sipped a bottle of Diet Dr. Pepper, sitting in a tavern called Dagwood's west of the Michigan State campus.

Shotwiff said, "David is the regional manager for USDA in central Michigan. He's a full-blood Haudenosaunee from a family with a long and interesting history. His ancestors were at Iroquois Point."

The man lit a cigarette and so, too, did Service. It was mid-afternoon.

"I speak the truth," Ohgwahoh began. "My ancestor was Ayonwaehs, Mohawk war chief at the founding of *Ne Gayanesha gowa*, the Great Binding Law, what whites call the Constitution of the Five Nations. Your own constitution is in part based on ours. My people, the Agnieronnon, were the most aggressive of the five nations. Our enemies called us the man-eaters, which was true."

"Iroquois Point," Professor Shotwiff interjected.

"My mother and my grandmother told our family how the Agnieronnon and the Onneiochonnon had gone to La Baie des Puants to persecute the Wendat, those who some call Huron. But the Wendat had warning and fled, and our people turned back to the east where they encountered the Noquet. A battle began, which continued up a river far to the north. We pursued them until they were all dead, taken captive, or had escaped. It was decided at this time to continue north to the big lake and travel east to find a village to eat."

"Bawating?" Service asked.

"It was well known by my ancestors that there was no longer a permanent camp there, their previous forays having driven the enemy west with fear and trepidation."

"Despite the fact that the Saulteur had won most battles against the Haudenosaunee," Shotwiff interrupted. He turned to Service and grinned. "David's people find the term *Iroquois* to be an insult and are thus called Haudenosaunee. By either name, they got their asses thrashed just about every time they came up against the Ojibwa. Remember, at this time there really was no grand tribe called Ojibwa. Rather, there were multiple small bands all through the area like the Saulteur who shared language and culture and rallied to help each other when threats arose. Only later, after the Iroquois wars had concluded, did the Ojibwa become one tribe. Still, the Indians in the 1650s all moved their families west, suspecting the Iroquois would keep coming back, and of course, all parties turned out to be correct."

The professor turned back to the Mohawk. "If your people knew Bawating was empty, why would they go east to find a village?"

"The story does not tell us this," Ohgwahoh said.

"Some contemporary French accounts claim your people were looking for a village to give them food," Shotwiff said, "not a village to eat."

"Double meaning," the Mohawk replied. "It can be translated as a threat or as a need."

"Did they *need* food?" Service asked.

"War parties were invariably on the edge of starvation. They would be gone for as long as four years, and some were forced to turn back because they could not adequately feed their warriors."

"Which is why your people ate captives," Shotwiff said. "Food that walks."

"It's true we ate enemy warriors, but most captives were kept alive to be adopted by families into the Five Nations."

"There were such people with them this time?" Service asked.

"Yes," David Ohgwahoh said. "The Noquet were captured in the skirmishes going north, and some others they had harvested en route from our home country."

Shotwiff looked like he had sent his brain elsewhere when he surprised Service. "Continuous warfare sent other tribes into flight, but the Haudenosaunee aggressors found their ranks being thinned by continuous war campaigns, and thus they were constantly taking hostages back to adopt. You couldn't make your woman preggers if you were a thousand miles away, so they needed replacement people to maintain tribal size. By 1670 an estimated seventy percent or so of the Iroquois war force was comprised of various adopted Algonquin and Huron. Trying to trace all this is complex, and virtually impossible, because there were—and are—no written records. What records we do have from Europeans all tend to have their own names for the same things. The name *Iroquois* comes from the words *hiro kone*, which means, 'I have spoken.' The first French people to hear this thought they heard Ir-o-quois." Shotwiff looked at David Ohgwahoh. "Go ahead, please."

"The people were moving east and decided to camp," Ohgwahoh said. "As was the practice, they sent scouts forward from the camp. The scouts saw Saulteur, but remained hidden, hoping they had not been spotted. But they had. The scouts continued on their mission and upon return some days later, they found their camp had been attacked, leaving headless bodies and the bones of those eaten by the Saulteur attackers."

"Captives too?"

"Presumably they were dead, but it's possible survivors were taken by the Saulteur to adopt," Ohgwahoh replied.

"Who buried the dead?" Service asked.

"The scouts, perhaps, but the telling does not address this. Even the Saulteur would honor enemy dead."

"You know this, or assume it?" Service asked.

"It is assumed."

"How many in your force?" Service asked.

"One thousand warriors," Ohgwahoh said with obvious pride.

"The accounts say one hundred," Shotwiff countered.

The Mohawk smiled. "Then you understand."

Service didn't.

Shotwiff turned to him. "The Haudenosaunee in those times used the number one hundred to represent any large, undetermined number. It is like most Native American representations: more figurative and symbolic than literal and precise."

"Then where does the thousand come from?"

"Other sources, mainly Saulteur. The scouts that day reconnoitered the main Haudenosaunee force and sent for reinforcements. Odawa, Nipissing,

Amikone, and others were in the area; all responded, even their women and children, assembling an ambush force estimated at three hundred, but not just warriors."

"What does that tell us?" Service asked.

"The Iroquois were looking to raise hell."

"Might the bodies have been left unburied?" Service asked the Mohawk.

"Unlikely."

"But your scouts found them unburied, headless, all that."

"That is true, but we do not know how many. It is more likely that most had been buried by the Saulteur to get their spirits away. Allowing spirits free run of Earth was a bad thing."

"Your scouts saw the Saulteur and did not go back to warn the main group?"

"A calculated risk. It was only bad luck that they were seen," the man said defensively.

Shotwiff added, "If the intent of the Haudenosaunee was a village, why did they not continue east along Lake Michigan the day they encountered the Noquet?"

The man lifted his hands. "The story does not tell us."

"Did the scouts bring any remains with them after finding the bodies of their brothers?"

Again Ohgwahoh lifted his arms.

Service saw the professor shoot him a look suggesting the meeting was over. "Thanks for sharing with us," Service said to the Mohawk.

"It is good to keep the past in the present," Ohgwahoh said, standing up.

• • •

"Bloody cannibal," Shotwiff said when the man was gone. "He has been sending me letters for years about having a story to tell. I kept telling him I was retired."

"But you called him," Service said.

"Long shot for us," the professor said. "All Mohawks give me the creeps. They're maniacs, always have been."

"He seemed fine."

"A diploma don't offset genes, son. The poison in those folks is always right up to the surface."

"Then why talk to him?"

"His family had the story of the battle. This is rare."

"It is hearsay," Service said.

"True, but we can compare it to other contemporary accounts and begin to develop some assumptions and theories. I think I told you that I have always harbored doubt about the Iroquois Point site. All sides then knew that the Soo site was largely abandoned, and that Mackinac was heavily populated with Saulteur, et cetera. To come up the St. Mary's from Point Detour would require the ascending force to come up the east bank, closest to a population site, and the river at Bawating is only a half-mile wide, which makes it impossible to ascend unseen. The straits presented a five- to eight-mile gap depending on how you came at it, a much better chance to pass unseen."

"But the Iroquois turned *north* after the Noquet."

"Mohawks! You see, they came for blood, and the chance to get it sent them that way. That's how they've always been: quick to fight, slow to think strategically. It was always my presumption they went north to seek a known Saulteur concentration, but if that had been the case, they should have gone up the Manistique to the Fox, and northeast to a place where they could portage to the Tahquamenon, then float down to the upper falls and go on the attack over land from there. The Saulteur kept camps at the lower falls and at the mouth of the river, a place once called Emerson. This route was the one the Saulteur used to go southwest on the warpath."

"There were villages on the Tahquamenon?" Service asked.

"Yes, and no doubt that's what the Haudenosaunee scouts were seeking. The Algonquin had villages at Whitefish Point, Shelldrake, the mouth of the river, and a rather large one further upstream. There was also at one time a concentration on Menekaunee Point, southeast of the mouth of the Tahquamenon. From your site you could hike to any of the Tahq sites. It would be less than ten miles crow-wise to the lower falls village."

This makes some sense. "They make base camp at our location and send out scouts. Where does that leave us?"

"The excavations will tell us."

"*If* anything remains," Service said.

"There is always evidence—if anyone cares to read it."

"Why did you call David Ohgwahoh now?"

"Well, we were headed here, and his story finally interested me enough to hear it firsthand."

"What about passed-down Saulteur accounts?"

"I've never encountered any. Most of what I hear are revisions of the Jesuit accounts."

"Which means the dig is everything," Service said.

Shotwiff grinned. "It usually is, son."

46

Lansing, Ingham County

FRIDAY, JUNE 15, 2007

Service's cell phone buzzed and he answered it.

"Yo, this you, Fish Cop?"

"Who's this?"

"You know who is this, hombre. You tell me I get something, we got deal, right?"

"If I lie, I die," Service said.

"You cool, Fish Cop," Hectorio said. "This line safe talk?"

"Sure."

"I ain't stupid, man. I don't trust nobody. You know dam, Gran' River, Old Town, like dat?"

"Not offhand."

"West side river. I see you there thirty minute. Not there, I figure you not serious person. Alone, no uniform, Fish Cop."

"I'll be there," Service said, looking at his Automatic Vehicle Locator system laptop and adjusting the maps until he reached Lansing. Service looked over at the professor. "You want to meet the most dangerous artifact dealer in the state capital?"

The professor grinned. "Are you serious?"

"Absolutely," Grady Service said.

• • •

He parked the Tahoe a block west of the river, on Washington Avenue, and got out, leaving the professor alone. "I call on the radio, you walk down that street to the dead end," Service said, pointing at the route. He handed his spare keys to Shotwiff. "Lock it if you leave."

Service got to a walkway along the river's edge. The Grand was a couple hundred yards across, he guessed, give or take, water the color of baby food gone bad, yet somehow this ugly, stinky water hosted robust salmon and steelhead runs. He looked around, found himself alone, and checked his watch. Five minutes early. He lit a cigarette.

"Hey, Fish Cop, who the old man in your ride?"

Hectorio stepped out from behind a large sycamore tree. He wore a loose black shirt, pegged black pants, a red Lansing Lugnuts ball cap.

"Historian," Service said. "A friend."

"He knows lotta shit, this historian you got?"

"Yeah."

"You test Hectorio, you fuck wid him?"

"I wouldn't do that. The man rode down to Lansing with me. I can't just cut him loose. He and I have business. How do *you* treat old people? What have you got for me?"

"Twenty-five K, stripend," Hectorio said.

"If your shit checks out."

"You don't say that shit when we talk back 'ways," Hectorio said.

"Do I look stupid? You got something good, I'll pay."

"Cash, no new bills."

"However you want it. Can I call the old man, ask him to join us?"

"You seeing my face is enough. I give you this."

Hectorio handed an envelope to Service. "Your guy look at them pitchers, you caw me." The man handed the DNR detective a cell phone the size of a cigarette pack. "Prepaid, man. No trace. Only got one number. You hit dial, I answer, we talk. Like dat."

Service nodded and walked west up the street, not looking back.

"Something wrong?" the professor asked.

"The guy is shy. A lot of shitballs are." Service handed the man the envelope.

"Should I wear latex gloves or something?"

"This isn't *CSI*," Service said. "This guy's too cautious to get caught by TV gimmicks. In real life the bad guys aren't all stupid."

Professor Ozzien Shotwiff studied the photographs and Service tried to be patient. He lit a cigarette and stood beside the truck, shuffling his weight between feet.

Finally Shotwiff looked up at him. "Am I supposed to think this is genuine?"

"That's what I'm asking you. Is it?"

"Do you know what it is?"

Service leaned down and looked at one of the photos. "A stick."

"It's a chief's cane, and it's carved with mnemonics, sort of hieroglyphics that recount Haudenosauneee history, starting with the league's founding. These canes are incredibly rare."

"And valuable?"

"Priceless."

"Does priceless have a pricetag?"

"There are only a few such canes around, and most of those were carved sometime in the nineteenth century. Based on the symbols in this photograph, I'm guessing this dates to the seventeenth century. There are none this old anywhere. It's one of a kind if it's real. This man you met, he has possession of this?"

"No, I think he's more of a middleman. He wants to know what we'll pay."

"The State's broke," Shotwiff pointed out.

"Never mind the State or the money source. How much?"

"Start low, one hundred thou," the professor said.

"That's *low?*"

"We'll see."

"What else can you tell me about it?"

"Ironically, it's Mohawk."

Service pressed the dialer on the diminutive phone.

"*Hola,*" Hectorio answered. "You like baseball, man?"

"Too slow for my tastes."

"That 'cause there still too many white guys in the game. You got a number for me?"

"One hundred thou."

"Don't insult me, man. I fuck you up good."

"Not an insult, just asking. How about you name a price?"

"You a clever bee-otch, Fish Cop," Hector said with a chuckle. "Okay, you want number, I say three hundred."

"No chance. One-ten."

"Hombre, you got to be serious here. This no game, man. Two hundred."

"One twenty-five."

"You loco, man."

"Hey, my guy says this is priceless. Who the fuck sells priceless? Only somebody feeling some heat. One twenty-five's the offer."

Hectorio didn't answer right away. "An' my fee, man. One-fifty."

"You takin' a fee from both ends?"

"My bidnet, man. Not yours. We got deal, Fish Cop?"

"How long until delivery?"

"Exchange this for dat, same time, *si?*"

"When?"

"I caw you back, hombre."

"When?"

"Neswick?"

"How?"

"You got phone. I got your card."

"What about security?"

"I trust you, Fish Cop. "One twinnyfie and my fee, *si?*"

"Depends on the exchange details and if the merchandise checks out. My expert gets to look it over first, *comprende?*"

"You lie, all dis shit," Hectorio said. "Make your cop stick harr. Okay, bueno, I call neswick. Remember, eh?"

"Lie, die."

"Beeleedat," the man said. "Neswick, man. You call me Aitch you want." Hectorio hung up.

Professor Shotwiff was staring at Service. "You're leading him on, right?"

"No, that thing's got to be hot. The owner wants to offload. There's opportunity here. I can smell it."

"Sounds risky."

"It could be. I asked that you examine it before we buy. I figure a man who feeds bears would find this pretty tame business."

"Sarcasm *not* appreciated," the professor grumped, his ever-present grin dissolving.

47

Pullman, Allegan County

SATURDAY, JUNE 16, 2007

"You doing okay?" Grady Service asked Professor Shotwiff as they rocketed across I-96 to Grand Rapids and headed southwest toward Allegan. They had spent the previous night at Chief Waco's temporary apartment in Holt, a Lansing suburb. The chief's wife was coming in next week to house-hunt, but wouldn't relocate until their Missouri house sold.

Father Fix-it, Charlie Nickle, had called late last night. "The family's name is Kerse, in Pullman. That's in Allegan County."

"Thanks, Father. We know."

"You *do?*"

"Annie, sons Andrew and Al."

"Remember, Detective, we're all human."

"You have the power to absolve sin, Father. Cops don't."

Service called Sergeant Lanie Wick, who supervised Allegan County COs. "Family named Kerse in Pullman," he said.

"Oh yeah, we know that crew," Wick said. "Allegan's a big county, but some families and individuals still manage to pop to the top of the cesspool. CO Red Ring has busted them for one thing after another, all of them: Annie, her old man Arno, especially the wingnutter boys Andrew and Al. The sons are nasty little pricks on their best day."

"Tell me about the parents."

"Annie is partial to sex with bipeds. I doubt Arno is that choosy. Red just told me a couple of days ago they're separated again."

"Again?"

"One of 'em goes astray and the other takes umbrage and moves out. They end up having makeup sex and the cycle starts all over again. Paragons of true physical attraction, those two."

"And the boys?"

"Running wild and fast with their fists. Classic bullies. Red had to wrestle Andy in Bear Creek the last time he had contact with them. Both boys can fight. One starts it and tires out the victim, then the other one jumps in and finishes, a real tag team."

"Nice."

"The next generation in near full flower. Why are you interested in the Clampetts?"

"Situation up in Luce County. They may be tied to it."

"You catch them on their four-wheelers? We bust them all the time for that in Allegan, Van Buren, and Ottawa. They rarely pay tickets, and we end up grabbing them on warrants the next time we catch up to them. There's *always* a next time with the Kerses, who seem genetically incapable of following rules."

Service said, "Could Red do a drive-by, look for life signs at their address?"

"I'll bump him. He thinks of them as special clients."

• • •

CO Othar "Red" Ring called. "Hubby Arno was busted last night, drunk and disorderly in Fennville. The local cops caught him urinating on the steps of a church. He's in the Allegan County lockup. Nobody's made his bail yet. Annie's truck is at her trailer."

The CO arranged to meet Service at the Kerse residence, a mobile home along a scrub-brush field and an eroded creek called Fungo Drain, on 110th Avenue.

Service offered Shotwiff the chance to stay in Lansing, saying he could pick him up on the way back, but the professor had refused. "I'm having way too much fun," the old fellow said. "Who knew all this stuff went on!"

A hand-painted sign in front of the mobile home proclaimed ANNARN-FUNGOGRILA. Service shook his head. *What the hell?* The Kerse place looked like the water-hole for motorhead outlaws: a battered gray camo duck boat; a bent and dinged-up metal bassboat; a trailer with four snowmobiles under tarps; another trailer for four-wheelers, but empty; four mud-caked 200cc dirt bikes; and two full-size Gold Wings that gleamed like polished tinfoil deposited among cigarette butts.

The woman who answered the door was barely five feet tall, with nose veins and nose rings, bloodshot eyes, dilated pupils. "Mrs. Kerse?" Service asked.

"No, I'm, like, her upstairs maid," she said curtly. "Who the fuck are you, big dude?"

Service showed her his badge. "DNR."

"What's Tweedledope and Tweedledumbass done *this* time?" she asked. "Or is it Tweedledad? They are *all* morons."

"Would you mind stepping outside?" Service asked politely.

"I think I like it right where I am," she said through the screen door.

"Please step out here," Service said, lowering his voice.

"Okay I smoke?" the woman asked.

"No," Red Ring said from Service's side.

"I don't mind," Service said, reaching for his own pack.

"You dudes want coffee?" the woman asked. "Ain't fancy-schmance, but it's fresh and hot."

"Appreciate it," Service said.

"No, thanks," Ring said, weighing in.

The woman disappeared inside and came back with two cups of coffee, a cigarette dangling unlit from her lower lip. She leaned against Service, an unspoken hint for a light. She set down the cups and lightly held the back of his hand when he flicked a flame on the lighter.

Annie Kerse had a tiny waist and long stringy brown hair. She was as tan as a coffee bean and wore tight shorts and flip-flops. Her toenails were painted black. Service could hear a tongue post click against her teeth when she talked. She was good-looking, dripping sex, and obviously not all that far up the human evolutionary scale from savage.

"Dudes, s'up, dis?" she asked, her voice not so edgy now.

"Godfroi Deslongshamps."

She immediately broke eye contact with Service and looked toward the street. "Whodat?"

"Your fingerprints are all over his cabin."

"He was a mistake is all," she said after a dramatic sigh. "You never made no mistakes?"

"How was he a mistake?"

"Dumb fucker, like told my old man he and I were hitting it."

The gist seemed clear. "Your husband disapproved?"

"Ya *think?*" she retorted, rolling her eyes. "It was like a joke, ya know, the chance to *do* God!"

"If you say so," Service said. "Where did you meet Delongshamp?"

"Kids tole me about 'im. Called him Frogman, like he was ugly. Only I think frogs is *cute,* and he's, like, hung, dude." She used her hands to approximate a size.

"Your boys beat him up."

"On account my old man went wang-chung. God's okay, ain't he?"

"He's disappeared."

The woman immediately lifted her hands in a defensive posture, stepped back, and shook her head. "I don't know nothin' 'bout *dat* shit," she said.

"How did your boys know the man?"

"They usta ride out that way."

"Four-wheelers?"

She shrugged.

"No legal trails there," Service said.

"They off in the fuckin' woods, what the diff'? People 'posed to keep mutts on leashes, but I got 'em shittin' all over my yard, dude. It ain't 'zackly murder."

"Why did your boys beat up Mr. Delongshamp and trash his place?"

She raised her eyebrows. "Duh . . . like, 'cause maybe the man was fuckin' their mama?"

"Where are your boys now?"

"Fuck I know, I ain't their PO. They come, they go, ya know, like that."

"You need to help us to help them, Mrs. Kerse."

"Only thing I *need* is my lawyer. Seriously, where's God?"

"We don't know. Maybe the mother ship beamed him up, or something."

"But he ain't dead."

"We don't know. You think he's dead? That worry you?"

"Dude, don't twist my fuckin' words. I liked the guy. We, like, had us a real good time is all."

"Do your sons beat on you?"

She laughed, genuinely amused. "I'd cap their sorry punk asses."

"I need to talk to your sons."

"And I don't, which makes that your problem, sayin'?"

"They come in voluntarily, it will make things easier."

"Them two don't do nothin' easy, sayin'?"

"Your husband gonna make bail today?"

She seemed surprised by this. "Bail for what?"

"Drunk and disorderly," Red Ring said. "Last night in Fennville."

"I ain't got no call," she said. "He okay?"

"I don't know," Service said.

"He ain't yet forgive the Frogman thing. He will. Just take time is all, with that one."

"Your husband ever beat you?"

"Nobody beat Annie Kerse lessen she mooded for the sex rough. Try beat me, I cap your ass."

"With what?"

"Got me a Wop Nine," she said with sudden enthusiasm. "Goes in size of marble, comes out like PBA bowling ball. *Bloopf!* Shit flies everywheres."

"What make?"

"Beretta," she said. "Want to see?"

Gun nuts were much the same, always gaga to talk firepower and other technical firearm trivia. "Sure."

She came back with the weapon, held it out handle first. The clip protruded from her other hand. "Shoots sweet," she said, "once you learn to dance the kick. I looked at one of them forty-cals like you DNRs carry, but I wanted knock-dudes-on-they-sorry-asses power."

Service hefted the pistol. *Freshly oiled, well maintained.* He had no doubt she practiced with it. "Yours or your husband's?"

"Sheeit," Annie Kerse said, "he a shotgun man."

"You got a holster?"

"Yeah, soft leather."

"Can I see it?"

She wrinkled an eyebrow momentarily, but went to fetch it and brought it to him.

"You got a carry card?" Service asked.

"I only pack it up north in the woods."

"The holster's rigged for concealed," he said, "and concealed from view is concealed from view. You got to have a concealed-weapon carry permit. Venue's not the issue."

"Maaan, this is chickenshit. Dude, why you hassle me?"

"We need to talk to your sons, Mrs. Kerse."

"Or you take my piece, thachersayin'?"

"That's up to you. We need to talk to your sons."

She seemed to ponder her predicament for a moment. "Fuck the little shits. They got a flop about a mile north on Van Riper."

"That's also Pullman?"

She nodded.

"Got an address?"

Service followed her inside and she grabbed for her cell phone. He covered her hand with his and took it away from her. "Unannounced," he said. "No head starts."

"I was, like, just gonna put the phone on the charger, dude."

"Right."

"Can't blame a mama for being a mama," she said with a pathetic grin.

A belated, ill-timed start at mothering probably beats no start at all. "You got a landline?"

"No, dude."

"Computer?"

"Dude, back off."

"We get there and they aren't there, we're coming back here and you will get to go visit hubby. Aid and abet, flee and elude, illegal carry firearms, unregistered weapon—there's all sorts of potential stuff on your menu, Annie. Felonies included."

She crossed her arms. "Like I said, fuck 'em both. They all yours, but make sure ya tell 'em they mama loves 'em."

Red Ring rolled his eyes as they walked toward their trucks. "You want dep support?"

"Think we need it?"

"Wouldn't hurt. This pair ain't the most steadfast dominoes in line."

"But they defend their mama's reputation."

"Ah, one redeeming quality," Ring said. "If that qualifies."

• • •

The address took them to a small one-story ranch house, neatly kept, lawn mowed, not at all what Service had expected. Overly enthusiastic deputies from Allegan County were already there and had made contact. The boys were on the sidewalk in cuffs, wriggling and grunting curses, their faces bright red. They wore long basketball shorts, no shirts. Service saw that they were big kids, six-fourish, bulked and ripped, obviously tasered into submission. Drool hung from their mouths, snot from their heaving nostrils. Delongshamp was lucky to have survived a beating from this pair.

An Allegan County deputy looked at Service and patted his taser. "Hard-asses. They forced us to go to old Flash Gordon and give 'em a ride on the lightning."

The brothers glared at Service. Two girls sat on a white wicker love seat on the porch. They wore string bikinis and had mussed hair, both of them smoking. "*Their* story?" Service asked the dep.

"Scrompdoggies," the deputy said dismissively.

"How *old* are they. They look twelve."

"How many twelve-year-olds you know built like that? This is Allegan-tucky, man. Girls grow up fast out here."

"Age of the boys?"

"Nineteen and twenty, you believe their licenses."

Service took the licenses from the deputy and compared photos to faces. Andrew was the eldest. "Andrew?"

"Fuck off," the boy said.

"These girls with you and Al, they're underage."

"Said they was over eighteen," Andrew countered.

"Inches maybe," Service said. "They're jailbait, Andrew, and I smell dope."

"Dude, it rude ask ta check ID wit' my dick inner mouth, true dat?"

What was it with white hillbillies trying to dress, talk, and walk like a lot of black city kids?

No reaction to the dope comment. The smell was heavy. "Who pays for your house?"

Andrew grinned demonically. "We work, dude."

"Doing what?"

"This, that, sayin'?"

"Like dealing skunk?"

"Fuck 'em," younger brother chimed in. "Don't say shit."

A dep came out of the house. "Baggies all over the place, and some very odd things in one of the bedrooms."

Service followed him into the house, which reeked of skunkweed, the cheapest and poorest quality of marijuana. An old door was laid between twin beds in a bedroom. There were three plastic bags filled with arrowheads and flint points. And two rusted ax heads.

"You got any idea about this shit?" the deputy asked.

"Native American artifacts."

"Legal?"

"Depends on how they came by them."

Back outside, Service said, "Nice collection in there, Andrew. You buy them or deal for them?"

"We don't do drugs," Andrew said.

"We do," one of the young girls volunteered. "You dudes got some?" she asked hopefully.

"Get Dad!" the younger brother shouted.

"Your father's in jail," Service said, "and you two are adults."

"Drunk tank," the deputy added. "I heard it on the radio last night. Pissing on church steps."

"We're placing you under arrest," Grady Service announced to the boys. He took a laminated card out of his wallet and began to read the boys their Miranda rights.

"Arrest for what?" Andrew asked.

"Grave robbery—to start," Service said.

"We did *not* rob no graves, dude," Andrew said emphatically.

"Stuff on the beds in there says differently."

"Dude, we just picked that shit up from the ground. We did not dig up no fuckin' graves."

"And that motherfuck stiff us on the job, too," younger brother chimed in.

"Who?"

"The Frogman," Andrew said. "We want a lawyer."

Service finished reading them their rights and stepped over to the girls. The girls stared up at him. "You sure you two are eighteen?"

"We don't look it?" one of them asked.

"I need to see some ID."

One of the girls snapped her string bikini bottoms and her gum. "Where we gonna carry ID, dude, like up our twat pockets? Whyfor you hassle them boys?"

"They've been robbing graves," Red Ring said.

"*Eeeeww!*" the girls said in unison. "That is so *nasty!*"

48

Allegan, Allegan County

SATURDAY, JUNE 16, 2007

Former DNR lieutenant Eugene McKirnan had retired fifteen years ago. He had a summer home near the Allegan dam, and wintered in south Texas. Service dropped off Professor Shotwiff with his retired colleague and headed for the county jail to talk to the Kerse brothers.

The two were still being processed into custody when Service got to the jail. The shift sergeant greeted him with a nod. "You want them booked?"

"Not if I can work a deal. They call a lawyer yet?"

"Nope. They're pretty quiet and behaving right now."

"Weed?" Service asked.

The dep said, "Was speed we'd be goin' rounds with 'em. You want 'em separately or together?"

"Together will work."

The sergeant pointed down the hall. "That room."

"Their old man still here?"

"Is indeed. Bail bondsman said he'd come see him Monday. You want him in this powwow too?"

"Sure, we'll make it a trifecta of assholes."

The sergeant laughed and left him.

• • •

The three sat at one table, not looking at each other. They wore orange jump-suits and paper slippers.

Service introduced himself to the father, Arno Kerse. "Your boys tell you what they're doing here?"

"Me and them two ain't got much to say."

"No gratitude for them kicking the ass of the guy who was *schtupping* your wife?"

The father looked at the boys. "You done that?"

"We wasn't lettin' him get off free," Andrew said.

"Stiffed us, too," brother Al added.

Service announced, "They're being charged with grave robbery, a federal Class A felony, ten years for each count."

Arno Kerse looked befuddled. "Them two ain't no angels, but they don't dig up no damn dead bodies."

"Artifacts at their place tell a different story," Service said.

The father looked shocked. "Arrowheads. This is about *arrowheads?*"

"Artifacts," Service said. "You can't take them off public land."

He had not had time to run down all the technicalities of charge possibilities and was making this up as he went. His gut said these three were meaningless, but that they might point him somewhere important.

"People pick up arrowheads all the time," the father argued. "You can buy them anywheres up there. Hell, the Boy Scout leader here has crates and bottles filled with that shit."

"I understand what you're saying," Service said, "but laws pertain."

"Look, my boys're all pussy when it comes to dead bodies, graves and shit."

The sons glanced at their father. "We ain't no pussies," the younger one said defiantly.

"What law did they break?" the father asked, ignoring his younger son.

"Archaeological Resources Protection Act, the Native American Graves Protection and Repatriation Act, and the Michigan Penal Code."

"Dude," the eldest son said. "There wasn't no bones. No bones and no damn graves."

"Which is a good thing," Service said quickly. "Otherwise the charges would be a lot more severe."

Arno's voice was rising. "Some dumb brave drops his goddamn quiver, the arrows rot, and my boys find the points like a million years later, and *this* is a fucking felony? Are you *fucking serious?* What's happening to this country?"

Service sensed an opening. "Why don't you tell me where the points were found. If it's different than the site we have identified, maybe we can make an exception here."

"Maybe we oughta get them a lawyer," Arno Kerse said.

"That's your right, Mr. Kerse, but no charges have been filed yet, which means we have time and space to talk. You bring in a lawyer, everything gets formal and no road leads home. Understand?"

Service could see that the man was trying to weigh his options. "What if my boys could tell you where and who they work for?"

"Depends on what they have to say, and how it checks out," Service said.

"They won't lie, will you, boys?" the father said, looking at his sons.

The younger son stared at the floor.

"Delongshamp," Andrew Kerse said. "We set nets for him and that other weirdo."

"Peewee," the younger son contributed.

"Nets?" Service asked.

"For the big buck," Andrew Kerse said. "Huge guy."

"You're telling me you both set capture nets?"

"Yeah, and we run some deer with our four-wheelers. Bolf, he'd come up on the radio and tell us where to go, and we'd go and yell and scream and drive crazy and run the deer at them nets."

"You get any?"

"Wun't let us see," the elder brother said.

"But you knew there was a big buck."

"They had pictures, ya know, from trail cameras over bait. A twelve-point."

"What were they going to do with the animal? It's in velvet, right?"

"They didn't tell us nothing 'bout that."

"How would they get the animal out of there?"

"Little crick over east of Vermilion. They usta put a boat up there and park their truck in the public tourist lot."

"In daylight?"

"Only night," Andrew said.

"How often did this happen?"

The brothers made eye contact. "Four times—five?" Andrew said.

"For pay?"

"Beer and twenty bucks each, but las' time, Frogman, he skip the lou on us, sayin'?"

Andrew added, "Then we hear Mom been scrompin' wid dat Frog, and we went and give 'im da what-for. He say Bolf would pay what we earned, that it was an overbite or something. But we never seen them guys again," the younger son recounted.

English as a second language. "So this happened recently?"

"Night before they defended my honor," Arno said with an odd touch of pride.

Arno's playing dumb. "Delongshamp told us we were done, that they was leavin," Andrew explained.

"And my old lady announced she was going *with* the Frog!" Arno shouted.

Service closed his eyes. "This is the sixteenth. You're talking about the night of the eleventh, yes?"

"Afternoon. Don't 'member date," Andrew said.

"Delongshamp say what he and Bolf wanted with the big buck?"

"They didn't talk much."

"Where'd the arrowheads and axheads come from?"

"From where we was settin' nets. They was just layin' all over the ground." Andrew Kerse seemed to describe the exact place Service and Sedge were dealing with.

"You saw a boat, or they told you about one?"

"We seen it. She was maybe twenty feet, had a deck built on the back, and two sawhorses on top the platform."

"Sawhorses."

"Looked like lat us," Andrew said.

"You saw the men in the boat, or with it?"

"Nope, we just seen the boat one night."

"Color, registration numbers?"

"Gray, a beater, we didn't notice no numbers."

"But the *truck* was black," the younger son said.

"They had a truck?"

" 'Lectrick. It was real weird, with a flatbed and more sawhorses."

"Like the boat?"

The young men nodded and shrugged.

"That Frogman nark on us, man?" Andrew asked.

"He didn't have to. If you cause physical harm and damage, the victim doesn't have to file charges. We can do it *for* the victim."

"We ain't got nothin' more," Andrew Kerse said. "What happens now?"

"You sit tight and I'll get back to you."

Service left them together and went outside and telephoned Sedge and filled her in. "You gonna kick them?" she asked.

"I'm going to issue written warnings for illegal possession of Native American funerary objects."

"We don't know if it's a burial ground," Sedge said.

"I just need some flypaper to get them back if we need them."

"You need cites from the penal code?"

"Yeah, but I'll turn the tickets in at the court, and one of the magistrate's people can help me find what we need."

"Don't bother," she said. "Nobody's gonna be working the weekend. Write them on 750.387 and 750.160. That will take care of it. Basically disturbing graves. Why were they out there?"

"Setting nets for Kermit."

"No shit? Ribbit, ribbit," she said happily. "They saw him use the nets?"

"Nope, they set them up and admitted to herding animals with their four-wheelers. Kermit and his pal Peewee had a boat stashed at Vermilion, and it sounds like it was outfitted similarly to the truck we heard about."

"You want me to head over that way and look around?"

"Can't hurt."

"You?"

"Gotta get Shotwiff back and find home myself."

"I'll call you after Vermilion," she said.

He and the professor would spend the night at McKirnan's and head north in the morning. It felt like a year since he had seen Shigun or Tuesday. *Balance*, he told himself. *Seek balance.*

PART III: BLACK WITCH

49

Strongs, Chippewa County

SUNDAY, JUNE 17, 2007

Sedge called as they were driving east of McBain angling toward US-127. "Katsu wants a meet at his place," she announced.

"When?"

"Where are you now?"

"Approaching Vogel Center, west of Houghton Lake."

"Okay then. Northbound is good."

"Did you get out to Vermilion?"

"Not only that, I found the boat."

"In the creek?"

"No, on a trailer on a road near old Whitefish Cemetery. Someone called it in."

"Plates?"

"Reported stolen from downstate."

"Where?"

"Okemos."

Near Lansing. "What's Katsu want?"

"He won't say. He sounded kind of edgy. He asked about Shotwiff, and wants to talk to him too."

"Good, we'll be his daily double. You want to give me some directions?"

"Better. I'll meet you at Strongs Corners on M-28 and lead the way. Bump me when you cross the big bridge."

"Three hours, give or take," Service said.

Shotwiff was watching him. "Sedge," Service told the professor. "She says Katsu wants to see both of us. You in a hurry to get home?"

"It'll still be there when I get there," Shotwiff said. "Have you any idea why the Five-Pack Creek Band hasn't gotten federal recognition?"

"It's a slow process, I guess."

"That's true, but were I a betting man, I'd wager the Sault Tribe is blocking them. The Sault group takes umbrage at any of their Native American brothers getting any gains in power, real or imagined. The infighting between tribes can be quite nasty, and it's vastly misunderstood and discounted by the government."

"But the Five-Pack Creek Band is real?"

"It *was*. Makes you wonder if the Sault crowd understands the potential downside of Katsu's site."

"It's that significant?"

"Not in the grand scheme of the planet, but in the American Indian world, it's a big deal for sure. The Saulteurs have already made out how they led the battle against the *Na-do-we-se* in 1662, even though history suggests it was a combined, thrown-together force; in any event, most Saulteurs were way over in Keweenaw and not likely to be back this far east in any significant numbers. The lighthouse at Iroquois Point attracts tourists from all over. They shop and eat in Brimley and lots of them gamble at Bay Mills and over to the Soo. Take the battle away from the lighthouse site and what happens? Only hardheads would make their way out to Katsu's remote site. The point is, word will spread that Iroquois Point isn't the place, and that's likely to concern Sault and Bay Mills leadership."

• • •

Friday called as they refueled in Indian River. "Where are you now—Jamaica, Shanghai . . . Mars?" She sounded happy.

"Indian River," Service said.

"Karylanne called."

"Everything okay in Houghton?"

"Little Mar and her mom are fine. She was just checking in."

"As in checking up on me?"

"Pretty much."

"How's our little man?"

"Hungry," Friday said. "At this rate he'll be six foot when he's five. Are you gonna have some pass days when you get back?"

"I hope."

"*We* hope, you dope. *We.* Home tonight?"

"We hope," he said.

Friday giggled. "See, old dogs *can* learn new tricks. Where are you headed now?"

"Strongs. I called Shark a few minutes ago. He'll be over to spend the night, take the professor home in the morning."

"God," she said. "I loathe delayed gratification."

• • •

Duncan Katsu's home was precisely as Sedge had described it: a one-story box in the woods. There were seven or eight dogs of indeterminate lineage running loose and barking excitedly. Their presence made Service nervous about getting out of the truck, but the professor got out and the dogs mobbed him, tails wagging, like he was some kind of pied piper.

Katsu met them at the door and invited them in. He pointed at a table in a breakfast nook, made fresh coffee, and heated frybread in the microwave. Service looked around. No artifacts, little decoration of any kind, few personal touches, but the place was spotless and organized. Somehow, not what he'd expected.

"You wanted to see us?" Service said.

"Try the bread, sip coffee, slow down," Katsu said.

Is he laid-back or uptight? Can't read him. This is a new mood. Something's changed.

"Very good bread," Shotwiff said, chewing slowly. "You get a visit from the Sault boys?"

Katsu was caught off guard and stammered. "You privy to tribal drums?"

"I'm old, and believe it or not, experience counts. They don't like your find, am I right?"

"They say I'm wrong—that tribal history says the original place was the site of the battle."

"They come with carrot or stick?"

"Both," Duncan Katsu said. "If I back off they pledge to throw their weight behind the band's recognition drive."

"And if you don't?"

"The opposite—unspoken and unspecified, of course."

"Their evidence for their site vis-à-vis yours?"

"Possession . . . tradition."

Shotwiff grunted softly. "They come on strong?"

"More direct than strong, you know, calm and businesslike. The strong-arm will come later, behind my back, hit and run."

"Your criminal history," Sedge said.

Katsu nodded. "One of their points, absolutely."

"Are you asking us to back off?" Service asked.

"I just thought we should talk about developments."

Vacillating, unsure. "How about this development? Our chief went to bat for you with the acting state archaeologist. With slight modifications Toliver will be allowed to test-dig."

Katsu's faced pruned.

"We know you don't trust Toliver," Sedge said, "but he *is* qualified, and this way you can sit right with him and monitor his work."

"I won't have a role," Katsu said. "Lac Vieux Desert, Keweenaw, Saginaw, Sault—these are the federally recognized Chippewa groups eligible for BIA services. Under NAGPRA the U.S. Park Service will be responsible for securing the site and will coordinate with BIA to determine cultural affiliation. If this is the battle site, they'll probably call in the Mohawk and Oneida too."

"NAGPRA's got no real authority on state land," Shotwiff announced. "NAGPRA applies only to federal and Indian land, and, in some cases, to private land with exterior boundaries of Indian reservations, whatever the blazes that means. Because this is state land, a permit will need to be issued under the auspices of the Archaeological Resources Protection Act, the state archaeologist, and the DNR. The feds will have nothing to do with it unless the state invites them in. The Sault Tribe has no legal transport into the game."

"They can delay with litigation," Katsu said. "Some call them the S-U-E tribe, and that's not meant as a joke."

"They can delay," the professor agreed, "but this is the sort of thing public opinion can play a role in. People will want to know the historic truth. In my business we call this the Indiana Jones legacy. People actually care about this stuff."

"With Michigan's economic problems, the Sault Tribe will claim the State can't afford excavation costs."

"Let them," Sedge said. "The state's not paying. Toliver's college is funding the dig."

Shotwiff held his cup out for a refill. "Might be some bumps ahead, but they'll be moguls, not mountains."

"*If* this is the place," Katsu said, not exuding confidence.

50

Harvey, Marquette County

MONDAY, JUNE 18, 2007

"Call me if you need me," Ozzien Shotwiff said as he headed west with Shark Wetelainen.

"And then there were two," Friday said, grinning.

"If we don't count Shigun."

"Work with me on this, Service. It's just us today," she beamed.

"You don't work?"

"Nope, and neither are you—at least not for the State."

"You working tomorrow?" he asked.

"Depends on how today goes," she said.

"I hate tests."

"Deal with it."

• • •

Shigun was down for his early afternoon nap when Service's cell phone buzzed. He looked for a nod from Friday before picking up. "Service."

"*Hola,* this Aitch, man. I tell you neswick, it neswick now."

"Barely," Grady Service said.

"My guy, he ain't so sure one twinnyfie cut id."

"The offer's on the table. There ain't gonna be any more, Aitch."

"This ting it priceless, like Dorothy's fuck-me ruby slippers, *comprende?*"

"I understand, but the bargaining is done."

"Mebbe my guy, he say I should find another buyer."

"Yeah, he might. Meanwhile, I sic the IRS and DEA and BIA on you, and tell them all what you have, and we'll see where it all shakes out when the dust clears. If it clears. That IRS shit hangs around like dinosaur farts."

"I tole you Aitch ain't got nothin', man. Like all them letters and such make me sick."

"Talk to your guy. You're a businessman; help him see the deal as a safe way to unload."

"He gotta stay behind his wall—you know that, right?"

"Aitch, what's with all the whining? I thought you were the man."

"I am the man," Hectorio said unconvincingly.

"Then act like it," Service said, cutting the line.

"Problem?" Friday asked.

"Nope." Something clearly was spooking Hectorio. What or who could do that?

Friday stood by the sliding back screen. "Have you noticed how dry it is?" She turned, grinned, and pointed at the backyard. "Out there, not in here."

51

Harvey, Marquette County

MONDAY, JULY 23, 2007

A training-class slot unexpectedly opened for Sedge at the Ram Center on Higgins Lake, and she had taken off downstate for a full week of special man-tracking training. When she returned, the initial summer invasion of four-wheelers had begun. Outlaw gearheads were tearing apart Luce County and kept her running around, writing tickets at the rate of nearly a book a day, which was a lot.

Grinda had called the museum man as arranged, but he'd given her a new number, telling her to stand by for a call from him. And not a word from Hectorio since their last brief conversation. Everything felt like it was grinding to a halt, except for life with Friday and Shigun; the three of them had lived together for almost an entire month in what he guessed was close to a normal daily life.

He liked it a lot. He had even managed to get all his Wildlife Resource Protection Unit files mailed down to Milo Miars.

During this period, he had talked several times with Master Sergeant Bearnard Quinn, and they had come up with an approach to evaluating personnel. Quinn would write up his evaluations and send them as e-mail attachments.

It had been a plodding, enjoyable time, but he sensed a change this morning when Sheena called as he was pouring coffee for Friday. "Clatchety called me from Trout Lake. Our museum guy?"

"I remember." Actually, he *had* forgotten the man's name, but it was somewhere in his notes . . . he hoped. "What's he want?" *Is it normal to be so forgetful?* He was having more and more trouble juggling lots of facts and details.

"Says he has a quote 'special viewing opportunity,' end quote, of a one-of-a-kind piece."

"Description?"

"You heard the whole thing. One-of-a-kind."

"When?"

"Friday, July twenty-seventh."

"What did you tell him?"

"I agreed, but told him I wanted my hubby with me."

"Simon?"

"No, *you.*"

"He agreed?"

"Remember how I described him as tentative the first time I met him?"

He did.

"There's been a sea change. Whatever this thing is that he's got, he's spewing major geek sweat for a sale. He didn't say so much, but I could sense it."

"You write your report yet?"

She laughed at him. "God, you *sound* like a sergeant. No, I haven't had time. When we need it, then I'll put it together; okay by you?"

"Fine." Good time management on her part. "What time's our meeting?"

"Thirteen hundred hours. One truck or two?"

"Let's hook up at the district office at eleven hundred. I'll drive my personal truck and we can use that."

"Sounds like a plan," she said.

"You run the Mercedes license plate?" he asked, suddenly remembering her visit to the museum.

"Steel-trap mind," she said. "Okemos address."

Hmmm. He wrote *Okemos* in his notebook. "Name?"

"Imago Neil Held. I called Bill Curry, asked him to talk to Ingham County, see what he can find out about Mr. Held."

"And?"

"No word back yet from Bill." Curry was a longtime CO in Lansing who somehow managed to keep his nose out of office intrigue and do his field job right in the city and local area.

"Keep me posted."

"See you Friday."

Service called Jingo Sedge. "That boat and trailer you found?"

"What about them?"

"Owner's name?"

"Let me check my notes." After a few moments she said, "Malcolm Fallkrome." She spelled it for him.

"Okemos, right?"

"Good memory!"

"Did you talk to him?"

"I did. He reported the trailer stolen last year."

"What about boat registration? Was that current?"

"Wasn't a number on the boat. Looks like one got sanded off. Mr. Fallkrome says the boat isn't his. He inherited the trailer from an uncle. He's never owned a boat."

"You check out those claims?"

"Should I?"

"Every detail, remember?"

"Okay."

"Do me a favor; call Bill Curry in Ingham. Sheena has him checking a name linked to the museum gig. Play your name by him, ask if he can look for connections."

"What connections?"

"If we knew that we wouldn't be asking for help. I'm not exactly sure. Linkage?"

"Are we in teensy-tiny straw-grope mode here?"

"Getting close, I think."

"Okay, I'm on it, Sarge. You there this week, or here?"

"Not sure yet. Let's hear what Curry comes up with."

Service dressed Shigun and dropped him with his daycare sitter. As he headed for his office at The Roof, Chief Waco called. He waited until he was parked in the office lot before calling back.

"Everything is signed and sealed for the dig," the chief said. "The assistant SA signed on Friday, and DEQ will sign this morning. You want to let your people know?"

"Yes, thanks. Your wife find a house yet?"

"An old place on the Grand River near Dimondale. Got some outbuildings, and forty acres on both sides."

"Sounds good. Thanks, Chief."

"You talked with Sergeant Quinn?"

"Several times. We've worked out a rough plan. We'll send it to you for comment."

"I look forward to reading it."

"You're going to announce what we're doing, right?"

"Yessir, after we finalize the plan. We move forward together, always together, Michigan man."

"Roger that," Service said. Eddie Waco had all the earmarks of a real leader.

Service hit the speed-dial number for Sedge.

"You lonesome this morning, or what?" she asked sarcastically.

"The dig permit papers have been signed. You want to let Toliver and Katsu know?"

"DEQ signed off?"

"DEQ signs this morning. The chief just called me. I think he has personally walked this stuff through the gauntlet. The OSA signed on Friday."

"I'll let Toliver know. He and his crew are already here gathering supplies and equipment, but he won't move out to the site until he has paper in hand."

"Does he know Katsu will be with him?"

"He will in a few minutes."

"And it's not negotiable," Service said.

"I hear you," she said.

"How long for Toliver to roll once he has paper?"

"Two days to move equipment into place and organize the site. Three days to break ground, he insists. He's acting really finicky and cautious."

"He'll have paper this week—Friday at the latest—which translates to July twenty-seventh, yes?"

"Sounds about right to me, but I'll verify when I talk to him today. I'm going to alter my patrol plans to stay close to the dig site," she said. "Sergeant Bryan will pitch in to help."

"Good thinking. I'll call when I know how my week is shaping up. Sheena and I have a meet at the museum on Friday."

"Both of you?"

"I'll be her husband."

Sedge laughed. "That's a concept to defy all logic."

Everybody has to be a comic. He hung up, looked at his notes, and called her again.

"*Now* what?" she challenged.

"Horses."

"What about them?"

"You follow that anywhere?"

"Sheena and I sent samples down to the lab at MSU. No word back yet."

"Got a name down there?"

"Arthur Causey, DVM. Why?"

"My mind keeps coming back to the damn horses. You care if I run with this one?"

"Knock yourself out. Before we end this conversation, is there anything else I can help you with, Sergeant Service?"

"Nope, that should do it."

"I hope so," she said, and hung up.

• • •

Dr. Arthur Causey was quiet and sturdy, deliberate. "You got the horse tissue samples?"

"We did," the vet said.

"Run tox yet?"

"Yes, but not the standard panel."

What standard panel? "I don't understand."

"It's along the lines of a hunch," the forensics man said.

"*What's* along the lines of a hunch?"

"The direction I took."

"Enlighten me."

"When I was a boy my father worked at a small college in northern California. My dad was a doctor, one of the pioneer transplant surgeons, and he was looking for drugs to stop or minimize organ and tissue rejection."

Causey would not be rushed. He had a story to tell. "Was he successful?"

"Not exactly, but he stumbled onto an approach, and when one of his collaborators left, he took the work with him. The result was that a large company got involved and commercialized the process and sought FDA approval."

"For the idea?"

"For ATG."

Patience. "Which is?"

"Antithymocyte gamma globulin."

"And this relates to our samples *how?*"

"Technically it is called horse antithymocyte gamma globulin. Horses are injected with various agonists to stimulate antibody production in their blood. Then blood is extracted from the horse and the antigens are separated and purified."

"So the horse is a kind of factory? The pure stuff is called ATG?"

"Yes."

"I think I'm with you so far, Doctor. What about our case made you think about your dad and his work?"

"Well, I might not have if Officer Sedge had not included photographs of the site. When I saw the disposition of the carcasses, a lightbulb illuminated in my head."

"Because?"

"My dad used to take me to see his horses. He and his team took great care of them, but when you use a large animal in this way, with constant blood agonist challenges and blood removal, a lot of scar tissue forms over time."

"Scar tissue?"

"Ugly scar tissue. Think Frankenhorse."

A joke? "And?"

"The animals weren't in pain, but they looked extremely bad, and when the project was completed the decision was made to humanely euthanize the animals and quietly and secretly dispose of their remains. There was great fear of antagonizing the antivivisectionists and creating a furor. So the disposal was done in the dark of night. The animals were slaughtered, and the remains were highly reminiscent of those your people discovered."

"What are you telling me, Doctor?"

"I ran a toxicology panel on your samples. The blood from those horses shows significant antigenic quantities."

"That ATG thing?"

"Highly possible."

"That's still being done?"

"The process has been commercialized and patents granted, but if you are a researcher on a limited budget in an academic setting, you might be concerned about even more venomous antivivisection extremists these days. The movement is virulent, and there are many ways to manufacture small quantities of ATG."

"How long ago did your father do his work?"

"Into the 1980s."

"Do your results show where our samples came from?"

"Science and toxicology do not yet provide such data on faunal samples."

"So ATG is all we know?"

"Well, there is another element in the panel results."

"Which is?"

"Somehow there were non-Michigan soil traces mixed in."

"You can tell this?"

"I identified nonindigenous microflora, so I called my wife in for a consultation. She's a soil scientist at the university. It took her less than two hours to give us an answer. The soil in the equine samples is green gumbo cleche clay, found mainly in Cedar Falls, Texas. Apparently that's in south Dallas County."

"Your wife is sure?"

"She knows soil like some people know sports statistics—it's her passion and her profession."

My wife, the dirt queen. "Meaning our horses came from there?"

"Of course not. It's not possible to determine point of origin, unless we have faunal reference samples, which we could then use to compare RNA. Absent faunal samples, we're left with what we have. The animals indirectly or directly picked up green gumbo cleche clay."

"Indirectly?"

"Off a shoe sole, or a truck bed," Dr. Causey said. "Or should I say boots in this instance?"

"Will there be a report?"

"Yes, but not with any great dispatch. We're barely staying afloat here with the state's budget crunch."

I feel your pain, pal. "Thanks, this is helpful," Service said, and hung up. *Close to something here, real close. It's in my gut.* He called Information to get the phone number of the Cedar Falls Texas Police Department. He dialed the number, and after a couple of intermediate stops, ended up with Chief Jackie Jay Emerson on the other end.

"Chief Emerson?"

"Yessir," the man said.

"Grady Service, chief master sergeant, Michigan Department of Natural Resources. I've got a sort of left-field question for you. It relates to a case we're investigating."

"Let 'er run," Chief Emerson said.

"Have you had horse theft problems down your way?"

Emerson chuckled. "Back when we hung horse thieves on the spot we didn't have too much of a problem, but we done went and got civilized, and there ain't no more capital punishment for horse thieves. We still get us the odd case now and then. Citizens still git all worked up over it, but we don't string 'em up no more."

"Are there drug companies or college labs near you?"

"Them questions related?" the chief asked.

"That's what I'm trying to determine."

"Well, son, the thing about Texas is that if there's a way to make yourself some money, legally or otherwise, you can bet some would-be cowboy will be doing it."

"What about cattle rustling, horse theft, and your local whitetail deer population?"

"Hold on, Sergeant Service. We got deer, but not like other counties. As for cattle rustling, that happens too. Anything else before I try to stitch together some answers?"

"That's it, so far."

"You mind I get back to you on this stuff?"

"Thanks, Chief."

"Call me Jackie Jay."

"Grady here."

"Glad to meet you, Grady. I'll be back at you soon as I can."

• • •

Sedge called. "I just talked to Toliver. He is overjoyed at the permission coming through, and ready to commit significant violence on my body over Katsu."

"Think we need to let Special Agent Jane Rain know the score?"

"I'm headed out to see her now. I'm sure Toliver will tell her, but I want her to hear directly what I have to say."

"I think I'll head over your way midweek," he said.

"That would be good."

52

Newberry, Luce County

WEDNESDAY, JULY 25, 2007

CO Bill Curry's voice sounded like it had been cured in pickle brine and coated with ground glass. "I gotta call you Sarge now, or Big Shot? Sedge asked me to give you a bump."

"Service works fine."

"You ain't heard of Imago Neil Held?"

"Just heard that name for the first time the other day"

"Republicommie, you know to each according to his need, from each according to his ability—as long as each is a fatcat rich motherfucker who would just as soon wipe his Eye-tye loafers on John Q. Public as give him one red cent of government assistance. Mr. Held owns a big hunt club in Hillsdale County, two full sections of land. You should talk to Milo Miars about him. He was inside-the-wire undercover there. Held claims the club is members only, but the buy-in seems awfully steep. Once you get inside you can sit in an overstuffed chair and shoot you a big-ass old buck."

"All raised right there on the property."

"That's the claim."

"Evidence otherwise?"

"Common sense is all. No evidence, and no reason to get a warrant to seize something. They butcher, cure skins, and do trophy mounting right there on the property. Held was one of Clearcut's asshole buddies. Reporters dubbed him the attack-ad king of America. And he's big with the gun rights people and the NRA."

"He owns a Mercedes."

"That a question or a comment? Sumbitch prolly owns a fleet."

"He into antiquities?"

"You mean like antiques, curios, gizmos of old?"

"Indian stuff."

"Never heard that, but wouldn't surprise me."

"You know anyone who has been into his home?"

"Not really."

"How about the name Malcolm Fallkrome?"

Long pause. "Well, that's one asshole surely been inside Held's pad."

"They're connected?"

"Fallkrome is Held's top copywriter, asshole buddy, you know, all that I-love-you-man-group-hug-modern-pussy-man bullshit."

"Hunt club member?"

"Wouldn't surprise me. Hey, I answered all this for Sedge already. What the hell is going on?"

"How did Sedge explain it?"

"Tight Lips? She wouldn't say shit. Keeps her cases close."

"But she asked you to call me."

"She did indeed."

"And you made the Fallkrome–Held connection for her."

"Sure did."

"What did she say when she heard that?"

"She said, 'Ain't that some shit.' Verbatim. It's nice to chat with you, Service, but am I supposed to do something more here?"

"Maybe. Held or Fallkrome know you?"

"I've met both, but I doubt either took note."

"You got a smooth-talking officer in your district?"

"Jerron Alwine."

"New?"

"From Nantz's class," Curry said.

Nantz, his late girlfriend, had attended the academy until injuries from an assailant had forced her to drop out.

"Too young. Someone with ten years, scar tissue."

"Lyydi Enojarvi."

"Yooper-born, right—Calumet?" Enojarvi had a solid reputation and was known to be fearless and clever.

"That's her."

"She never struck me as a gold-tongue."

"Guess you got to work with her to see it. She's smooth, smart, listens, and never panics. Not ever."

"Think she could handle Held's club?"

"Don't see why not. Looks alone will open most doors for her."

"Talk to her and mention Milo, or I will talk to her about a possible UC job."

"I can do that. We done now?"

"Yep."

Held allegedly runs a pay-per-kill operation, but calls it a club. The lawyers will have to look at the charter, see how it's set up. Or I can take a shortcut.

Grady Service called Zhenya Leukonovich of the IRS, got her answering machine, and left a message for her to call him.

He called Chief Jackie Jay Emerson in Sweet Cedar, Texas, and deadended to another machine. After the beep, he said, "Grady Service here. Joseph Paul Brannigan. Add that to the mix of subjects."

Marquette County sheriff Sergeant Weasel Linsenman took a long time to answer his cell phone, eventually uttering a tentative "Yes?"

"I need a little favor."

"I heard they gave you stripes," Linsenman said. "Congrats and condolences. All your favors scare the shit out of normal folk like me."

"Cops aren't afraid of anything."

Linsenman chuckled. "This one is afraid of everything, man. What do you want?"

"Thought you'd never ask. Limpy Allerdyce."

"Stand by one," Linsenman said and set the phone down hard. Service could hear him rustling around in the background and then he was back on the line. "Okay, I took my Zantac. That name alone turns on my heartburn like a faucet."

"I need for you to drive out to his compound and ask him to call me."

"If he's got a phone to call you, why can't you call him?"

"Weasel."

"I know, I know. It's Allerdyce. Regular rules and logic never apply. Man, that cannibal camp creeps me out."

"It's not like the old days," Service said.

"Maybe not for you. The rest of us aren't on a first-name basis with the asshole."

"You'll do it?"

"Shit. But you owe me."

Linsenman had once saved Service's life and this left a debt Service doubted he'd ever be able to repay.

"Call you on your cell, eh?"

"Yep."

"Youse around here?"

"Newberry."

"Okay, man. I'll head down there tomorrow, first thing. Needs to be daylight before I go near *that* place."

53

Paradise, Chippewa County

WEDNESDAY, JULY 25, 2007

Delmure Arcton Toliver had rented four small, rickety tourist cabins on Whitefish Bay. They were south of Paradise and north of the remains of the old lumber town of Emerson. The cabins were made of logs and painted pink. Toliver had been on Sedge's case since she'd told him about Katsu's status with the dig.

Jane Rain pottered in a small kitchen while Service and Toliver sat in a narrow sitting room. "The man has no credentials, no experience, no education, and no role in this," Toliver insisted.

"He has roots at the site. You don't."

"That is not relevant and you know it."

"Professor Ozzien Shotwiff thinks differently," Service said.

"Is that psychotic windbag still alive?"

"Not just alive, he's examined the site."

Toliver's color drained. "He'll be there *too?*"

"To visit."

"It's *my* dig."

"Yes, it is, but it's also state land, and the professor's presence is not your call. You are there at the pleasure of the people of the State of Michigan, and Katsu will be with you, and Shotwiff and any number of other individuals may be there as well—as the State decides. Officer Sedge has a job that encompasses a lot more than you and your narrow interests. You keep giving her a hard time and I'll tell her she can stop being polite."

"You call her attitude *polite?*"

"See her in a temper flare and then you can tell me."

"I don't like this."

"You don't have to like it. You have your dig. Be happy with that. How long to break ground?"

"We started moving equipment into place yesterday. It will be done by Friday. The rest of my team comes in Sunday. If I have the permits in my hand Friday, we'll start digging Monday."

"See you out there," Service said.

"You'll be there too?"

"Just for grins."

●●●

Zhenya Leukonovich called and Service stepped outside the pink cabin to talk to her. "What is his desire?" she asked.

"I'm on my cell phone."

"Is this to be a sensitive conversation?" the IRS agent asked.

"Yes."

"Can you get to your computer?"

He was driving his personal truck, not his state vehicle. He had the laptop, but no way to connect. He needed to get back to the district office.

"It will be more secure over the computer," Leukonovich said. "Zhenya will talk more after she is made aware of what is wanted."

She was a beaut. There was a time when the sexual tension between them was right to the edge, but that seemed to have dissipated. *Because of me, or her? More likely it was Friday.*

Sedge's truck pulled into the cabin driveway and she rolled down her window. "You talk to Toliver?"

Service nodded. "I told him to shut his yap."

"If he doesn't?"

"Wait until he gets some holes dug, then kick his ass off the dig and appoint one of his people to run the show. We need to know what the hell is in the ground out there."

"I have that authority?"

"You do now. And while you're at it, ask Katsu to please tread lightly. There's no need to put fresh sparks to dry tinder."

"This whole thing's sort of exciting," she said. "Three hundred and forty-five years after the fact and maybe we're about to learn the truth of what happened."

He was less enamored than interested—if it linked to DNR business. If not, well, he didn't want to think about other implications. He kept this bottled inside. No need for her to hear.

"Dinner at my place tonight? Six?"

"Sounds good."

"I talked to Sheena. She's rolling in tomorrow afternoon and will bunk at the Bomb Shelter. You guys going to brief me on the museum deal?"

"In time. Toliver said he's already started moving equipment out to the coast. Where are they coming in from?"

"Near where you and I parked that first time."

"Less cumbersome to use a boat around the point."

"I suggested that, but Toliver doesn't like boats."

"Each to his own."

• • •

Cedar Falls Chief Emerson reached him as he was passing the entrance to the upper falls of Taquamenon. He pulled to the side of M-123 and answered.

"Joseph Paul Brannigan," Emerson said excitedly. "Boy, that name sure got my attention. Mostly we deal with kids and trailer-park half-life yahoos from tightly packed gene pools, but old J. P., now, that boy is pure royalty among scumbags. You ever seen a pitcher of him?"

"I met him."

"No shit?"

"He was using the name Godfroi Delongshamp."

"You don't say."

Service explained the circumstances, including the Kermit BOL, and the sheriff laughed so hard he ended up in a coughing fit. "I gotta get that one for our bulletin board," he said. "That BOL was thinkin' *way* outside the box!"

"How do you know Brannigan?"

"Back around Y2000 that sumbitch stole cars, trucks, cattle, sheep, dogs, horses, and more damn wives than I could count. How does a man who looks like a frog have that sort of effect on womenfolk?"

"Chemistry?" Service offered.

"Okay, he's the devil. You say he's been using the name Delongshamp?"

"Yes."

"That's the name of a fancy restaurant up to Plano," the chief said.

"We don't know how long he used it, or where. Do you have a sheet on Brannigan?"

"Yessir, and it's long. You want it?"

"Please."

"What's he up to way up there?"

Service said, "We're not exactly sure," then took the chief through the litany of events and possibilities.

"Now I think I see how all your questions tie together. Far as I know, old J. P. never messed with deer down this way."

"You said he stole cars and trucks?"

"He surely did."

"Can I get descriptions?"

"Want them now?"

"With his sheet will be fine."

"Let me have your e-mail and your fax number. We'll get it off to you."

"I'll be at the office in thirty minutes or so."

"What's the weather like up your way?" Emerson asked.

"Hot, still."

"We got us some hot, but you could float your inner tube on the humidity here. You catch that ugly little sumbitch and I will personally fly up there and fetch his sorry butt back down here. Course, that depends on what you folks get him for. Way I see it, we should agree he should belong to the State, which will give him the biggest boot up his behind."

Service smiled. He liked Emerson. "I agree, but I assume your local prosecutor, my department lawyers, and our attorney general people will weigh in pretty heavily on that decision."

"Was a lot easier and cheaper when we just found a big old tree and strung 'em up."

Service didn't doubt it. "Thanks, Chief."

"You are most welcome, son."

• • •

He called Milo Miars from downtown Newberry. "Curry told me you did plainclothes at Imago Held's hunt club in Hillsdale County."

"Never could get the inquiry to go anywhere."

"You couldn't pass the bank-book test?"

"Not sure. Held was polite and superficially gracious, but it just sort of fizzled. I spent two nights at their clubhouse."

"You see any artifacts?"

"Such as?"

"Indian stuff."

"There were some items, but I wasn't really paying close attention. You looking for something specific?"

"Not yet. How would you feel about sending in Lyydi Enojarvi?"

"It's an old boys' club," Miars countered.

"What I hear is that it's a money club, and money doesn't have a gender, Milo."

"Are you trying to do my job?"

"I was, you think we'd be talking on the damn phone, Milo?"

"I'll organize it and run her," Miars said.

"That's your call, but I'll make sure she can pass the bank-book test."

"How will you do that?"

"Don't worry your pretty little head." *Territorialism. It pissed him off.*

• • •

Captain Elise McKower was standing at Reception when he walked into the district office. "We found a place to live," she announced. "Two miles from Chief Waco. The girls love the house."

Service didn't ask about her husband, whom he considered a slug at best and a leech at worst.

"I hear you're around here a lot. Work with Sedge going all right?"

"You were right. She's good." *And weird,* but he kept this to himself. "I need to get online."

"Use the machine in my old office. Are you ever going to put on a uniform, Senior Sergeant?"

"When it seems appropriate, Captain."

McKower rolled her yes, winked, and smiled at him, shaking her head.

• • •

Service typed an e-mail to Leukonovich and sent it.

Sergeant Bryan ambled into the cubicle and lowered his long frame into a chair. "You meet that Toliver dude?" he asked.

Service nodded.

"Creeps me out," Bryan said. "You seen his girlfriend, Jane?"

Service nodded again.

"Him and her, what's *that* all about? I hope this damn gig doesn't go Moby."

Service stared at the young NCO. "Moby?"

"Large, immense, complex—like the white whale, Super Sarge."

"It won't. Obsessive-compulsives digging holes. What could complicate that? Go away, Jeffey, I've got work here."

The towering sergeant drifted into the aisle outside the cubicle and immediately engaged a fish technician in lively conversation.

A note popped up from Leukonovich:

Platinum Rack Hunt Club, LLC, a 503(c) organization, organized as a nonprofit in 1978 with 40 shareholders. The club runs as a camp for disadvantaged youth from southeast Michigan. INH has been a person of interest this office for some time. Past efforts have gone Heisenbug. What is the senior sergeant's precise interest in INH?

How did she know about his new job?

Service could still hear Bryan and stepped into the aisle. "Jeffey, what the hell does *Heisenbug* mean?"

"Scope-dope term for a bug that disappears or changes tactics as soon as you try to probe it."

"Like a moving target?"

"Smarter, and more elusive."

Service returned to the computer to wait for Chief Emerson's information, but nothing came through, so he typed a note back to Leukonovich:

Past suspicions PRHC is unlicensed, for-profit, put-take hunt operation. No reasonable cause developed in past, but possible new leads may be opening. Will keep you informed.
G.S.

54

Newberry, Luce County

THURSDAY, JULY 26, 2007

Service bunked at the Bomb Shelter and drove into town first thing in the morning while Sedge stayed behind, intending to start her day's patrol later so she could make contact with trout fishermen at dusk. Service's cell phone rang as he was passing The Old Bank building in downtown Newberry.

"Sonnyboy."

"Linsenman must have been out early."

"I speck I mebbe make dat boy stain 'is 'wears, eh. Speck the dep din't speck nobody walk my trails first light. Called me bunch nasty names, he did."

"I'm sure you've heard them all before."

Allerdyce chortled. "I ain't no cherry when comes get bad-mouthed," he admitted. "Weasel say you want me call. Here I am."

"You set us up with Clatchety at the museum."

"Not me, my chum."

"Okay, your chum." *Games.* "If we were to ask him about Clatchety and the so-called museum, what do you think he'd tell us?"

"Dat guy don't talk so much."

"Is Clatchety a hired gun or the main man?"

"Depends. Where you at?"

"Newberry."

"DNR office?"

"Right, north of M-28."

"Good time, mebbe you me talk," Allerdyce said. "I'm over datway. See youse dere."

Why not? He'll fit right in with Toliver and Katsu. "Call me when you get to town."

Grinda showed up around noon. "Sedge wants to meet for lunch at the Falls."

"The park or the hotel?"

She grinned. "Hotel, smart-ass."

He cared little for U.P. restaurant/bar food, most of it tending toward fat and grease. "What time?"

Grinda checked her watch. "Half-hour. Want to ride with me?"

"Sure."

"You bring other clothes?" she asked, appraising him.

"You got a problem with my ensemble?"

"I just thought we might want to make this guy think we have means."

He grunted. "I'll think about it."

His plan was to bring heavy pressure on Allerdyce to find out everything he could about Clatchety and his museum. As they headed down the hill into town a name popped into his head. *Honeypat*. If Imago Held's the big shot in Lansing everyone claims, might she know him? Or at least *of* him? *Worth following up.*

Sedge came in and the three of them sat in a booth in back of the bar. Service ordered a grilled cheese sandwich with sliced pickled jalapenos on the side. The women talked and his mind wandered. Sedge was going on about something called Howling Diablos and shaboogie trash can blues. The sandwich floated in grease. His phone burred.

"Sonnyboy?"

"You here already?"

"Whin we talk, eh?"

"Falls Hotel, downtown," Service said. "Pick me up?"

"Ten minute. I look you out front or come in?"

"I'll be outside."

"Don't like our company?" Sedge asked as he got up and went to pay his share of the bill.

"Allerdyce is picking me up," he said.

The female officers sat with open mouths. He paid his bill and went outside into the sun and a blinding blue sky. Allerdyce was the enemy. That he was being fetched by the old poacher caught them all by surprise and made him smile inwardly.

A shiny green Hummer pulled up to the curb, Allerdyce behind the wheel. Service got up into the wide vehicle, asking, "Where's your old Ford?"

"She good in woods, but long trip, dis better."

Service looked around. The vehicle looked and smelled new. "A little ostentatious for your line of work."

Allerdyce made a snorting sound.

"Head north out of town," Service said. "We can talk while we drive."

"Your head plugged?" Allerdyce asked as they cruised over the railroad tracks. "Most time I tink you sharp as Finn knife."

"What?"

"Youse call me 'bout errorheads, dat right?"

"I didn't call you. You showed up at my camp."

"What I tell youse?"

"You asked me a question."

"No, I axe youse's got plugged-up head."

It was a headache to talk to the old man, a delicate, frustrating dance, or feigned moronics, and Service knew when to surrender and just listen. "Okay, you said arrowheads are all over the place and not worth shit. And I asked if you knew that from experience, and you said maybe you just heard it in the woods."

"See," Allerdyce said, "dere's problem. Youse 'member everyting words got said, but youse don't tink 'bout what was I tole youse."

"You told me about Hectorio."

Allerdyce mashed the braked suddenly, throwing the Hummer into a violent stop, causing vehicles behind him to veer left and right, honking horns, making obscene and threatening gestures. He ignored all of them with a frown on his face.

Allerdyce tapped his temple. He said, "Use dat bloody noggin', sonny-boy," and accelerated as other vehicles skidded behind him. Service tried to ignore the outside world's chaos, and think. "The stuff is all over the place. You told me that."

"Holy wah."

"But they shouldn't be all over the place up here?"

"Youse tell me, Mr. Dickteckative. Four Mile Corner here, which way I go?"

"Left, toward Deer Park."

"Okay we stop Bear Ranch?" Allerdyce asked.

"Sure, why not," Service said. The more he thought about things, the more cluttered his mind seemed to get.

After a few miles they turned down the driveway of Oswald's Bear Ranch. Allerdyce paid the entry fee, parked, and was out of the Hummer before Service could even undo his seat belt. He found the old man standing in front of a ten-foot-high chain-link fence with a sign that said MALES.

Allerdyce stood with his arms crossed, staring at a huge animal with dirty fur. Beyond this one, Service saw eight more bears of varying size. The ranch had been in operation for years, and sometimes had as many as four dozen animals in residence.

"See dat?" Allerdyce asked. "Plain as dose bears got noses."

Stuff all over the place. Not worth shit. Plain as a bear's nose. Bingo: Bears were solitary creatures, and all these together in pens made for an artificial situation, one created and arranged by man for profit. But it wasn't artificiality exactly that Limpy means. Maybe it's quantity. In the wild you'd never see this many bears together.

"There were never many Indians up here on Superior south shore," he told the old poacher. "Soo, Bay Mills, Tahq, Grand Island, Keweenaw, Ontonagon."

"Why you tink dat?"

"Fish in Superior, lake trout and whities and perch, they spawn in close. Some furs in the swamps, but not much big game way up here because there's not enough food for them. Without fish and fur bearers up here, there's no reason to be here."

Allerdyce nodded. "So how come dere's all dem bloody errorheads?"

"Well, we know they made a lot of stuff for trade purposes."

"Did dey?"

"Yes, of course."

Allerdyce grunted. "Youse might want check dat, like where dat flint come from, eh?"

"We have flint."

"Mostly crap chert is what we got, not much flint 'cept down Burn Bluff, an' mosta dat's ten feet down in lake water. Indians dive for flint, you tink?"

Service looked at the old man, who was a lot smarter than most people suspected. "Locals traded for the flint. They traded for everything."

"You still blind."

"They traded for stuff, then made things from the flint."

"Not so many red niggers, 'member. If not many, how come so much stuff? Why dey need all dat shit?"

"Are you telling me people are manufacturing artifacts?"

Allerdyce shrugged. "Some say dat how it is."

"The museum's a scam?"

Allerdyce shrugged again. "Not all. You run scam, youse got have some stuff legit, eh?"

"I hear you," Service said.

"Din't say nuttin', sonny."

"Clatchety the main man or a hired gun?"

"Hear both. Hear neither. You pick."

"You know Imago Held?"

"I 'posed to?"

55

Trout Lake, Chippewa County

FRIDAY, JULY 27, 2007

They bunked with Sedge at the Bomb Shelter, and when Service saw how Elza Grinda was dressed for their meeting with Clatchety, he felt like a slug. She wore a flowery sundress and paper-thin sandals, her hair in a neat French braid, nails done, makeup, and all he could say was "Uh-huh."

"You look good, too," she quipped.

"*Not,*" Sedge intervened. "The least you can do is shave."

"These are informal times," he countered weakly, but both women were pointing at the bathroom.

He started to say something and his companions said, "Don't even," in one voice. Knowing he was beaten, he grudgingly shaved, but suspected Clatchety would be so dazzled by Grinda he would barely glance his way.

He had called Honeypat Allerdyce in Lansing the night before.

"Youse," she greeted him. "Figured I'd be getting dis call."

He didn't want to plumb her reasoning. "Imago Held," he said.

"What about 'im?"

"Client of yours?"

She laughed out loud. "Dere's privacy laws," she said.

"Not for illegal activities."

"Everybody knows Held."

"Power broker, right?"

"Bozian's old asshole pal," she said.

"I'm trying to find someone who's been in his house, or his hunt club down in Hillsdale."

"Dat could be arranged," she said.

"How much?"

"How bad youse need it?"

The price she wanted was one he wouldn't pay. "Don't go there, Honeypat."

"Youse're one called me."

"Probably a mistake," he said.

"We all make 'em," she said. "Dere's worse things. You and Hectorio got something working?"

"Aitch tell you that?"

"Not in so many words, but he's got that peso-glow thing working."

"Peso-glow?"

"Dude lights up when he thinks bonus money is coming his way."

"Bonus, in contrast to non-bonus?"

"You know, his regular gig. That sort of income we all come to expect, but the stuff that comes in above and beyond, that's bonus."

"What about Held?"

"Slick as swamp water, poisonous as Massasauga. Youse know da type."

"Be specific."

"Got a squeeze, real easy glove, hear what I'm sayin'?"

Easy glove? She is a piece of work. "Yes. This glove got a name?"

"Skyler Verst."

"Who is?"

"Off the table, Mabel, quarter's for the beer. Was married state senator from East Grand Rapids who term-limited out. Her ex old man runs company, Opinion Twenty-Four Seven."

"Political polls?"

"Politics, opinions, marketing—youse name it, he does it."

"Elephant or donkey?" he asked.

"Big elephant, but he gave money to Timms."

"And his wife ran off with Held?"

"Weird world, eh? Wasn't no run-off. She just pushed Verst out the door. And she runs to Held whenever he wants, but he ain't exclusive."

"Verst a grudge-holder?"

"Aren't we all?"

"How do I get in touch with this woman?"

"When I said she ain't exclusive with Held, I didn't mean, like, she's available to walk-in traffic."

"I really need to know about Held's house."

"That could be arranged."

"Not at your price."

"How can you possibly know my price?" she countered sternly, and Service heard the change in inflection. Honeypat had become Honeypet. A chill swept over him.

"You're right," he said. "I don't know."

"I assume youse got a case."

She had him in a quandary. "Let's leave it at that. I would really appreciate talking to someone who has been into Held's place."

"All right," she said. "What would you like to know?"

"*You've* been in there?"

"Yes, of course."

"Recently?"

"Is time frame important?"

"Depends on when you visited. It could be."

"St. Patrick's Day, this year. He has the Great Green Gala every year, calls it the Three Gee Ball."

"I didn't know that."

"You're not an insider."

He didn't ask how she ranked. "Obviously." *And thankfully. Something different here, her voice, tone, something.*

"You know where Held's money came from?" she asked.

"No."

"Coins."

"Like, rare coins?"

"Old, rare, whatever. He tells the world he attended Central Michigan University and sold his coin collection while he was there, and made so much money he was forced to drop out and manage his investments. He gives major donations to politicians, and to all major universities in the state."

"Luck sometimes comes into play," he said.

"Nonsense. In Held's time in Mount Pleasant, which amounted to only four weeks, a man in Nashville, Tennessee, had his coin collection stolen."

"Are you calling Held a thief?"

"I'm saying the FBI investigated him, but never indicted."

"Investigated at the time of the robbery?"

"No, years later, after the statute of limitations had closed."

"And no indictment."

"Feds initially judged it was a political allegation by one of his many foes, but more importantly, someone intervened with the FBI."

"Let me guess," he said. "Sam Bozian."

"Why do you say that?" she asked.

"I'm guessing he was Bozian's pollster. Sam didn't shit without polls."

"I find your language both rude and insulting."

"I'm sorry," he said quickly. "About the house," he added.

"*What* about it?"

"Antiques, original art, artifacts, that sort of thing?"

"All over the home. Artifacts in display cases."

"What sort of artifacts?"

"Civil War, Native American, that sort of thing."

"This was as of this just-past St. Paddy's Day?"

"Yes, March seventeenth."

"Photographs on the walls?"

"More stuffed-animal heads than anything. You know, man-cave wall of death."

"You find such things objectionable?"

"Hey, I don't have all night ta shoot shit wit' youse, Service. Youse want ta know 'boot Held's place, youse know da price. Anyting else I can do?"

Service stared at the telephone. *What the hell just happened? Is she for real, or is this some sort of put-on?* "No, that's it. Thanks," he said.

"One last ting, free," Honeypat said. "Hectorio ain't one you want to play wit', hear me? He don't give but one warning," she said, and hung up.

Driving to Trout Lake the conversation with Honeypat/Honeypet was troubling him. Stolen coins, Indian relics, stuffed animal heads. *What the hell are we into—if anything?*

• • •

Clatchety was tall and thin and walked with a slight limp. The man had cloudy gray eyes and a heavy five o'clock shadow. Grinda introduced him as Andrew but Clatchety ignored him.

"You mentioned something special," Grinda said.

His smile was thin. *Nerves?* He handed her an eight-by-ten color photograph that he tapped out of a manila envelope.

Grinda passed the photograph to Service, who felt his stomach churn. *This is the same cane Hectorio showed me. Jesus! What gives?* "What about it?" Service asked the man, passing the photograph back to him.

"Make an offer," the man said. "Availability of this item is extremely limited."

"We're in the market for something more . . . local. The item in this photo is Iroquois, specifically Mohawk."

The man's eyes went buggy.

"Are you *serious?*"

"We collect what appeals to us," Service countered.

The man stared at him, said, "Local? Wait here." And he left them.

Ten minutes later he was sliding the top off a wooden box two feet long and ten inches wide. Top off, the man set the box on a table.

Breakhead. "Is that handle bone?" Service asked.

"The striking head is pure agate, very hard, the handle's made from the leg of a bear."

The bone was chalky yellow, the agate head pink and pale green. Service pretended to study the weapon, but he saw soil particles in the box and these interested him even more. "Local?"

"Iroquois," Clatchety said. "But discovered locally."

"Provenance?"

"These are one-of-a-kind items, picked up on private land and passed down through generations of families."

"A Mohawk war chief's cane isn't local, and, more to the point, it's not unique. I've seen others. I may, in fact, have seen this very one."

Clatchety was blinking wildly, fighting to control his emotions.

"It is unique."

"No, the symbols show eighteenth century, and this time period is common."

Clatchety said, "I think you are mistaken about the symbols. This clearly is seventeenth century. May I ask where you saw it?"

"Passed down through families," Service said. "You understand."

"I see."

Service tapped the wooden box. "How much?"

"Twenty."

"Eight," Service countered.

The man eyed him with a slight grin. "Twenty, hard."

"Ten. Last chance or we're out the door," Service came back.

The man exhaled. "I'll be back. Please wait."

"Hired gun," Service whispered. He checked his watch, told her the time. "Help me remember this."

"Ten *thousand* dollars?" Grinda said.

"Don't worry your pretty little head, honey," he said.

She rolled her eyes in disbelief.

The man came back somber-faced. "Ten, but only for cash."

"Deal," Service said, opened his wallet, pulled out and counted off twenty crisp McKinleys.

The man stared at the money. "You want the box wrapped?" he asked.

"Nah, the wooden box is fine, "Service said. "Receipt?"

"You want a paper trail?" the man asked.

"Suit yourself."

"What about the staff?"

"Not interested," Service said.

"Thirty, special deal just for you."

Aitch has asked for twenty-five plus fifteen handling fee. The owner isn't Hectorio. Is this guy one of Hectorio's competitors? "That include your handling fee?" Service challenged.

"It's customary," the man said. "The offer is thirty, this day only."

"Thanks, but no thanks." Service tapped the box. "This is sweet."

Out in the truck Service said to Grinda, "Take the box to Forensics in Marquette on your way home, ask them to analyze the soil for content, and ask about carbon dating." They double-checked the time the man had left them, presumably to use a phone.

"Subpoena phone records?" she asked.

"If it comes to that."

"You were almost drooling over the war club."

"I think it's very rare, the same one the USFS described to Sedge and me."

"The feds are involved in this?"

He nodded.

She stared at him. "Grady, where did all that money come from?"

"I got it legally. That's all that matters."

"Do we have a plan here?" she asked.

"Put bad guys in jail," he said. He saw she was not smiling. "I'm hoping the soil in that box will match our site. I've seen this before," he said. "So has Sedge. Katsu had it at one time. It came from the site, he said, and I want to confirm that. And if they can carbon-date, that might tell us something more."

"I didn't even notice the dirt," she admitted. "This is another strange case you've latched onto."

"I think this one came looking for me," he said.

"Any notion why?"

Wish I did. "No, ma'am."

56

Halfway House, Chippewa County

WEDNESDAY, AUGUST 1, 2007

Things had been hectic and complex, like the gods were frowning and thumb-ing their noses on the area and the project, though Service didn't believe lit-erally in higher powers. DEQ sent the signed permit to Toliver in Paradise, but the messenger had a heart attack, wrecked his government vehicle near Gaylord, and ended up in the hospital in Traverse City. Sometime during the emergency and resulting chaos, the permit had disappeared, causing a new one to be issued and signed and sent, the second messenger finally delivering the goods, which served to finally settle a seriously rattled Toliver.

No word from Marquette on the soil sample from the war club box. Ser-vice had not shown the weapon to Toliver and did not plan to do so.

Shark Wetelainen again fetched Professor Ozzien Shotwiff from Silver City and promptly disappeared to secret brook trout water allegedly some-where south of Newberry, which might or might not be the truth. Shark was a master of misdirection in his outdoor forays; when hunting he would walk a mile the opposite way of his blind, then double back two miles just so it would be a chore for anyone to follow him. His ways made Service shake his head.

Toliver's people had erected a giant new Cabela's wall tent at the dig site, and ten smaller three-man shelters around it, reminding Service of a goose and her goslings. His team was comprised of college kids, happy to be, in Toliver's words, "on the verge of trying to bring clarity to history."

Limpy had gone who knew where. Katsu was being polite and attentive to Toliver. Tomorrow the archaeologist would begin organizing the excava-tion grid. "We should be sifting sand by Monday," he'd announced officiously to Sedge.

On the surface the whole scene was one of peace, organization, and pur-pose. Toliver and Shotwiff were even talking to each other like respectful colleagues.

Service plopped down on a driftwood log by the edge of an uncharacteristically quiet Lake Superior. Sedge came down and stood beside him as he lit a cigarette and took a hit.

"Careful with those ashes," she cautioned.

"Everything okay at camp?" he asked her.

"For the moment. Jane Rain and I talked."

"She reveal she's a fed?"

"Too professional for that. Right now, everyone seems to be playing nice."

"Then why does it feel like a tsunami of shit is rolling our way?" Service retorted.

• • •

The dig team wanted a campfire at dusk, but Sedge told them no. They had small butane stoves to cook with. The land was too dry for open fires. The college kids weren't happy, but accepted her declaration.

Right at dusk Service saw a figure in the gloaming to the southeast. *Allerdyce.* Where the hell had he come in from?

"Scary dry out here," the poacher greeted him through tight lips. "You know dis Lost Boy Point, eh?"

"Who calls it that?"

"Nobody knows trute," Allerdyce said. "Is real name, Lost Boy Point."

Service was confused. "This is the halfway house area," he said.

"You know you-pee, eh. Lost Bay on some old county maps never got fixed back up. 'Pose to be Lost Boy. Long time back Indi'n pipples lost some kid, come here find 'im, but come up on dere enemas an' shit hit fan."

Enemas? "Right, this is the place." Service pointed at the camp area.

"Dis place, sonny? Geez oh Pete, who tole dat?"

"It was here, not at Iroquois Point."

"Dat lighthouse tourshit place? Not dere eder. Ain't near no water. Bad guys leff canoes here mebbe, but da fight was back in woods over dat hill I just walk down."

Oh God. Crazy old fart.

"You tink Limpy don't know trute?"

"You're the only one who thinks this."

"Bullpucks. Pipples out here woods long time, dey all know trute."

"You're telling me this is common knowledge?"

"Old clans, sure."

"Your chum from Raco an old clanner, as in Ku Klux?"

Allerdyce grinned. "You funny, sonny. My chum, he knows. We all know trute. You want to see?"

"You can take me to it?"

"Not dat far, just over hill dere."

Service debated a cigarette and felt lightheaded. "Tell me your fairy tale again."

"Not my story—trute," Allercyce insisted, and repeated the story of the lost boy and the alleged chance encounter that led to a battle.

"Wait here," Service said, and went to fetch Professor Shotwiff. "Got a few minutes?"

"Got forever," the old professor said with a grin, and Service led him out of the camp to the woods. "Limpy Allerdyce, Professor Ozzien Shotwiff."

"Ding Dong Disney, bear-man?" Allerdyce said, grinning widely.

Shotwiff's face darkened. "Ding Dong Disney?"

"Don't mean spittley-spot," Allerdyce said. "Glad to meet youse. Youse teacher man?"

"Retired."

"Me too," Allerdyce said, causing Service to choke.

"Tell the professor your story."

"Local kittle gone missin'. Chips here look for him, see bad boys, set up ambush, kill all their asses."

"Right," Shotwiff said, "This was probably the place."

Allerdyce jerked his thumb toward the hill. "Not down here. Up *dere*."

Service and Shotwiff exchanged glances. "He says he can take us to the location," Service said.

"Might as well look," the professor said. "Nothing to lose, eh?"

"What're the chances?"

"In my time I've learned not to overlook any reasonable possibilities."

"I'm not sure I'd call this one reasonable," Service said.

"How far to the place?" Shotwiff asked Allerdyce.

"Not far, just over hill."

"You've seen the place?"

"Go now?"

Shotwiff laughed out loud. "How about we wait for daylight?"

Service said, "Shall we let Toliver know?"

"Would you?" Shotwiff asked. "The man's a horse's ass."

• • •

Service later pulled Sedge aside and told her what was going on. "Jesus," was her mumbled response. "Let's talk to Katsu," she said.

"Why?"

"He seems so sure about this site, and Ladania Wingel pinpointed it too."

"*If* she told the truth," Service said. "Let's hold off on Katsu until we see what Allerdyce has."

"You think he could be right?"

"It's taken a lot of years, but I've grudgingly learned not to bet against him."

Service had had enough experiences with the old man to know he probably knew more about the physical U.P. and its detail history than anyone he had ever met.

"Ironic," Sedge whispered.

"It's always ironic with this guy," Service said.

"Where's Allerdyce?"

"God knows," he said.

"God or the devil?" she came back.

"Take your pick," he said.

57

Halfway House, Chippewa County

THURSDAY, AUGUST 2, 2007

First light and no sign of Allerdyce. Service looked at Professor Shotwiff and shook his head. "Coffee?"

The professor smiled. "If the man's not here, what was last night all about?"

Service had no answer. Limpy's mind was not like others, and he was entirely unpredictable. The two men watched Toliver assemble his youthful worker-bee team. Toliver talked while the others made breakfast on small backpacking stoves. One of them offered their leader a cup of coffee and he tasted it, made a sour face, and threw the liquid on the ground. "The plan is a walk-across survey. Flags are already set at the corners of the perimeter. We'll record all visualizations and graph each on the master and section charts. Georgie will do the sketches for the record." Toliver pointed to a small redhaired woman nearby. "I have marked twenty shovel test pits, which after gridding will be our initial tasks. Five teams of pairs, each with four shovel sites. Questions?"

The young people looked eager, if half-asleep and a bit droopy-eyed. One of them asked, "If we go blank on all twenty shovel sites, what then?"

"We won't," Toliver said confidently. "But if that happened, we would declare the site sterile, pack up, and go home. I doubt that will be the case here. Artifacts can be seen on the sand's surface. Other questions?"

He looked around. No takers. "Let us remember our cardinal rules, people, the main commandments of professional field work: First, everything is important at this juncture. Second, we work from the surface down, top to bottom, known to unknown. Third, our eyes are our primary tools; don't just look, you must *see!* Questions?"

Silence still reigned. Toliver pointed to a canvas tarp on the ground, went over and pulled off the cover. "Grid materials. We will lay out five-foot squares. Once the grid is strung and pegged we will begin shovel tests. From that point on it will be full trenches, which I will demarcate at the time. Everyone knows their job for gridding, yes?"

They all nodded obediently as he looked around and adjusted his stained, worn Tilley hat. "Here we will uncover the past, dear colleagues," he said solemnly. "Bear this in mind with every task. Nothing you do here is unimportant."

Service watched an impassive Katsu squatting off to the side and wondered what was going through his head. The sand is bleeding, Santinaw had exhorted him. If Allerdyce was right, the bleeding wasn't here.

Toliver clapped his hands loudly. "Go to it, people!"

"Where the hell is Allerdyce?" Sedge whispered.

Service shrugged and said nothing. "Everything look right here?" he asked the professor.

Shotwiff stifled a yawn. "Blowhole epizootics aside, this is all standard fare in my business. Toliver is obviously experienced and confident, a dangerous mix with being a pompous ass."

58

Halfway House, Chippewa County

THURSDAY, AUGUST 2, 2007

Allerdyce drifted toward the edge of the grid just after lunch. Service looked at his watch.

"You're late."

"Went ta talk ta my chum."

"The mystery man in Raco?"

"No mystery me, sonnyboy. I know dat bird long time, eh. He tell me, '*Naa-din esh-pen-eaag-wak*'—you know dere singy-songy-jibberingo lingo?"

"Some."

"Me I know pert good. Dis means get back what dey tink important."

"Your Raco bud is tribal?"

"Never said *dat*," Allerdyce chirped. "He said stay back from hill dere. I show youse dat place, gone rain bad luck from sky above."

Shotwiff looked at Service and said to Allerdyce, "If you believe that, we'll stay away. Time has probably eroded and destroyed the site. It usually does."

"Da place right dere all right, skulks, all dat stuff."

"If that's true, our knowing where it is can help us to protect the site."

"Dose Shinob tink dere gods do dat for dem pert good, I tink."

"They're probably right," Shotwiff said.

Allerdyce cackled. "No dey ain't. Shinobs don't know shit! I'll show youse, but just youse two."

"Is two the critical mass for the tipping point on bad luck?" Service asked.

Allerdyce gave him a sour look. "Sometimes youse ain't funny, sonnyboy. We gone go, les get went, eh."

• • •

The site was in shallow swale at the bottom of a fairly large and eroded hill, with remarkably little sand on top. Through the swale there was a trail sunk in bedrock, an enfilade in military terms, a sort of shallow draw that would let you move unseen, or create a death trap for those unaware that you were on their flanks. As soon as Service saw the lay of the land his gut tightened. This was the perfect place for a lethal ambush, today or three and a half centuries ago. Some things don't change.

Shotwiff looked around, hardly moving his head. What had Toliver told his young team—the eyes were the primary tool?

Allerdyce picked up a four-foot-long stick and poked in the sand. "Here," the old poacher said, his voice barely a whisper, and difficult to hear.

Service saw the skull top and nudged Shotwiff, who said, "I can see parts of four of them from here."

"He's right, then?"

"We'd have to excavate carefully to know for sure."

"Toliver can't move his dig to here. His permit won't cover this site."

"When I was doing this business, this is the sort of site I'd walk away from, make notes in my journal and leave it be unless sometime in the future there would be a reason to reveal it."

Allerdyce whispered, "We need ta skedaddle. Ain't good stand in grave-yard, piss off ghosts."

"People been helping themselves to things from here?" Service asked as they climbed back up the hill.

"Dunno," Allerdyce said, nervously glancing back at the place where the skulls lay in the sand.

• • •

Sedge caught his eye back at the dig site, but he ignored her.

The site of the grid was sheltered by trees, the air hot but not humid. The young people had stripped down to the bare minimum in clothing. "We weren't here, they'd dig buck-naked and smoke their junk at night," Sedge said with a chuckle.

She was undoubtedly right. Many CO stops of anyone under forty produced dope and/or alcohol violations, often both. It made him wonder if today's dope was akin to Prohibition's booze.

The grid had grown steadily since morning. Toliver worked tirelessly and patiently with his diggers, carrying a handheld GPS and now and then getting on his knees with a measuring tape and a plumb bob. The sound of mallets pounding metal pegs sounded like muted cymbals in the forest.

Service lacked the knowledge to judge, but to his untrained eye it looked like Toliver knew his business.

Service looked around for Allerdyce, but he was gone again, and Service had no interest in knowing where to.

Late lunches were passed around in boxes. Peanut butter on fresh limpa rye bread from the North Star Brick Oven Bakery on M-123. In Service's mind it was a sin to put peanut butter on such great bread, but it wasn't his call. He had enough to think about. He rejected a sandwich offered by Sedge.

"There's another site," he whispered to Sedge when they drifted away from the group with Shotwiff. "Just over this hill. We found skulls."

"And?"

"Toliver's only permitted to dig here."

"Katsu's wrong?" she said.

"Time will tell," the professor said quietly. "But Toliver's correct; he won't come up empty at this site. He thinks this was some kind of temporary refuge and fishing village, and he's probably right."

"I've got other things to do," Service told the professor. "You can head out with me or stay here with Sedge. I'll be back."

"Always liked field work," the old man said. "I miss it. So I'll stay and watch."

"Where are Toliver's vehicles?" Service asked Sedge.

"One mile due south," she said. "There's a forty-acre landlocked state parcel inside a Little Traverse Conservancy half-section. I remembered this, and that there was an old two-track to the state land. I called the conservancy and they gave Toliver permission to cross their land to stage from the other location. It's a lot closer than where you and I parked."

"This is north of LOL?"

"Yeah. It took two phone calls to get permission. Where you going?"

"I want to swap my private ride for the Tahoe. I'll call Friday. She can drive the Tahoe over here and take my truck back."

"Want to meet her at the Bomb Shelter? It's private," Sedge said, raising an eyebrow.

"What's this week's exhibit, Pocahunkus?"

She laughed. "Cinder blocks only. When are you leaving?"

"I'll spend the night, take off first light, come back the next day to give you a break."

Service pitched tents for himself and the professor, away from Toliver's tent city but with a low ridge between the two shelters and the lake, to prevent them from being sloshed if the lake got exuberant.

"I adore the sound of Superior," Shotwiff said.

"This time of year it should be fine, but when the *Edmund Fitz* went down in seventy-five, a friend of mine had a place west of Deer Park, thirty feet above the beach. The waves broke over the cliff in his yard and pushed his kids' bikes fifty yards south up his driveway. This is not the place to be when Superior gets into a snit."

"That doesn't change my feelings for the sound," the professor countered.

The area was parched the whole forest a bed of tinder, and the professor was, until recently, someone who thought nothing of feeding large predators. Service studied the sky. Yellowish thunder-bumpers had been building since late morning. "We might get a shower," he told the professor. "Let's recheck the tents, make sure they're secure and that the rain-flies won't blow away."

• • •

It drizzled for twenty minutes around 4 p.m. Thirty minutes later the sky turned black and exploded with rumbling thunder crashing in all directions. Service watched as the sky turned dark, variegated blue and white lightning columns arcing downward, leaving the air sizzling and the taste of iron in his mouth. Two strikes were close, the interval between flash and thunder less than a second. Both strikes made him jump. The professor just stared up at the sky with his mouth hanging open.

Sedge trotted down from the big camp. "Jesus, one of those was less than a mile away by my count." Her eyes were wide, chest heaving, but her voice was calm and controlled. "We're bone-dry out here," she said.

"You fix the loke?"

"Close, and south southwest," she said.

"That's toward my truck. Get on the radio, call Station Twenty, ask them to alert the county."

"My 800's not working out here," she said. When the DNR had gotten the 800-megahertz system, officers were promised the radios would work everywhere, under all conditions. It turned out to be just another semi-empty promise. "We are so damn isolated here, a fire could get a big head south of us and push up here, and we wouldn't know it until it was on us."

"I'll check the closest strike," Service said. "Stay with the group. Professor, go with Officer Sedge."

She held out a family band radio, Motorola, red. "Ten-mile range, Channel One, backup on Ten. Let me know about the strike before you head for your truck."

"Channel One," he said, nodding. "Or Ten." The term, number *ten*, had meant everything bad and evil in his Southeast Asia days.

Sedge didn't need to provide directions. Following the course line he could smell smoke, and soon came upon an ancient eight-foot black stump, sluffing fresh smoke. It was surrounded by black swamp water. Even if it fell over, it couldn't reach dry fuel. Still, he waded out thigh-deep through the muck and used his hat to scoop as much water and sludge on the smoldering wood as he could manage. He called Sedge on the radio. "Found it. An old stump in a little marsh. I put it out but it's still smoldering. Who says lightning doesn't strike twice in the same place?"

"Should I think about evacuating the group?"

"Not yet, but tell Toliver what's going on, and that he may have to leave everything and bug out PDQ. If you end up having to go, don't even try for your vehicles. Just foot-boogie due east down the beach to Vermilion and set yourselves up there. You got spare radio batts?"

"Yes."

"Good; conserve them. Save them for Vermilion if you need to go that route."

"You talk to your woman yet?"

"No bars here," he said of his cell phone.

It was 6 p.m. when he reached his truck and saw a Hummer coming through the woods at a pretty good clip. It stopped and Allerdyce jumped out.

"I just come up One Twinnytree. Youse see all dose lightens up dis way?"

"All around us."

"Bunches down south, too. I stop truck, take sniff. Got heavy smoke up dere norta One Twinnytree. Murp'y Crick. I tink youses mebbe got a burn goin.'"

"There was one small smoker north of here."

Allerdyce looked him over. "You wade swamp?"

"Tried to douse the stump. It should be okay."

"Where you want me go, sonnyboy?"

"Do you know where the others' vehicles are parked?"

"Yeah, mile nort'easta here."

"Park your vehicle with theirs and report to Sedge. Help her if she has to evacuate. I told her if she has to go, to hotfoot it east to Vermilion." Service handed the family band radio to the man. "Reach her on this: Channel One primary, Ten the backup. Be careful, old man."

"Youse too, sonnyboy. Looks like da Indi'n god done send us whole kick yer caboola!"

● ● ●

Service made his way south. The forest roads felt strange under the dark sky. Eventually he crawled down CR 500 to M-123 and turned southeast toward where Limpy had smelled smoke. The Bomb Shelter was in the other direction, but not far.

Down the road he thought about the area, which he knew as intimately as any in the U.P. If there was fire north of M-123 and west of Murphy Creek, it would be the middle of nowhere and impossible to handle easily. He turned off M-123 and skirted Chesbrough Lake to where the road dead-ended into a massive Nature Conservancy peat marsh. South of him were the headquarters of the East Branch of the Two-Hearted, and Sleeper Lake, both less than two miles southeast of his position.

He could smell the smoke and feel the wind in his face. There looked to be a little ash in the air, but not much yet. *Bad*, he told himself.

He toggled his 800 and was surprised when it blooped to life. "Twenty, this is Twenty Four Fourteen. I'm on Chesbrough Road at the Nature Conservancy property, Luce County. There's a fire southwest of my position somewhere in the direction of Sleeper Lake. Twenty Four Fourteen clear."

"Twenty Four Fourteen, we just had another call on the same event. The alert is going now. You close to the fire?"

"No."

"Be careful out there, Chief Master Sergeant. Congratulations on your promotion."

"Thanks," he said.

• • •

By the time he got to M-123, smoke snakes were slithering across the highway. He met a Troop and a dep both rolling with their gumballs tinting the rolling gray smoke. Service pulled alongside the Troop, rolled down his window, and showed his badge.

"Looks like a bad boy," the Troop said. "Be careful—the gawkers are already rolling, and I damn near clipped a big bear just south of here."

Service tried to reach Sedge on the 800, but she was not answering. Instead he called Sergeant Bryan on his cell phone, which miraculously had two quivering and questionable bars. "Sedge is up at the dig site. Where are you?" Service asked.

"Home."

"There's a fire near Sleeper Lake, and I'm headed to the district office."

"Roger that, I'm rolling."

Service passed multiple law enforcement vehicles as he sped south toward town. He called Friday on her cell phone.

"Finally," she greeted him.

"We have a fire over here. Can you drive my Tahoe to the district office and swap for my personal truck?" Even with Service obviously speeding, the eyes of the officers were all to the north.

"Now?"

"If you can."

"Meet at the district office?"

"Right."

"Be couple of hours," she said. "My sis can watch Shigun. They're just starting to talk about your fire on the radio here."

Great. There had been no cell phones or Internet during the Seney fire in '76. He wondered what effect such devices would have this time. Everyone up here feared fire.

God, don't let it be like Seney. That fire had been a monster, burning 75,000 acres, and everyone who'd fought it or been anywhere near it knew for certain it was a *real* monster, not some slick trick conjured by Hollywood special effects people.

59

Newberry, Luce County

FRIDAY, AUGUST 3, 2007

McKower pulled into the lot the same time he did. There were trucks all over, a red fire pumper at the door, men in yellow Nomex coveralls and green DNR shirts huddled in the parking lot.

"I heard you on the radio," McKower said. "Look bad?"

"Can't really tell. Lots of smoke, and the wind is in high-hoot, so it's probably building fast. I never actually saw any flames, but I sort of mopped up a lit snag to the north. I was with Sedge and the archaeologists between Crisp Point and Vermilion. We had lightning all over the damn place, Lis. It was everywhere."

"The radios are jammed with traffic," she said. "Here's where we'll pay the price of all agencies not being on the same commo system and over not having enough fire officers. Is Sedge going to evacuate those people?"

"Not unless she needs to. I told her to just hike east on the beach to Vermilion and regroup there. That's a long way from the fire if it jumps big."

She said, "Let's get inside, call the chief, and see what the fire people want us to do."

"Is there an event commander yet?" he asked.

"Do we have an event yet?"

"Let's hope not," he said, but felt down deep they had something ugly taking shape north of them.

• • •

McKower worked the phones and Service sat in front of her computer radio console.

"All right, Chief," McKower said, flipping on the speakerphone.

"I talked to Wassoon," Eddie Waco said. "He's got scouts evaluating the fire as we speak. How far from town is it?"

"Seven or eight miles north," Service said.

"Tahquamenon State Park?"

"Ten miles east of there."

"I just heard there's a fire at the Upper Falls," the chief reported. "They got right on it."

Bad bad bad, Service told himself. *The park's not that far south of Sedge's group. How many lightning strikes had there been in that corridor?*

"Wassoon has asked the governor to release a couple of Guard choppers—just in case. What's our role in this?"

"Do what the incident commander needs," McKower said. "A lot of routine law enforcement work, traffic, notifications, evacs, patrols—all that."

"If you want people from other districts, go direct to their lieutenants. We'll tack overtime onto the fire bill. I'll alert everyone you may call and let them know they are to pitch in. Keep me in the loop as best you can," Waco said, and hung up.

"Who the hell is Wassoon?" Service asked.

"Do you pay attention to *anything?* Wassoon is Spiggot."

"No shit?" *I didn't know he had another name.* Spiggot was the nickname of the State's wildfire supervisor, a warhorse among fire officers.

Fire Officer Gar Fox stopped at McKower's cubicle. "It's lightning, Sleeper Lake, and this one will be a very tough nut—hard as hell to get to. The wind's pushing it south toward 123. I'm going to put the Incident Command Post at Four Mile Corner."

"You the incident commander?" McKower asked.

"No, Kerry Brownmine out of Baraga. He's en route."

"What do you need from our people?"

"Let's start with a meeting up at Four Mile. Kerry will run everything from there. We'll probably have to 'doze a couple of tracks into the fire in order to get on top of it. A statewide 800 line is going in and will be debugged as quickly as we can make that happen. Fire decisions and status will all be done from the CP. Service field office personnel will work phones, back us up and take overflow. Other law enforcement is short of bods. Your people can jump in with traffic control. I'm probably going to preemptively close 123, and we're thinking about County 407 up to Pine Stump, too. I want as much of this doped out as we can for Brownmine so he can jump right into the dance. We'll probably also want your guys to escort fire division commanders on recon runs. Make sure your people draw fire suits. See you at Four Mile."

"We're on our way," McKower said. Her phone rang and she answered. "Okay, that will help. How many?"

She was making notes in her little notebook. "Send them to Four Mile Corner, north of town on 123. The command post will be there. Thanks."

To Service: "Let's move. The west side is sending six officers to help spell our people. Let's get out to Four Mile. This is all going to unroll really, really fast," she added.

It already seemed to him that it was.

A small woman with pigtails stopped at the cubicle as they stood up. She had two large red canvas bags marked DNR FIRE. "Fire suits," she said. "We had one made special for Sergeant Bryan and it ought to fit you," she said, flipping the jumpsuit to Service. "There are helmets, harnesses, canteens, and respirators in the big bags. Make sure you turn the stuff back in or it will be on my butt."

Service looked at his captain. "We supposed to wear these banana suits?"

"It's your call, but I'd keep it close."

They walked outside and got into her Tahoe. "Where's your state vehicle?" she asked.

"Home. We worked a plainclothes deal last Friday."

"You've been here since then?"

"Grand, ain't it?"

"God, your new woman must be a saint," McKower said, backing out of her parking spot.

"What's the radio situation here?" he asked as they headed north into town.

"Mishmash. Our people will stay on the district 800."

"Special event?"

"Too much trouble. We'll all use the main one, but try to maintain discipline. I don't want chitty-chat going on. Please help me enforce it, especially with the younger officers. We'll monitor 48P911, Luce County's law channel. It runs through dispatch out of Kinross and works good. Monitor Eighty for Troops out of Negaunee. It'll be a weird mix complicated by all the fire personnel. No idea what they'll have. I'm guessing High Band and 800 and God knows what else." She looked over at him as she raced north. "You all right?"

"I hate fire," he said.

"Good. Let's help our fire folks get this sonuvabitch out."

• • •

They found Four Mile Corner cluttered with dozens of vehicles and all kinds of fire trucks. A mobile command post trailer had been placed on the grass triangle that separated the highway from a grocery store that had gone bust years back, and never come back to life.

"Do you know Brownmine?" Service asked.

"Moved up from the Detroit area, rising star rep. He led the team that got national accreditation for Critical Incident Management. He's the number-one short-team leader." McKower looked over at him. "Don't be so damn skeptical. You don't have to be born in the damn U.P. to have the inside track on righteousness or competence."

"I didn't say that," Service said.

"You didn't have to," she said. "Have you met our new director yet?"

"What new director?"

She laughed at him. "You are one of a kind, Grady. Chief Waco told me he told you about Belphoebe Cheke."

"Oh yeah," he said. "Wyoming, wildlife type."

"Apparently she and the governor know each other."

"Great—that will help the state."

"Governor Timms is *your* friend too."

"Right now she needs all the friends she can get," Service said. The state was in the economic tank, fiftieth of fifty in most economic categories. The freefall had come on Timms's watch. Most of it was not her fault, but it had come during her watch, which in politics amounted to the same thing.

Service and McKower stood outside the command trailer as others joined them. There were uniforms of various state law enforcement agencies, and various DNR and federal units, park service, fish and wildlife fire personnel, USFS law enforcement, tribal police from Bay Mills, and DNR specialists checking in: logistics, safety, plans, information/PR—even a financial specialist to help oversee the spending of money the State didn't have.

Gar Fox raised his hands for silence. "Kerry Brownmine's coming. Until he's here, I'll coordinate. Time's short. Don't sit on your damn concerns. Get everything on the table as soon as possible so we can take it off just as fast. You're all experienced. National Weather Service is sending us a fire weather guru from somewhere down south."

"Would that be like Berrien Springs, or are we talking, laahk, way down in Mississippi?" some joker drawled.

"Okay," Fox said, "knock off the crap. And spare the man any of your half-baked Yooper weather jokes. Let's do this thing right."

He began: "The ICP is this trailer. The old store next door will house the Red Cross and Salvation Army, and warehouse donations of clothing and food, tools and miscellany. Any evacuees will be directed to the center being set up at the high school. Mo-Neeka, you here?"

A woman raised her hand. "That's Mo-Neeka," Fox said. "She'll handle accommodations for evacuees. There will also be a place for evacuated animals across the street from the high school. Luce County Animal Control is taking care of that show, up to and including horses and cattle."

"Moo," somebody said.

"How big is this thing now?" a voice asked. It was the Luce County sheriff.

"We estimate it's already at four thousand to seven thousand acres, and it's got a shitload of fuel above- and belowground. If it gets as big as Seney, we'll need an army to fight it. Better to plan big and not need it than to plan small and be up shit creek. Other questions?"

None. "When you come to the ICP for daily briefings, don't park here. Find a place elsewhere. Keep this area open for the incident commander and emergency vehicles. We'll probably meet twice a day, early morning and again late evening. If you can't get here, send a rep in your place, and make sure we have a list of your replacements before we break up today." Fox paused to catch his breath. "I've *seen* this fire. 'Dozers will have to surge a couple of roads into the area. You know the drill. Stop it first, then crush it. For now we're in the stop-it-any-way-we-can phase. Winds are gonna push it toward 123, and that's where we're gonna make the first big fight," he said, and paused for emphasis.

"I don't need to tell you that the town is south of us, and all those folks expect us to have their backs, and by God, we do and we will. Section chiefs, if you have someone who can't cut it on their job, get their ass out posthaste. This is neither a training exercise, nor a dress rehearsal. This is the real goddamn deal, ladies and gents. We either produce or we are out, no hard feelings, and that includes everybody here. The incident commander will designate fire divisions, alpha, bravo, Charlie, and so forth." Fox turned to McKower, "The IC may want your people to provide personal escort for division chiefs. Got enough people to cover it?"

"Six coming from the west side," she said. "We're good. Sarn't Service will supervise COs, I'll liaise with the incident commander and other law enforcement at the planning and allocation level. If you need help quickly, go directly to Chief Master Sergeant Service."

Gar Fox smiled. "Thanks, Captain."

This said, Fox moved on to the roles of other law agencies, methodically talking to the lead representative of each group, outlining probable duties and priorities, asking about what they needed or wanted. He was calm, rational, organized, and deadly serious.

Jeffey Bryan arrived and Service went to greet him as other CO trucks began pulling in. McKower stayed with Fox.

"Where's Sedge?" Bryan asked.

"Still east of Crisp at the dig." *I already told him this. Is he being overly nervous?*

"Do we need to get her out of there?"

"Not yet. There's a twenty-mile gap. If she has to evacuate, I told her to hike east to Vermilion and we'll recover them there."

Bryan nodded.

"I'm not taking over for you sergeants," Service told him. "McKower will work with the short team and I'll fill in for her with you. I'm not going to micromanage your shit. You know what to do, so do it. When the western guys get here, give them familiarization rides in key areas over key routes, then turn them loose in their own trucks."

COs were gathering, looking at him expectantly. "This thing may melt into chaos, but it will be *controlled* chaos. Stay calm and help people who need help. Most important, if you need help, ask for it."

Service's cell phone vibrated and he stepped away to answer it. "I'm at the corner by the district," Friday said.

"Come through town north to Four Mile Corner. There are lots of gawkers. Be careful."

Service walked over to McKower. "A Troop I met earlier tonight nearly hit a bear on 123. This is dense bear country. Make sure Gar tells everyone the facts. The fire's gonna have the animals scared and running, and they may be acting stupidly, especially the young males."

She patted his arm and his phone vibrated again. "Sergeant Service, this is Goldie at the lab."

"Have we met?"

"No, I'm the dirt guy," the man said brightly. "That sample you sent over?"

"What about it"

"Not enough. Silica is all I can tell you. Without more to work with, I'm SOL."

"Silica—like sand?"

"Sort of, yessir, but that's not why I'm calling. Don't know if you meant for us to look at this, but you had a fair amount of *Ascalapha odorata* traces in the wooden box."

It was getting noisy. Service pushed a finger in his open ear. "What did you just say?"

"Black witch."

Service held the phone away from his ear and stared at it. "Is that like a rock band, or what?"

"No, no, sorry—it's a giant moth. Some people see it fly at night, which is when it usually flies, and thus they think it's a bat! Thing has a six-inch wingspan."

"This is significant?"

"That's for you to say, sir. *Ascalapha odorata* is native to the Deep South and to the tropics of Central America. On rare occasions they have ventured into the Upper Peninsula. I know of only two places where they've been found, but both are well documented and both are in Chippewa County: Vermilion Point, and a couple miles west of there."

"West toward Crisp Point?"

"You'd know that better than me. Does this help?"

"If you're the dirt guy, how come you know about moths?"

"Hobby for the wife and me. Truth is, working on once-alive stuff is a lot more fun than inanimate substances. I mean, dirt has organisms and all, but hey, it's not the same."

"What do you mean by 'working with them'?"

"You know, radiocarbon-dating and stuff. Not us, but we have a vendor in Florida, and we can get results in a few days. They're good."

Service closed his eyes: *Dumb*. "They can date stuff like a bear bone?"

"How much you got?"

"Couple feet."

"No problem. You want to send it over?"

"I will, but don't try using it as a fly swatter."

"Huh?"

"You'll see. Thanks, Goldie."

• • •

Friday winked when she slid out of the Tahoe, marched directly over to him, and planted a honker of a kiss that brought everyone in the area to an unbreathing standstill.

"Whew," she said, separating.

Service introduced McKower and watched the two women make nice and sniff each other. *Neutral—good so far.* Service led Friday over to his pickup and gave her the keys and the bear-leg breakhead. "Jesus, that looks awful. Is it real?"

"It's real enough, but the real question is, how old? This goes to Goldie at the lab."

She rested her head against his chest. "You need to get your big butt home—all of it," she said gently, and got into his truck. She slid the window down. "Call your granddaughter. I told Karylanne you were in Newberry, she told the kid, and the kid heard about the fire on the TV, and now she's petrified that her Bampy's gonna burn up."

"As in the fires of Hell?"

"No, you dope, like a *marshmallow*. She's a kid, not a sky pilot."

He saw her look past him toward the fire smoke billowing in the north and he could see the concern in her eyes.

"Call me," she said, blew him a kiss, and left him to do his job.

60

Chesbrough Lake, Luce County

SATURDAY, AUGUST 4, 2007

The officers from the western U.P. had shown up after midnight and this morning were riding with east-end COs to get a look at the road systems and help start evacuations, which had been ordered at 0500 that morning.

Incident Commander Kerry Brownmine had taken charge. Gar Fox was with a CO up County Road 407, trying to assess the need for an evac up that way, and gauging where and how to cut a road into the main fire area, which was a little north and east of CR 407.

Service spent the night sleeping in the back of his Tahoe. It was a little cramped, but not bad, and he had slept deeply. He woke rested and immediately went through his truck to inventory and organize his gear, and to start the chain saw to make sure it worked.

A working chain saw could save lives in a fire, especially his own. He had a spare fuel can, which he would fill when he got coffee. There was a spare chain in the plastic carrying box for the saw. He tried on his banana suit, helmet, and goggles. The suit fit well enough and had huge thigh pockets. He pulled his Tahoe over to the fire garage, which was empty of vehicles, and grabbed a double-bit ax and Pulaski from a barrel, signing a paper on a clipboard indicating he'd taken gear.

He drove from the fire garage to Pickelman's on M-28, where he filled up the spare fuel container, making sure to leave it on the ground when he filled it. He went inside and handed the clerk a thermos. "Black coffee, please," he said.

The woman filled the thermos and brought it to him. "Got any Styrofoam cups?"

"You on the fire?" she asked.

He nodded.

"Coffee cups and gas are on the house for you fellas. Be safe out there, eh?"

A man with a shaved head wandered over to him as he got to his Tahoe. "Your fire guys up dere don't know shit," he said.

"Who're you?"

"Russ Cheeker, I been loggin dis county since fifty-two. Dat fire, she ain't goin' nowhere but where she is. Ain't no place she can move to. All they gotta do is guard roads. I logged dat hull damn area. Just peat and swamp. How come then they got all them damn people up here running all over the place?"

"Better too many and not need them, right?" Service said to the man.

"Someday taxpayers gonna get pissed enough make you state boys toe the line, eh." *Why did emergencies seem to bring out the disgruntled?*

There were still vehicles all over Four Mile Corner, but he parked north on M-123 and walked back to the mobile command post and stayed outside. The air was dry and warm, the humidity up. Humidity always seemed to elevate at night. He had no idea why.

Elise pulled in and walked over to join him. "It is very weird to sleep alone in your own home," she said quietly, her eyes half open. Her house was on East Lake, which was west of town. She wore surplus military BDUs and scuffed heavy brown field boots.

"Ain't captains 'pose to look spiffy and pressed?" he ribbed her.

"Only those who patrol office buildings."

The organization had been battling for a long time to acquire some sort of Class C field uniform—battle dress, fatigues, whatever—and so far it had been a no-go. As it was, they worked in the field in uniforms that had to be dry-cleaned, which made no sense from any angle. All other cop outfits had fatigues of some kind. But not the MDNR.

Gar Fox arrived with a man in blue jeans and a faded green DNR shirt. He had beat-up hands, a homely, leathery countenance, and needed a shave and a haircut.

"Brownmine," Elise McKower whispered.

The incident commander waited until everyone had arrived. He seemed secure in silence, not feeling the need to socialize and glad-hand. When the crowd had grown he looked at his watch. "Zero seven hundred, people. We will start all meetings on time. If you're not here, ask someone to catch you up later. Remember this: All politics are loco, and a fire, technical definitions aside, is the ultimate political football. Every move we make out here will be second-guessed by someone somewhere and we are not going to worry about that crap. Just do your jobs and I'll CYA."

Brownmine looked for a response, got none. "Fire in strangmoor is tricky business. Let's be clear: Our goal here is, one, to put out the fire, and two, to do it with no loss of human life and minimal structural damage. If your people get into a situation where they feel tempted to act heroically and in doing so risk their lives, tell them to get the hell out of that position. We have equipment rolling in. We have manpower coming in. This isn't the old days. We know how to fight these monsters, so tell your people to play safe. This monster will eat us if it can, so let's just not serve ourselves up to her. Grady Service here?"

Service held up a hand with a cup of coffee.

"You're gonna be my shotgun. We'll talk more when we're done here."

Service nodded and looked at the ground.

McKower whispered, "Know the diff between a Finnish introvert and a Finnish extrovert?"

Service squinted. "Do tell."

"The introvert looks at his own shoes when you talk to him. The extro-vert looks at *your* shoes."

He chuckled and could see this pleased her immensely. "He check with you about putting hooks on me?"

"Never before laid eyes on the man, but Gar asked me last night who would be the best person to hold Brownmine's hand, and I volunteered you."

"Thanks much."

"Always trying to help, Sergeant."

Brownmine came over after the briefing concluded. "I met Eddie Waco at a conference in Reno a couple of years ago. Helluva man. He called me last night and suggested I use you as my personal escort, and your captain concurs. That gonna fuck up your plans?"

"Twenty-four seven?"

"Just when I need to kiss the fire. I'll need someone who won't drive with his foot on the brake all the time, and Chief Waco says you're that man. You got fire gear?"

"In my truck."

"Go about your business, but make sure I can reach you quickly. If we can't hook up, who should I grab?"

Service pointed at McKower.

"Captain?" Brownmine said.

"Yes," Service said. "But Lansing ain't rubbed itself all over her and dulled her field edge yet."

Brownmine's eyes twinkled.

Gar Fox left the meeting to head up County Road 407, trying to find a way to cross to the fireground, which was a hair east and north. Brownmine issued an order at the briefing for all COs to contact all dwellings between Halfway Lake and Pine Stump and evacuate the residents. Same for all people around the Chesbrough Lake and Widgeon Creek areas, which were east of the Two-Hearted Headwaters Preserve.

Service gathered his COs and sent them out. Sergeant Bryan asked him if he could check camps and help with evacuations around Chesbrough Lake. There weren't enough officers; Service passed this to Elise, who said she'd arrange for additional personnel from other districts.

In the interim he headed toward the lake area to urge people to leave. He let Brownmine know his destination before bugging out. Up on M-123 just south of Murphy Creek there were fire vehicles everywhere, parked helter-skelter. This part of the road was closed north to County Road 500, but the park at Tahquamenon remained open. If tourists needed to escape, they could go east into Paradise, then south to M-28 to get out of the danger area. A fire this time of year would kill tourist businesses, many of which were already on the brink of economic death.

Overhead, Blackhawks carrying 700-gallon Bambi buckets were dropping water along the road. The communications frequencies were cluttered with anxious but businesslike voices. It smelled, felt, and sounded like a small helping of war, right down to the incessant *thump-thump* and whine of the choppers working overhead.

He found himself alone, bumping along deeply rutted two-tracks, smoke curtains wafting like ghosts through the woods. He kept his windows up and air blower going to breathe clean air as best he could. His Automatic Vehicle Locator was going in and out of service, which made it impossible to know exactly where his colleagues were. The rolling map worked, but there were no markers from other COs.

By noon he had hit all the main cabins on the lake and started methodically working named and unnamed side lanes and trails, looking for tents, trailers, or isolated buildings. There were an astonishing number of them, and so far he had sent a half-dozen families packing.

One geezer had told him he was going to remain at his house and help fight the fire. Service took his digital camera out of his pocket, and said. "Show me your hand."

The man did as instructed and Service took a photograph.

"What's that about?" the man asked.

"Needed a picture of your ring and watch to help us identify your charred remains—if we can find your body."

The man gulped and decided to shove off.

Another man wanted to know about his cats.

"How many?" Service asked.

"Twelve or so," the man said sheepishly.

"I think they'll be just fine," Service told the man. "They are born with survival instincts we don't have." He didn't tell the man that most of them might end up as coyote snacks.

He drove up on a young couple humping wildly in the back of a rocking Volkswagen van. When he pounded on the van, a young man opened the side door. "We're putting a priority on which fires to put out first," he told the man. "And yours isn't one of them, pal. Get thee elsewhere or go to jail. Your choice."

"Elsewhere," the man said, reaching for his pants.

"Can we at least finish up?" his girlfriend asked. "I'm, like, *really* close?"

"Move or jail," Service said again.

"That's *so* rude," the girl yelped.

• • •

By early afternoon, it seemed that most people were gone. He was about to head back to the ICP when he saw a man stumbling along a two-track ahead of him. He stepped on the gas to catch up; at twenty yards the person turned around and looked at him. *Kermit?* The man bolted north into the brush and Grady Service ran right behind him, but in less than five minutes his lungs were filling with fire smoke, and he knew the man could easily hide in this miasma. *Not smart to make a foot chase in a smoker.*

So much for end-stage macular degeneration! Lying little fucker! Faking blindness.

Service called Jeffey Bryan on the district's 800 channel. "I just saw Kermit," he told the young sergeant.

"Where?"

"Between Chesbrough and Widgeon Trail," Service said, coughing.

"Smoke getting you? Take a shot on your respirator."

"It was him."

"You sure?"

"Absolutely. He took one look at me and ran."

"Pretty good for a blind man," Bryan said. "You want help?"

"Thanks . . . I'm tempted, but my gut tells me we'll never find him in this smoke. Spread the word that everyone needs to keep an eye peeled for him."

"My AVL's in the crapper," Bryan reported. "I'm just north of you . . . I think."

Service said, "I'm using an old plat book, marking off the roads as I check them."

"People resisting?"

"Some, but not bad." *If Delongshamp is rustling deer for hunt clubs, why is he still here?*

On another two-track, five minutes later, he came up behind a naked woman carrying a rifle with a scope. She wore high-top Converse All-Star red tennis shoes.

"Uhh, ma'am?"

The woman turned around and glared at him. "That *thing* took my T-Bone."

Service stepped toward her. "Why don't you let me hold your rifle while we talk. I'll try to help you, but let me secure the rifle, okay?"

She didn't resist when he took the weapon and eased the safety on. "Where do you live?" he asked her. His maps showed no properties in this area. This was state land.

"Back 'ere," she said, looking back into the woods. "Oh my."

She reeked of booze. "How much have you had to drink?"

The woman exhaled dramatically. "Either way too much or way too little," she said. "Where's my T-Bone? I just want my T-Bone."

"Who is T-Bone?"

"Companion and protecker. Wanna see pitcher?"

She groped around and a sheepish grin fell into place. "Left my purse at camp. Lesgosee purse—you wanna drinkie?"

"No drinkie. Go *where?*" he asked.

"I dunno," she said seriously. "I *usta* know."

"Was it a bear?"

"T-Bone?" she said. "No, he's my poochie-woochie. Boy!" she added, "I really need a drinkie. You got drinkie?"

"Water."

She made a gagging sound. "Not *that.*"

"Where are your clothes, ma'am?"

"Don't need 'em on private property."

"That's true when you're on *your* private property, but this is state land."

She closed her eyes, said, "I do not know where my camp is. I want my T-Bone. And I want drinkie."

"It's dangerous here," he told her. "We're evacuating all residents to town."

"But I don't got no clothes," she said.

"We'll take care of that for you."

"You will? Can we get drinkie-winkie too?"

"We'll see," he said, humoring her. "What's your name?"

"My mama said don't give that out to strangers."

"My name's Grady."

"Mine's not," she said mischieviously, and quickly added, "I am Lois Lane."

He raised an eyebrow and she thrust her chest up. "Only with *great* tits!"

Booze, he thought.

"I like parties," Lois Lane said.

"What about T-Bone?" he asked.

"Who?"

Fire smoke and booze. Lovely combo.

"My name's not Lois Lane," she said quietly, and then she took off into the woods.

Service toggled his 800 and called Jeffey Bryan. "I've got a runner headed toward Widgeon Creek Road. Can you head this way?"

"Got a description?" the sergeant asked.

"Yeah, she's naked with red high-top sneakers," Service said. "She has good tits and she's real drunk."

"Oh good! *Your* mammary scale?"

"Nope, hers. I don't have a scale."

"I'm headed your way—I think."

Moments later Bryan was back on the radio. "We just saw a bear carrying a little white foo-foo dog."

Service got back into his truck. T-Bone, he guessed, was about to become a snack.

What the hell is Delongshamp doing here? He tried the 800 again for Sedge and she answered. "Uh-huh," she said. "How bad's the fire?"

"Where are you?" he asked.

"Just coming off CR 500. Toliver's team went ballistic over the fire. There was a small rebellion this morning. They heard about it on a cell phone, or iPod or some damn thing, and wanted out. I sent them east to Vermilion with Katsu and Limpy. The professor's with me."

"Good call. I'm at Chesbrough Lake, evacuating residents."

"You want me down there with you?"

"That would be good."

"Rolling," she said.

Radio discipline is going straight to hell, he thought.

61

Chesbrough Lake, Luce County

SATURDAY, AUGUST 4, 2007

Bryan came bumping along from the north and Sedge from the south, the two filthy black patrol trucks converging on Service's Tahoe.

The lanky sergeant got out of his truck, leaving his door standing open, and walked over. "Your lady friend is in a red cabin a quarter-mile back," he reported.

"You saw her in the area, or going into a place?"

"I saw her in all her glory going into the red cabin. Totally starkers."

Sedge wandered over. Professor Ozzien Shotwiff remained in the passenger seat of her truck, but waved a puny salute at Service.

"What happened to Toliver and his diggers?" Bryan asked Sedge.

"Like I said on the radio—revolution. They bugged out and wanted to go back to their pre-dig quarters in Paradise. It was like yelling *Fire!* in a crowded room. The word spread like wildfire, and they were like . . . outta there, most quick."

"Katsu and Allerdyce?" Service asked.

"I asked Katsu to keep an eye on the dig team. He can get in touch with me on the cell phone. Allerdyce? No idea. He was behind me and the convoy, and when I pulled onto pavement and looked back, he was gone. But he was a big help Grady," she said. "He really was."

Will I ever figure out that old sonuvabitch? "How's the prof?"

"Disappointed, I think. He likes being in the woods, and I think he's lonely."

"Katsu or Toliver get wind of the other site?"

"Not that I could tell. Did I hear the word *naked* on the radio?"

Service told her what had happened.

"What got into her?"

"Devil rum and analogs, I'm guessing."

"How close is the fire?" she asked.

"Less than a mile out in the peat and fens." Service felt the wind shifting toward the south. "If the wind holds it will push it away from here, but the damn wind is swapping around like crazy and without warning. We need to get people out of this area while we can."

"He saw Kermit," Bryan told Sedge.

"No way! *Today?*" She looked at Service with unmasked astonishment.

"Thirty minutes ago, maybe, about a third of a mile west of us. He looked back at me and rabbited into the smoke. I started to follow, but figured we have higher priorities."

"Let's go fetch Lady Godiva," Sedge said. "This I have to see."

"She'll want a drinkie-winkie," Service said.

"I bet she will."

"Don't mention that a bear was seen carrying her little dog away."

"Any idea why Kermit is here?" she wanted to know.

"None."

To Bryan: "Again, Jeffey, you saw Ms. Nudist go *into* the red cabin?"

The sergeant nodded and smiled. "Most people should never sashay around in public in the buff. But this lady is in that small minority who can pull it off, so to speak."

Service told the sergeant to continue his patrol.

The red cabin was old and made of logs with yellowing broken chinking forming crooked mosaics between the logs. There was a porch on all sides, a couple of small outbuildings, and a large garage-pole building made of aluminum and set on a large cement slab. There were two old buck poles near the large building.

"Want help?" Professor Shotwiff asked as Service walked over to Sedge's truck.

"Thanks, we're good," Sedge told him. "Keep an eye on the fire for us and your ear on the radio. If something happens, honk the horn. We have to gather up an unwilling evacuee. She might be a bit on the drunk side."

Shotwiff smiled.

Sedge went to the south door and Service went to the north side and stayed back so he could see both the east and west porticos. If she came out he could easily run her down here.

There was gray-white ash curling in the air again, beginning to put a light dusting on the landscape. *Keep your goggles around your neck*, he reminded himself.

"Got her," Sedge said over her 800. "She's out, cold as a cod. I'll fireman-carry her out to your vehicle. Can you jump in the cabin and find some clothes for her?"

The cabin was cluttered in a loving, ancient way, the walls covered by photographs of hunters with dead deer and bears and birds and strings of trout. Forty or more small deer antlers mounted on plywood shields had been nailed along the ceiling line throughout the cabin. It was an old place with a lot of history and memories for someone. It would be a damn shame if the fire ate it.

He found a bedroom with an open suitcase on a twin bed. Woman's clothes. He grabbed a pillowcase and threw stuff into it, including ankle-high hiking boots. He started out of the room and noticed a framed glass case on the wall filled with arrowheads, shaped like a giant fan. Was this proof of what Limpy had claimed—that this stuff was all over the place up here? He paused to look. Some of the points were copper, turned green shades.

The woman had vomited on herself and his dash by the time he got out to his truck. There was a hose attached to a spigot sticking up from the ground and he stretched the hose to the vehicle. Sedge propped up the woman and Service hosed her down, and when Sedge said, "I think that should do it," he flipped her the pillowcase and went to shut off the water. "Get her dressed," he said over his shoulder.

"She's a looker," Sedge said. "Sure you don't want to do this?"

"Just do the damn job and let's get the hell out of here," he chirped at her.

As he and Sedge struggled with the woman's largely dead weight, trying to fasten her seat belt, he said, "The soil sample didn't work out."

"You want to cuff her?" Sedge asked.

"Nah, she'll be okay."

"So the soil sample was no good?"

"Right, but the techs say there is evidence of a black witch."

She stared at him. "You mean like the evil sister of Glinda the good witch, or what?"

"It's a moth," he said, "size of a bat."

"I'm not into bats," Sedge said.

"Need drinkie," the drunk woman slurred. She looked Service in the eye. "You pack Dr. Ruth?"

What the hell was she talking about? "Yep, she's in your bag."

"Okay," she blathered. "Gone *need* her." The woman narrowed her eyes and stared at Service, her head bobbing. "I don't like your attitude one bit, Bubba." With this, her chin hit her chest and she was out again.

"You continue to make a big first impression on people," Sedge said.

"It's a gift from God. What the hell is Dr. Ruth?"

"Only the most powerful electric vibrator in the history of civilization," the young officer said.

He was unable to think of a suitable rejoinder. "Follow me into town to the high school. We'll dump Lois Lane and the professor there."

"Her name is Lois Lane?"

"That's what she said earlier."

Sedge grinned and patted his arm.

Service drove less than a hundred yards when a small white dog came scampering down the two-track toward him. He braked, put the truck in park, and got out. "T-Bone!"

The little dog launched itself into his waiting arms. Service rubbed its ears and put the animal on the floor at the woman's feet. There were pink spots in the animal's white fur, probably blood from his ride in the bear's jaws. But it was just pink, not dripping. "I think you'll live, mutt. It's your human I have serious doubts about."

"Kermit sighting," Sergeant Bryan announced over the radio. "At the intersection of Lang Trail and Widgeon."

Service stared at the computer's rolling map. Based on where he had seen the man, he seemed to be heading northwest into some really nasty, hard country.

"You want us to pursue?" Bryan asked.

"Stay with priorities," Service told his friend, and followed Sedge toward M-123.

62

Over Luce County in a Blackhawk

FRIDAY, AUGUST 10, 2007

Grady Service had flown in a lot of helicopters, never in circumstances that allowed him to sit back and enjoy the ride, and this time was no different. At least this time there was no one on the ground looking to put a lucky shot into the bird.

Governor Lorelei Timms was dressed in chic blue blouse and black slacks, her hair pulled back, an Army Guard camo flight helmet pulled over her head. Service had never before noticed what intense, lively eyes she had as she listened to Brownmine describe the ugly, blackened, twenty-five-square-mile fire scene below them. "We have it at fifty percent containment, Governor. That doesn't mean it's out. It just means we have a ring around it, and with a little luck it will stay inside that ring. Peat and roots could very well burn until fall rains set in and snow comes. There's a remote but very real possibility we could have some flare-ups next spring, but it's not likely. In any event, Gar Fox is the local fire officer, the best in the state, and he won't let this thing jump up on us."

"No serious injuries?" Lori asked.

"Not so far. Just some minor stuff, and everyone will recover. And only a couple of structures lost. We've been real lucky on this one, given the conditions. We turn total squirrel with a fire index of three hundred. It was twice that when this happened."

Governor Timms reached over and affectionately patted Service's knee. "You look like crap," she said. "When's the last time you slept?"

"A full night? Uh, I can't remember." *With somebody? Even longer.*

The governor chuckled and rolled her eyes. "How come you aren't wearing your uniform?"

"No time to get it, and it's not practical for this kind of work."

"Why aren't you wearing a fire suit?"

"Why aren't you?"

"We're not in the fire."

"There ya go," he said, earning another laugh.

"You know your new chief, Eddie Waco?"

"I do."

"You gonna tell me the NRC made a good choice?"

"Do you think you did?"

"Absolutely."

"There you go," he said again.

"You pissed at me?"

"Nope, but if I could get Sam Bozian up here, I'd mash his ugly snoot into the ashes and hold it there till he stopped kicking."

"Are you threatening a former elected official?"

"No, ma'am, just dreaming. Dreams are still legal, right?"

"Some of them," she said. "I think."

"I'm sorry things are so bad," he said to her, and she looked at him and nodded. He thought he even saw the hint of a tear, but Governor Timms, as ladylike as she seemed, was also as tough and resilient as tempered steel.

"When we land and can find a quiet place, there's something I want to talk to you about," he said.

She nodded and turned her attention back to the fire scar and smoke tendrils and clouds below.

• • •

Back at Four Mile Corner the governor had just finished a radio broadcast in a local radio station's mobile broadcast trailer. Service saw that her anxious handlers were all vying for her attention, but she made eye contact with him and motioned for him to join her.

"Let's go see the Red Cross people," she said, and led him into the old store, which had become a warehouse for donated goods. The Red Cross people were immediately fawning, but she waved them off. "Could we have the room alone for a few minutes, folks?" she asked.

Just like that, they were alone.

"Nice to have power," he said.

"I wish. What is it you wanted to talk about?"

"It's not fire-related."

"Fine, tell me."

He took her through the situation with the state archaeologist, and how conservation officers were charged with protecting antiquities, but the State would not reveal locations unless a crime had been detected and the officer thought to ask if it was a state archaeological site.

"You're making this up, right?"

"No, ma'am. It's real."

"You're supposed to protect something you can't even know is there?"

"Catch-twenty-two," he said. "Sort of like that."

"You realize I'll have to get the attorney general on this. These damn rules never seem to operate on common sense. I'm not promising I can change it through the legislature. The Republicans there would vote to keep me from ever taking another crap in my own home if it would win them imagined points with voters. But I *can* issue an executive order. The next governor sitting in my seat can also quickly undo that."

"Anything would help. It's not fair to ask our people to do something, then handicap the doing."

"I agree with you, Grady. You know anything about some very strange billboards that popped up all over the state—like morels?"

"Nope," he said.

"Why is my skeptic-meter full right?"

"Don't know."

"Any other business?"

"No, that's it."

"Good. The billboards made me laugh out loud! How's our Little Mar?"

"Precocious."

"I am not surprised. Your new lady, Detective Friday. When do I get to meet her?"

Obviously she had somebody watching him. "When will you be in Marquette?"

"Maybe after the Labor Day Bridge Walk. I'll call ahead. It'll probably be a rush thing. This life is all about rushing around. My kids hate it."

"And you?"

"I thought I'd be able to do more than I've been able to do, and I don't much like that feeling, Grady. I love this state. There's a helluva lot of politicians in this state that give lip service to that, but I mean it."

She added, "I'm buying some top-line Yooper swampers for the next governor and will tell them to be prepared to wade through shit every single day. They should look at the teamwork on this fire to see how things should work," she added.

The fire "event" had not gone as perfectly as it looked to the governor. A controlled back-burn near Pine Stump Junction had nearly gotten out of control and taken out everything in that area, but nature in the form of another wind shift had saved them. The radios didn't work for shit. People two hundred yards apart resorted to sending runners to pass orders, like World War I or something. Different agencies couldn't talk to each other at all. And of course cell-phone coverage was virtually nil in most parts of the northern county.

Far from perfect, but the thing had been beaten. So far. Downstate the state police were rumored to be warning all citizens to stay out of any part of the U.P. because of the fires, and at least one toll attendant at the big bridge had been warning tourists away from anywhere in the eastern U.P.

Governor Lorelei Timms looked at him. "Do you know that local people are doing laundry for firefighters?" She shook her head. "This place . . . ," she said. "These people . . ." Her eyes were clearly tearing up, and she was unable to finish.

Suddenly she stiffened. "You're *sure* you don't know anything about those billboards all around the state?"

"Heard about them. Even saw one."

"I bet you have," she said with a taut jaw. She squeezed his arm. "Okay, let's get our butts back to work, big boy."

They stepped out of the room to be greeted by a growing gathering of Red Cross workers and citizens and firefighters, and she began to mingle, which she did with such ease and with such genuine feeling, it was hard to understand how anyone like Lori had ever ended up in the damn swamp of state politics. The state didn't deserve her, and she sure as hell deserved better from the entire state.

Brownmine walked over to him. "Good lady, eh?"

Service said. "For a politician."

"You want to ride the circuit with me today?" the incident commander asked.

"You da boss. Something up?"

"Flying over a fire with the governor and dancing the edge are different things. I like knowing from close-up what I think I'm seeing from above. Make sense?"

"Absolutely."

"There's still a lot of burning over in the Two-Hearted Headwaters, and I want to hike in that way and see what I can see," the incident commander said.

|||||||||||||||||||||||||||||||||||||||||||||||||||||||||||||||||||||||||||||||||||||||||||||||||||||||||||||||||||||||||

63

Two-Hearted Headwaters, Luce County

SUNDAY, AUGUST 12, 2007

Kerry Brownmine was young, cool-headed, logical, analytical, supportive of his team, and the best fire boss Service had ever worked with—which was saying a lot, because back when he'd started as a CO, he had worked with the great Gar Fox. Brownmine knew how to manage a complex process and how to lead people, both individually and in a group. He could make small talk, but there was no bullshit in the man.

There was supposed to have been rain the night before, but it had never materialized. The I-Met said today's temperature would hit the high seventies, with more low humidity. The morning winds were eight to twelve miles per hour, but I-Met predicted they would flip over to northwest by late afternoon and blow at fifteen to twenty miles per hour, with thirty-mile-per-hour gusts. This day was going to be a huge test for everyone, and for the twenty-seven-mile perimeter line dug out by 'dozers and hardworking hand crews.

The summer Perseid meteors were supposed to be in full display last night, at sixty meteors an hour, but smoke and heavy cloud cover had prevented anyone from seeing meteors, much less any stars, and most minds were on the fire, not what was above it. Today's clouds were tinged with ominous yellow and sickly grays and looked to Service like they led to the portals of Hell.

This morning Service had hauled the fire boss to the end of County Road 420 and they had hiked south into the Two-Hearted River headwaters property owned by the Michigan Nature Conservancy. They had stopped at the remote McMahon Lake Plains area and checked out the location and results of a backfire Brownmine's people had set the night before.

"We've got good black here," the fire boss said. "We're right in the middle of the fens, the strangmoor country. No way we can fight the beast in here. We have to block ahead of it and beat it that way. So far, our line's good," he added. "Our people have been working their butts off. Relief crews are coming in from all over the country."

In the distance, Service could see small tongues of flame and rising smoke. It stunk and got into his pores and clothes. Heat rolled over them from the fire and the hot ground under their boots.

Brownmine was on his radio, talking to the pilot of an army National Guard Chinook, carrying a two-thousand-gallon bucket. "Roger, dump right in front of us, Army," the incident commander said as the Chinook whined low toward them.

Both men got down on a knee, put a hand on top of their yellow helmets, and looked down, their chins tucked into their chests, waiting for the bolus of falling water. If two thousand gallons caught you standing, it could matchstick your back.

"Danger close," Service told his companion.

"Let's be glad it's water and not napalm," Brownmine said. "Director Cheke's coming in tonight. She wants a meet."

"Got other duties."

"You can't be a hard-ass all the time, Sergeant. Everyone in Lansing is not the enemy."

"I know," Service said. "You're in Baraga."

The incident commander laughed.

The high-frequency fire radio squawked. "Fire Six, Bravo Six."

"Fire Six," Brownmine answered.

"We've got a few slops over toward Halfway Lake. Have you had contact with Alpha Six?"

"Negative on Alpha Six. Were you able to step on the slops?"

"That's affirmative, Bravo Six. We're on watch. This wind is crazy. Just thought you'd want to know."

"Your team need anything over there?"

"Negative, we're good. Bravo Six."

Brownmine said, "Alpha Six, Fire Six."

"Fire Six, we've been seeing unauthorized personnel over this way all day. The evac order is still in effect, correct?"

"Affirmative. That order remains in effect until we revoke it. You have law enforcement present?"

"Yes, but spread way thin," the sector chief reported.

"Twenty Four Fourteen will roll over your way as soon as he can find a ride for me. Fire Six."

"Alpha Six, thanks. Tell Twenty Four Fourteen we're due west of Chesbrough Lake at this time."

"There," Brownmine said to Service. "Now you have a legit reason to skip the meeting."

"Why's the director here?" Service asked. "Flag show?"

"I'm passing the baton to a new incident commander. This thing's holding at fifty percent. We want as many people as we can to get firsthand incident command experience. Find me a ride, and I'll get out of your hair."

Brownmine hooked on with a water truck heading back for a refill and handed Service his HF radio. "Old but reliable," the incident commander said. "Just like you. The Nature Conservancy sent people and radios. It's damn nice to have at least one organization in this state that's driven first and foremost by science."

"Who's the new IC?

"Fire Supervisor Maximillian Stinson."

"Stumphumper Stinson, from Durand?"

Brownmine nodded. "You know him?"

"Long time. Old carrier rustpicker picked up downed pilots with a chopper crew off coastal North Vietnam."

"Rustpicker? That makes you a jarhead."

"Semper fi."

"Drop the HF with Stumphumper when you're done with it. Do you know Director Cheke?"

"No."

"She once told the vice president of the United States, 'Bite me.' Cheke's a pro, fearless and dedicated to science. Our legislators are *not* going to enjoy trying to play bullshit games with her. You and I are gonna have ringside seats for one helluva scrap."

"I hope she doesn't underestimate the staying power of full-time, overpaid professional assholes," Service said. "Science is sometimes vastly overrated by those who believe in it most," he added.

Brownmine waved, jumped into a red truck, and was gone.

Service's 800 came to life. "Twenty Four Fourteen, Two One Thirty."

"Twenty Four Fourteen." His new call number sounded odd to him.

"Your location?"

He glanced at the rolling map on the AVL. " 'Dozer line running south off the end of County 420."

"I'm headed back to Lois Lane's little red house."

"Say again?"

"You heard me. She ran from the evac center last night."

"You want backup?"

"We finally got an ID on her," Sedge said. "The name Skyler Verst ring a bell?"

God, Held's easy glove. "Affirmative, Twenty Four Fourteen. The subject drinking again?"

"Unknown."

"Anyone see her depart?"

"It's not a POW camp," Sedge said. "No. The professor noticed this morning that she was gone and called me."

"Rolling your way," he said. "Where are you?"

"Just turning north on South Chesbrough Road, if that's the name. I'm not sure what it's called. How's the fire?"

"Some hot spots southwest toward Halfway Lake." Service looked east into the fen country and knew somewhere east there was a sportsman's club that might have some two-tracks, but with fire lurking he couldn't risk getting stuck. "I'm going to have to come all the way around; call it thirty miles and close to an hour."

"Two One Thirty copies. The professor wanted to come."

"You told him no, right?"

"You bet I did, and he's sitting right next to me as we speak."

Service pulled up to the watertruck with the IC aboard and signaled for it to pull over. "I've got to go back through Four Mile," he told Brownmine. "You might as well ride with me."

Brownmine slid into the Tahoe, took off his helmet, and pulled a pack of cigarettes from his jumpsuit pocket. "You got a light?"

Service laughed and handed his lighter to him.

Goldie caught him on the cell phone after he'd dropped Brownmine at the Four Mile command post. "Sergeant, I'm sorry this took so long."

Service tried to remember the date and day, but couldn't. "What have you got for us, Goldie?"

"Mid-seventeenth century, give or take twenty-five years."

"That's certain?"

"Yessir."

"Thanks, Goldie."

The weapon fit the time period, and if Smoke Ghizi was correct, the same weapon could very well have been in Toliver's hands. But who had found it—and where, and when? This goddamn case was just one question after another.

He picked up his hand mic. "Two One Thirty, Twenty Four Fourteen."

"Two One Thirty is on foot," she answered.

"That item we sent to Marquette tested within the time tolerance."

"I can't believe this idiot woman came back here," she said angrily.

Service smiled and accelerated. *She is a lot like me*, he thought. Except for the painting thing.

64

Chesbrough Lake, Luce County

MONDAY, AUGUST 13, 2007

A lot to sort out in this thing—maybe too much. Focus. What had Smoke Ghizi said about nighthawks sometimes staging diversions so they can loot national park relic sites? Could Delongshamp have set this fire for such a reason? No evidence. Don't let your damn mind run loose. You've got plenty of reality. Don't soil it with fantasies. Still . . .

Service called McKower on the 800. "Are you with Fire Six?"

"He's briefing Director Cheke."

"Ask him if we're certain that lightning started this thing."

"Are you entertaining other possibilities?" she asked.

"Probably not, but you know how my mind works."

"I doubt that, but I'll talk to Fire Six. You're at Chesbrough, yes?"

"Heading that way." No doubt Brownmine had told her—more evidence that he knew how to follow and lead, which showed they had a lot in common.

"Two One Thirty, you still on foot?"

"Affirmative. No sign of our girl yet, but the smoke's not too bad out this way, and right now that's a good thing. Where are you?"

"Just turning north on the same road you took."

"I parked about three hundred yards south of the cabin. No idea where our friend is, but I don't want to spook her if we can avoid it."

The vaunted 800-megahertz radios, once thought secure, were now subject to inexpensive scanners, resulting in back-and-forth messages between officers that exchanged information more scant than substantive. Technology advances were always temporary. The bad guys always caught up quickly.

"I'll do the same. Twenty Four Fourteen."

"If you see a pale blue Datsun pickup, it's Quinn Beard's. I recruited him to help us."

Quinn Beard had been a horse blanket, a long-retired old-time CO. Service had served briefly with him as his own career was getting under way. *Got to be eighty now. At least eighty.* "You checked the cabin yet?" he radioed to Sedge.

"I decided to sit on it for a while. Seems reasonable she's headed here."

Service stopped his truck and checked his plat book. *Undated. Shit. Most counties have the publication year on the cover. Not Luce.* He flipped to the area and found the property on the east side of the lake. The plat book said, "SV etux." *SV and wife? Shit. One lousy bar on the cell phone.* He dialed Honeypat Allerdyce's number and mentally crossed his fingers.

"Thought youse was puttin' out big fires," Honeypat answered.

How does she know that? "Skyler Verst's ex-husband's name."

"Sid."

"He own property in Luce County?"

"I ain't his realtor, darlin'."

"Describe Skyler."

"Why?"

"Honeypat."

"Five-two, thick dark hair, big plastic boobs, hundred pounds soaking wet."

"She have a drinking problem?"

"Don't we all from time to time?"

"*Honeypat.*"

"*Okay*, youse don't gotta get your skivvies in a knot, and youse don't have to yell! Little bitty thing like her, she don't hold it so well."

"When she left her hubby, did she get property in the settlement?"

Honeypat chuckled. "They never divorced, eh. She just kicked 'im out. I told youse that, 'member?"

Service rubbed his eyes in frustration and tried to remember their conversation, eventually recalling Honeypat's exact words: "She just pushed Verst out the door." *Jesus, man. Follow up, listen, get the wax out of your ears. Stop being lazy. Do your damn job.*

"Thanks, Honeypat," he said, and disconnected the cell phone, which now showed no bars. *Damn UP geography!* He radioed McKower again. "Can you get in touch with the County Register of Deeds?"

"It was lightning," McKower said.

"How can they know that?"

"They can't really, but it's a logical assumption based on how events unfolded."

"There's *no* possibility of arson?"

"Some, but very, very slight, which is to say improbable from the standpoint of odds. What do we want from the Register of Deeds?"

"Sid Verst of East Grand Rapids. Is he the current owner of a property on Chesbrough Lake?"

"Back at you," she answered, and broke contact.

He found Quinn Beard and Professor Shotwiff leaning against Beard's truck. Beard wore a small automatic in a belt holster and didn't look much older than when Service had last seen him many years ago. "Long time," he greeted the retired officer.

"Winters in Arizona," Beard said. "My bones can't handle U.P. winters anymore."

"You look fit enough to put on your uniform."

"Appearances deceive. What's the score with this tootsie we're looking for?"

"Mandatory evac. Last time we found her she was drunk and naked."

Beard raised an eyebrow. "Was a day when that would pretty much define a high old time for me. I gather she's back here."

"We think she's headed this way, but we don't know if or why. Excuse me."

Service toggled his 800. "Two One Thirty, Twenty Four Fourteen is with Sergeant Beard. Did Lois Lane grab her dog when she bugged out?"

"Negative. I checked." *Why was Kermit here? Where is that little asshole headed?*

"No sign?"

"Not yet. *Relax.*"

"You want us on foot up there with you?"

"Negative. Just hang there for a while."

"Twenty Four Fourteen," he said. To Beard: "You know Sedge?"

"Yep. Introduced herself to all the retirees when she moved into the area. Good gal, good CO. We all like her. Straight shooter."

"Where's your place?"

"In town, down the street from Joy Hospital."

"You know the area out this way pretty well?"

"Good as anyone," Beard said.

"If you hike northeast from here, what do you hit?"

"Little Two-Hearted Lakes country. Mostly heavy cedar swamps. If you keep going, you'll hit Pike Lake, and more cedar swamps, hemlock—you know, the eastern U.P. in all its swampy glory."

"Pike Lake built up?"

"Some. Hell, there's even a country stop-and-rob and a phone booth out there."

"Deer populations?"

"Still real low from too many consecutive bad winters."

"You know of any Indian sites in the county?"

"Close to here? Nope, but an old-timer once told me that Indians used to have a winter camp on Brimstone Pond, which isn't on any map. It's a deep water hole in the middle of black spruce peatlands between Sheephead and Betsy Lakes. Lots of wild cranberry marshes, squatloads of muskeg, real badass footing. The old guy told me he used to use modified snowshoes to hike out there in summer. The pond's springfed and used to be loaded with big native squaretails. There's a half-mile-long drumlin with a bunch of maple trees so the Indians could camp on hard ground, trap the area, shoot moose in winter, tap for syrup in spring."

"You've been there?"

"Not on foot. Flew over it when we used a plane to work night shooters. Only person who ever talked about the place was that old man, and he's dead twenty years."

"Why'd he go out there?"

"Brook trout and arrowheads. Had him a helluva collection. Always wondered what happened to all that stuff after he died."

Service walked over to his truck and checked his computer map. "That's inside Tahquamenon Park's borders," he said over his shoulder.

"Seems about right. I guess I never thought about that," Beard said.

"Twenty Four Fourteen, Cinderella has arrived and she's even dressed this time."

"Quinn says that breaks his heart."

"I bet it does. I'll wait for you guys."

They approached the cabin as they had before, but Beard stayed with Service.

"Empty," Sedge reported on the radio. "I'm doing an inside walk-around right now."

Two minutes later. "She's not here, Grady. She must've walked in the front door and right on out the back. There's a pile of clothes inside the back door."

"We'll check the lake," Service said, and he and Beard headed north through a popple grove toward the lake, a hundred yards away. Service peeked out before stepping out of cover.

The naked woman was waist-deep in water, beside a dock, a shotgun in hand.

"Hey there, Lois Lane," Service said, stepping out.

The woman stared daggers at him. "I *loathe* the clothes you picked!" And added, "*Men.*" *Probably not a compliment.*

"What's going on here?" he asked, advancing slowly toward her.

She tilted her head to the left. "I hate messes. This way I don't ruin any clothes, there's no mess for anyone to clean up, and all the fishies get fed."

Suicide. Shit! "You should slow down, think about this," Service said as calmly as he could manage.

"Right—if I slow down, I'll get cold feet. Just make sure you tell that asshole this is *his* fault."

"Look, Skyler—"

"You *know* who I am? Oh sweet Jesus! That clinches it."

"You pull that trigger and there's no turning back," he said.

"That's the whole point," she said, took a deep breath, exhaled loudly, placed the barrel under her chin, and a cloud of pink spray lifted from her shoulders before the concussion of the report made Service flinch. Then another round thundered out of the gun as she fell backwards and both Service and the retired officer went flat on the ground.

"Jesus!"Sedge shouted, coming through the woods. "Jesus!"

Professor Ozzien Shotwiff emerged from the trail Service and Beard had taken, looked at the water, said, "My Lord," and sank slowly to his knees. He lowered his head, put his hands on the ground to steady himself, and began to vomit.

Service and Sedge moved out on the dock. There were small rings on the lake's surface as small fish began to feed on morsels of human flesh. Sedge was on her radio, calling the district office, asking them to pass word to the county medical examiner, and to send a bus—cop talk for an emergency vehicle.

"She say anything?" Sedge asked.

"She hated the clothes I picked out for her."

"She's naked," Sedge pointed out.

"I'm merely the reporter," Grady Service said.

"I think I want to go home now," Professor Ozzien Shotwiff said behind them.

65

Paradise, Chippewa County

MONDAY, AUGUST 13, 2007

They left the remains in the water and Sedge stayed at the lake to await the medical examiner's people. Service was surprised that she had enough bars to call Katsu on her cell phone. After a brief discussion she looked at Service. "Toliver, his diggers, and Jane Rain are still with him at the cabins in Paradise," she told him before he left.

Service wasn't sure how he was going to cull Rain from the others, but when he pulled up in his Tahoe he saw her sitting on a bench by the shore of Whitefish Bay, smoking a cigarette. He stood beside the bench. "Seat taken?"

She didn't even look up at him. "Help yourself," she said. "You smell like fire."

"Ya think? Listen, it's just us government drones here, so let's not play ring-around-the-bullshit-pole."

Rain's face remained impressively impassive. *Has control of herself.*

"Ghizi told Sedge and me about Toliver and some war clubs and a Milwaukee dealer and all that stuff, and how Toliver sanctimoniously told the government his college didn't want tainted artifacts, which subsequently disappeared, making the point moot. But guess what? An agate breakhead with a bear-bone handle surfaced in Trout Lake of all places. How many clubs like that could there be? And no two agates are identical."

Rain looked him in the eye. "Clatchety's ersatz museum?"

Good, we can collaborate without games. "I bought the weapon for ten grand."

"It's worth more," she said, "a whole lot more to some collectors, not necessarily residents or citizens of the US of A."

"Cash is sometimes king in the land of fencing," he said. "Clatchety tried to sell me an Iroquois chief's cane. Mohawk."

She grunted. "We're familiar with that item."

"Me too. A guy in Lansing tried to sell me the same piece."

"It's not authentic," special agent Jane Rain said, "but it fools almost everyone."

"Manufactured?"

"A nineteenth-century con job, not contemporary."

"Let me guess: Your people had it and put it into circulation."

"Some pumps require more priming than others."

"Is the bear-leg club part of the priming work?"

"Nope, that's for real, and it's also out of left field. We lost track of it in 2006."

"Clatchety was speechless when I passed on the cane."

"Why are we having this talk?" the U.S. Fish and Wildlife special agent asked.

"Delongshamp turned up at the fire."

No acknowledgment of any kind.

"Skyler Verst offed herself."

Jane Rain shuddered.

"Ate a shotgun," he added. "I watched it happen."

Rain stifled a gasp.

"You *know* her?" he asked.

"Her ex, who is technically not her ex, narked on her little relic biz with Imago Held. She scouts, he finances, others do the selling, marketing, and risk-taking."

"Others, like Clatchety?"

"And Hectorio. The two of them are partners, but their business relationship as of late has been shaky, we hear, and we've suspected a permanent schism in the works. Hectorio doesn't like—or leave—messes."

Messes. The same word the Verst woman used. "Held's network?"

"Presumably. A real scum-line. We know six or eight names, real lulus, but meticulous lulus. Held knows how to play with bad boys, big and small."

"Has the IRS got their nose into Held?"

"You know the IRS. They like to Lone Ranger it."

"How close are you to moving against Held?"

She shrugged. "Hard to say."

"Is Toliver part of Held's field force?"

"We're not sure. If he is, we haven't found the angle yet. Where's the agate-head club?"

"At Michigan State Police forensics lab in Marquette."

"Are they checking for prints?"

"I didn't ask."

"Could you?"

"Sure. You don't know Delongshamp, aka Kermit, aka Brannigan?"

"No. Should I?"

He believed her. "What about Peewee Bolf?"

"Who's that?"

"Our frog's partner. How does Katsu fit into this?"

"You are a very odd man, Chief Master Sergeant," Jane Rain said. "Katsu is more of a bystander than anything else. Maybe."

"That's not what Ghizi told us," Service came back.

"That was then, this is now. Things change," she said.

"Why are you shadowing Toliver?"

"I don't think I can talk about that."

"Look," he said. "We're either partners and collaborators, or we're not. It's as simple as that."

He sensed her weighing a decision. "Ghizi's afraid you'll break the case and leave us with nothing. Our management is pretty insistent that we spend money only on cases where big results will be forthcoming."

"As far as we're concerned, you can have the case, the bust, all of the credit. I'm not even sure our state AG would have a clue how to prosecute something like this."

Sedge's experience with Elvis Shields, the former assistant attorney general, seemed to support his assumption.

"To some extent you and I are engaging in bar talk without the booze," Rain said. "There's a maze of federal law pertaining, but there are not many prosecutors at state levels who have much experience in these things. A hell of a lot of work and expense goes into enforcing what amounts to very low visibility laws, and you know prosecutors at all levels of government prefer high-profile cases with positive publicity when they unholster their guns."

"Are you telling me this is a waste of our resources?"

"I'm not saying that. And I'm also not denying it could end up just that way. Look, you can go after these people on the buy or sell sides. Most states have some sort of legal sanctions and prohibitions, generally on the premise that anyone with a relic ought to know where it came from, and if it's stolen, they ought to know that too. You can get after auction houses and dealers, but like gun dealers, it's damn hard to control or even monitor what goes on at their so-called legal swap meets. The bottom line is that the public doesn't know shit about this stuff, but it's a big global business, ranking behind narcotics, illegal animal parts, money laundering, and arms trafficking. Federal investigators like me have to think and act like lawyers and noodle out the pathways in a case that can be successfully prosecuted. It's not enough to find the crime and bust a bad guy. Those days are long gone."

"Are *you* a lawyer?" he asked.

"I am, with a PhD in anthropology to go along with it. I was an academician for a while, but it was too much like counting angels on the heads of pins. I worked for two years with the Department of Justice in Miami, and then Fish and Wildlife recruited me from DJ. I like this work a lot, but that doesn't make it less frustrating or restricting in how we move. Sometimes I feel like a snail carrying a boulder."

"You said maybe Katsu's a bystander. Explain?"

"He's got a sheet, he's leading a national recognition effort for a very obscure band, and a brouhaha over relics might get his group the kind of publicity they need to get the government's attention. The government loathes any publicity that seems to cast it in the asshole role."

"Professor Shotwiff says his band is historically valid. Are you going after this with NAGPRA?"

"Justice will decide, but NAGPRA's got a lot of political baggage, and there are some serious exemptions that complicate things, such as all the stuff the Smithsonian has is under a separate statute, and NAGPRA doesn't cover anything found on state land after 1990, or any private collections before 1990, or anything found on private land. NAGPRA's about Indian and federal land. The better instrument is NSPA, the National Stolen Properties Act, but like I said, Justice will make the call, not us," she said.

"All I can do is look at the case from the viewpoint of both laws and see what we can do to pull in evidence to build a case down either road. The problem, in part, is that NSPA has not been used much federally, and not at all by states. Bottom line: Antiquity theft doesn't meet the priorities of pressing public policy or public safety with this administration. To be fair, it's not just this one—it's any modern administration. It takes a lot of money to make one of these cases. If someone had the *Mona Lisa* you might be able to stimulate strong political support. But Indian trinkets—they just don't make the cut most of the time."

"But you *are* on a case," Service said.

"Because of Ghizi, not me. He's crude but persuasive. Ganking artifacts is like stealing evidence from a criminal case: When the evidence goes, the case goes with it. A lot of politicians are lawyers. They understand this logic and Ghizi uses this to build support, but it's a delicate balance, with tentative support at best."

He did not envy her position. "What about RICO?"

She gave him an extended puzzled look and lit another cigarette. "You want to explain?"

"I'm not a lawyer," he said. *Thank God.* "But I read and pay attention to some stuff." *Not as much as I should, like e-mail.* "RICO's been used to get organized crime, white-collar insider traders and scambams, terrorists, anti-abortion demonstrators, even local cops. One size fits all with RICO, right? Have I missed some?"

The Racketeer Influenced and Corrupt Organizations Act, or RICO, was passed by Congress in 1970. Since then it seemed like the feds were using it for all sorts of cases that didn't have anything to do with the Mafia.

"There are others, but that was a pretty good list," she said. "Maybe the powers that be have thought about the RICO route, but I haven't. You're a game warden, so you might have heard of the Waltham Black Act of 1722?"

"Vaguely. That's the one where it became illegal to poach with black-face—or in a disguise."

"Not just illegal. It carried the death penalty, which seems pretty damn extreme for poaching. The Black Act is a classic example of legal mission creep. It started out with the death penalty for poaching in disguise, but eventually came to cover fifty or sixty infractions, all of which carried the death penalty, the majority of which didn't warrant such severity. RICO's grown the same way the Black Act grew, with similar results. Eventually the rights crusaders will force limitations, and that probably will be a good thing."

"Are you telling me that even if arrests are made the perps may walk?"

"I'm not saying the *suspects* won't walk," she said.

"This whole thing pisses me off," Service said, not bothering to mask his feelings.

"You are in good company," Rain assured him.

"I'm going to talk to Toliver," he said.

"Why?"

Because I can, he thought. "I want to hear the breakhead story."

. . .

He found Toliver sitting knee-to-knee with a young woman who was look-ing at him with worshipful doe eyes. "Got a minute?" he asked Toliver.

It was clear from the professor's look that he preferred the young wom-an's company.

"Fire out?" Toliver asked.

"Control first, then comes the out part. We're about fifty percent there. How come your people bailed out of the dig?"

"Panic," Toliver said. "As simple and complex as that—fight or flight. What do you want? Our not being on the dig site does not mean we are without tasks."

Yeah, I can see your tasks with the girl, asshole. "I want to talk to you about a situation involving some stolen war clubs."

Toliver didn't blink. "I got taken in, end of story."

"Isn't that sort of a professional black eye?"

"Patently unfair," the professor said, "but accurate."

"Like life. Tell me the story."

"I'm sure there are transcripts."

"I prefer a live voice."

"Which part?"

"There are parts? How about you tell me all of it?"

"I don't know all of it, only the things I was involved in."

"That'll do. Talk."

Toliver sighed. "In the summer of 2005 I bought five breakheads of Iro-quois origin. I bought them for the museum at my institution."

"Just war clubs?"

"There was a stone knife as well, elkhorn handle, ornately carved, stone blade. It was exquisite."

"What month that summer?"

"August, I think."

"Bought from whom?"

"A dealer."

Service was tempted to say *late* dealer, but refrained. He wanted the man to talk, and silence was sometimes a better catalyst than questions.

"You probably want his name," Toliver said after a long pause. "William Wildhorse, and yes, presumably a Native; I never knew which tribe, or if he was legitimately Native."

Service let silence hang in the air like an impending storm.

"He had a gallery in Kraut Town in Milwaukee. Pure chance I stopped in one day and we talked, and so it went from there."

"Other galleries in that area?"

"I really can't say. This was a long time ago."

Two years long ago to an archaeologist? Bullshit. "Go on."

"The artifacts were stolen and Wildhorse was arrested by the FBI."

"Charges?"

"Interstate commerce violations or some such thing. It didn't really matter to me, and the FBI would never tell me how they knew the artifacts were stolen, or from whom or from where, or when. I still don't know."

"What happened to Wildhorse?"

"They had to let him go. Not enough evidence."

But they were sure the artifacts were stolen. This doesn't track. "And the relics?"

"Returned them to Wildhorse, the apparent rightful owner."

"But *you* had bought them."

"I had indeed, but I never took possession, and after all this happened I told the FBI my institution did not want them without proven provenance. The FBI gave them back to Wildhorse."

"Are there photographs?"

"Ask the FBI. I don't possess any."

"Did you have the weapons?"

"Nossir, I did not. Never. I just saw them in the photographs Wildhorse shared."

"And you bought based on photos?"

"Technically, yes and no; this is fairly common. The deal was contingent upon my approval once I saw them in person. If I didn't want them then, the deal would be terminated."

"But money changed hands?"

"Yes, but not the full price. It was more like earnest money in a real estate deal."

"This is standard practice?"

"I wouldn't call it standard, but it happens. It's not rare or unique if that's what you mean."

"But you bought based on photos."

"I'm an expert. I saw what he had."

"Seems pretty liberal on his part." He wanted to say *desperate,* but didn't.

Toliver shrugged.

"And then you had dinner with Wildhorse after he was released from custody, and he keeled over dead."

"I don't know your source, but that is way off base. William felt bad at dinner. I drove him to the emergency room and they admitted him to the hospital. He died later that week."

"Poison?" Service asked, wanting to see Toliver's reaction.

"Campylobacter in his cabin's water."

"Did he ever present provenance on the stuff you bought?"

"Only his word that the things had been in his family for generations."

"And he told you this after the FBI let him go?"

"Are you implying something?"

"I'm just trying to get the timelines straight in my head."

"That's the story, all of it," Toliver said. "When can I take my team back to our dig site?"

"When it's safe out there."

"But the fire's at least twenty miles south of our excavation."

Odd fact for someone who opens the conversation asking if the fire is out. "You realize this is a peat fire and it's burning below-ground? It's not likely to be entirely out until we get our heavy fall rains and snow."

"Meaning?"

"You may not get cleared back to the site until next spring."

"Not until April?"

"Realistically, it could be May up there on the shore. The snowfall is huge and stays a long, long time."

"This is unfair."

"Would it be more fair if you took your crew back up there and the fire jumped up and killed them all?"

"You're exaggerating the risk."

"That's what cops get paid to do. We don't take meaningless risks with innocent civilian lives. It tends to piss off the taxpayers."

"Just a few days could make a huge difference," Toliver said, probing for some negotiation space.

"It's in Mother Nature's hands now, Professor. If we get significant rain, we'll see what can be done."

"What are my options?"

"Wait."

"Is there an appeal procedure?" Toliver demanded.

Grady Service pointed a forefinger up at the sky and smiled. "Try *Him*."

66

Newberry, Luce County

TUESDAY, AUGUST 14, 2007

The reduced speed limit on M-123 was still in force at 25 mph, and Service made his way slowly west and south, driving cautiously. He called Goldie before leaving Paradise and asked for fingerprints, chastening himself for not automatically doing this himself, or asking Sedge to do it. *Some super sergeant.* Traffic was sparse.

The area around Murphy Creek was still littered with pumper trucks, fire paraphernalia, and firefighters milling around in their yellow suits smudged with black soot. The fire had burned to within sight of M-123 but was only smoldering at the moment. Hoses snaked into the open area as water was pumped from the creek to the fire in hopes of drowning it underground.

Service found incident commander Max Stinson at the command trailer, and the two old pals embraced like two bears. "Weather's staying hot and dry. We've got this sucker ringed and we're moving in the hand crews now." Max's Vietnam had been spent on a carrier, crewing a chopper picking up navy pilots who splashed into the Gulf of Tonkin, and sometimes into North Vietnam itself.

"Seems like it's going pretty smoothly," Service said.

"If you don't look too close. We set a backfire up by Pinestump and that sonuvagun turned on us like a nasty snake. Luck prevailed. Yeah, real *smooth.*"

"Any new activity today?"

"Here and there. The Troops are sending us a chopper with infrared and thermal-imaging capability. They're overhead as we speak. Once we get a picture of hot spots we can have our crews beat-feet into them and put them down."

"Road closings and evacs?"

"The 420's still closed, and I have manned barricades to cut down on gawkers. The evac for Chesbrough and Widgeon is still in effect."

"Any more reports of unauthorized personnel out by Chesbrough?"

"Heard you were out there for the suicide. How many in your career?"

"I haven't kept count." *One was too damn many.*

"Your job, I don't blame you," Stinson said. "Some people just snap. We're going to run hose and piping out to the fire and pump water. Wisconsin loaned us some six-by-six ATVs with water pumps. They're real handy for this kind of work, great force extenders. Rest of the U.P.'s getting our weather. Got nine or ten other burns going, all under control so far. It's all late this year. Usually spring's the annual burn circus."

"The drought," Service said, and his friend nodded. "Brownmine used me as his escort to the line."

"McKower's here and Jeffey Bryan's close, so I'm good to go. You can go do whatever it is you do now. I heard they filled your sleeve with stripes."

"Stripes, yeah. Weird, Max. I'll probably be northwest of Chesbrough."

"How far?"

"Little Two-Hearted Lakes, maybe."

"Bump your folks on your 800 and make sure they know where you are."

• • •

Grady Service took M-123 northeast to Duck Lake, and drove the curvy back road to a place close to the lake on the west perimeter of the Little Two-Hearted Lakes country. He got his ruck out of his truck and strapped his fire suit and helmet to the outside, just in case. His intent, loosely drawn, was to hike northwest, but he found himself sitting on a stump burned over by some long-ago and now-forgotten fire. No cell-phone coverage here—at least, at the moment. An hour from now this could change. He had no idea why this was so and didn't care.

At least the 800 was working today. Goldie could get him on the state police 800. "Two One Thirty, Twenty Four Fourteen. You have cell coverage where you are?"

"That's affirmative, Two One Thirty."

"Could you give Goldie a bump, tell him there's no cell coverage where I am, and he can pass results over Channel Two on the 800."

"Two One Thirty, clear."

The desire to move and expend energy, even if it was wrong and wasteful, ate at him, but he remained on his log perch. Why was Delongshamp here? He'd seen him near Chesbrough, and Jeffey had seen him northwest of there; he had concluded that Kermit was headed northwest, but now as he sat and relaxed, he realized the truth was that the man could have turned around and gone anywhere. He had made an unwarranted assumption, yet something about Delongshamp was eating at his subconscious and telling him the man was the key. *To what?* That was the real question.

Sleep tickled at him and he tried to resist, but a nap sounded good. "Twenty Four Fourteen, you available?"

"Affirmative."

"Two One Thirty. Meet me at my place?"

"Twenty Four Fourteen, clear."

• • •

She was seated on a battered wooden bench on the Bomb Shelter's front porch.

"Goldie faxed these to us," she said, proffering a sheaf of papers. He fought the urge to speed-read and made himself work his way slowly through the pages, sheet by sheet. At one point he put the papers under his arm and lit a cigarette. "Wingel," was all he said.

"She probably has an explanation," Sedge said.

"Or can't remember."

"That's even more likely. What now, Chief Master Sergeant?"

"We need to think like lawyers."

"Ooh. That sounds painful."

"No pain, no gain."

"Clichés suck," Sedge said.

"I met with Jane Rain yesterday, cop to cop."

"She acknowledged her status?"

"I didn't give her a lot of wiggle room. You said you had to bring that AAG Elvis what's-his-name up to speed?"

"Elvis Y. Shields."

"Right, that guy."

"I put a lot of work into that jerk."

"Work on what?"

"NAGPRA to some extent, but more on 324-point-76, 102 to 106."

"Plain language?"

"Natural Resources and Environmental Protection Act Number 451, from 1994, or NREPA for short. It all has to do with handling and recovering aboriginal remains and antiquities from state land, and covers human and animal matter."

"NREPA." Jane Rain had not mentioned this one.

"And there's always grave robbing," Sedge added.

"Is that a joke?"

"No, I'm serious. I even told Elvis about it: 751-point-160, and I quote: 'Declares that a person is guilty of a felony who, not being lawfully authorized to do so, shall willfully dig up, disinter, remove, or carry away a human body, or the remains thereof, from the place where that body may be interred or deposited, or shall knowingly aid in such.' The penalty is ten years and five grand."

"What did Shields say?"

"Nothing. The asshole just shook his head."

"I'm thinking a lawyer would say a war club isn't a body."

"I'm just trying to convey what I know that might help us. I can't get it out of my mind that Wingel found a body out there and reburied it, and can't or won't say where. Jesus, the photo we got from Oregon shows she's a damn thief. She balled her sensei at Oregon, got caught by his old lady, and Wingel, nee Ence, boogeyed eastward. I keep asking myself, why McGill and Canada with so many good schools in the U.S.?"

Service listened politely, his own mind churning. "Wingel ends up in Wisconsin at Whitewater State. Toliver's late dealer was in Wisconsin. Toliver visited said dealer in Wisconsin."

"We need more on Toliver's background," Sedge said.

"I'll bird-dog it," Service said.

"When this case began, you said it was mine."

"It still is."

"Then why do I feel like it's slipping away from me?"

"Federal involvement."

"Is that supposed to appease me?"

"It's supposed to make you shut up so I can think, and so you can get back on patrol."

"Your NCO bedside manner needs serious work, dude," she said.

"Sergeants don't do bedsides," he retorted.

"I'll bet your old lady would confirm that," she said, and headed for her truck in a huff. He halfheartedly sailed his ball cap at her.

67

Marqutte, Marquette County

FRIDAY, AUGUST 17, 2007

He had been home two nights. Friday called Service from her office in Negaunee. "I just put salt in my coffee, thank you very much!" she said.

"Jell-O mode?"

"Ya think? Geez, Grady, I sometimes think being together full-time could kill the both of us."

Jell-O mode was a sort of spaciness Friday went into for up to eight hours after lovemaking. Her ob-gyn recently diagnosed it as a phenomenon called SIPAS, Suspended Intellectual and Physical Ability Syndrome. It affected fewer than 1 percent of women, the doctor had told her. *Together full-time? Where is that coming from?*

"You get word on the burn ban?"

"What's that? I've been digging."

"All counties except the southernmost tier are on fire ban, first time this widespread since 1998, including no smoking outside."

"Bullshit," he said. "Unenforceable."

"My sister's coming for dinner tonight. You're the chef, eh? You know I can't cook when I'm in this condition."

"Hot dogs work?"

"Don't be a goof."

He meant it; he was of no mind to cook, much less socialize.

"Karylanne's bringing Little Mar for the weekend. She has to do something in the Soo tomorrow and is leaving Mar with us."

This made him grin. His granddaughter was a hoot—most of the time. And a load. Sometimes she was also a PITA in training—pain in the ass.

"I'll cook something." He had no idea what.

He called McKower and she said, "We're at sixty-two percent and holding. Evacs remain in force. Big wind gusts blew all morning, but the line seems to have held so far."

"Sedge?"

"Somewhere on the northern fireline with Jeffey."

He ended the call and pushed his cell phone to the side of the computer. He hoped the calls were done. He needed to concentrate.

This morning he had tried to talk to Hibernian College in Velvetick, Ohio, but the human resources queen there had been an unvarnished bitch and refused to confirm or deny anything about Toliver, whom she slipped and referred to as Tolly, and just as quickly got lockjaw, saying it was because of "regrettable Republican-driven privacy rules. I'm afraid you will require a subpoena for any records. This is a private, not a public institution." The phone call left him scratching his head and seething. He started to surf the web without a plan but suddenly decided on a different route. He found Smoke Ghizi's card in his wallet and called him.

"Hey," he greeted his one-time marine comrade, "Service here."

"What's up?"

"Working the case's backstory. Where the hell did Toliver go to college? I called Hibernian and they dribbled me against the academic stone wall."

"Give me a minute to pull the file," Ghizi said. Moments later, "Okey-doke, Sarn't, what can we do you for?"

"His college degrees."

"All of them?"

"Please."

"AA degree in 1980, from LCOO Community College, Hayward, Wisconsin; in 1983, BA in history, University of Wisconsin–Whitewater. Two years later, 1985, MA in anthropology, U Wisconsin Madison. In 1990, doctorate in Native American studies, Oklahoma State University, Stillwater. Want his thesis title?"

"Sure."

"*Seventeenth-Century Iroquoisian Militarism in the Great Lakes.*"

"Okay, got it."

"Anything else?"

Service kept underlining U Wisconsin–Whitewater. *Is this the same as Whitewater State?* He had lived most of his life in the U.P. and had never heard the Wisconsin college called anything *but* Whitewater State, which did not mean he wasn't behind the name curve. "I'm good; thanks, Smoke."

"Keep your knife sharp, your powder dry, and your hand grenade in your belt, son."

No mention of the conversation with Jane Rain. Had she not told her boss? *Was* he her boss? *Odd.*

He typed his initial search information into Google and stared at the first result: "Lac Courte Oreilles Ojibwa Community College." *LCOO is a Native American school, and Toliver went there?* The site said that 75 percent of its students were Native. *Huh.*

You could access a catalog by clicking on a small icon, which was so tiny he couldn't make out any of the words. All he could see was something that looked like a shiny smiley face.

He dialed Ghizi again, who answered, "Figured you'd be calling back."

"Toliver's Native?"

"No tribal card, but some of his closest friends carry them. He grew up right there in Hayward. His old man ran an antiques store, and he went to the community college for two years and transferred to—"

"Whitewater State."

"Officially it's the University of Wisconsin, Whitewater, UWW; this is a bit of a sore point because most people confuse all the parts of the Wisconsin system with the flagship campus in Madison."

"Why the hell didn't you tell me about Toliver?"

"You said you had enough information."

"Okay, what else do I want to know?"

"Guess where Katsu went to college?"

"Same time?"

"Pretty much."

The two men clearly disliked each other. "Does *their thing* date back to their LCOO days?"

"Wouldn't surprise me, but this has never been confirmed."

"Which means you've talked to people about it."

"More than plenty."

"At the community college?"

"Uh, they are not real welcoming of federal badges. You might have more luck."

Service knew he wouldn't. The problem was being *wabish*, not the carrying of a badge.

"You want Toliver's employment history?"

"Please."

"In 1991, he was a history instructor at UWW, and moved as an associate professor to Oberlin College in Ohio, in 1994. From there he moved to the Stella Sixkiller chair, a lifetime appointment which automatically gave him the department chairmanship at Hibernian."

"Instructor to department chair and full professor in eight years?"

"Whoosh, just like a rocket," Ghizi said, "but Custer went up faster. Anything else?"

"Did Katsu earn a degree?"

"He did indeed, and went to the University of Illinois where he eventually graduated from dental school."

"Katsu's a dentist?"

"On paper. He's got no practice."

Jesus. "Toliver was an instructor at Wisconsin–Whitewater?"

"Yep. Isn't that something!"

"Did—"

"Yessir, he was an instructor, and working on his master's. Wingel supervised his master's thesis."

"And moved from there to Stillwater?"

"Presumably. That's what the record says."

"His record at Oklahoma State?"

"Stellar, like everywhere he went and everything he touched. The man was a rising star right from the get-go."

"Whole lot of weird coincidences here."

"Gotta ask yourself—what're the odds?" Ghizi said sarcastically.

The two men went silent. "Stones in your gizzard, Sarn't?"

"How *close* was said supervision?"

"Officially, strictly according to Hoyle. Unofficially around the water-cooler, a whole lot of smirks and rolled eyes."

"You interviewed people."

"We did."

"You think they're in cahoots?"

"I don't think there's a law that clearly defines that as a legal term."

"Have you got people bird-dogging Ladania Wingel?"

"No comment."

"Thanks, teammate."

"No call for that tone of voice. I can only attest to that which I control, and that Wengel broad sure ain't part of my brief."

"Strict constructionist?"

"I'm not obstructing, Grady. I just don't know, and that's the truth. I can speculate, but I prefer not to. You need anything else?"

"Not at the moment."

"Have yourself a nice day," Ghizi said.

Service started to leave the building to smoke, but remembered that the burn ban was in place, which frosted his ass. Captain Grant's administrative assistant Fern LeBlanc was in the reception area, pottering around.

"Where are we supposed to smoke?" he asked her. They had always rubbed each other wrong until Nantz and Walter had died, and then she seemed to have softened toward him.

"Outside, like always," she said.

"What about the burn ban?"

"Bans don't apply to cigarettes," she said. "Unenforceable."

Goddamn Lis! She had set him up. He stomped outside, got into his truck, lit a smoke, and inhaled deeply. *Need to settle down and think. Damn Lis!*

Marquette County conservation officer Bradley Wurfel pulled his black patrol vehicle into the parking spot in front of the Tahoe. The black Chevy was coated with fine orange dust.

So Wingel knows Toliver, and Toliver and Katsu were at the same community college together. Good God, this is getting denser than an interstellar black hole.

Wurfel got out of his truck with a briefcase, waved, and headed for the front door of the office building.

Service's cell phone warbled. Caller ID said it was Chief Waco's number.

"Chief."

"You're in Marquette?"

"For now. Came back Tuesday night."

"Do you know a man named Heywood?"

Service said, "Heard of him. Writes bullshit books about COs."

"Novels, Grady. Have you read them?"

"Who has time?"

"You might want to make time, because he's asked specifically to spend some time with you."

"Like what, an hour? What the hell for?" *I don't need this. I don't want this.*

"Days, so he can see how you work in your new job."

"No way, Eddie!"

"It's 'Chief' when we're conducting business, Chief Master Sergeant."

"Goddammit, Chief."

"This is a good thing, Grady. Good for us, good for you, good for the state. Besides, his hearing aids are brand-new, and he only stutters a little bit. You get used to it quickly. He was here this morning. I told him you'd be glad to partner with him."

"When?" *Partner?*

"Up to you. I gave him your telephone numbers. He'll be in touch. By the way, he has his own vest."

"I heard he's like a hundred."

"Nah, he can't be a day over eighty."

"I suppose he has his own walker."

"Just a cane," the chief said, "and it looks like he handles it pretty good, at least in an office building."

"A vest. Where am I supposed to take him?"

"Wherever your mission takes you. Working with our men and women helps him make the stories seem authentic."

"But he's making it all up."

"Of course; that's what fiction is."

"*Good God,*" Service said in frustration.

"The author will call you. Play nice. That's an order."

"I can't wait," Service said. He hung up, flung the cell phone out his window, and watched it skitter and bounce across the blacktop parking lot.

Fuck. He got out and bent over to pick up the phone. Out of the corner of his eye he saw that someone had used a finger to draw a smiley face in the dust on the back gate of Wurfel's truck.

He couldn't stop staring. He got up in a daze and was almost to the front door when it registered. What came into his mind was a business card left by a woman with a tight, bright-red top. The name on the card: Marldeane Youvonne Brannigan. And she had neatly written in immaculate script, "Have a nice day."

Holy shit. He scrambled to his cubicle and found the phone number for Cedar Falls Texas police chief Jackie Jay Emerson and punched it into his cell phone, which was suddenly dead. Damn! He grabbed the landline and punched the number into that.

Be there, be there, be there.

"Chief, Grady Service up in Michigan."

"How y'all doin', partner?"

"Good. Got a question: Joseph Paul Brannigan. He one of your local folk?"

"Nossiree, that ole boy's a damn carpetbagger, hails from the cheese state—Minnesota, is it?"

"Wisconsin."

"Yeah, yeah, that's it."

"Thanks, Chief. And he was active down your way around Y2K?"

"Yessir, but he just sorta drifted outta the pitcher. His jacket don't say he got busted or nothing, so who knows."

Service called Friday. "I have to go to Wisconsin."

"When?"

"Today—now."

"What about my sister, or Karylanne, or your granddaughter?"

"This can't be helped, Tuesday."

"Okay," she said. "I'll hold down the fort. How long this time?"

"Not sure. I'm taking Allerdyce with me." *If he could find the sonuvabitch.*

Silence on Friday's end. Then, hoarsely, "Now, *that* scares the hell out of me, Grady."

68

Sheboygan, Wisconsin

SATURDAY, AUGUST 18, 2007

It took him until midnight to find Allerdyce and get him into his truck and on their way. Having the old man there was like having the company of a bobblehead doll, chuckling to himself, lost in his own world. No questions, no conversation, not even his stupid grin.

That morning Sedge had called on the cell phone while he and the old man were eating breakfast at a truck stop.

"I'll cut right to the chase. I'm so damn tired I can hardly keep my eyes open. Where are you?"

"Sheboygan, Wisconsin."

"The late Skyler Verst?" she said, with a hitch in her voice. "Her maiden name was Brannigan. Think that has anything to do with our little pal Kermit?"

"Here's some more for you to chew on," he told her. "Katsu and Toliver knew each other at a community college in Hayward, Wisconsin. And Toliver's supervising professor on his master's thesis at Wisconsin Whitewater was none other than Ladania Wingel. The night I met Wingel in Jefferson she was with a lady friend, name of Marldeane Youvonne Brannigan."

"Holy shit," Sedge said wearily. "My brain's too tired to even start processing any of that."

"Sleep—I'll call you back."

"Are you alone?"

"Got Allerdyce with me."

"Oh my God. I'm in a nightmare," she mumbled, and hung up.

69

Jefferson, Wisconsin

SATURDAY, AUGUST 18, 2007

Aunt Marge Ciucci knew Marldeane and Skyler Brannigan. "Sisters," she told Service while giving Allerdyce a suspicious look. Wayne had arrested the girls' brother for poaching from the time he was a kid.

"Deer, ducks, turkey, bear—you name it, the man hunted it and killed it, and usually sold it, too," Marge said. "For most people hunting's a deep-seated drive, a compulsion from the genes, but for J. P. it was a disease, something he had no control over."

"Had?"

"Till the day he died."

"J. P. Brannigan is dead?"

"Yessir, died in September 11, 2001. He was one of those unfortunate folks in New York City."

"This was reported in the news?"

"The girls reported him dead and told the story. It was all in the paper. They even had a funeral, though there weren't nothing to bury, just a box."

"What can you tell me about the sisters?"

"Both good-looking and both like men; they started early on that. Skyler, she's living around Lansing in Michigan, and Marldeane's still here. Marldeane got her a taste for the vino."

"No recent news about the women?"

"None I heard or read. Why?"

"Skyler committed suicide last week. I was there."

Something about Marge's face. "You don't look surprised."

"Not a bit. All three of them kids have been out of control their whole lives."

"What does Marldeane do for a living?"

Marge Ciucci opened her hands. "Nobody knows, but whatever it is, she lives high on the hog—long winter vacations to Key West, the Canary Islands, places like that."

"She hangs out with Ladania Wingel."

"Wingel runs the school board, and Marldeane is the school's biggest and most consistent benefactor. Who's this fine fella with you?" she finally asked.

"Allerdyce," Service said.

Allerdyce bowed his head but said nothing.

"He doesn't talk much," Marge remarked.

"He doesn't have much to say that's worth hearing," Service said.

"I guess its good to know someone that well," she said sarcastically.

• • •

Service dropped Allerdyce in town and went on alone. They would reconnect later. He got to Brannigan's address, a huge older home on a multi-acre manicured lawn set on the banks of the Crawfish River, just south of Aztalan State Park. Service was met at the door by a woman of indeterminate age and short blonde hair. He showed his badge. "I'm looking for Marldeane Brannigan."

"She's not here," the woman said.

"And you are?"

"Not Marldeane," the woman said.

"Do you know when she'll be back?"

"Her sister died. She went to collect her body," the woman said. "I'm looking after the house."

Service got back to his truck and called McKower, who was still at the fire. "Skyler Verst. Her maiden name was Brannigan. Her sister's en route to claim her body. Has the medical examiner released it yet?"

"I don't know. I'll check and get back to you. Cell coverage?"

"I'm good." He immediately called Sedge, who sounded groggy. "Listen, I'm in Wisconsin. Marldeane Brannigan has gone to Newberry to claim her sister's body."

"Where's she staying?"

"No idea, but you might want to check the red cabin."

"Okay. And you?"

"Heading back, probably. McKower's checking to see if the body's been released yet."

"I doubt that. Our medical examiner had a stroke the day after the suicide. They put him on a medevac to U of M. Nothing's getting done in that office for the moment. It's frozen. They never even got to an autopsy on the woman."

"You know that how?"

"My turf," she said. "I try to keep track of everything in my territory."

"You know some jerkwad named Heywood?"

"Sure, I've read his books. Why?"

"Just wondered."

McKower called back. "The coroner's out of action. There's been nothing done with the body and there may not be for a while."

Service drove back to Brannigan's house and the same woman answered again, drink in hand. He showed his badge again. "Where's Marldeane staying in Michigan?"

"Where she always stays—ya know, the place where she can talk to God. Your badge isn't good here, is it?"

"I'm a federal deputy too," he said.

"Oh" was her sole response.

"You remember the name of the place where she is?"

"No, just that it's way out in the woods and it's real quiet."

"Lands of the Lord?"

"That's it," the woman said. "They don't have no phones there. Not even running water. Seems to me you should be able to get close to God with a clean behind. You want a drink?"

"No, thanks." He cringed as he left.

Service called Sedge again on his way to fetch Allerdyce. "A source says Brannigan stays at the Lands of the Lord compound when she's up that way."

"You still want me to check the cabin?"

"To be thorough. I'm heading back. Should be there late tonight. I'll bump you when I get close."

"Do you want others involved?"

"Can Max Stinson spare you guys?"

"I'll check with the captain. Two or three do it?"

"Two plus us should be plenty," he said.

• • •

He wanted to chastise himself for making a long and unnecessary drive, but he wasn't sure how he would have gotten the information otherwise. The question to Marge had just been a matter of making nice. Could have called Marge to start, he decided, but done was done.

Allerdyce was seated in what used to be called a fern bar, drinking a red drink from a martini glass. Service sat down across from him. "We're going back."

"We ain't done nothin' here."

"The Brannigan woman is in the U.P."

"I heard dat," Allerdyce said. "Prolly up to the Lands Lambs of the Lord place. Folks here say she likes booze, God, and men—in dat order. She sounds like a pip. Want snort for da road?"

"What is that?"

"Razzieberrytini," the old man said, smacking his lips.

"Down the hatch. We need to roll, fine fella."

"Don't call me dat name."

"You didn't mind it with Marge."

"Dat was differ'nt."

Allerdyce chugged the rest of his drink, left a ten-dollar bill on the table, and trundled out in front of Service.

"We gonna use sireen, mebbe?"

"No. Shut up and get in the truck."

"Too bad," the old man complained. "Always wanted ta run sireen from da udder side a tings."

My partner, Service thought, pulling into the street and heading north to connect with I-94.

70

Lambs of of the Lord, Chippewa County

SUNDAY, AUGUST 19, 2007

The officers assembled west of the religious retreat: Sedge, Sergeant Bryan, Chippewa County CO Korfu, Service, and Allerdyce. Korfu looked like a serious iron-pusher with huge shoulders and a bull neck. Service had never worked with him before, knew nothing about him.

"She was there yesterday," Sedge told the group. "I know the guy who owns property to the south of the place, and asked him to go up there and look around. There will be outdoor mass at noon today. Unfortunately, the Kerses are there too—all of them."

Shit. "How?" Service asked, shaking his head.

"I don't know. Apparently Allegan kicked them."

"Just great," Service said glumly. "What about the fire?"

Sergeant Bryan said, "Eighteen thousand acres, sixty-five percent control, two hundred and sixty souls on the ground. A recon flight spotted a new smoke near Hulbert midday yesterday, and the incident commander diverted resources off the south line. Fifteen acres, no structures. They knocked it down fast. Rain is forecast for today."

"Rain or wishful thinking?" Service asked.

"Sixty percent chance," Sergeant Bryan said.

Service said, "Let's hope we're not in the sixty. They need rain on the fire, but we don't." Most people never understood that when weathermen announced rain percentages, it meant there would be rain in that percentage of their area. Even COs sometimes forgot this.

"All previous forecasts have been off on quantity and duration," Sedge added.

Service thought about their situation, where the fire was. "What's our buffer?"

"Ten or twelve miles, crow fly," Sedge said, "but we could order an evac for the retreat, pick off Brannigan when we go in to notify them to leave because it's unsafe."

"I believe in sneak attacks and ambushes," Service said, and they all grinned. "If we get runners, I'd prefer *we* influence their routes and directions."

"Creep it or George it?" Korfu asked.

"Both. Jingo, you come in from that south property. Bryan and Officer Korfu come in from here, from the west. Limpy and I will block between their boundary and Kermit's camp on the Betsy. Make a radio call if anyone splits. Alert those the runner will head for. Where's Toliver?" he asked Sedge.

"Bitching about lost time, calling Lansing every day. He calls Dr. Ledger-Foley and Director Cheke," she said, raising her eyebrows.

"What are they telling him?"

"Nothing. They both stopped taking his calls, and that *really* frosts his ass."

"What's our timing?" Sergeant Bryan asked.

"When's mass?" Service asked.

"Noon," Sedge answered.

"Okay, noon it is," Service said. "That gives us three hours, and we should catch them bunched up. I'll check in on the 800 ten minutes before noon. All of us need to be within two hundred yards of your target by then."

"What kind of people are we dealing with?" Korfu asked. "I know Father Charlie, and he's a good guy."

"We're looking for a woman named Marldeane Brannigan, attractive, fortyish—she'll stand out. She won't be a problem," Sedge said.

"The Kerses like it rough sometimes, but they are incidental to our mission," Service said. "If they get in the way, smack them down fast and secure them for pickup later, then get on with business. Any other questions?"

Silence. They knew what they had to do.

• • •

Service and Allerdyce were in position early, and both looked around for worn trails that might indicate possible escape routes for runners. There was one faint path toward the little river and another to the west, neither particularly well traveled. Service had watched Allerdyce as they hiked to their area. He seemed to grow younger with each step he took in the woods. He was stealthy, alert, and tireless. It was a creepy and disturbing observation.

He checked in with the others at ten till and said only "Go at noon."

"Youse like dis stuff," Allerdyce observed. "Jes' like youse's old man."

"Shut up, Allerdyce."

"Is good ting," the old poacher said. "Youse tink we get dis gal youses want?"

"No idea."

Service's cell phone vibrated. Six till. He was shocked to have coverage, almost afraid to connect. "Yeah?" he answered.

"Ghizi here. Jane called. Toliver's missing."

"When, and what's that mean?"

"Couple hours ago, and we don't know. He took one of his chickie-poos and left."

"What's Jane want us to do about it?"

"She just thought you should have a heads-up. She's questioning the rest of dig team right now."

"Katsu?"

"She didn't say."

"We're sort of pressed right now," Service told the U.S. Fish and Wildlife man. "Give us an hour, okay?"

"Roger that. I'll tell Jane," Ghizi said, and hung up.

Service grinned at his phone. *She's the boss, not Ghizi.*

Service waved Allerdyce to the west and he walked east toward the Betsy River.

Time seemed to stand still. Service's adrenaline was topped out and he was ready. Allerdyce was hunched down, watching south. It struck Service that the old man looked like a calm, battle-scarred predator accustomed to ambushing victims. It was a less-than-comforting observation. At least he's on our side this time, he told himself.

71

Halfway House, Chippewa County

SUNDAY, AUGUST 19, 2007

Service had given the signal and the radio had gone silent. It had been thirty minutes since the pinch was supposed to have happened. Finally, he heard Sedge's voice.

"Those damn Kerses were kneeling piously one moment, eyes toward heaven, and the next they were on us like rabid dogs in heat," she said. "The whole damn family—mom Annie included—are major pains in the ass. We have got to get tasers, Twenty Four Fourteen. Two One Thirty, clear."

Rabid dogs in heat? Okay, then, things didn't go as planned.

"You got her?" Service asked.

"Negative. The Kerses went from Hail Marys to kick-ass at light speed. We just now got them under control. Barely. I'm *serious* about tasers!"

"Ask Father Charlie about Brannigan."

"I did. She left early this morning."

Great.

"What do you want us to do?" Sedge asked.

He could hear frustration in her breathing. "Calm down, Jingo. Take a deep breath. What's your status?"

"Korfu's called for Chippewa County deps for backup and transport. We're going to charge the Kerses with obstruction and assault and battery; every damn one of them has a pocket full of speed, and the old lady's purse is loaded with weed. It exploded when she smacked me in the head with it. The deps aren't close yet. This is going to take a while." Service heard a rustling sound. "Dave, sit on her! She just tried to head-butt me again."

To Service: "Can I get back to you?"

"Get things taken care of there. Where did Marldeane go?"

"Father Charlie's not sure. She was staying in a tent, never showed for coffee this morning."

"Meaning she could have left last night."

"Pretty much."

Damn. "Allerdyce and I will push north, Jingo."

"To the frog's hut?"

"Roger that. Twenty Four Fourteen clear."

If Captain Grant is listening to this radio work he'll be wigging out. The captain demanded that his officers always sound in control and professional.

Service saw that Allerdyce was already nosing his way north and he turned to parallel the old man, who was alternately pointing at his eyes and at the ground. The old man was letting him know he had cut some kind of sign.

Service stepped up his pace and kept parallel to Allerdyce. Twenty minutes later the old man flicked a hand and pointed at an angle intersecting Service's route of travel. *The trail is coming my way.*

Allerdyce continued north. Service did the same, head down, looking for the trail, assuming Allerdyce was moving toward him. He found a track, at least size twelve, less than a day old, definitely not a woman. *What the hell?* He looked up. *No Allerdyce. Shit! Should have told him to stick by me. No, I should have left his miserable ass in south Marquette County.*

"Two One Thirty. You still punksitting?"

"Affirmative. No Chip deps here yet. They caught a vehicle accident on the way out."

"Can you move up with us? I'm nearing the frog's cabin."

"Problem?"

"Not at the moment."

"There quick-like, Two One Thirty."

"I'll wait, Twenty Four Fourteen."

While he waited he moved up to the camp and looked around. The big prints had angled past the cabin and down to the river, where the person appeared to have crossed. He started working a circle pattern, spiraling out from the cabin, and eventually saw a print. Pure luck that he did. Allerdyce knew how to move in the woods.

Sedge showed up on the run, sweating, and Service explained what had happened.

"You think the old man was trying to lose you?"

"No idea." *With Allerdyce I can't rule it out.* He told her about Toliver and Jane Rain and Ghizi.

"Where's Katsu?" she asked.

He shook his head. "Tell me again what Father Charlie said about the woman."

"She was there last night, but not this morning."

He was moving along, following Allerdyce's prints.

"Can you see sign?" Sedge asked.

"Bent grass, slight impressions, not much. This guy's good at hiding himself."

"Is he hiding from us?"

"I don't think so. I think it's habit."

She looked at the ground. "God, I don't know how you can even see it. I couldn't see it at tracking school either."

He stopped and showed her and she rolled her eyes. "For real?" she asked skeptically.

The tracks were meandering north. "You recognize this place?" she asked.

He didn't.

"This is where we tussled with Toliver the night we met." She pointed northeast. "There's an old two-track that runs past West Pond. Toliver used to drive up Vermilion Road to where it branches north. He'd continue west to where the road eventually peters out, but you can see where it once was. It cuts diagonally across Michigan Nature Association property."

"I didn't think we were that far inland."

"We ran several hundred yards in that charge," she recalled. "The main hill is north-northwest of us, and that landlocked state forty is southeast of us. You really ought to carry a GPS," she chastised.

Advancing north, they reached a small but sharply angled sand hill, and along the lip saw Allerdyce on his back, looking away from them. As they came forward he looked back, raised an eyebrow, and made a patting motion with the palm of his hand. They crawled toward him and Allerdyce pointed down in front of him. Service scanned around him first. This looked like the area the poacher had shown Professor Shotwiff and him. Below he saw Marldeane Brannigan in a halter top and shorts, her skin red from sun. She seemed to be looking down at her feet into what appeared to be a hole. Service looked over at Allerdyce. The poacher dragged three fingers slowly across his eyes.

"Hole?" Service mouthed.

Allerdyce nodded, made a ladling motion with his hand. Brannigan seemed to be talking softly and swatting at insects as dark clouds began to sweep in from the big lake, and Service heard thunder dragooning in the distance. Weather up here could change in a blink, any day of the year.

As he reflected on rain, a new figure appeared beside Brannigan. Jesus! It was Ladania Wingel, holding a clipboard and jawing at her companion. Service mouthed to Sedge: "Wingel."

Both women seemed focused on the hole.

Service tapped Allerdyce's shoulder. "Can you get close enough to them to see what's going on?"

Allerdyce nodded. "Want clipperbird?"

"Take a look only if you get a safe chance, but right now, just see what they're doing and we'll work our way in from another direction."

The old man slid backward on his belly and crab-crawled westward along the hill's military crest. Service motioned Sedge back. "What's he doing?" she asked.

"Recce."

"And us?"

"Get below—get ready to move in from the east."

"Is there a third person down there?"

Service said softly, "Probably."

"Digging?"

He wasn't sure, had no answer.

"Wish we were closer to see what they're actually doing," Sedge said.

They lost sight of Allerdyce, but moved to the cover of leaning white cedars, paused, listened, and tried to see.

Nothing. The air was dead. Sedge held out her hands, her eyes questioning.

"Predators strike when they're ready, not before," he whispered.

"I thought this was recce?"

"Nothing is ever strictly anything with that old man."

When it came it was explosive, and almost too fast to take in. Wingel seemed to make a violent motion to her right with the clipboard as Allerdyce popped into view, twisted the clipboard away from Wingel in a single fluid motion, and smacked her hard in the side of the head with it, sending her out of sight.

The Brannigan woman shrieked, seemed nailed to the ground.

Service and Sedge started forward, but there was another shout and two men with shotguns appeared from the north, pointing their weapons at Allerdyce, who was grinning and nodding.

"Kermit?" Sedge whispered.

"And his faithful companion, Peewee."

Nobody had bothered to mention that Bolf was six and a half feet tall and massive. Service used his arm to hold Sedge back. "Slowly," he whispered, easing his .40 caliber SIG Sauer out of its holster.

They had good cover to within thirty feet of the assemblage. "My signal," he told his partner, and urged her to spread out to the right so they would present two targets and force choices.

Wingel struggled back to her feet and began slapping Limpy, who neither cowered nor said anything. Kermit pulled Wingel away.

"Hands behind your head," a shaky Delongshamp told the poacher.

Bolf pointed his weapon at Limpy, who chuckled. "Go 'head. Ain't same ta kill man look in 'is eyes, eh. An' youse're all under arrest."

Deslongshamp said, "You're crazy. You're not no cop."

Marldeane Brannigan said, "I don't like this, J.P. Go ahead and shoot the man. He smells bad."

"Move!" Service said hoarsely, and he and Sedge charged forward, racing into the opening as fast as they could move, both of them shouting in unison, "DNR! Put the weapons on the ground! DNR! Do it *now!*"

The armed men hesitated and glanced at each other, neither seeming to know what to do next. Allerdyce pivoted swiftly and planted a kick between Bolf's legs. The huge man gasped and went down, and Allerdyce twisted the man's weapon away from him as he fell, turned it around, and rammed the butt into Kermit's neck, making him scream, clutch his throat, and fall away.

Allerdyce was suddenly standing over them, brandishing the rifle. "Youse two split-tails shut your big yappers. Asswipe down dere in 'ole, crawl up here wit' us human beans."

Toliver edged sheepishly out of the hole. He was sweaty and covered with dirt. There was an explosion as lightning struck just east of them and rain began to come down in sheets. Service peered into the hole, saw two skulls.

"Naughty, naughty man," Service told Toliver.

"This, I will remind you," the man said haughtily, "is a state-approved excavation."

"Not here it isn't," Service said. "At this site it's called grave robbing."

Marldeane Brannigan screamed and flung herself toward Service, but Limpy intervened and cross-checked her with the rifle, sending her down into the hole, which was quickly forming into mud. Allerdyce looked down at her. "Hey, girlie, grab dose skulks while youse're down dere."

The Brannigan woman cursed him

Limpy said. "I can see youse's nippults wit dis rain."

More cursing.

• • •

Korfu, Bryan, and Booker, another Chippewa County CO, met Service, Sedge, and their prisoners on the remains of the old two-track that cut across the Michigan Nature Association parcel. The first thing they did was cuff all of them with disposable plastic cuffs. The suspects would be booked in the Soo.

"Coming?" Sergeant Bryan asked.

"We'll be along. You want to check them into the hotel?"

"Charges?"

"Resist, assault, and grave robbery."

The sergeant looked confused. Service handed him two skulls in plastic evidence bags. "Grave robbery," he repeated.

"I'll make sure our guests get rooms with a view," Sergeant Bryan said.

• • •

Service, Sedge, and Allerdyce returned to the site. "You," Service said, poking Allerdyce in the arm. "Stay right *next* to me."

"Youses're welcome," the old poacher said disconsolately.

"You are a felon," Service said. "Under the terms of your parole you may not possess a firearm or be with anyone with a firearm."

Allerdyce grinned and his eyes twinkled. "Guess youse're in cahoots wit' dis felon. Youse invite me go 'long, an' *youse* got guns, sonnyboy."

Service looked at Sedge. "You get to be the hero in our report."

"Me?"

"Can't say it was dickhead here. They'll send him back to jail."

"Who youse call dickhead?" Allerdyce said.

"Shut up," the officers said in unison.

"Toliver brought a girl but I don't see her," Service told Sedge.

"What are you thinking?"

"I'm not. I just want to account for her," he said, leading them toward the scene of the confrontation.

They scoured the area and found several holes and two large black plastic bags filled with various artifacts and remains.

Service held up a hand, and a voice said, "Decision time."

Service looked up. Duncan Katsu towered above them. He was wearing deerskin breeches and moccasins, his hair loose, face painted grayish-white and streaking from the rain, which continued to pound down.

"Dr. Katsu," Service said.

"I prefer Four Hawks," Katsu said.

"You knew all along that the site was here, and not at the fishing village."

"I did," Katsu said. "But I also knew it wouldn't take long for Toliver to expand his search. I guessed Wingel already knew, but I couldn't figure out how she fit. I figured she got away with some stuff, got scared, and backed off." Katsu looked left and right and twenty men stepped into sight, dressed as he was, painted the same and carrying shovels, and bags. Jane Rain, in a T-shirt, shorts, and and hiking boots, was last to step out.

"Toliver had a girl with him when he came out this way," Service said.

"She's fine. We have her," the U.S. Fish and Wildlife special agent said. "We saw the whole thing here. I was just getting ready to move in when I saw Bolf and Delongshamp, and decided to let it play out." She grinned. "Got sort of dicey, eh? Good thing you had that old-timer on your team."

Allerdyce muttered *old-timer* in a tone of utter disgust.

"It seems clear now," Service said to Rain. "You didn't have *someone* in Katsu's camp. You had Katsu."

"He's not a felon," Rain said. "That was fabricated to help us."

"He hasn't lost his dental license?"

Katsu looked at Service. "I never had one. I realized there were more important things in my life."

"You have a plan here?"

"Rebury my people."

"*Na-do-we-se* are yours too?"

"They deserve no less."

"Who buried them originally?"

"We did," Huronicus St. Andrew said, huffing up to his son, breathing heavily. "All that stuff about a road of skulls and such, that was all crap made up by those few who ran away from the fight, got back to their people, and didn't want to come back this way again. Even after the battle, it took twenty, thirty years for our people to move back to Bawating. I told you my son was a good boy, Service."

"Your vision for the future working today?" Service asked Santinaw.

"It don't work that way, paleface."

EPILOGUE

Sault Ste. Marie, Chippewa County

FRIDAY, SEPTEMBER 7, 2007

Sedge knew the judge, convinced him the whole lot were flight risks, and no bail was allowed.

Delongshamp began to crumble first. He claimed he and Bolf had not been involved in the artifacts business to start with. Their sole interest had been big cervids for a dealer in Texas, but the big deer they had trapped died en route, and they had buried it near his late sister's cabin. One day Service drove him out there and he pointed out the grave immediately.

The horse parts were from the vehicle they stole to transport the live deer. Because they had the animals, they butchered them and sold them in Milwaukee to a Hmong restaurant owner. They buried what was left at the site of the old fishing village.

"Planning," Delongshamp said. "Ain't our forte." He'd learned from his late sister that Marldeane was making beaucoup money from stolen arti-facts, and he tried to wedge his way in by using Skyler to help him, but she couldn't take the stress and checked out. He showed no remorse over her death. He knew nothing about Held or Clatchety, or anything that had hap-pened downstate.

This morning when they got back to court Service was amazed to see Wingel and Marldeane being represented by none other than the infamous Sandy Tavolacci, the favored mouthpiece of U.P. scumbags, east to west.

Tavolacci greeted Service with a sneer. "Grave robbery? Youse has really lost 'er dis time, bub."

"Dream on, Sandy."

Service and Sedge testified to events at the old graveyard that day, and both painted Sedge as the prime mover in the action. The suspects accused Allerdyce of assault, but when he took the stand he looked like he didn't have a care in the world.

"So," Tavolacci said, "from defendant to plaintiff."

Allerdyce blinked. "I ain't no plane ticket," and laughed out loud. "You drinkin' moose juice again, Sandy?"

The judge had to gavel the courtroom to order.

"Did you or did you not take weapons away from Mr. Delongshamp and Mr. Bolf?"

"Nope, sure din't," Allerdyce said solemnly.

"Our witnesses will testify differently," Tavolacci said.

"What dose game wardens tease-to-fry? Was girlie dere took dose fellas' guns."

"Why should we believe you? You're a felon."

"Right," Allerdyce said with a hearty chuckle. "Which is why I wasn't gonna grab no bloody guns. I been prison, but I ain't stupid, Sandy. Holy wah! *Youse* know dat."

• • •

The judge eventually released the group on bail. The grave robbery charge was dropped and replaced by charges from statutes governing the removal of artifacts from state land. The case got lots and lots of media attention, across the state and even nationally.

Grady Service was invited to appear on *The Late Show with David Letterman*. Chief Waco encouraged this as a way of bringing light to the problem and when Service resisted, ordered his top sergeant to go on the show.

Letterman said, "So let me get this straight: In Michigan, it's the game warden's job to protect historical sites?"

"That's right," Service said.

"But the state authorities who know where these sites are won't tell you where they are so you can take care of them."

"Right again."

Letterman gave one of his looks to the camera and stammered. "Is anyone trying to change this?" the famous host asked.

"I hope so," Service said.

Letterman grinned. "That is one sharp uniform you've got there, Chief Master Sergeant. I understand you're the first officer at that rank in state history, going all the way back to 1887."

Service nodded and Letterman said, "Big hand of appreciation for Chief Master Sergeant Grady Service of the Michigan Department of Natural Resources."

Service was met in the green room by Karylanne, Little Mar, Friday, and Shigun.

"You were funny, Bampy!" Maridly squealed.

"I wasn't trying to be funny," he said.

Friday poked his ribs. "Just one of your many gifts."

AUTHOR'S NOTE

It borders on surreal to write these words, but I have now been working with and writing about Michigan's conservation officers for more than a decade. A former DNR spokesperson once referred to me jokingly as "the DNR's embed." I have always liked that label, and yes, I have unabashedly defended the people who manage and defend our natural resources. Too many people are quick to criticize despite having no clues about what really goes on, and why.

For the record, and as written, the State Archaeologist's Office does not proactively disclose archaeological site locations to police officers or COs. It's a sad but true bureaucratic comment on what low regard our own state bureaucracy has for our peace officers.

Shame on the state.

Shame on *us* for allowing such prejudice and shortsightedness.

I've ridden with officers in all fifteen U.P. counties, and approximately forty more counties below the bridge. I've gotten some very intimate looks at our state, and remain convinced that we have one of our nation's great repositories of natural beauty and mostly accessible wilderness. When our state will ever learn to properly promote this great asset and our prodigious history is beyond my ken. I just hope our artifacts are not all stolen and destroyed by the time the state gets around to it.

Here I would like to thank all the officers who have shared their trucks with me, either in solo patrols or group efforts (sometimes called "goat rodeos" for good reason), often in uniform, occasionally in plainclothes, and regularly far from the truck on foot, or being directed in a truck by an aircraft buzzing overhead.

Without the guidance and encouragement of a lot of people, this series would never have come to life. I especially want to thank retired captain Tom Courchaine and Sergeant Mike Webster, along with the late chief Rick Asher and former Natural Resources commissioner Bob Garner. These four opened the doors and their files to me.

I also thank Lieutenant Tim Robson, and sergeants Steve Burton, Pete Malette (Ret.), and Darryl Shann, each of whom contributed mightily to the effort, as did COs Dave Painter, Grant Emery, Paul Higashi, Nick Torsky, "Sunshine" Hopkins, Sgt. Jeff Rabbers, and "Bigfoot" Dan Bigger, the officers who have silently suffered my presence more than others.

I also give huge thanks to the following retired officers: Detective Rick Ackerberg, Sergeant Kathy Bezotte, Chief Herb Burns, and Lieutenant Walt Mikula; Walt has more information about cases in his head than an encyclopedia. I hope he gets it all on paper sometime so future officers can learn from him and his experience. Our Michigan DNR law enforcement operation does a lousy job with institutional memory and keeping a good history of all they do and accomplish, both good and bad.

In addition to the few spotlighted above, there are many more officers who deserve thanks, and here they are alphabetically: Ryan Aho, Brian Bacon, Sergeant Mike "The Force" Borkovich, Matt Eberly, Sergeant Arthur Green, Brett "Gus" Gustafson, Doug Hermanson, Chris Holmes, Mike Holmes (Ret.), John Huspen, Bobbi Lively, Patrick MacManus, Warren Mac-Neil, Dave Miller, Jason Niemi, Kellie Nightlinger, Pete "Night Train" Purdy, Lacelle "The Gentleman" Rabon, Jeff "The Bouncer" Robinette, John "Weasel" Wenzel, Jason Wicklund, Lieutenant John Wormwood (Ret.), and Sergeant Pete Wright.

Others who earn a tip of the cap (also alphabetically): Nick Atkin, Kyle Bader, Sergeant Troy Bahlau, Mike Bomay, Brad Brewer, Mark DePew, Mark Ennett, Mike Evink, Jarad Ferguson, Pat Grondin (Ret.), Mike Hammill, Mike Hearn, Dan Helms (Ret.), Captain Dan Hopkins, CFS Ken Johnson, Detective Mike Johnson (Ret.), Sergeant John Jurcich, Brandon Kieft, Kris Kiel, Mark Leadman, Brain Lebel, Ken Lowell, Joel Lundberg, Lieutenant Dave Malloch, Corporal Steve Martin, Jason McCollough, Mike McDonnell (Ret.), Mike McGee, Derek Miller, Sergeant Chris Morris (Ret.), "Mighty" Mike Mshaar, Brian Olsen, Steve Orange, Greg Patton, Ivan Perez, Tami Pullen, Gary Raak, Dave "The Meat Eater" Rodgers, Reed Roeske, Lt. Dave Shaw, Ben Shively, CFS Terry Short, Chris Simpson, Jon Sklba, Jason Smith, Steve Spoegl, Rich Stowe, Sergeant Jackie Strauch (Ret.), Todd Syzska, Chuck Towns, CFS Shannon Van Patten, Dave Vant

Hof (Ret.), Jeff Walker, Danny Walzak, Shane Webster, and Phil Wolbrink (Ret.).

Sorry if I missed anyone.

Quite the list, quite the time, and one helluva ride from then to now.

Of all the Woods Cop novels, this one has perhaps been the most fun to write because it delves into an area many people are interested in, but, like me, have little knowledge of.

Be advised: Grady's not done yet, but that time will come as it surely does for all of us. Meanwhile, embed clear.

Over.

Joseph Heywood
June 20, 2010

Joseph Heywood is the author of *The Snowfly* (Lyons), *Covered Waters* (Lyons), *The Berkut, Taxi Dancer, The Domino Conspiracy,* and the eight novels comprising the Woods Cop Mystery Series. Featuring Grady Service, a detective in the Upper Peninsula for Michigan's Department of Natural Resources, this series has earned its author cult status among lovers of the outdoors, law enforcement officials, and mystery devotees. Heywood lives in Portage, Michigan.

For more on Joseph Heywood and the Woods Cop Mysteries, visit the author's website at www.josephheywood.com.